Justin Cartwright was born in South Africa and educated there, in America and at Oxford University. He has directed documentaries, films and television commercials. He is the author of four previous novels and lives in London.

Justin Cartwright

LOOK
AT IT
THIS WAY

published by Pan Books
in association with Macmillan

ACKNOWLEDGEMENTS

I am indebted to George B. Schaller's *The Serengeti Lion* for facts about lions. I have also drawn on E. H. Gombrich, *Art and Illusion*, Basil Taylor's works on Stubbs, and Bruno Bettelheim, *The Uses of Enchantment*. Thanks, also, to the *Independent* for permission to use their masthead above a fictional article.

I would like to thank Alan Gordon Walker, Roland Philipps, Leonie Fox and all the many people who were involved in the skilled business of producing this book.

I feel, too, an urge to thank London for providing the material, but I am not sure where to start.

First published 1990 by Macmillan London Ltd
This Picador edition published 1991 by Pan Books Ltd,
Cavaye Place, London SW10 9PG
in association with Macmillan
9 8 7 6 5 4 3 2 1

© Justin Cartwright 1990

ISBN 0 330 31769 5

Printed in England by Clays Ltd, St Ives plc

For my old friend Garry Southern

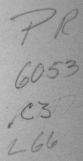

Et saves bien qu'il fut contrefaise al vif
(You must understand that it was drawn from life)
— Villard de Honnecourt, 1235, of his drawing of a lion

THE INDEPENDENT

LION'S VICTIM IDENTIFIED

Police today issued a statement identifying the body found in Regent's Park, believed to have been a victim of the lion which was recaptured yesterday after disappearing for four weeks from London Zoo.

The victim was Mr Miles Goodall, 31, unemployed City dealer. A police surgeon confirmed that Mr Goodall's injuries were consistent with having been severely mauled and partially eaten by a lion.

Police have not confirmed an earlier report by park attendant, Mr Abdul Dunwoody, who first discovered the body, that the victim had a hand-gun on him when found. Any connection between this incident and Vice-President Danforth Quayle's private stay at Winfield House, the US Ambassador's residence, was pure speculation at this stage, said a police spokesman. None the less, reliable sources confirmed, an urgent internal enquiry is being launched into security at Winfield House, which occupies twelve acres bordering on Regent's Park.

A friend of the victim, Mrs Joyce Rolfe, of Windy Corner, Farnham, Surrey, said that Mr Goodall had been suffering from considerable stress since losing his job at First West City Merchant Bank some weeks ago.

1

CHAPTER ONE

The sky is the colour of a mullet's skin, grey with flecks of minerals. Outside my windows, the park is subdued. It's been trying to rain all day, as they say around here.

I am faxing a message to New York:

Bums. Arses. Fannies. Tushies. Sit-upons. Derrières. Khyber Passes. Botties.

I believe you can chart a nation's social history by the shape of the nation's bottom. In Victorian times there was a theory that the criminal classes could easily be identified by the science of phrenology. Their eyes were set too close together; their occipital lobes were constricted; their rational impulses were squeezed out by poor development of the skull. It was scientific. In this spirit I launch my enquiry into the disappearance of the small and wiry Londoner. The jockey-shaped Cockney, he of the fast fingers and the pipe-cleaner limbs, is an endangered species. Bottoms, and breasts (bristols, boobs, knockers, etc.) are growing unchecked. Londoners are eating McDonald's, Burger Kings and Kentucky Fried Chicken. They live entirely on these protein-packed foods with the consequence that they are becoming bulky. The little pickpockets, purse snatchers, chimney sweeps, and sneak thieves have vanished in one generation. Like much of London, they will only be a memory soon.

Boys tower over their traditionally formed parents and grandparents. They have muscles and bellies where their parents were held together with bits of string. And the girls! They are ballooning into fantastic shapes. The fattest of them have huge pear-shaped butts, which they none the less compress into stone-washed jeans or short black skirts. Even the least

3

stout have ducks' bottoms waggling beneath them as their legs struggle to carry the additional weight. They seldom run, but when they do the whole construction totters dangerously. And they are always eating. If they are not actually sitting to eat, they are snacking on bags of cheese-and-onion-flavoured potato chips, or 'crisps' as they call them. Even children on the way to school carry these little bags of poison.

In the more expensive parts of town, women are working their bodies. In these areas they eat sensibly – fish, salad, pasta with fresh tomato sauce – and they have their hair done frequently. Hairdressers in high-rent Chelsea specialize in the glossy look. The women with the tight, under-control bottoms also have gleaming, under-control hair. In the other, and more numerous, neighborhoods – dreadful places like Peckham, Kilburn and Holloway – perhaps despairing of their unmanageable bottoms, women are tormenting their hair. They want to look (like Annie Lennox of the Eurythmics) interesting and independent. But they forget *la loi du canard*: short hair emphasizes the burgeoning backside. No matter: they shave the area above their ears, they tickle the front up into little spikes, they wear crew cuts, brush cuts and table cuts. Out in the suburbs, the encircling darkness, they still tease their hair into ringlets so that it flaps all over their heads like a poodle's on retrieval duty.

The City is changing too. The streets are a bedlam of building works and excavation. 'Cladding' is all the rage. Brutal sixties office blocks of leprous concrete with blue panels of a plastic compound called 'quartzite,' once fashionable, are being 're-clad.' This requires a glamorous new glass skin and a pediment on top of the building to hide the lift shaft and services. On ground level the building must now 'interact' with the passers-by. The theory of noted London architect, Richard Rogers, that essential services should not be denied but exhibited – like breast-feeding in public – finds no favor with the corporate mind. The corporate person is still in the ascendancy. He is in league with the real world; he uses the expensive seats on airplanes; he eats at restaurants which set a lot of store by 'presentation.' This presentation involves fancy work with ingredients, forced marriages between fruit and flesh, the pressing into service of obscure berries and arson with expensive liqueurs.

4

Other, older buildings are becoming penthouses, lofts, work-spaces, drawing stations. The emphasis here is on brightly colored beams and exposed brickwork. (I have a former hay-loft myself.) Wonder of wonders: After all these years of neglect it has been discovered that London has thousands of acres of derelict warehouses, chapels, smokehouses, rope factories, chandlers, pulley makers and grain stores. Professional people are moving into these spaces – 'space' is a big word – previously occupied by barometer makers, brewers, unitarians, sea captains, fishmongers, watchmakers, shipbuilders, lascars, rice merchants, spice traders ('the smell of cinnamon pervades the place'), coopers and a myriad more, all forgotten. The river is making a comeback. Colorful galleries (aka *'galleria'*), harbors, marinas and wharves are appearing everywhere. Little waterbuses skim up and down the Thames from Docklands to Chelsea. There are regattas of ancient barges and steam vessels. Old things are in, but they must be fully restored. 'Restoration' is a big word too. It is surprising, therefore, that the mania for restoring the body has not taken more of a hold. The body is enjoying the benefit of affluence all too clearly.

That's enough. They'll cut it anyway. I write for *Manhattan* magazine every fortnight on London: arts, theatre, politics, literature and restaurants. It's a great job; reasonably well paid, amusing, and with (free) entry to almost anything or anybody in town. At the same time I am free to pursue my private thoughts.

I have become a minor celebrity back home, a bush league Alistair Cooke or Garrison Keillor, mildly ironic but at the same time essentially reassuring. This celebrity has allowed me to appear in a commercial for American Eagle credit cards. (I have to be careful: they are litigious to the point of madness.) In my role as Euro-savant I am supposed to lend lustre to this crude computer credit operation. The thesis is simple: by using this card, you too can be accepted all over the world – like me – in places where you really have no business poking your nose. The world is changing fast. Instant acceptance can be purchased. People are no longer willing to wait a few generations. The folks from Cedar Rapids feel more relaxed in the Ritz with this little plastic card in their wallets.

The seagulls wheeled curiously as I stood on the balcony of a penthouse apartment (previously a brewery), overlooking Tower Bridge. I said the following words to the camera, while walking awkwardly past the skyline with my neck craned at forty-five degrees:

'London. My kind of town, for the last ten years now, and it's still just as full of surprises. So I always take my American Eagle card with me whenever I leave home.'
(Shot of me leaving picturesque mews cottage in Belgravia in a taxi.)
'You never know when you may need it.'
(Shot of me being confronted by flower seller in Edwardian dress.)
'From the opera (shot of me at Royal Opera House for Pavarotti) to fish and chips (shot of me with rubber-faced character actor called Bernie, as he dips cod inexpertly into bubbling oil) you know you are in good company with the American Eagle card.'
(Close with shot of me escorting sophisticated woman into the Savoy. Her motivation not explained.)

For the thirty seconds, which took five days to film, I was paid $375,000. It turns out I could have got more. American Eagle's advertising agency lied. They said they were negotiating with John le Carré for this slot, and I accepted too quickly. I could have got half a million. I bought a Mercedes. It is one of the new S series, costing £48,000. It has changed my view of London: I seldom use the Underground or the buses now and I see people – my fellow Londoners – from within its warm embrace.

Bernie's line was severely cut in the editing. He had to say: 'Coming up in half a tick, guv, every one a little beauty', as he retrieved the fish from the lethally hot oil. This was, I could tell, far too complex for our little saga, even before they recorded the line. Bernie had plenty of suggestions for alternative lines, which he tried out on Ed Kaplan, the director.

'How about "Every one a coconut", Ed?' he said desperately. 'That's a bit shorter.'

'It's not working. Bernard,' said Ed.

And later: 'This is good, Ed. Me mum used to say this: "This'll put 'airs on yer chest, me little darlin'."'

And then, desperately, '"'Ere's a little of what yer fancy, guv." That's short. Do you like it more?'

In lieu of dialogue, Bernie was reduced to using his vast range of facial expressions but Ed Kaplan was not really paying attention. He was wondering if he still had time, as the shoot was running over, to get up to Newport Pagnell to find some parts for his 1964 Aston Martin DB5 which was on blocks in Bridgehampton. He was keen to get it going for the summer. Ed had been a Rhodes scholar back in sixty-nine, but somewhere along the way he had got lost in advertising. Ed remembered taxi drivers with woolly mufflers and flat caps, and policemen who smiled; it was his familiarity with all things British which had secured him the job. Anyway, Ed got the rocker arm and the tappets for his Aston Martin, I got my Mercedes and Bernie scalded his hand in the oil. He tried to sue American Eagle, with predictable results: lawyers' letters as thick as scripts showered upon him. He enjoyed the attention. An actor's life can be lonely.

After the film-gypsies departed – their encampment of Winnebagos, catering trucks, generators, camera cars and support vehicles mysteriously dispersed – I felt lost for a few days. I now understood Fellini's love of his crew: his ordered, busy world with its own hierarchy and its own jokes. Perhaps a fish in an aquarium feels the same way about the lack of reality outside.

Whenever my daughter Gemma is in town, I take her to the aquarium at London Zoo; it is one of her favourite places. It is a gloomy cavern under the goat mountain. We ignore the goats and head straight for the small, bright tank which houses the coral reef effect. The fish there are as bright and virulent as tropical fruit.

Sometimes as we leave the aquarium we hear the lions roaring. Lions, it seems, are not very intelligent. They roar to announce that they are going hunting, even though their evening meal, donkey quarters, is about to be delivered in a wheelbarrow by an assistant keeper. Their roars reverberate none the less across the goat mountain, but the goats are too astute to worry about empty threats and the people in the expensive Palladian villas are seldom at home.

CHAPTER TWO

William 'Simba' Cochrane had once been famous for having been attacked by a lion. He had been dragged from his horse, severely mauled and survived. Even that was perhaps not enough to ensure his fame. What had clinched it was the fact that as the lion was eyeing him contemplatively, holding him pinioned with one massive paw, he had managed to release his penknife from its sheath. At the very moment the lion rasped his face with its huge tongue, as a prelude to its first serious mouthful (the way people will toy with the olives and the breadrolls) and its carnivorous breath – rotten gas swirling round an empty stomach – played on his face and its huge teeth (yellow with leonine plaque) prepared to bite into his throat (rather red from the sun), Cochrane plunged the penknife into the lion's hairy neck. The lion grunted, but seemed merely surprised at first until its dark blood began to pump fiercely through the thick black ruff which decorated its head and leaked on to Cochrane's shoulder.

'What did you think then?'

'I was frightened the bugger was going to get really angry. . .'

'I'm not surprised.'

'But 'e didn't nor nuffink. 'E looked sad. And then 'e walked orf. Then me 'orse got up. 'E was just stunned like, and I caught 'im as fast as I blooming well could and I buggered orf, I can tell you.'

'Were you in pain?'

'I felt nothing (nuffink) at all as a matter of fact. Not a dicky bird. Not till later nohow.'

This was the interesting part. He had felt no pain at all even though the lion had bitten right through his shoulder blade

9

and gouged away a section of his chest; the scars, sixty-one years old, he showed me now, pulling up his shirt and the yellowing undershirt. They had done a neat job at the surgery, considering it had taken a day and a half to get him there, delirious but determined to retrieve his penknife. Looking at the scars was part of the ritual of an interview with Cochrane. Interviews with Cochrane had become scarce in the last thirty years, but he knew the form. His chest was lopsided, as though he had been pared, like a potato peeled carelessly.

'That's where the bugger bit me first, after 'e 'ad knocked me 'orse over. You can still see the perfect teeth marks. Like a dental plate said this young girl what come to see me from the television. The knockers on 'er, you shoulda seen 'em, like ripe bloody cantaloupes. You ever eat a cantaloupe? Lovely. Juicy. We used to eat them for breakfast out in Africa. And watermelons. A penny each. Bloody great whoppers, like 'er tits.'

He bared his gums in a lewd chewing motion. He was a difficult man to like unreservedly; old age had not lent him charm. Instead his semi-celebrity had left him with an inappropriate little legacy of self-regard.

'It's five pounds for an interview,' he said, suddenly. 'Fifteen dollars in your money.'

The exchange rate had obviously stayed fixed for some time in his mind, perfectly set like the dental record the lion had left on his back.

The building Cochrane lived in was suppurating. The walls outside were oozing; the rainwater pipes had spawned strange chemical florescences, like the crystals which children grow in jars, on the brickwork around them; inside his flat the wallpaper, which was heavy and florid, bulged uneasily as though something biological was striving to be born behind it, and the linoleum on the floor bubbled uneasily with the effects of damp. The building was owned by an obscure charitable trust which had neither the right to sell for redevelopment nor the ability to raise money to improve it. In this chemically impure building huddled a few hundred elderly people in their crepuscular apartments which mirrored – I was well away – the twilight of their lives and the world in which they lived.

William Cochrane, the man who escaped becoming a lion's

breakfast by such a narrow margin, was the most celebrated of these residents, although (as I had found when I asked the lady caretaker for his whereabouts) not the most popular.

'You interested in that cock-and-bull lion story too? What a load of rubbish. Six D. If you ask me the closest 'e ever come to a lion was at Regent's Park Zoo . . . Still that's just my opinion. Six D. 'E never goes nowhere.'

The caretaker had a terrible mortal cough. Like Cochrane she belonged to an era that was passing, an era of saturated food, sixty cigarettes a day and damp apartments, heated by prudent use of gas fires. All around the tenement, old buildings were undergoing wonderful transformations into more desirable and up-to-date accommodation. But in Jubilee Buildings the old ways were alive, at a subdued level, certainly, but with a quiet persistence, like the fungus growths on the skirting boards.

Cochrane's horse had been retired after the incident. It had suffered an equine nervous breakdown. The slightest noise frightened it and it shied at bushes. This, I could well understand, was a considerable handicap out in Africa. Cochrane had worked for the 'PWD'. It took me a while to figure out that PWD meant Public Works Department. He had been in waterworks, so the damp of his present abode was perhaps not as noticeable to him as it was to the visitor. Actually horses had soon afterwards been withdrawn from active service in the Public Works Department. The mounted water worker had been eliminated by a decree from the Colonial Office, so no one in the PWD was ever able to duplicate Simba Cochrane's extraordinary adventure. None the less other people have been taken from horses by lions.

A German professional hunter, Fritz von Schindler, was taken in Kenya from his polo pony while flushing lions and killed.

After recovering from his encounter with the lion, Cochrane had been given a small disability pension and a desk job back in London with the Metropolitan Water Board. It had not suited him. Nothing in his subsequent life had been as much fun as being eaten by a lion.

'It didn't hurt at all?' I asked again.

'Didn't feel a thing. What I remember most is 'is awful foul

11

breath (bref) breathing on me face. It were disgusting.'

The scars showed pink where the lion had bitten him and white where the doctor had sewn him up, so that his torso, with its little squiggles and hieroglyphs, looked like a painting by Miró. And on his back the perfect dental impression – which had so enthused the ample television researcher – showed a faint blue.

The lion had died soon after the encounter. Trackers had recovered the knife which was displayed in various exhibitions around the world. There was not much call for it now and Cochrane had recently offered it to the *Guinness Book of Records* exhibition in Piccadilly Circus for a modest sum, but they had rejected it on the grounds that it was not a record.

'It was unique that's all. The one and only, that's all it bloody was. Stupid gits.'

Waning celebrity, Cochrane had discovered at leisure, was not much of a commodity. It wasn't much of a penknife, as a matter of fact, with a white inlay of bone on the handle and some crude chasing. On the blade were the words: *With this knife, William F. Cochrane killed a lion, Oct 5, 1931.*

The engraving took up most of the space on the blade, which Cochrane had great difficulty closing with his knotted fingers.

'It's me arthritis (arthuritis). These bloody flats should have been condemned years ago. I applied to the council but they don't take no notice of us. They give all their flats to unemployed lesbians and darkies. It's the damp. It's gone right into me bones.'

I helped him do up his shirt. The leering boastfulness had gone now. He lit a cigarette which clung to the damp on his lips like a gecko to a wall.

'When did you feel the pain?'

'Not until I woke up in the 'ospital in Thompson's Falls. Then they gave me morphine. It's lucky I'm not one of them junkies as a result.'

The way Cochrane spoke was dying too. It was Cockney of the music-hall variety which became moribund – along with cab drivers in flat caps – about fifteen or twenty years ago. The new Cockney was just as rich a language, but its focus had moved. It was concerned with easy money and fancy cars and it took a less romantic view of life in the smoke. The word 'fucking' had entered the vocabulary in a big way. In fact it was moving into all sorts of territory previously thought to be immune. Perfectly ordinary conversation in the street employed the word constantly. On the way to see Cochrane I heard a mother say to her child: 'You left your fucking brains indoors again (leftyer fu-u-k-kin brains indoors agen)?' for some small misdemeanour.

Cochrane's little flat smelled of defunct aromas too, like carbolic soap, eucalyptus chest rub, throat linctus, sweet sherry, fishermen's cough drops and overcooked vegetables. His face, at this lull in the conversation, crumbled. Confusion not so much reigned as camped there. His body and his face were almost hairless, yet his head was covered in a baby fuzz as if his hair was making a return after many years of absence. The language was changing, but the facial types persisted; this was the small, wiry, humorous type. Although the faces were still around, the bodies of their grandchildren had grown larger and fleshier, the legs longer and straighter and their hair permanently barbered and dyed. Indeed some of them seemed to have microwaved their hair, subjecting it to harmful rays so that it appeared to have been scorched or fried unnaturally. Whenever I go to the airport in the summer, I see groups of these people who have taken their hair in for drastic treatment in preparation for their holidays. To me these faces and bodies do not go together, like old master painters who started a portrait and left the pupils to fill in the hands, torsos, spaniels and hawks.

The flats were dark. We had not been talking for long but it had grown even darker. Thicker cloud, I guessed, had passed over the habitually grey ceiling outside bringing with it the spitting of rain – like an old man trying to piss – which in turn caused the bricks and stones to suppurate, the water leaching out the salts, the spores and the mineral deposits which had accumulated there.

Cochrane had a photograph of the lion's corpse. It was huge. The head was propped up on a rock and its mane was thick and dark. It was a miracle that the knife had gone through this hedge at all. The askari stood next to the lion in the photo with his .303 rifle on his shoulder, rigidly to attention, whether out of respect for the late monarch of the jungle or at the behest of the photographer (a senior waterworks official known as 'Stinker' Forsythe because of his legendary expertise with sewers), I had no way of guessing.

'Stinker was a dab 'and with (wif) a camera. He took pictures of most everything (everyfink) what we done out there.'

Cochrane let me look at his newspaper cuttings. His brush with death – his good long look right into the face of mortality (with its halitosis) – had been big news in East Africa. But it had also found its way by the wire services to all the papers of the Empire and beyond to New York and Paris. He had been given an Atlantic crossing on the *Queen Mary*. He had been awarded a medal in Canada. He had met the Duke of York. He had made a guest appearance at Barnum and Bailey's circus at Flushing Meadow, even entering the ring with the lion act for a stake of $500.

'Were you frightened?'

'Frightened? Terrified more like. This lion tamer geezer, 'e said the lions could smell fear. 'E was dead worried, 'e was, in case they went for 'im an' all.'

Here he sat in the damp twilight as I leafed through his cuttings. The moisture had got into the scrapbooks too, so that the pages were covered with a soft green powdery mildew. Maybe the growth on Cochrane's head was mildew. The one small window was running half-heartedly with sulphurous rain. I thought of Barnum and Bailey's, all colour and light and girls with thunderthighs doing those curious little leaps and emitting muted shrieks, as though they had been goosed by a bat, and I imagined the intrepid Simba Cochrane, lop-sided but plucky, entering the lion cage and scuttling behind Salvatore Corleone's, the lion tamer's, back, the whip snaking through the air, the lions snarling, wondering who this bow-legged little interloper was (and whether he was edible) and Cochrane getting a whiff of their meaty breath (donkey offal) at the same time as the lions got a whiff of his overactive sebaceous glands.

'It would have looked well 'ere on the floor, the lion skin. Unfortunately as it appeared it was too far gone (gorn).'

By the time Stinker and his askaris had reached the lion's

body it was beyond redemption even by the Indian taxidermist, who took care of hunting trophies. It was difficult to imagine what an enormous lion skin would have looked like here, head raised, glass eyes flickering malevolently – if intermittently – in the weak flame of the single gas heater. Old people become very attached to the most dilapidated furniture. It seems to acquire a comforting value in their estimation; but Cochrane's furniture – a small spindly table, a kitchen chair and a heavily pockmarked armchair – in his imagination would have been shown to good advantage by the lion skin. There was also a glass-fronted cabinet which displayed Cochrane's memorabilia, and a carpet of brown and orange dahlias. Cochrane offered me tea, but I had experienced elderly English people offering to make tea before: a long interval was punctuated by the clashing of chipped cups before the eventual appearance of a teapot, formally dressed in a woolly outer garment, an ecological nirvana for mites and spores, then an orthopaedically clamorous period of pouring and anxiety about the sending in of depth charges of sugar lumps. *One lump or two? You did say two? Oh no sugar. I can always make some more. Oh I am a silly billy.* These old people take an immense amount of sugar. Cochrane probably ate it by the bagful, judging by the state of his mouth. The tea ritual, as with the Japanese, has deep symbolic meaning. I declined.

'When the lion knocked you off your horse did you think you had a chance?'

Cochrane's features sprang to action stations. The lion world was the real world. His small, jockey's body leaned forward as if he were in the starting stalls on Epsom Downs. I sympathised with the little man with breadmould on his head. There are periods in my own life – in everybody's life probably – which seem more vital and therefore more real. He had feared that our conversation about the limpid past had ended.

'I didn't feel nothing (nuffink) at all except I was winded so as I couldn't breathe (breeve) nor nothing. That may of saved me life.'

'Were you frightened?'

'I've often given that some thought. Turned it over in me mind like, and I can honestly say,' (he aspirated the 'h') 'I weren't frightened at all.'

15

'Even when he bit you?'

'It was a dream. I was thinking (finking) clearly like in a dream.'

Shock. The sudden constriction of the blood vessels, so strong it completely blotted out the pain and the fear of that moist mouth and its three-inch teeth, every one a canine (or perhaps a feline) and the indolent eyes, the colour of corn stubble, apparently fixed negligently on something distant, the paws the size of designer dinner plates, the thick mane, darkening with age, the looming muzzle scarred by a hundred fights, each whisker as thick as a piece of mackerel line, and the warm, sullen, poisoned breath, coming in short, searing blasts after the exertion of leaping on to the horse and detaching this monkey from its perch. And the little man, despite the blood and the crushed shoulder and the pain in his face which was being rasped by a huge tongue, quickly unsheathing his cheap knife and plunging it through the thicket around the lion's neck with such force and accuracy that the brute bled to death, its paws – like Androcles's lion – ill-equipped to deal with a medical emergency as the blood pumped on to the dry, sandy soil. It was shock, the chemical surge, the magic mushroom, the dervish, the Gurkha, the frenzy which the little people of this country must have within them; which sent them over the top at Ypres, or into the Zulu assegais, disdaining fear, feeling no pain. To feel no pain is to be drunk in Cockney.

'The lion recognises the true prince,' I said.

He didn't hear.

'It was a dream. To be honest when I woke in the 'ospital I was not one hundred per cent sure what 'ad 'appened to me. I thought (fought) I had as like as not dreamed the 'ole business, particularly (partikerly) wif the morphine and all.'

Some dream.

The streets outside are not dreaming. They are like a wet dog anxiously trying to shake off the moisture. The lights from the Masonic Lodge, where bank managers and senior policemen are gathering for a gin and tonic, are shining yellow against the gaseous backcloth of the City. I should never have brought the car. It will have been vandalised in the onrushing gloom. But now I find it unmolested, no ticket although time was up hours ago, no mazy screwdriver lines down the side, in fact all its handsome Teutonic features intact. As I unlock the doors, above me in the Lodge I can see them: their faces are the faces of butchers, bakers and candlestickmakers, as they bask in the warm conviviality of a world without the poor and black. Not that I can talk. In ten years here I have hardly met a person of colour. None of my friends is starving. You can't go out looking for these people; they live on another planet but pass around the edge of our lives occasionally. No point in feeling guilty about it; that way lies madness.

As if in response to my thoughts a group of tall black boys come shambling along the kerb, holding a black dustbin liner over their heads, like those Ashanti chiefs. They walk like moonwalkers with exaggerated bend and lift, as though the damp streets are sticky and walking is somehow demeaning. They would rather be in a car like mine, although they favour the bad man's wagon, the BMW, given a choice. Three of the five have Walkmans. I get into the car quickly and light up the space-age controls, ready, if necessary to get going. They pass, the tinkling from their headsets, like small scratchy wind-up toys, left behind them. I lurch out into the damp road. I haven't quite got the hang of the power steering. Someone is shouting at me: 'Why don't you look where you're fucking going you fucking dickhead?' I shrug Italian style. He's a minicab driver. This *métier* seems to attract the psychically disturbed. With one push on the pedal I leave his old Ford Granada trailing. No doubt he's still in there screaming away. It's mostly ritual, but you have to be careful. Somebody was thrown under the wheels of a huge truck the other day after a minor altercation. The driver is probably a Greek Cypriot. If you took a snapshot of a London street any day, you wouldn't find a scene from Dickens, that's for sure. You would find neat Chinese nurses, Rastas in knitted caps, Pakistanis in shiny leather jackets, Japanese tourists in matching raincoats, backpacking students and the occasional Arab in a burnouse – outnumbering the natives.

I set off down Farringdon Road past the *Guardian*. The dome of St Paul's, the grey streaked with copper slug-trails, is briefly visible, like an umbrella held up against the rain. The five-speed wipers (there may be more) make light of the rain. There are little wipers on the headlights too, going like the clappers. I pass the bookstall on its iron wheels where *Guardian* journalists, I imagine, go to buy second-hand books. The man who runs the stall is packing up, disconsolate. He has this pitch on a busy street once a week; it must be an ancient licence. I know where he keeps the books; it's a little warehouse near the church in Clerkenwell. It would make a great apartment. I've honestly thought about asking him if he wants to sell. I've caught the itch now; wherever I go I think about buying some property and doing it up. It's not a disease, it's more a fungus, a sort of mildew of the soul, like the stuff that's squatting on Cochrane, the lion killer's head.

I fight my way down towards Fleet Street, past the site of the Fleet Prison, now the Memorial Hall, past the defunct newspaper buildings, past the Law Courts with their menacing gothic turrets and spires, past the little Air Force church marooned in the middle of the road, past the Indian High Commissioner just climbing into his Ashoka limousine at the back of India House, a couple of bodyguards moving sideways like hermit crabs on either side of the car, and down the wide stretch at Charing Cross Station and out into Trafalgar Square. The huge lions which lie there are wet; the bronze is showing green in patches so that they, too, appear to have mildew. When Landseer cast them he made only one body and two heads.

CHAPTER THREE

Londoners love fish. At Billingsgate, the ancient fish market, the fish lie in boxes, on trolleys, on stalls and on cascades of ice. The air is rich with their subaqua, seaweedy fishiness. The eyes are bright, the fins lustrous, the skin (not every fish has scales) moist. They come in all shapes and sizes from the sleek torpedos of tuna and swordfish to the knobbly excrescences of monkfish and the pink wings of the furtive skate. These cold northern waters are alive with fish. Long before fish and chips, long before the arrival of the potato from the New World, Londoners were eating fish in abundance. Wherever the remains of a Roman camp are uncovered by archeologists, there they find the remains of immense shellfish dinners. In the nineteenth century, apprentices to their dismay were fed on oysters, by the barrelful. Porter and oysters. The porter arrived from the River Douro in Portugal in sailing barges . . .

No, wait a minute. I think I'm getting muddled here between port wine and porter, which was surely some sort of ale. Anyway, I'll look it up later.

Bernie took me to Billingsgate Market at four-thirty in the morning. At the end of the shoot I gave him my phone number, which was a mistake. He has taken it upon himself to show me London:

'Real London. You know, not your poncey clubs and that.'

His true motive is to advance his career. Like all actors he believes in the break. He certainly doesn't see himself dipping cod into bubbling oil in commercials for ever. Not at all. You must be joking. He pictures himself in a far more heroic role,

19

demonstrating the triumph of the human spirit over adversity, a theme which he has persuaded himself is universal. I do not completely agree with him on this, but there is no point at all in arguing with Bernie, because he is adept at incorporating your thesis into his own world view. In fact without knowing it he is probably one of the leading proponents of the Hegelian notion of thesis and antithesis leading to synthesis, which, it happens, is the view ('based on fifty years of living life as it is, Tim') he held in the first place.

'You wanted to see the fish market, Tim. I'll pick you up at four-thirty.'

'In the morning?'

'Time and tide wait for no man, as the bard said. I've got a good mate what runs one of the biggest traders down the market. He can get you lovely Dover soles for a couple of quid (luvverly Do-oh-vah so-o-ls for a couplaquid).' The 'o' in Dover soles took wings for a coupla moments into his roomy nasal cavity. When Londoners talk a deal, the vowels take a terrible beating.

Bernie has a great idea for a musical. It's based on his childhood in the East End. To me, despite the refurbishment, the yuppie mice nibbling at the edges of the huge stale cheese, the East End is a solidly blank, depressing place of crumbling, weeping buildings and exhausted little shops selling third-rate goods. Its inhabitants seem equally tired; if they are white, they are crushed by the realisation that they will never be able to afford to get out, and if they are Asian, they are exhausted after the struggles of emigrating from Bangladesh. Bangladesh seems to be under water most of the time, so perhaps the East End with its (merely) damp and suppurating buildings appears a haven of stability, the proverbial high ground, to Bangladeshis.

Anyway, as we powered along the Commercial Road, there was a surprising amount of traffic in the pre-dawn gloom: newspaper trucks and vans, refrigerator trucks, out-of-town buses and rusted cars. This is the time of day when cleaners and dustmen and street sweepers and construction workers and shift workers are about. At bus stops, little, dispirited groups of Asian women waited, whether on the way home from work or on the way to work I could only speculate.

Against this not very colourful backdrop, gliding by, Bernie told me the idea – the big concept which was going to free him both from bit parts and humiliation at the hands of producers. I hadn't told Bernie that the car was bought with the proceeds of our American Eagle commercial. After all he had a far more labour-intensive part than I did. If Marx is correct about the surplus factor of labour in any industrial compact, then Bernie should have been paid more than me.

Strangely enough, I hardly needed to listen to Bernie to know the plot. Against all the evidence, musicals celebrate the triumph of the individuals over the system, in all sorts of improbable ways. I was ahead of Bernie. Before his large elastic mouth got there, I could see the tenement buildings, the market traders, the fish porters, the not-so-lovable bobbies, the raggedy (lovable) children, the beautiful Lady Bountiful, the synagogue in Bacon Street, the doomed love affair, the heartbreak, the disturbing social ructions, the scene in the Salvation Army hostel, the swaggering blackshirts, the cama-raderie of poverty (as nothing, in my experience, to the chumminess of wealth), the chorus line of washerwomen and fishwives (contralto and soprano), the barrels of jellied eels, the pubs frequented by boxers and criminals, the whores with hearts of gold, and so on. And so it proved. The twist is that Bernard Koppel rises from the ashes of the Blitz to become a famous entertainer. In this case life is definitely lagging some way behind art, but Bernie is quite prepared to give life the necessary kick up the backside.

'Up the Khyber, know what that means?'

'No,' I say, although of course I do.

'Rhyming slang. Khyber pass, arse, gottit?'

I glanced at him. For a potential world-beater, the Chaplin *de nos jours* (or even something less ambitious), he needs to do something about his nasal and aural hair. It's growing like rhubarb. Also his breath is none too good at this time of day. (Whose is?) Perhaps Bernie lives on jellied eels. Certainly there's a whiff of the sea – or more specifically the riverbed – adorning his early-morning monologue.

Bernie can see the romance in anything. His wife died twenty years ago, worn out, I should imagine, by his opti-mism. This gloomy East End whizzing by with its saree importers, its Eldorado Night Clubs and Golden Gate Bingo clubs, its second-hand car dealers (Japanese minibuses a speciality), its massage parlours, its grimy tower blocks, its pubs advertising Australian lager, its litter, its squalor – this will become in Bernie's retelling, a fabulous wonderland of plucky little Cockney folk, fighting cheerfully against the odds until Hitler, Uncle Adolf himself, sends his buzz-bombs and whizz-bangs screaming over the narrow, cold Channel to obliterate the workhouses, the almshouses, the bawdyhouses, the public houses and the rest; buildings on which the sun never shone, out of a sky without a rent in its leaden canopy. Nothing will crush their spirit; certainly the weather hasn't a hope where Adolf and Hermann (who had no balls at all) failed.

'You've got to look on the bright side, rise above it, ain'tcher?'

In his imagination Bernie is not the dilapidated actor with the mobile face who is sitting next to me, but a little boy again, a wiry little street urchin stealing apples from the market, running errands for the prozzies in the tenement, attending yeshiva, winning Boys Clubs awards for his recitation, hanging about the Empire where he is getting an education from life as well as the education from books, courtesy of his angelic, artistic mother, who was on her way to being the first woman neurologist in Bosnia or Latvia – I forget which – until the dreadful repression which meant she was thrown out of medical school in Omsk or perhaps Minsk, and the devoted couple – Bernie's parents-to-be – shipped for New York, but were diverted to Liverpool, owing to a bureaucratic fuck-up, or perhaps even a conspiracy among the high-ups who run the world. In Bernie's demonology the high-ups are WASPS with Teutonic features in their country houses, racquets clubs and panelled boardrooms. Politicians are playthings in their hands. Putty. It was ever thus, as the bard said.

The fish smell rose as we parked the car in the reserved car park. Reserved for the big boys. The traders who have held the rights, clasped tight to their chests in fact, since Elizabethan times. Even from the grandees' car park the fishiness was strong. You could grow healthier just breathing this air, it was so full of iodine and ozone and all the other things that fish are famous for. Actually fish have enjoyed a startling comeback in this regard. My perfunctory researches show that fish were eaten by the poor until very recently. The rich ate the good old roast beef of England. Fish was cheap. Now fish is fashionable and beef has slumped in the index of popularity. The same sort of thing has happened to doctors and lawyers.

Bernie steered me towards the vast hangar of fishiness.

'Roll up yer trousers, otherwise you'll go home smelling like a flounder.'

I was hoping for a more colourful spectacle, to be honest: the air loud with the famous foul language of Billingsgate rising about the fish in chaotic medieval profusion. In reality the fish lay not on old-fashioned barrows or in barrels or even on slabs, but in styrofoam boxes, many with the lids on. There were a few sharks, tuna and giant halibut and some interesting tropical fish – pomfrets and angel fish – but the whole place was unexpectedly calm and prosaic.

Bernie touched my arm lightly and guided me down the central aisle to his friend's stall. His friend was speaking on a mobile phone held in one hand and making notes with his other hand in a ledger. He was taking an order for Icelandic cod, twenty stone.

'No can do, old son. Twenty's the limit. The gulls have been diabolical. No, even that's going to be a bastard. What? Fucking gulls.'

He coughed asthmatically.

'Gulls?' I asked Bernie. 'They eat that much?'

Bernie started to laugh. His eyes watered.

'Gulls: storms, wind. Not seagulls.'

Gales. He meant gales but he said 'gulls' with a little extra liquidity thrown in to distinguish them from the sea birds of the same name.'

'Hello, Bernie old son,' he said, putting down his telephone. 'Not much in today.'

'Because of the gulls,' I said.

'That's the one. Pleased to meet you. Jimmy Tibbs. Any friend of Bernie's is a friend of mine. Is that right, Bernie?'

'That's right Jim. This is Tim Curtiz. He's a writer.'

'I've got a book you can write. I've got loads of ideas and stories, but I ain't got the talent. Want to do it?'

23

'Give it a rest, Jim, he's not interested in your sex life. What's nice today?'

Jimmy Tibbs may have had a two-thousand-dollar mobile phone, but he came straight out of the catalogue. His legs were short and slightly bowed as though he had been riding dolphins on the side; they are ideal for stepping daintily over boxes of fish. His facial skin was red with a spider-web of burst blood vessels, and his face was lively, almost as lively as Bernie's. Between them, at five in the fishy morning, they pulled more faces in a few minutes over the price of a coupla skate wings – huge and ribbed like a Chinese umbrella – than the great Grimaldi himself. Their bushy eyebrows danced *pas de deux*. Jimmy Tibbs's skin appeared to have been chafed. Perhaps he was once a fisherman in the North Sea himself, hauling in the nets in the stinging cold. Now he was a pocket-sized fish trader, a stockbroker of fish, standing surrounded by skate, hake, plaice, mackerel and haddock certainly – but dealing also in trawlerloads yet to be landed and truckloads still to be loaded. Yet the skate wings were obviously equally important.

'Just the skate, Bernie. The rest is not prime quality. The weather's (the wevver) been fucking diabolical.'

'Do Billingsgate people still swear?' I asked. To talk Billingsgate was for centuries to have a foul mouth.

'Not fucking much, we don't,' said Jimmy cheerfully.

His frame was small, but under his white overall he was carrying a hard, prominent little paunch. I guessed he was about sixty, but judging from the difficulty he had getting a deep breath of the life-enhancing, fishy air, he may well have entered his last decade.

Bernie has an eye for the picturesque. In truth you needed it here. The place looked like an airport terminal in Eastern Europe that had been invaded by fish. The picturesque old fish market in the City has been converted to a currency-dealing floor.

'Look, see that old geezer?'

'Yuh.'

'He's a fish porter. Carrying fish in the traditional way.'

A man in a white coat was walking past with a box of fish balanced on his head. Alongside this one relic of the old days (his head crowned with styrofoam) Bernie saw a hundred porters in leather jerkins and bobbing hats, carrying boxes of herrings and eels or flounders, dancing, probably in clogs, to the jaunty music of Lionel Bart, or Andrew Lloyd Webber if he wasn't too busy.

'OK, Jim, we'll take the skate. We're just going to Mavis's for breakfast.'

We left little Jim, a tunnel showing between his legs, talking to Grimsby on his phone. In the corners of the market were cafés, serving eggs, bacon, sausage, toast and tea in any multiples or combinations required. The bacon smell had vanquished the fish smell here, but it was a small victory, a corner of a foreign field. I wondered what on earth I was going to do with a pair of skate wings the size of those flippers kids wear at the beach.

Bernie knew everybody. He introduced me to interesting characters. After each introduction he gave me a brief biography. Everybody seemed to be rich.

'Loaded. Broke his leg falling off his wallet.'

''E don't look much but 'e's got a villa in Cannes (Cans).'

'Villa' gets the treatment too. It's a word to be savoured, like pickled herring or chopped liver, before swallowing. It's a rich, flavoursome word. Bernie's conversation is larded with these words. As a matter of fact 'tasty' is a London word. It means both good-looking, as in 'tasty little number', and a good purchase (probably crooked) as in 'tasty little deal'. In the City the barrow-boy swaps dealers have been getting into trouble with tasty little deals. It's all over the papers.

I forgot to retrieve the skate from the Mercedes. As a result of this its balanced heating and ventilation systems – continuously scanned and adjusted by its microchip brain – had accelerated the skate's progress from the fresh, briny state to the early stages of decomposition. I had to throw it away and then look up skate recipes in case Bernie cross-questioned me. Pure research. *Skate with black butter. Skate poached in a court bouillon. Skate à la crème. Croustade de raie. Skate knobs. Skate mayonnaise.* Who would have guessed there were so many ways? I decided that skate with black butter sounded satisfactorily tasty for Bernie and memorised the recipe. Even here the recipe could be approached from different routes, like mountain climbing – like life come to think about it. I opted for the poaching. When you live alone you can become obsessive about details: train times, flights, restaurant bookings, out-of-date library books and much else. Perhaps it is because you are spared the trivia of family life and something has to take up the surplus capacity. A friend of mine is doing research into the cerebral cortex and he claims that the brain has a life all of its own, an independence from the conscious being – the proprietor of the brain after all – which makes its own decisions about when it's bored and when it's intrigued.

My phone rang. It was Cochrane, the lion killer, from a call box. I could hear him as he struggled with the technology, but he could obviously not hear me. The phone went dead. As I put the receiver back I sniffed it. It had acquired the smell of skate from my hands, which I had washed twice. Despite Bernie's advice, my trousers did smell of fish. In fact all my clothes smelled of fish. My car was impregnated with the odour too. The leather-clad steering wheel would probably smell for ever. I felt all my pre-enlightenment loathing of fish rise. Fish stank. Fish were nasty. Fish ate sewage. Fish fucked in water.

Then I thought of my daughter Gemma's love of the fish in London Zoo. They induced in her a state of serenity, her little intense china face lit from the other side of the plexiglass, her tiny hands contracting, almost undulating, with the pleasure of watching their endless progress around the tanks. There was one large freshwater tank full of mirror carp with distinct nacreous scales the size of dimes attached like sequins to their naked bodies, swimming effortlessly in balletic patterns, like the *corps de ballet*, knowing instinctively where they were going next, a flowing torrent of fish in the verdigris waters of their tank. Gemma watched them with an intensity which reminded me of a great concert pianist at work. Maybe she was conducting them. Maybe she wished to be in there with them floating free. Dreams of the womb and all that stuff. I couldn't hate fish if Gemma loved them.

On the way back from Billingsgate we drove through Docklands on what Bernie, predictably, said was the Yellow Brick

Road. We turned a corner and the skies parted. The sun had not yet risen but it had done something more beautiful: it had leaked out behind the ribs of cloud, back-lighting them so that they acquired a mother-of-pearl sheen, the colour – well – the colour of mirror carp, the colour of tarnished silver by candlelight. In front of this luminous backdrop, the gantries of a hundred cranes rose into the sky and a railway carried a toy train high above the dock between the cranes and the middle distance. It was a scene from *Metropolis*, yet the sky behind was unmistakably by Turner as it melted into the glowing water of the dock.

'They're building the biggest new city in Europe here,' said Bernie.

What price the singing fish porters now, Bernie me old son? I thought to myself.

'You want to go to Smithfield now?' he asked.

'Have you got a friend who is selling off ribs of beef?'

'As a matter of fact, come to mention it. And it's historical. You should know about this. A fishmonger stabbed Wat Tyler there in 1381.'

'Forget it, Bernie. You've been a pal. I've got to file tomorrow. My public expect it.'

So I wrote the story. Naturally I did not mention the boxes of domesticated salmon and trout from fish farms, with their curiously alien look, like castrati or capons. I laid on the local colour pretty thick. As Bernie says, it's all there if you know where to look.

When I had finished I wrote to Cochrane:

Dear Mr Cochrane,

I enjoyed meeting with you very much. I think your story, and the great courage you displayed all those years ago, is still fascinating. Thinking about your story, I realise there are more questions I would like to ask you. I would like to arrange with the zoo for us to meet again, at the lion terraces. Would you like to do this? The fee will be more than £5 I assure you. More than $15 even.

I believe you tried to telephone me earlier today. If you

27

can't get through to me trust me to come and see you soon, within a fortnight. We'll aim to go to the zoo three weeks on Friday. I'll pick you up at 8.30.

Yours sincerely

Timothy Curtiz

What I had in mind was a confrontation between Cochrane and a large male lion, those lanceolate, piss-coloured eyes surveying the former lion's breakfast as a counterpoint to our conversation. Boxers who have been knocked out never forget. In another context, it has been said that once you have been tortured you stay tortured. The synapses have been cauterised by the experience; a neurological path has been created, like a watercourse through a desert. And who knows what lions have buried in their race memory? Man on his two spindly, pink legs, the unspeakable monkey who somehow has achieved dominance over everything. Christ, what a fucking joke that must be to a lion!

CHAPTER FOUR

Victoria did not know how to adjust the microchip controls on the heating. The house was cold. The decorating, which had seemed so right at the time, looked cheap and unskilled. The strawberry-mousse rag-rolling on the walls was crude and pretentious. The curtains, run up by the wife of a Turkish Cypriot minicab driver, hung at peculiar angles, like the first ball-gown her mother had bought her all those years ago. Thirteen years, to be precise. She sat at the limed-oak kitchen table, a cup of coffee cooling in front of her. She was counting. She had reached seventy-six. She could hardly believe it. Seventy-six, and maybe more! She had slept with seventy-six men since she was sixteen. Jesus. Of course, seventy-six divided by thirteen was only six and a half a year. Or one (and a bit) every two months. But there had been nothing mathematically regular about it in real life. Some months there had been none at all. Seventy-six was nothing like a record among her friends, yet this morning it seemed a disgustingly long list. All that passion and tenderness (and even a little subversive violence) were as distant as the surf heard in a seashell held to the ear, which is, of course, only the pounding of the cardio-vascular system. The trouble with sex is that it is nine parts illusion.

Seventy-six men and boys, most of whom she had not seen for years. Some she had never seen again, after the event. You couldn't just blame men. Women were complicit in the whole arrangement. But seventy-six of them. Oh my. Seventy-six (plus) willies, dicks, John Thomases. Why do they have affectionate nicknames, when the women's have little animal names or worse? You didn't have to be a paid-up feminist to draw a few conclusions about the alloted sexual roles.

29

As she finished her – inconclusive – count, she thought with bitterness how quickly the decade had passed. At nineteen she had set off to Sussex University, and at twenty-nine she was sitting alone on a Sunday morning in London, wondering where those years had gone. A decade had simply vanished. In that decade she had lost the bloom of youth. Worst of all was its predictability: her anxieties were of the obvious variety; you could read about them in *Cosmopolitan* every month: anxious women, anxious about their lack of breasts, their abundance of breasts, their lack of achievement, their over-achievement, their lack of children, their surfeit of children, their lack of a career, the tyranny of a career. You could also read about the trap that women had so blindly walked into by accepting, even courting, new responsibilities and expectations. Which, of course, they could never satisfactorily assume. And so on. The trouble was, like cheap music and shallow novels, they often had a certain potency. Her mother, a finely tuned antenna of anxiety, had taken to calling to ask what she was proposing to do now. The word 'proposing' was given an ironic stress, the second vowel had a little extra charge, which, in the perfectly honed nuances of their relationship, was as good as electro-convulsive therapy.

Her mother's hope had been that her 'relationship' with Miles would 'work out'. 'Working out' in this context meant marriage. It hadn't. Her mother had liked Miles. She found him charming, which was code for sexy. Almost everyone found Miles sexy. Being sexy was Miles's *raison d'être*. He walked around in a cloud of sexiness, like a beekeeper carrying the queen bee.

Miles had come in from the opera at four-thirty one night.

'Hope you don't think I'm being a nag, Miles, but doesn't the opera end at about eleven? Pavarotti likes to get to bed early.'

Miles was carefully buttoning his nightshirt.

'Nnh. The bottom line, Victoria, is that I am not ready to settle down.'

'The bottom line, Miles, is that you think bonking is a religious activity. You see yourself as having a calling from on high. Which, if I was talking purely in terms of technique, I would have to say is not true.'

'You would know, of course.'

She had tried to hide the extent of her sexual knowledge from Miles, naturally, but he still referred to it in moments of strife.

Miles talked in a way that had begun to irritate her. He was like blotting paper, lexical blotting paper. She suspected that knowing the latest words – 'golden parachutes', 'proactive' and 'dysergy' were a selection from his current repertoire – made him feel close to the centre of things, and consequently a long distance from Victoria who had somehow spun out to the periphery of things. Not only did Miles's verbal promiscuity irritate her, but the way he enunciated made her angry, particularly when he was sitting in front of his 'screen' at the bank, with long pauses punctuated by the occasional, sceptical, 'Yhh', or 'Nhh', or 'Mhh'. Where her mother tickled up the vowels, Miles had taken to eliminating them altogether, so that in answer to her enquiries he made a noise like a dentist's drill just before it struck a nerve, or perhaps, she once thought, like a Vietnamese expleting. This little noise suggested at once that Miles was bored by the question and that it was not a proper question anyway, but a rhetorical device to catch him out. His suspicions on this score were often justified. But then so were hers which prompted the enquiries.

Miles had taken to opera. Victoria, who had seen herself as the educated and creative half of their partnership, was particularly incensed by this. Before Verdi his great love had been Bruce Springsteen. Now, courtesy of the bank, he was always off to Covent Garden with clients, apparently other dealers. Miles was in a SWAPS team. Victoria had no idea what it did, but it sounded incredibly juvenile, like Monopoly by telephone. And Miles, aged thirty-one, had started affecting hand-made shoes at £300 a pair, shirts at £120 each, worn with braces that cost £75 a pair. His hair was cut in a new and interesting way too, with little wings and carefully sculpted sides, so that he looked not like an English gentleman but an English gentleman in a foreign film.

'Soon, Miles, you'll be playing golf.'

Long pause.

'Yhhh.' (The dentist drill struck an obstruction.) 'Mhh. I've been thinking.'

'Well hurry up.'

'I've got to take the work situation more seriously, mhh.'

'Than what?'

Slight dry laugh, air emitted sparingly:

'M-hhh. Than I have been.'

Victoria could sense trouble, like a swallow sensing the onset of winter.

'I can't wait, Miles. Let's hear it.'

'It wouldn't be fair on you with the commitments I'm taking on. The bank is profit-led to a point where there are no para-chutes.'

'What does that mean? In English. I know it's dog eat dog out there, in the Church's handmade shoes, but what exactly are you trying to say, in English?'

'Don't take the piss, Vic. Arnie's keeping me very busy. It isn't fair on you, I know.'

'Who are you bonking now, Miles? Katia Ricciarelli? Ricardo Muti? You pompous prick. Get out.'

There were two problems when Miles moved out. The first was purely financial. The house in Wapping was expensive. Interest rates had risen and since they had bought the house a new development called Curlew Rise had largely obscured their view of the river, so removing its unique selling prop-osition; in the meantime the market, even for houses with an unobstructed view of Father Thames, had collapsed. Miles wanted – as he put it – out, but he was prepared to continue paying half the mortgage until Victoria had found her feet. Half the mortgage was one thing, but what about half the gas, half the electricity, half the taxes, half the repairs on the roof? It cost just as much to heat one person. Probably more. For a start it had been his idea to buy somewhere down here, a million miles from civilisation. Property prices were rising faster here than in Tokyo, he said. Unfortunately something had gone wrong. The plethora of Heron's Beats, Mariner's Walks, and Sandpiper's Reaches had oversupplied the market. A hiccup on the graph, said Miles in his Olympian manner. People in the City were always pretending that what they did was scientific. They employed the language of mathematics and science to lend respectability to their gambling.

The second problem was that, aware as she was of Miles's shortcomings, she found herself brooding on the fact that Miles, at thirty-one, was beginning to find his feet, while she had obviously lost her footing altogether. Miles was sexy, good-looking, and just becoming rather rich. With the huge bonus he was expecting, he would earn nearly £70,000 this year. Although she despised him, she sometimes shared her mother's unarticulated opinion that she might not do any better, at twenty-nine and a half. Without Miles around to despise in person, this realisation was doubly painful.

Framed in the small amount of vista left to her by the encroaching buildings, she could see a slice of the river, indifferent to her, indifferent – it seemed – to London, to its misery, to its history, to the meaningless strivings of the citizenry. It simply flowed on. You could never set the Thames on fire, as Miles was confidently expecting to do (in the work situation). The Thames was not combustible; it was old, bored and cold. Its surface was scoured by winds blowing all the way up from the estuary, scudding viciously over its boiled tripe surface. Curlew Rise was vandalism. Its fancy fretwork of variegated bricks and cast-iron balconies had slashed her view of the river. Her Turner had been wantonly defaced by a maniacal property developer, leaving her with just the very edge of the picture, a useless piece of canvas, as useless as a five-pound note without the serial numbers.

As she looked at the river morsel, she took comfort from one fact anyway: she did not miss Miles himself, with his ivory-handled and badger-bristled brushes and those brogues with the acupuncture holes all over their hand-sewn toecaps. Even his willy – number seventy-three chronologically – had lost its place in her affections. She was surprised how little he had left behind; it confirmed her low opinion of him that he had been wafted away so lightly.

She pulled her overcoat over her nightdress and set off to get the newspapers from the corner shop. The white locals called it the 'Paki shop' although the proprietors were dark, furtive people from Bangladesh. The popular myth was that the Bangladeshis were simply a new generation of upwardly mobile immigrants to the East End of London, an area which

33

had – in this mythology – played host to waves of immigrants over the centuries in some inexplicably altruistic fashion. As far as Victoria could see there was an altogether more basic reason, a law of physics, namely that water finds its own level. The East End had thousands of acres, perhaps even square miles, of dereliction. Miles's mistake had been to assume that the logic of the Nikkei Index applied in this disordered topography. No upwardly mobile Japanese in his right mind would want to live down here. Nor did Victoria. She wanted to live in South Kensington or Hampstead, back among the English. Nothing personal. Perhaps a few years ago she would have found it interesting, even challenging, to live among people who, in their swampy homeland, had barely seen a tap and lived exclusively on rice. Perhaps she would have felt some personal responsibility that the gas in her hairspray, however unwitting she had been, had contributed to the melting of the Himalayan snows and the consequent flooding of Bangladesh, leading, with a certain amount of symmetry, to the arrival of Mrs Chowdray and family in the corner shop. Now, if she was honest, she didn't give a fuck.

The shop stood pluckily in a forlorn block that had largely fallen down. No doubt the developer of Curlew Rise was about to build Sandpiper's Reach here, though with any luck interest rates had killed more development. On the other hand, if rates continued to rise, she would never be able to sell. She should have moved out first, leaving the financial wizard to handle the financial indigestion.

Miles's top lip acquired a little frostiness in discussing finance, as if his face were suffering from a dose of Novocaine. He imagined it was icy composure, the product of an inner calm. He saw himself as the sage of the marketplace. Underneath his good looks and his declamatory custom-made clothes ('custom-made' and other Americanisms were common in the City), Victoria saw emerging the sly self-esteem and vanities of a certain type of Englishman. Life prepares these people for a comfortable, misogynist middle age. Middle age is their heyday: Their contact with women is reduced to the formalities of a Japanese in a geisha's parlour. Their self-esteem is lavishly catered for by chauffeurs, share options, dining clubs, directorships of companies, boxes at the opera, and charity sporting events. While their children moulder in boarding school, they have long conversations with their hairdressers who libate them with exotic extracts of plants and fruit; they also cultivate cosy relationships with doormen and headwaiters. Their wives are drained of succulence as they wax more prosperous. (There seems to be some physical law at work here, that each couple shall only have so much juice between them.)

By the time she had bought the Sunday papers from the quiet, dusty woman with a large bust, she could barely believe that she had managed eleven months with Miles in this ghastly, desolate landscape of shabby old buildings and presumptuous new ones. There was always a smell of burning oil and pitch from the building sites, which added to the sense that she had been living in a war zone.

'Thank you, Mrs Chowdray,' she said calmly, despite the seething of her blood, which matched the turbulence of the river's surface as she walked back along the embankment behind the park.

The tide was turning and the waters were undecided about their true destination. They chopped and bucked and heaved irritably. Victoria sometimes made no distinction between sentient and inanimate objects in respect of feelings. The river was angry, no question of it. Essentially, human beings were not as far removed from the primal soup as they liked to imagine; they were only a collection of cells which had somehow acquired a sense of self-importance. If she ever had children – which now looked unlikely – she would value them most for this lack of self-esteem.

The wildness of the river – the open land on the other side with the gulls wheeling excitedly over the rubbish barges and the piled bricks and twisted exoskeletons of bulldozed factories – stirred her. She was pleased to realise that she did not miss Miles the person, even if Miles the institution had left a gap. She had feared parting with Miles – she had thought about it often enough – in sick expectation of that desolation and jealousy. Yet there was none, only anxiety about being twenty-nine and a half. And she was a perfectly capable person, well paid, sexually attractive (to the power of seventy-six) with a few temporary financial worries only. She was due to start her course at the Tate next week and at the same time the Agency had moved her on to the American Eagle account which meant lots of travel. The creative work was not very interesting, but they were working on a new commercial with a journalist stiff who wore phoney English tweeds and was a poor man's Gore Vidal back in the old US of A. The scripts were wooden to the point of caricature, but she could sort them out. Victoria would deliver.

At the same time she would cultivate her other-life, which she had neglected to her cost; she would study her Stubbs conscientiously. Stubbs had spent seventeen years working on his horse and lion pictures and many, many more studying anatomy. Sometimes he worked on cadavers which had been dead for months. To Victoria his lions looked woolly and cuddly, but someone had told her that Stubbs had studied the anatomy of Asiatic lions, common in menageries then, and perhaps they were more cuddly, like the sort of toy you could win at a fair by throwing darts or shooting air rifles or ringing ducks. His dogs were good: to the life. And the horses, those eyes of amber with adrenal squirts of fear. She would join a gym down there too. Her bottom was in danger of deflation after eleven months of sitting about waiting for Miles to come back from his meetings and opera and wine bars and shoemakers.

By the time she reached her front door she had cheered herself up with her own resolve. The phone rang. Her mother's extra-sensory perception had picked up trouble – just a little cumulus formation on the radar at first, then a major storm front bearing down. But Victoria felt proof against anything her mother could throw at her.

'Hello, Mum. No. He's out. In fact he's out of my life. Yes. For ever.'

Her mother's intake of breath and a small girlish 'Oh' suggested that she was upset as much for her own sake as Victoria's.

'Would you like to come down for lunch, darling?' she asked bravely.

'No thanks, but let's meet next Monday when I'm up at the Tate and I'll give you a blow-by-blow account.'

'He hasn't been hitting you, has he?' She sounded quite excited.

'Not that sort of blow, dear.'

Her mother had almost no awareness of the winds of change which were buffeting the English language.

'Are you feeling all right?' she asked in the small voice.

'I feel like someone who has had a ten-ton weight lifted off their shoulders,' said Victoria. 'And by the way, why are you speaking in that squeaky voice?'

Victoria recognised the voice. She herself deployed it sometimes when the occasion demanded. Her mother often used it when speaking to Miles. It was a regression to a more innocent, a more coquettish, self. At twenty-nine Victoria had begun to realise that people are not just one self – the self their outward appearance and circumstance suggest – but previous selves and imagined selves. Women, particularly, were prone to a notion of a preferable self. It was all hopelessly mixed up with the harsh facts of childbearing and desirability, the very same things she had been brooding on earlier, so she decided not to be hard on her mother.

'Victoria, I'm upset. I thought possibly, this time, you would settle down.'

'Why are mothers so keen on their daughters settling down? Do you think they're envious?'

'Don't be provocative, Victoria. Miles always seemed so nice.'

'Appearances are deceptive. Miles is a dipstick. It's taken me eleven months to realise it.' ('Dipstick' was one of Miles's new transatlantic words.)

'But he's doing so well.'

'Exactly. That's what they want in the City: numbnuts in Paul Smith suits. He's simply being fed into the mighty engine.'

'I realise you're upset, but aren't you being a little unfair to Miles?'

'Unfair? Good joke. He's the one who persuaded me to live down here in Bangalore and now he's gone, leaving me to find a roofer, a plumber, an estate agent and God knows what all. And as it happens I'm not upset, not in the way you would like.'

'I thought you were against racial jokes. You used to be. As for your last remark, I'll try to ignore it. I don't know where you get this twisted mind. Probably in advertising.'

'Probably from you. Goodbye.'

Victoria slammed the phone down. (These new phones were too light for such gestures.) Now she *was* upset. Her optimistic mood, created on the bracing riverside walk in her nightie, had gone. It had been dissipated by her mother's determination to squeeze the juice out of her quandary. Girls and their mothers, she thought, what a fuck-up. Of course girls and their mothers feed off the same bits of DNA, little strings of human essence handed down from generation to generation. Their relationship was probably predetermined five hundred or a thousand years ago somewhere in rural Sussex.

She decided to get dressed immediately before self-pity set in. This was not as easy as it might have been. Her wardrobe was in a period of transition. She had never felt completely happy about the black and grey look – the Joseph look – nor with the severe hair which went with it. Now she wanted to give up dressing to a theme. She wanted to dress, somehow, in her own way. The problem was she had not decided what that was. London fashion was so extraordinarily eclectic (read 'scruffy' she sometimes thought) that the moment you abandoned a look – Joseph, Versace, Brown's or whatever – you ended up like everyone else: eclectic. Girls in the agency were still going round in artfully torn jeans and Western belts and black Doc Marten's, all looking as if they had just casually thrown this combination together. Her mother, of course, would have liked her to wear floral print skirts by Laura Ashley. She settled for untorn 501s, clean white Converse and a heavy workman's shirt of washed-out pink. She made herself up, just enough to emphasise her so recently older and wiser eyes.

She had nothing to do. London was hers. She could do anything. But, she thought, you couldn't do anything with London. It was too big to comprehend. It was like the universe which we now know for sure to be infinite, without a beginning either in space or time. In some places she had been to – Amsterdam, Florence, even Paris – the city was a comprehensible whole. Not London. You could barely grapple with the notion. For the people who lived down here, the indigenes, Belgravia and Chelsea were as far away as Rawalpindi or Cincinnati. Heal's and Harrods might have been nothing but specks in the firmament dimly observed on a clear night. If anyone was looking.

Outside, at the end of the narrow alleyway of her vista, she could see the river begin to glint as the scudding clouds passed over and allowed the sun, or at least its refracted alter-image, to kiss the water's surface with silver, one of those brief and unenthusiastic little French *bisoux*, where the lips barely touch the cheek (and French children try to avoid the stab of grand-mère's whiskers). It was enough for Victoria. She had the urge to practise the art of divination by firing arrows into the sky. She fired one hopefully upriver where the sky above Heron's Beat was for a moment not leaden but argent. The silver clouds looked like lions crouched to spring on the terrified cumulus horses. She fired another arrow from her seeping, owner-occupied duplex towards the lion shapes, before they tumbled into the savannah of clouds.

She had never been to Africa (or Asia for that matter) but the lionscape was instantly recognisable.

CHAPTER FIVE

Zoos are concerned – there are fashions in zoo-keeping as in every form of human endeavor – with gene banks and pools these days. They see themselves – they use the metaphor freely – as arks for the survival of various species. You could grade species in zoo-keepers' esteem in inverse proportion to the amount still at large in the wild. The Mauritius pink pigeon and the pygmy hippopotamus are stars in the zoo-keepers' firmament, where the conventionally sized hippo and the drabber pigeons have mere walk-ons. It follows that African lions are not very popular because they breed anywhere with indecent haste, and especially in zoos. There is an over-supply of lions. What to do with the annual surplus is a perennial problem for zoos around the world. They have resorted to vasectomy, birth-control pills and sterilization. A zoo-keeper's nightmare is another litter of cute cubs with the puzzled demeanor and disproportionately large feet.

London Zoo has decided that its African lions will now be replaced with rare Asiatic lions. Not even lions are immune to the dictates of fashion. The black-maned male lion, Chaka, is to be 'euthanized'. (There are fashions in terminology, too.) The news has leaked out to shocked Londoners by way of an innocent publicity release. The older of the two females, Suku, is also to be euthanized. A good home is sought for the younger female – Doris to its keeper, Dukwe to the public. None of these lions has been anywhere near the wild. They would not know a wildebeest from a London bus. They are like actors who have not made it to the Broadway transfer, after faithfully playing out in the sticks in summer stock – what the Brits call 'rep' – for months. Bigger stars, the Asiatics, are coming to occupy the lion terraces. But wait, there is a glimmer of hope for the incumbents: genetic tests show that the new lions are not genetically pure. The DNA proves conclusively that back in the 1950s a careless Rajah, the Wali of Swat or the Maharajah of Jaipur perhaps, allowed an African male to wander at will amongst the females of his menagerie in parched Rajastan. Alarm and despondency in zoological circles! These Asiatics, previously believed to be the single largest genetic pool, are tainted with African blood! The search is on at Gir in India, the only lion sanctuary in Asia, for purebred Asian lions. And as for Doris, her likely destination at the moment is the Bronx.

Who knows what a lion thinks about? What premonitions are troubling the Cockney lions as they perhaps sense a little coolness entering their relationship with their keepers? Do they have the feeling – like old actors – that their agents are looking elsewhere to earn a crust?

Like my friend Bernie in fact. He has been struggling to find a new agent. His former agent, Lennie Weinreb – a fellow survivor of the Blitz and much else besides – has lost heart. His son-in-law, who is a successful developer in Wapping, is building a villa in Spain. At the back of this villa he is building a small apartment, all on one level, for Bernie's seventy-four-year-old ex-agent. Lennie has had it with showbiz. The fun's gone out of it. The schlemiels who pass for actors these days you wouldn't believe it. The young comics who can't sing a note – they don't even have a theme song – the high-ups in television who have lost touch with real people – the whole thing stinks.

I wonder if this protestation, relayed to me by Bernie with mimetic gestures, isn't just an elaborate way of getting rid of his last client, an old guy in golfing trousers with hair growing out of his ears and nose; an old geezer who has failed to see the writing on the wall. Lennie hasn't the heart to say – I am making this up – 'Bernie, they don't want sixty-nine-year-old comics with 'airy ears what can tap dance while singing the hippopotamus song in Yiddish. And to tell the truth I don't think they care too much what 'appened back in 1940 no more. Call me stupid if you like, Bernie, but I think you should save youself a lot of balls-ache. Give it a rest, my son. Use some grey matter. On eighty-five quid a week you can live like a king in Nerja, Mervyn tells me.'

Bernie, it goes without saying, doesn't see it quite like this. I am his best hope at the moment. He knows there's another American Eagle commercial coming up in a few months. (Research on my image and impact will soon be complete.) He sees himself – if not exactly starring – at least sharing billing with me. He's going to be showing me around London, just the way he's been doing it in real life, and, of course, the US public are going to go a bundle on this lovable East End character. No kidding, this is what Bernie believes. He tries to be subtle about his gameplan, but it comes bursting out from behind any subterfuge. Bernie cannot keep his feelings to himself. In this respect he is completely without dignity: *I'm an open book. That's me trouble. I'm too straight. I've had so many of me ideas nicked you wouldn't believe it.* There's another explanation for this apparent honesty, but I don't have the honesty to suggest it.

'Big mistake, Bernie. Work your ideas up first. That's the rule. Ask anybody,' I said.

Bernie made a show of noting this advice. But there is a curious ambivalence in our relationship: Bernie needs me, in his contorted estimation, but at the same time he sees me as a minor character who has got lucky. Conversely he is a major character who has not yet had the breaks.

'Nice cups,' he said as he slurped my high-roast Arabica from the Algerian Coffee Store. The cups are those chunky green and gold things, favoured by cafés in France. Noisily he took another sip.

'Bit thick, but nice.'

'Bernie, I've got to file.'

'I'm going. Don't worry. Stay not upon the order of thy going, as the bard said. Nice place. A false ceiling would make it more cosier. You're losing a lot of heat up there.'

'I like those beams, Bernie.'

'If you don't want a suspended ceiling, I've got a mate who could give them a more attractive wood finish than that.'

'Than wood? Nice idea. But not at the moment. Bernie, New York is waiting for my words of wisdom.'

Bernie stood up, in stages.

'How was the skate?'

'Fantastic. Numero uno. Beurre noir and capers.'

'Whatever turns you on,' said Bernie in his (poor) Nathan Detroit voice. 'Personally I like skate fried in matso meal.'

'Good stuff. Sounds great.' (No mention of matso meal in Julia Child.)

I stood up, keen not to let the opportunity pass, but my knee knocked one of the cups on to the granite slabs. It shattered.

'You drink too much coffee, if you want a word of advice, Tim. Too strong. It makes you nervous.'

'Probably. Sorry to hear about your agent anyway.'

'Not to worry. Between you me and the gatepost, he was past it anyway. Any news on the ad?' he asked as he edged reluctantly towards the door. We were like magnets that repel. As I advanced towards the door, he shifted away. When I stopped, he stopped.

'I'll let you know. I'm just a front. They do all the thinking.'

'Top dollar for a front, as I hear tell.'

Bernie's slang was years out of date, but his information was always up to the minute. I walked firmly towards the door, my magnetic field forcing him out of the door and towards the beautiful, roughly cut stone steps. I was half expecting him to offer discount carpet squares as he pulled his camel-hair coat, cut short of his knees, around his lumpy frame and jammed a black PVC Homburg on his head. This discordant dressing (the absurd hats and the elderly but cherished coats) seems to be a necessary characteristic of people with refugee antecedents.

'You mustn't let the bastards grind you down,' he said as his upper body, the legs already severed, descended from my view.

I was not sure if this was an all-purpose maxim or a specific instruction. Although he left a faint fishy smell behind him, he also left a little human warmth crackling in the air like the static you get in Japanese cars.

In preparation for my next meeting with Simba Cochrane, I had been to the lion terrace to see the lions feed. It was all highly organised. In catering this process is known as 'portion control'. The lions were fed not donkey quarters as I had imagined, but large pieces of horseflesh, weighed and doctored carefully to ensure health and avoid obesity. The male was thin. He had a hunted look; perhaps he was expecting the hyena to realise that his time was up and arrive, as they had always done, shuffling and diffident at first, but increasingly impudent as they recognised the symptoms. Perhaps the uncontrollable gushing of his semen had dried up. Perhaps he was just dreaming lion dreams of a state of grace out on the endless savannah. In any event, his ribs showed through, great joists of bone which had once supported muscular, sexually imposing flesh. Now they were hangers for the worn carpet of his skin. Yet his head was still magnificent, the way old senators, Supreme Court judges and orchestral conductors preserve a lifetime of egotism in their grand heads while their bodies atrophy just like any other old chap's. Like successful actors for that matter, the Laurence Oliviers rather than the Bernies of that trade.

The head keeper said that Chaka was no longer friendly. In the old days he enjoyed a good old scratch and would come when he was called. Now he was aloof. I asked if he thought lions had extra-sensory perception (a favourite topic of the *Reader's Digest* in my youth); presentiments of mortality. He didn't think it was a question of that. He thought the old boy was in pain from a worn vertebra.

The keeper himself could not have been less leonine. Like many conservation-minded people, he was essentially a herbivore, with a beard admittedly, but a beard which brought to mind a goat rather than something carnivorous like a lion. Euthanising the lion was not going to cause him any heartache. All part of the job. He was looking forward to the arrival of the genetically desirable Asiatics. Zoo-keeping had changed from the bad old days where Joe Public simply came and gazed at the adorable animals, and he for one was not sorry.

'Any way I can get Cochrane and the lion together?'

'What do you mean?'

'Well, actually standing next to one another for a picture?'

'I don't think so,' he said primly, his mouth closing like a fridge door with a clunk. Unscientific notion. Clunk. He was not a Londoner; he came from the outer zone somewhere, with a faint whine to his voice, church bells distantly heard. We talked about lions. He saw himself as the centre of things. He was saving the planet, for Chrissake, while all the blind capitalists and industrialists, the whole industrial military complex as a matter of fact, were pursuing the profit motive which led inexorably to the stripping of the rain forest, the thinning of the atmosphere, deforestation of the Himalayas, the flooding of Bangladesh and the inundation by immigrants of the East End of London. His social notions, expressed with a tinny note, were as unscientific as the most zealous fundamentalist's; but then whose are not? As we spoke he injected into the meat vitamin complexes, worming powders, mineral supplements and, probably, birth-control hormones. He used a huge syringe. Outside on the terraces, the lions were restless. The male walked stiff-legged around the perimeter. He roared. The roar was loud enough to cause the Petri dishes and tin trays of meat to clatter. I watched him through the keeper's observation window. Round and round he walked, looking beyond the children in nylon parkas, beyond the goat mountain, beyond the mosque, towards the middle distance. Nothing within hundreds of yards interested him. He skirted the edge of the moat, ignoring a small family of ducks which dabbled there recklessly. He roared again.

'He's hungry,' said the keeper. But as the lion marched awkwardly, like a veteran on Remembrance Day, he seemed to be seeing something in the distance. The females stood up and looked in the same direction. They began to mill about, caught in his turbulence. Perhaps they saw Simba Cochrane on 'is 'orse, happroachin' at a canter, his little body in khaki leggings and bush jacket looking unmistakably like something to eat.

The keeper called out loudly and banged open the iron gates to the inner cages where the lions were fed. In a moment the lionesses appeared hungrily but warily in the iron tunnel.

'Come on, come on, come, come, come.'

He spoke to them the way farmers talk to cows or cowboys to horses, with a professional tone. With deft prods and pushes on levers he separated them into their respective living quarters where the chunks of meat were waiting. They did not eat immediately, although they each placed a paw on a chunk of meat as if to prevent it escaping.

'Old bastard,' said the keeper gruffly. 'Come, come, come.'

'Perhaps he's not hungry,' I said.

He gave me an unscientific look.

We went outside to a little alleyway between the lion terraces and the leopard cages. The keeper called and banged the chain-link fence with a tin plate. The lion ignored him. A siren sounded and the few families still left in the gathering gloom under a sky as poisonous and mottled as the skin of a toad-stool, hurried off to the exit, perhaps afraid to be trapped in this otherworld of monkeys with dandruff hair, toucans with beaks like giant beanpods, restless probing snakes, quirky antelope with yellow teeth and an elderly lion roaring queru-lously. Night was falling, and with it the animals began to squeak and squeal and shriek; the peaceful, rustic zoo was becoming an uneasy dreamscape.

'Bloody old fool,' said the keeper.

The old lion stood with his front legs on a log, his huge sham head silhouetted, and roared again. The lionesses were restless. They began to eat guiltily as though expecting a rep-rimand from their sovereign, outside on important business.

'How do you get him in now?'

'He'll come soon. I think you had better go now or they'll be locking up.'

'OK. Thanks very much.'

I was wondering how he was going to get the lion in. There did not seem to be any obvious way if the lion went on hunger strike. He was still there as I hurried off, also anxious to be out before they locked the gates. I took a wrong turning and found myself in a dank, unlit tunnel. On the other side of the tunnel was the Zoological Society's building; with a little explanation I was able to leave the zoo through the Fellows' entrance. Three men in dinner jackets were mounting the staircase. Outside a family was piling into their car. Two boys of about sixteen were fooling about, throwing chestnuts at each other.

''Ere come on, will yer,' shouted a muffled voice from inside the car. 'Come on, pull yer finger out.'

'Did yer see them baboons wanking?' asked one of the boys as they walked past me. He had two or three earrings and strange

46

microwaved hair. The second boy was wearing stone-washed jeans and a leather jacket with a picture of George Michael on it. He too appeared to have had some radiation or incubation problem.

'It woz fucking purple, its dong woz, like a Mr Tastee, them purple rocket ones.'

'Come on, 'urry up,' shouted the underwater voice as they tried to push chestnuts down the back of each other's necks.

'Silly old cunt,' said the second boy.

They had loping walks, which suggested extreme lassitude, perhaps from the very activity they were attributing to the baboons. Untidily they climbed into the car, whose windows were fogged from the inside.

I walked around the circular road, past the American Ambassador's residence, Winfield House. I have been for dinner there twice. The lion's roars were throttled in the damp air, but I could still hear him, his voice hoarse and tired. Obviously he was not yet hungry, or perhaps he was proposing to camp out for the night.

When Sir Edwin Landseer, the sculptor of the huge recumbent lions in London's Trafalgar Square, required a model, he approached the Zoological Society. The secretary replied:

'The lion who has for so long been the most noble ornament of the Society's collection, is now suffering from so acute an attack of inflammation of the lungs that I fear there is little chance of saving his life.

'As he is certainly the finest example of his species now in Europe, and it is scarcely possible to expect that we shall ever obtain another equal to him, it has occurred to me that a study from this animal might be desirable to you. If the event which I cannot but regard as most possible should unfortunately occur, I shall be happy to send him to your studio while yet warm and leave him with you for two or perhaps three days . . .'

When the lion died it was delivered to Landseer's house where Charles Dickens happened to be dining. Dickens reported the manservant entering and asking: 'Did you order a lion, sir?' Dickens loved the story and repeated it often.

47

It is a good story. My father, who was lost in the mountains of Africa somewhere, was always looking for a story. I wonder what my little daughter who loves fish, and lives with her hare-brained mother on Long Island, will be? Perhaps she doesn't love fish any longer. I have not seen her for seven weeks. Children change their allegiances with bewildering speed. Last time she came she had given up cheese, which I had bought in in loads. Perhaps she has made a complete volte-face and forsaken fish. I can bring her to see the lions feed instead. The intense feeling I have for her disturbs me. I ask myself sometimes, if we had been a Victorian family with eight or ten children, many of them disposable to enteritis, influenza and all the other little ailments that took them away to the arms of the angels in the night, could we have afforded this intensity of emotion? Is it in inverse proportion to the likelihood of anything happening to her? Certainly she has the best physicians and specialists Park Avenue can supply, if the bills are anything to go by.

Sir Edwin Landseer, as part of his preparation for the lion sculpture, had wanted to spend a whole night in the lion house at the zoo. It was not allowed because another painter called Mulready had entered the lion house to find a lioness at large. He was cornered for nearly an hour before the keeper returned. What did he feel, I wonder, as he gazed into the horribly inexpressive eyes? Perhaps, like Simba Cochrane, he was cocooned by shock.

Outside it was raining. Where I live in Holland Park the houses are protected from the rain by coats of white paint so thick they are like bathtub enamel. Nobody scratches my car here; its fifteen – or twenty-eight – coats of German paint make light of rain. I could see the raindrops bouncing vainly on its hood. They only added a little sparkle, like the fountains of Tivoli, to this gorgeous object. My place was once the hayloft in the stable block of a huge mansion which no longer exists, courtesy of the same people who brought me my Mercedes. After the bomb fell, the grounds became a park where the children of the newly rich mingle with the children of the old rich. All around live investment bankers, futures traders and stockbrokers, with wives whose succulence is draining away as their husbands jet about the world, plumping themselves up with self-importance. One of these chaps actually plays polo. I see him set off, his car full of saddles and boots and polo sticks, piled apparently at random into the Volvo like an ad for Ralph Lauren. His wife comes to see him go, waving wistfully from under a magnolia tree by the rich, burnt umber front door.

The phone rang. It was the advertising agency for American Eagle. A woman introduced herself as the new creative group head. Could she run some copy up the flagpole and see if I saluted? It would have to go back to New York, if I gave it the OK, for final approval and research. They were hoping to shoot before Christmas.

'Could you give me dates as soon as possible, Victoria? My daughter is coming to visit.'

'I'm afraid I don't know yet. We'll have to get the copy agreed, the director lined up and so on. Let's say a month from now at the earliest.'

'Try and bring a schedule when you come round with the copy.'

'Right. I'll get the men in suits working on it. I'm looking forward to meeting you.'

'Me too,' I said. 'I mean I'm looking forward to meeting you, not me.'

She had a quick nervous laugh, pent up, ready to go perhaps a fraction too early.

'Let's have lunch. On American Eagle,' she added.

We made the arrangements with a frisson of complicity. We were indulging ourselves in the most commonplace of frauds: American Eagle were going to pay for a lunch which was not necessary at all. But then they couldn't care less. *Aquila non captat muscas.* The eagle does not hawk at flies. Interesting, too, that the American imperial symbol should be the eagle and the British, the lion, with his colleague the unicorn in a supporting role. And of course everyone knows the powerful charm the unicorn exercised in the sexual arena.

49

CHAPTER SIX

The horse's nose began to vibrate, to resonate like a musical instrument made of living skin. The whiskers on its soft, firm lips trembled with static electricity and the gentle flap beneath its mouth, which closed over long yellowish teeth – teeth like the piano keys of an old upright Steinway – developed a tic. The horse was gulping at the air, devouring it, feeding on the strong terrifying lion odour which flooded its geranium-pink nostrils and stung the sensitive membranes of its nose. It was as sharp as iodine applied to a graze. The whole animal began to shake and its legs stiffened; it began to hop on all four hooves at the same time in epileptic movements. Its neck and shoulders began to sweat uncontrollably and the sweat started from its cheeks, producing a cappuccino froth from under the bridle.

Suddenly the horse farted. A horse's farts are pleasant and vegetable and the noise is loud and leathery, like the slap of a razor strop. A moment later the lion charged, perhaps provoked by the fart. It was only yards away. Before the horse could get fully into its stride, before it could shake the stiffness from its legs, before its wildly rotating eyes could settle on an avenue of escape, the lion was flying through the air. The horse had made only two floundering movements, going nowhere, like a rocking horse, when the lion landed on its back, hurling Cochrane to the ground and pitching the horse violently forwards on to its nose.

Cochrane, unlike the horse, had no intimation of danger. He imagined that his horse was suffering the first symptoms of the African horse-sickness, and he was wondering if it would survive long enough to get him back to camp. As he lay pinioned by the lion's huge paw, he asked himself if the horse would have done better if it had not been gelded. The lion – my supposition – wondered why the prey had fallen apart in this peculiar way and why he had been left in possession of these little unappetising bits, dressed in khaki. The lion had taken a knock himself. He had been expecting some resistance to his spring. He had never seen anything like this. He stopped his half-hearted chewing as, ten yards away, the horse began to rise unsteadily to its front legs. While the lion's attention wandered, Cochrane slowly reached for his penknife. Cochrane was lying face down, with the lion pinioning him. The horse was having difficulty standing up. It was dazed. The lion was caught in two minds. In depictions of crusaders who have died in battle, a lion lies at the feet of the deceased knight. In this case the story had taken a novel turn: Cochrane lay at the lion's feet, appropriately, because it was the lion which was about to die. Watching the horse's efforts, the lion stiffened, squeezing Cochrane unbearably. The horse stood up shakily, its head presumably clearing. The lion turned Cochrane's head roughly and licked the side of his face. Lions like to eat eyeballs, lips and testicles first. Luckily for Cochrane, his khaki drill breeches were still intact; the lion had no view of his cajones or the whole story could have turned out differently.

The horse stumbled and fell on its knees again. The lion ceased rasping Cochrane's face to watch. Cochrane freed the knife from its pouch and gently opened it out. Although he could see the lion only out of one eye, and that was filmed over with his blood and the lion's saliva, he struck in the direction of its ear (which was surprisingly ragged) with all his force. The knife and his hand disappeared into the thick, greasy ruff around the lion's neck. The lion started – more, it seemed, out of surprise than pain. Cochrane lay still. Blood began to drip from the lion's neck on to Cochrane's shoulder. Soon the lion stood up and walked away towards the horse. Then it lay down, staring coldly into the middle distance. Now the horse stood up and trotted drunkenly away. The lion growled once, which brought the red flower on its throat into full bloom. It tried to stand but could not. It crawled a few yards and its huge head sank to the ground, which incidentally was alive with red ants. These ants had no trouble at all in penetrating Cochrane's khaki camouflage.

Now Cochrane rose to his feet. What a rising and falling had gone on! He felt desperately thirsty. The lion appeared to be sleeping fitfully for it stirred as Cochrane tried to walk, but it could do no more than raise its massive, stricken head slowly and fearfully. All down its shoulder the blood was trickling, little rivulets rising in the dense forest of its mane. The lion's head sank between its monumental forepaws.

Cochrane skirted it warily and called to his horse. Rare is the horse which comes when it is called. Despite the pain in his torso and head, he undid his heavyweight breeches, a difficult feat at the best of times, and rummaged in the tropical underwear where the ants were seeking – and finding – his balls with great determination. He walked off in the direction his horse had taken and eventually found it plucking nervously at some grass, the sweat on its flanks drying and its eyeballs steadying. Cochrane could not mount, but he rested his wounded arm by slipping it through a knot in the reins and, bound together in affliction, they walked to camp, a Cockney Quixote and an African Rosinante.

When Stinker helped Cochrane into his tent to bathe his wounds, he learned only that Cochrane had been attacked by ants. He put this down to delirium; in fact it was the suppressive power of shock which had allowed him to forget the appalling events of a few hours earlier and to walk the eight miles to camp after having been half eaten by a lion. In the process he had joined a select club, those who have survived an attack by a lion. Cochrane was actually in the most select club of all, those who have survived by killing the lion. There is a common factor in all these improbable escapes: the lion is distracted from the task in hand. Lions are easily distracted.

Thus David Livingstone whose arm was almost wrenched from its socket was saved by his servants who drew off the lion before it could kill the great man. The Tswana of his time used spears with bunches of feathers just like cheerleaders' pom-poms to attract the lion's attention when they were hunting. (Simba Cochrane was not the first to be attacked on horseback. A German professional hunter in Kenya, Fritz von Schindler, used to flush lions on his polo pony. This Clausewitz of the hunting fraternity relied on his pony's speed in the turn. Unfortunately the pony one day turned the wrong way and von Schindler was killed.) The next day Stinker and his trackers set out and found the lion carcass and retrieved the knife, the very one which the *Guinness Book of Records* exhibition had rejected in their blindness.

'You're a proper hero, Bill,' said Stinker.

It was a few months later that the newspapers named him 'Simba'.

I couldn't wait to see Cochrane confront the male lion, Chaka. I had arranged for a photographer to come alone, although *Manhattan* magazine prefers line drawings to actual everyday photographs. Here at least, we proclaim, vulgar reality is kept at a distance. Of course this kind of harmless affectation is no longer lost on advertisers who understand the wide commercial appeal of exclusivity. Exclusivity and clubbiness are very big sellers. Even in London, the home of the gentleman's club, new clubs are being dreamed up to cope with the demand. These range from rooms set aside at airports (which provide free peanuts and are called 'ambassador clubs' or 'clipper clubs' and so on) to expensive credit-card clubs. American Eagle, for whom I am a spokesperson, is launching its Golden Eagle Club. At our lunch, Victoria the agency person, explained that they were researching the viability of this concept. Research showed that I was ideally suited to push this exclusive club. A limited number of these cards would be offered to people with sufficiently large expense accounts. (American Eagle were famous for the speed with which they withdrew cards from executives who had lost their jobs. This was known as a 'withholding of privileges', which sounded like a phrase borrowed from the gulags.) It was some time later in one of those little fizzes of intuition that I wondered if this meant that I was not suitable for the mass-market card. I suffered the actor's anxiety: where had I gone wrong? A careless word from a producer can give an actor sleepless nights as he ponders its semiotic significance. Perhaps the tweeds were a mistake. They were very hairy.

The encounter between the lion killer and the lion had to be postponed. The lion was ill. His restless brooding was caused not by atavistic longings, but by an infection of the lumbar region. He was being treated with antibiotics and kept confined to quarters. I suspected that this was a case of the dissident-and-mental-hospital routine. For antibiotics, read tranquillisers.

I visited Cochrane again. He appeared listless and subdued as we recorded a long conversation. Cochrane had had a black woman in the Northern territory. He had left her pregnant after his stint with the PWD. It had preyed on his mind. He might have a son living out there. He would be fifty-one by my reckoning. It seemed to me to be rather late to be worrying about his boy. When Cochrane left East Africa, Hitler had just burned the Reichstag. Old people find the sins of their youth rising to the foreground of their memories, even as the possibility of repenting at leisure diminishes. Cochrane spoke with a stilted quality when the recorder was running, the way one does with answering machines. He seemed to think, probably with some justice, that this was his last shout. All sorts of things had troubled him over the years: his isolation, his diminishing fame, his congested chest, his rejection by *The Guinness Book of Records* and most strongly now – as the flickering sky outside produced deeper shadows in his flat – the thought that lying under a thorn tree somewhere was his son, a robust mulatto, who could perhaps save his old dad from this cold death by a thousand drips.

As he talked – mostly drivel if I am honest – I was thinking myself about the speed with which things change. Hardly original, but in Cochrane's lifetime Lenin had been alive, Hitler had risen and gone, leaving a bad stain on history, and now the communist empire was in disarray. In fact Cochrane had been in these flats, slowly decaying, since Khrushchev banged his shoe on the table at the United Nations. I can remember seeing pictures of that in *Life*. The years between Cochrane's encounter with the lion and his photocall with Chaka would span some of the most extraordinary events in the history of the world. (If, of course you were prepared to go in for that sort of grading of history.) A very brief period compared with evolutionary time, which covers the whole span from the first stirrings in the primal soup to the development of echo-location in bats and dolphins (and possibly elephants), but that is beyond understanding. We are equipped with brains which comprehend size in terms of body-length and strides and time in terms of days and seasons, yet we also have this aberrant ability to speculate about tens of thousands and even millions of years. Cochrane himself saw life since his near miss with mortality as a string of wrongs, a sort of frogspawn; it had a shape, but it was composed of individual injustices. The villains in this history were a series of malevolent individuals, rather than institutions.

''E was a right bastard if you'll excuse my French. 'E 'ad no time for me, not from the day I met 'im. 'E was jealous of me notorability.'

This was his superior at the Metropolitan Water Board, I think. Cochrane had spent the war in London. There was a great deal of work, even for a disabled man, in trying to keep London's water supplies going. There had been a brief relationship with a girl called Doreen Butt, who was in the Women's Royal Air Force, but she had gone off with a sergeant in the Grenadiers, who had got himself killed, of course, wouldn't you know it.

'No better than she ought to have been, mind you. I couldn't dance because of me wounds. So of course she was off like a long dog. What can you expect of women?'

Difficult question, in any context.

Victoria from the advertising agency appeared to be about thirty. She was fevered at first but calmed down quickly. She wore a short dress, something which looked like curtaining from an expensive country-house decorator, one of those shops where there is always a painting of a horse on the wall to warn the impecunious that they are not in Habitat, in case they were under any illusions. In England, enjoying familiarity with horses is the most important (of all the many) indicator of class.

Victoria was nervous but it was a skittish, sexual nervousness; she was conscious of the effect of everything she said and of her slightest movement. It was as if the air above the table was contested territory; her hands entered it fearfully. English people of a certain class often display extreme sensitivity to the small change of social life, like the Japanese. The dress was new, she said, and she felt like a sofa in it. Joseph must have gone mad. She quickly made it clear that she was not just some advertising bimbo who thought about nothing except ads and clothes and design and stuff like that. She was studying art history at the Tate and would probably do that full-time one day.

'Sorry. I'm talking too much!'

But she kept on. The American Eagle ads were very well received by the public in America apparently. Perhaps we could loosen up a little. The Cockney character, the one who dipped fish in the oil, was also liked. Quite a lot of people had expressed an interest in seeing more real characters like him in the ads. 'Although God knows how the research was worded to get that result.'

I was looking at her lips. Close to they were full and lightly ribbed as she smiled. Her eyes were set quite far apart. When she leant forward I could just see some black lace as the Joseph upholstery parted from her chest. (It is no good pretending that men, even the most evolved, don't look down girls' fronts given the opportunity.) Victoria probably noticed my eyes wander, for she relaxed. Our lunch arrived. She started quickly on her salad of variegated leaves chosen more for their artistic impression than their nutritional value. Her self-esteem had taken a knock, I surmised. Whose doesn't, from time to time? But I believe women practise a more constant self-appraisal, like radar scanning the sky or a sniffer at an airport, constantly testing the air for signals imperceptible to the male eye and ear. When I was a small boy I longed to send off for one of those whistles which could be heard only by dogs. We didn't have a dog, but I was entranced by the idea of communicating with canines on secret frequencies. Women are blessed with this ability to operate on frequencies denied to men. Victoria could echo-locate with the best of them, that was for sure. Behind her bright and well-decorated front I thought I saw a softness. London girls are closer to the recent, gentle past than girls in New York and Paris; they have never quite adapted to the street.

On the purely sexual level of judgement, which is the one always made first, I guessed that she burned a little too bright.

The social sensitivity of the English is repeated in their vowel sounds. Victoria's vowels followed an erratic itinerary around the Underground map, from Whitechapel to Knightsbridge. Before the arrival of my Mercedes, as potent as Siegfried, I regarded the Underground map as the only true map of London. Since I quit Niflheim to cruise the streets in my Merc, I have missed its simplicity.

It was important to Victoria to know the buzz words, but she gave them enough spin to suggest that she did not take them seriously. She spoke certain words with so much fastidious disdain – 'golden hellos' and 'personal organiser' are two I remember – that she seemed to be conducting a personal vendetta against neologisms. For all her brightness, she did not quite have the confidence which her conversation suggested. I suspected a broken romance and tried to steer the conversation in that direction.

'Are you married?'

'No. You haven't been talking to my mother have you?'

'I just wondered.'

'Are you?'

'Not any more. But I have a small daughter.'

'This small?' she asked, holding her knife and fork about a yard apart. A piece of radicchio (or was it arugula?) flew off her fork and landed on the next table where two men were lunching together with a cell phone between them. We apologised but they were tolerant. They glanced at us from time to time with conspiratorial smiles. The flying greens had drawn us all together.

'What do you really think of the campaign?' she asked before I could get back on the more interesting tack. Her voice was small and girlish now, and she touched my arm.

I drove her back to the agency in my starship. We set off up towards Notting Hill Gate, past the Eastern European Czech Embassy (why are they in love with concrete?), and smoothly into Hyde Park where the gloom of the afternoon was pressing down on the blitzed trees and on four late horsemen jogging by. The horses' trotting was bored and clumsy as if they were wearing boots, easy prey for a lion hiding behind the bushes. The horses passed by safely and we accelerated up towards

Marble Arch, the site of Tyburn gallows. I could see Victoria's knees and some of her thighs which had emerged from the rich dress as she settled herself in the leather seats. It was nice to be in here, in the microchip-controlled temperate zone as we sped down Park Lane and into Mayfair. When you are sitting next to someone in a car, you get a view of that person's face which can be unexpected. Victoria's face was sharper in profile, more vulpine and more sensual than from in front. Her eyebrows were quite thick and darker than her hair. I wondered if this had any bearing on her bodily hair.

'Where do you live?' I asked.

'God, I live miles away. In up-and-coming fucking Dock-lands,' she said. 'It's a day's march to get there and when you do you wonder why you bothered. But not for long.'

'Where are you going?'

'Anywhere, as soon as I can sell the place. My boyfriend and I split up a week or two ago.'

'I am sorry,' I said without much conviction.

'Why?'

'Well, that's the sort of thing you say. And then you say, "He must have been crazy."'

'Thanks.'

We turned into Berkeley Square. She jumped out after giving me a small scented kiss. The scents were of her leafy lunch and her perfume, a spicy and pleasant combination.

'I like your car,' she said. 'But you shouldn't eat fish and chips in it. Bye.'

Before I could incriminate Bernie she skipped off towards the pink marble hall of the agency. Inside two thousand people worked, well paid, modishly clad and expensively shod. They had computers and word processors and coffee cups by Rosenthal and they were, like the zoo-keeper, at the centre of the universe. Their world was somehow more charged than other people's, because they were nearer the magnetic forces. Whatever else they did, these magnetic forces repelled old people. I've been in there and there isn't a person over forty visible in the whole place. Aural hair is definitely out. Eel breath is out. Dralon golf trousers and short camelhair coats are out. They may be all right for characters in commercials – like Bernie – but no employee would enter the giant marble-slab entrance, with its interesting incised name running vertically in sans serif bold, wearing anything which had not been blessed by a sadhu of fashion. Victoria in her little old-rose dress was not immune. As she was swallowed by the huge pink marble slabs, I thought perhaps that her bottom was just a little large for her own self-image, or perhaps Joseph's skimpy dress created this illusion. A traffic warden, with tinder dry hair, looking like a careworn Hollywood actress, like Carroll Baker or Mamie van Doren, appeared in my sightline. She had a voice which combined a touch of knees-up down the Old Kent Road with a hint of menace.

'Come on, darling. You can't stop 'ere moonin' all day.'

'Mooning? Who's mooning?'

She coughed and pretended to write my registration number in her notebook as I glided off into the expensive traffic, traffic so cloyed with rich ingredients that my Mercedes suddenly seemed glaringly mass-produced. The other cars had been custom-made by craftsmen; mine had merely had the once-over from Germans in white overalls. Sometimes in London you get glimpses of enormous wealth, great piles of money, if you know where to look. It shows itself in the bow windows of gentleman's clubs (of the sort that American Eagle is trying to conjure up), at regimental dinners of the cavalry, at memorial services for the aristocracy, at one or two select kindergartens in Kensington, at the portals of merchant banks in the City, and here in Berkeley Square, where it can be seen scuttling down the steps to Annabel's late at night. This is money of the old sort, but money which has grown by leaps and bounds in the last ten years as everything, the very fabric of the country, has reached the point of critical mass. This wealth appears to have no physical limits. Low-temperature nuclear fission of wealth has taken place, on a scale which is a surprise even to the beneficiaries. People who had one or two million ten years ago are worth twenty, thirty, a hundred million sterling. How has it happened? Nobody really knows. It is necromancy, it is alchemy. The philosopher's stone has been found. These people, who can now buy up islands in the Caribbean and fabulous racehorses and jet aircraft, don't themselves understand how it has happened, so they keep – in one of their favourite phrases – a low profile. They don't really approve of the wide boys and the barrow boys in the City becoming rich too, but they can see the irony of that position and anyway none of these new chaps owns thousands of acres or whole streets of Georgian houses. They will never catch up, in fact.

Chastened by my abject poverty, I set off for an evening of Thai boxing.

Tracy is shorter than Cheryl. Tracy's family are in security. That's her brother Steve, her brother Scott, her dad Joe and her mum, Angie. The family have a close-to-the-ground look about them, which is useful in security. You don't want to be knocked over too easily in that game.

Cheryl could not be described as willowy, but her satin shorts end just about at Tracy's waistband. Tracy is the South East champion and Cheryl is the challenger. Thai, or kick, boxing, for girls is new to London but it has an enthusiastic following. You won't find it reported in *The Times* or advertised too widely. That's because it's not strictly legal, know what I mean? Well put it another way, nobody's got round to registering it nor nothing like that. The girls – gels – get £300 a fight, four rounds and all the advice they can use from their brothers in the corner.

Cheryl also got a fractured skull. But then, what can you expect, Tracy's been to Thailand to Rungit, and trained under – funny name – Payup Rugchart, the world-famous coach? She can do the Buddhist prayer bit and all.

The fight was held in the old Seaman's Mission, Limehouse, opened, says a stone near the front door, by the Earl of Balfour in 1906, a place where seamen and lascars could get a bath, a lecture and a cheap meal. Now it is for sale, but while it awaits a purchaser, its damp main hall, the scene of many a successful recruiting campaign for both world wars, it is used to stage Thai boxing. What is it about Thai boxing which appeals to these Londoners? I am afraid your reporter has been unable to fathom its charms. It is nasty, brutal and not always short.

For the first round Tracy stalked the taller girl with the subtlety of a mastiff. She landed four or five vicious kicks on Cheryl's blotchy, pale legs and one punch right on her nose. Cheryl kicked back ineffectually. Kicking is designed to weaken the opponent's legs. From the moment they came into the ring I could see that Cheryl had no chance. As she sank on to her stool after the first round, her nose was bleeding and her urchin haircut was stuck to her small fragile skull with sweat. Her dad Fred in the corner is in plumbing. Perhaps he should have handed her a short piece of lead pipe for the second round. Round Two lasted a few seconds. Tracy suddenly got both hands behind Cheryl's head and jerked it forward on to her knee which was travelling in the opposite direction. Cheryl fell back on to the canvas with a mineral thud. Fred tried to get her to stand up and fight, but a stretcher was summoned instead. Fred shook his head sadly as she was carried out. The Cockneys loved it. 'Didn't know gels could fight like that. Fuckin' amazin', that was. Jesus, did yer see that one wif the arse on 'er like an 'orse, 'ands like fuckin' lightning. And then some. I wonder what she's like on the job. Tear yer dong off I should fink.'

Wait a minute. Those last few sentences will have to go. As a matter of honest record, I also speculated about the girls' sex lives. (One does with female athletes.) But those two were like boys who had escaped from a reform school. Their physiognomy spelt delinquent. In their corners the dads and brothers had tattoos. There is a breed of person at loose in London with lank hair and tattoos which must be avoided at all costs. If there is any truth in the theory that people with tattoos are compensating for personality deficiencies, then it is clear why these people also favour large dogs on choke chains. They walk the streets, alternately encouraging and threatening these immense dogs, which pull at the chains like carnivorous ponies, like the horses of Diomedes.

I attribute all this to a picturesque persistence of the vicious degradation for which London was always famous. Londoners took pleasure in bear-baiting, cock-fights, dog-fights, rat-pits, bull-baiting, bare-knuckle fights and of course public hanging. Perhaps there is an irreducible amount of violence in all big cities which lies dormant in a sub-clinical state, and waits opportunistically for its moment. Great cities, like so much else, can only be described in metaphor.

There were other fights, between two clumsy black men and between an elderly Thai, who appeared to have had his brains

61

and his face battered by countless kicks and blows, and a thin, lethal Cockney boy whose skin was almost translucent in its paleness. The Thai eventually sank in a corner in a praying position to signal his surrender. The Cockney boy watched him coldly for a moment as his handlers jumped into the ring to congratulate him and towel him before leading him away.

I left soon after. The pavement was stained with sodium lights, the mean streets and the Mission mottled and blotched like poor Cheryl's legs.

CHAPTER SEVEN

This period before dawn was unlovely. The streets were neglected and dark. They would be dark for some hours yet. The remains of the night's activities – cans, pizza boxes, papers, vomit, broken bottles – had not yet been cleaned up. It gave Miles satisfaction to be up and speeding away – dressed, shaved, scented – when the streets were still quiet. He had left Jacci lying in bed. Also in the bed was her collection of colourful stuffed animals. He imagined what Victoria would say if she found out that he shared a bed not only with Jacci, but with eight purple, green and pink day-glo animals, every one of which had a name. Moving in with Jacci had perhaps been a mistake. He should have found his own flat when he and Victoria split up, but Jacci was so small, breathless and eager, that it had seemed easier. Anyway, it could not last: she had an accent like a fishwife's.

He reached the Embankment and sped past the elegant, sleeping houses of Cheyne Walk in his BMW. German cars. Everyone in the City drove German cars. German cars were somehow in tune with the times – fast, stylish, opulent and yet serious. After Christmas he would be getting a new BMW, bigger than this little convertible. He would also be getting a record bonus, nearly £40,000. He was doing well for the bank, even in these difficult days. Being good at his job was a great comfort to Miles. He had tried to explain the calmness and generosity which his modest success had given him. It was not just a question of money, as Victoria imagined. Nor was it being part of the City. Sometimes he actually despised the City. Finding himself able to take decisions quickly and profitably had given him a self-possession which he had lacked.

It had plugged some holes in his self-esteem. Victoria had never taken his job seriously. It rankled with Miles that she dismissed what he did so lightly.

He sped past the Houses of Parliament, round Parliament Square, past the amiable statue of Abraham Lincoln on the left, and past the strangely listing statue of General Smuts on the right. Here at least the street cleaners were hard at it. Big Ben said it was ten past six. Breaking up with Victoria had been made easier for him by his success. He felt that he had to get away from her, even though he believed that he probably still loved her. Life with Jacci was less complicated and more functional, more suited to the demands of his work and his present condition. Although she would have denied it, Victoria was thinking about marriage. Marriage had become an unspoken sub-text in all their disagreements. Marriage flowed darkly through her brooding silences. And yet.

The river was low, invisible from the car. Some mornings it was brimming right up to the retaining wall. He raced past the oldest artefact in London, Cleopatra's Needle, down into the tunnel, and swung up past the Monument towards the bank. At this time of day you could still surge powerfully around London, before the traffic began to snare and snag your progress. The car park was empty. Ashley, the attendant, was not yet in. Miles was the first. His parking space was usually tricky to back into, between the lift shaft and a concrete pillar. Now he could simply swoop in forwards.

He arrived in the dealing room just before six-thirty. He tried to raise Chua in Singapore, but for once Chua was not at his desk. He waited until seven before calling Victoria at Heron's Beat, but she was not there either. He felt a flash of irritation. He tried Chua again. Chua's number rang unanswered. It was only three-thirty in the afternoon there. They had many religious holidays in Singapore; perhaps Chua was off lighting joss sticks or performing as the back end of a lion in a lion dance. Miles had a picture of Singapore based on shots from airline commercials.

Singapore had been good to him. Some of the other dealers found it too speculative, but Miles had made the bank nearly a million last year in cahoots with Chua. It was Chua who had suggested a little personal trading. So Miles was keen to know how the Nikkei Index had affected their deal, because his screen showed him that there had been a violent dip in the night. When he was dealing personally with Chua he came in very early, before Arnold Zwitters.

The dealing room was huge, with each of the dealers sitting like a battery hen taking nourishment from the screen and the phones in front of him. Miles had overheard his boss tell a visitor that none of them – the hotshot dealers – had a future; none of them had management skills and none of them would last more than a few years. They were specialised worker bees with limited talents and a short life expectancy.

Arnold Zwitters was American. His face had the texture of an expensive alligator wallet. He had come to supervise the bank's preparations for Big Bang and he was one of the few successes of that period. As a result he had a seat on the main board now, up with Lord Zetland and the others who lived on Olympus but didn't have a clue about capital markets. You could not teach old dogs new tricks.

Miles tried the advertising agency, but they didn't even open the switchboard until nine o'clock, could you believe it. The dealing room was beginning to fill up. Everyone glanced at their screens intently before they sat down with their few personal possessions. On two floors there were 150 worker bees. Victoria had never understood what they did here. She regarded the City and its myriad activities with amused indifference. Once Miles had told her that his dealing room turned over larger sums in a week than the Tate Gallery, the Arts Council and the National Gallery saw in a year.

'Exactly. There's your problem,' said Victoria complacently. By this she meant that the City had an inflated idea of its own importance.

A man called Bob came around every Monday and Thursday to clean shoes. He crept around the dealing-room floor polishing the calf, brogue and kid, exchanging the odd word with his clientele. He had reached Miles. Miles could feel his shoes vibrating. Miles looked down at Bob's head. The skin of his scalp was pinkly visible through his short, no-nonsense haircut. Some of the dealers had had haircuts like that a few years ago, but most of them had taken to a more romantic look, like Miles's.

'That'll be a quid, thanks. Mind you, shoes like that should be more,' said the voice from near Miles's kneecaps.

'Mmh,' said Miles, reaching into his pocket, 'you're breaking my heart, Bob.'

He tried Chua at home, but his wife said he was out and put the phone down quickly. The shoe cleaner was continuing his crustacean movement along the line. Miles fiddled with his calculator. Bob cleaned about ninety pairs of shoes on this floor alone in a morning. If he kept that up all day he was making eight, nine hundred pounds a week. That was forty-five grand a year, just maintaining footwear. Perhaps he was dealing on the side too, with the information he could pick up.

The estate agent had rung to ask if they would put the price down fifteen thousand. Nothing was moving. Miles needed to speak to Victoria, although it was with a sense of foreboding. She was supposed to be getting the roof fixed. The last person to look around – the only person – had told the agent that there was a nasty leak in the attic. Victoria had no idea how to get into the attic. The pipe to the water tank would burst. Chua usually never left his telephone. On a day like this, with so much riding on it, Miles could not understand what he was up to. He called the agency. Some lout (they all spoke as if they had just got out of bed) said, 'Nah, she's not here. No idea. Nah, I can't take a message. Nah. Me pen's broke. Nah. I'll try an' remember. Oh, it's Miles. I thought you fell off the end of the pier a few weeks ago. Sure. Sure, sure. I've got it.'

It was her art director, Mike. He might just as well have said, 'Piss off you stiff, I'm busy.' Victoria had probably slept with him too.

He tried Chua at home again but this time his wife was very terse. She said, 'He's not here OK lah,' in that lawnmower accent, and put down the phone before he could say another word. Miles looked at his gleaming toecaps and then out of the plate-glass window which sighed and groaned in the wind; it gave a smudged view of St Paul's. The dealing room was considerably higher than the spot to which Christopher Wren had been winched in his basket. The dome had never been intended to be seen from this height. It was streaked with green from the copper, like ribbons of algae. The bank's was the second highest building in the City. It looked like a piece of space junk in the wrong orbit from outside, but from here it gave a commanding view of the City which Miles always enjoyed. He imagined the information from the markets flowing straight in over the stooped buildings below.

Zwitters walked around, a knowing smile on his well-seasoned face, to see how the workers were doing. Miles scanned his screen busily. He could do a little business with Union Bank on a swap, so he rang Zurich. His heart was not in it. His heart was between Singapore and Tokyo with one thousand tons of soya beans, which would cost him £72,000 if they were forced to close the contract today. He spoke to Ueli briefly. No problem. That was six thousand more than he had earned last year after his bonus. What was that little bastard Chua playing at? Chua's ticket was simply in the name of a computer number which pretended to be an institutional client, but in fact the client was Miles. By the close of business in Singapore, in – he looked up at the row of clocks – one hour's time, he would have lost £72,000 unless Chua had sold the contract. Miles couldn't sell it himself because officially it was marked down to Chua. If the price dropped, Chua was supposed to land one of his clients with the contract. The timing depended on close co-operation. He waited another half-hour, swapped Swiss francs for Deutschmarks listlessly, then swapping them back again. He thought about trying to pass the deal on to one of the bank's clients, but that was easier said than done. He would have to try to retrieve his tickets from records. Anyway, his discretion was restricted to a certain amount of exposure per day and nobody was going to allow him to buy a thousand tons of soy at any price. The riskiest thing he was supposed to do was interest-rate swaps, and then only according to the Zwitters patented formula. Soya beans were for madmen.

Victoria rang back when he was looking at the closing Nikkei price. It was disastrous. The Chua plan involved a hedge against the soya bean contract by taking a forward position on the rising Nikkei. Rising that is until the Finance Minister had a stroke in a massage parlour. He was now ten thousand out on the Nikkei as well. That was eighty-two thousand in all.

'You rang,' said Victoria.

'Mmh. Yhh. Look the agent says we're overpriced. Can we drop the price fifteen grand?'

'Largely academic, I'm afraid, Miles. The only person who has come round so far was a madman who wanted to crawl around in the attic for an hour.'

'Don't piss about, Vic, this is getting serious.'

'Has the old Index got the wobblies?' she said with insouciant precision.

'Nhh. It's just getting expensive.'

'And so's the bimbo, I bet.'

'Where were you last night, by the way? I called at seven.'

'Out and about. The truth is Miles, I can't stand Docklands another minute. Why don't you and the airhead move in until it's sold?'

'It'll never be sold unless you get the roof fixed.'

'Boring. I hear she wears sneakers with pink laces,' said Victoria, as she put the phone down.

Victoria had a talent for getting in the last word. But Miles did not have time to be angry. Fear was rising unchecked. It made him feel cold. He pulled on his jacket and called Singapore again. This time nobody answered at Chua's apartment. He and Madame Chua were both out burning joss sticks, for good luck.

Bob was ten yards away now, like a penitent at Compostela, dragging a box decorated with the Cross of St George, containing his brushes and polish, behind him. The dealers hardly noticed him, but today Miles realised for the first time that Bob's left hand was deformed. He held the shoe he was working on pinioned with his left hand, but the fingers were bent at a peculiar angle.

He called a contact at Drexel on the exchange in Singapore, trying to sound relaxed. He had a special voice for dealing on the telephone.

'Hi. Have you seen Richard Chua? I don't think his phone is working.'

'He's been arrested lah.'

'Jesus, what for?'

'They took him away first thing this morning.'

'What's going to happen to his contracts?'

'Don't worry lah, the Commission got them all. Do you want Euroyen, six years, three and a half, for dollars?'

'No.'

He felt icy cold. He was in terrible trouble. Not only would the SIMEX Commission close the contract at the end of the day, they would also look closely at all Chua's dealings. It would only be a week or so before they traced some of them back to Miles. Miles had done nothing illegal, but Zwitters would show him the door without wasting any time. People went into the glass fishtank of Zwitters's office and emerged scorched and lifeless within minutes. There was never anything to pack that would not go into a briefcase and a carrier bag. Miles decided to borrow the seventy-two grand tomorrow anyway and resign. Once they had sold the house he would more or less be in the clear financially, even after they had dropped the price. Because of the success of Zwitters's team he had had lots of job offers, but he had better get in quick before Zwitters put out the word on him.

He and Jacci were going to a charity ball that evening, in aid of the Asian tiger or something, tickets a hundred and fifty the pair. He could not have cared less if the whole rain forest was cut down and planted with soya beans. But he would have to go. He had bought Jacci a new dress from the Emanuels. That was a couple of grand. For a man who had just lost his whole fortune, £2,000 loomed very large. Jacci was proving to be a bit more demanding than he had expected. But she had stupendous knockers, floating, almost orbiting in front of her chest. Even after a month he got a hard on just thinking about them. She was also in the markets, making almost as much as he was. She was from Whitechapel, as sharp as a tack, with a big family who were all on the make. Her accent was atrocious, but he found it fashionable. It gave him a sort of glamour, like going out with a black girl. Jacci had no artistic pretensions. Victoria always managed to imply that the world she lived in was a more sensitive world, while the world he inhabited was simply a worthless by-product of the capitalist system. What was advertising, for Chrissakes, if not a service to the system?

Zwitters walked by; Miles studied his screen intently. Near record loss in one day for the Nikkei. When Zwitters had gone he punched up commodity futures. Soy was rising! He could hardly believe his luck. It was something to do with the Nikkei. Clever little bastard, Chua. Too clever it seemed. Soy futures were rocketing as news of the troubles in Tokyo reached the European markets. He had never fully understood commodity prices, but it seemed the markets wanted a forward position on anything that would allow them to get out of their exposure to yen. He called Singapore back and swapped some yen for dollars. If SIMEX kept his contract open, he could make fifty thousand by the opening of tomorrow's trading for himself.

'How're you doing, Miles?'

Zwitters had a habit of appearing behind your back and looking at your screen when you least expected him. Miles accessed the Euro markets quickly.

'Did OK on the yen stampede, Arnie.'

'You got in quick, nice work.'

'Sure, I saw the news about the Finance Minister at six-thirty.'

'Good work, sport. Teach us to stay out of massage parlours, eh?'

'Don't need it yet,' said Miles.

'So I've heard. I'm surprised you're got the energy to get in so early.'

All Arnie's pleasantries were loaded with menace.

Miles decided to bring up the subject of Chua before it was raised.

'Arnie, my guy in Singapore has been arrested. What do you fhink that means?'

'Is all your paperwork in order? All the tickets gone through?'

His alligator mouth was pursed. Arnie played a lot of tennis. He always had a warm ochre tan, which sometimes showed slightly yellow.

'Yuh. It's just that I'm concerned in case he has been using our name or something.'

'Don't worry about that. SIMEX values our business too much. If he has, we'll dump on them for being lax, and I mean dump. As long as you haven't been screwing about with Chua, Miles. You wouldn't do that now, would you?'

'Good God no.'

It surprised Miles that Zwitters even knew Chua's name.

There were a hundred and fifty dealers, each with scores of contacts. Perhaps he knew before Miles that a dealer had been arrested in Singapore. Perhaps he had just wandered past Miles's desk to probe him. Miles guessed that the Singapore police didn't worry too much about the right of suspects, so it was unlikely Chua would be able to make a public statement. All his dealings had been taken over by the Commission who would, as Zwitters had said, want to protect their reputation. Miles could stick to his story that Chua was using his name. On the other hand the contract was still open and making money.

Victoria called: 'I've found somebody who will do the roof. He says it's going to cost fifteen hundred, minimum. Have you got fifteen hundred, because I haven't?'

'We had better do it. Go ahead.'

'Seven hundred and fifty in cash this evening.'

'Before he does the job?'

'If you know a better way, just say the word.'

'No, no. OK, I'll get some cash over to you by bike tomorrow morning. I can't do it any sooner. Nhhh.'

Knowing Victoria, the man would be an unemployed sculptor who would screw up the job and run off with the money never to be seen again.

'Can't you get it to me tonight?' asked Victoria.

'No I can't. I'm going out. And I haven't got time to go to the bank.'

'You work in a bank, don't you?'

'It's not the kind of bank with cash dispensers and free cheque books for students, Victoria.'

'Bye bye, Miles. Before eleven, at the agency.'

Miles would have liked to talk to her a little longer. He would have liked to tell her his problems.

As Miles was going out to meet Jacci for a quick sandwich at the skating rink, Zwitters called him into his office.

'Miles, what time do you think it is in Singapore?'

'It's seven-thirty.'

'That's correct. Seven-thirty in the evening and they are working hard on the Chua case. It seems Chua used your code to buy a thousand tons of soy futures. You didn't have anything to do with this, did you?'

'No, no. Nothing.'

'That's what I told them. I also told them that we would accept the contract.' He punched his screen. 'I'm not in love with commodities, far from it, but the way this thing is going we stand to make sixty thousand by the time Singapore opens in the morning.'

'Is that kosher?'

'According to SIMEX, we bought. They offered me the option to pull out, but I decided to honour the deal.'

Miles tried to laugh cheerily.

'What are you doing now, Miles?'

'I'm going for a quick bite.'

'Well take your things, because you don't need to come back.'

For a few moments, Miles did not understand what Zwitters meant. He felt, as he stepped out, as if he had been drowned. Arnie knew all the details. Chua's dealings were already in the hands of the Commission in Singapore.

By the time Miles met Jacci, he felt as if his blood supply was dwindling. He could feel the constriction in his arteries. Not only had Zwitters fired him, he had turned him over for £60,000.

''Ere, fuckin 'ell you look like you've seen a ghost,' said Jacci just before her viperous tongue slipped into his mouth. He burst into tears. She quickly withdrew her tongue.

'What's the matter, darling?'

'I've been fired.'

'Come and sit down.'

They sat together on a granite bench as the skaters went by, round and round, some expert – with those sudden, show-offy changes of direction – some hopelessly, happily, inexpert – laughing and calling to each other before falling. An elderly man skated serenely, hands behind his back.

Miles was suffering from submersion. He wanted to swim to the surface and break free. Down here he could not breathe. Jacci loosened his collar and then fetched him a cup of tea and a sandwich. He had his briefcase – alligator-look like Arnold's face – and that was it. His whole professional life was in there. He explained to Jacci what had happened; her small face, a depraved child's face really, churned.

'The bastard. The whole fucking lot. What a bastard.'

Miles was racked by sobs again.

'Come on, darling. You're a big boy. Take me hankie.'

He could feel her weightless breasts as she hugged him. This close he could see a faint moustache on her upper lip, distinct golden hairs, on to which his tears were trickling. They stayed glued together for a minute or two.

Finally Jacci stood up. He could feel her warmth for a moment after she detached herself. Her small face was concerned and maternal. How quickly relations can change. That was the last thing he wanted from Jacci. She had promoted herself.

'Got to get back. Don't worry. You go and get on the dog. By the time I get 'ome you'll have another job. You'll see. And don't forget to pick up your DJ.'

What did she mean by the dog? She didn't even have a cat. She was gone, through the crowd watching the skaters and eating their sandwiches. Dog and bone. Telephone. Usually they only took a few minutes for lunch, but he had plenty of time. He watched the skaters too. The rink was surrounded by a sort of amphitheatre of marble and granite, and behind that exciting buildings which housed new banks and brokers. Many of the big names from New York and Tokyo were here. Some had come and gone already, so uncertain were things in the City. But the City of London was a trough into which they had to get their snouts, whatever the risks. The old gentleman's club had been invaded by cads and bounders. And he was one of them. He felt a sickening, shuddering shame. Yet he had done nothing illegal. Some of the Japanese banks would have him. Maybe the less successful foreign banks would even applaud his enterprise. There were at least three hundred foreign banks in the City. Gradually he felt the circulation of his blood return to normal and the oxygen reach his throbbing head. All his credit cards had been cancelled and he was only getting a month's pay. Arnie had specifically said that he was not entitled to his bonus, although Christmas was just a few weeks away.

He walked to Next to pick up his new dinner jacket. It was only £120 and they had done a good job with the buttons, but it seemed to him a heavy burden to carry on a day like this, as obtrusive as a party hat at a funeral. He entered the bank building by the garage ramp. As he got into his red BMW the attendant, Ashley, came over.

'No can do, bro. It stays.'

Ashley had seen this many times. He was sympathetic. He plucked Miles's sleeve fleetingly. Miles got out of the car.

'Keys, please. I'm sorry, man.'

'That's OK, Ash. It's not your problem.'

'It don't make it no easier. Be seeing you around, bro.'

'I doubt it.'

Ashley kicked his sneakers gently against the car's front wheel. *It's only a car, Miles*, he seemed to be saying.

Miles walked to the Underground and joined the flotsam which was scudding about under the streets of London on their aimless journeys. None of them would be at the ball to save the Sumatran tiger or whatever it was, that was for sure. They all looked half cracked as the chiaroscuro played on their faces. They looked as though they had been embalmed. They were stiffs, and he had joined their club. Only last week American Eagle had sent him the new Golden Eagle Club card and today he had been asked to hand it over. The deliberate humiliation was like the process of being admitted to jail. Chua was actually in jail, without shoelaces, glasses or wallet. Victoria would quickly find out about his problems. He dreaded speaking to her tomorrow, which he would have to.

The stations crashed by. They were a litany to his former life as a dweller in the sunlight before he had had to take to the catacombs and sewers.

By the time Jacci came home from work, Miles was drunk. He had made a few phone calls, but perhaps there was something in his voice which alerted his prospective employers. He had not really thought out what he was going to say in advance either.

'Hello, Gordon. You remember you said to give you a call if ever. Yhh. Oh. How many are you losing? That's bad. Nhh, nhh. I've just had enough of Arnie. Nhh. Resigned. Nhh. OK. Thanks anyway, Gordie.'

It was one thing being asked to join when you had a job.

74

For some reason it was quite different when you did not. He opened a bottle of champagne.

Jacci treated him like an invalid. She made him coffee and spoke to him as though he were ill, which in a sense he was.

'We've only got an hour. I'm going to do me hair. Will you be all right?'

'Of course I'll be all right. Do you think I'm going to slash my wrists?'

'Don't snap. 'Ow did you get on with the jobs?'

'Couple of good reactions. We'll see. It's early days.'

'That's the way to look at it. You got to look on the bright side. Every cloud and so on.'

Jacci was very keen on the bright side. She had the day-glo animals in the bedroom and a bright red Renault Five Turbo.

'Miles,' she shouted from the bathroom, 'where did you park?'

'I forgot the car keys in the office and I didn't want to go back, so I took the tube. Jesus, it's full of deadbeats and weirdos these days.'

He caught a glimpse of her through the bathroom door, as naked as a small fruit which has been removed from its integument. She was only twenty-three. Naked she was extraordinarily fragile. She was whipping her hair up into a frenzy in there.

'Could you turn me rollers on, Miles?' she shouted above the noise of her dryer.

Miles felt sad. He shouldn't be here at all. Now Victoria would have her low opinion of the City confirmed. It was – to use one of her little phrases – a self-fulfilling prophecy. Sadly, but bravely, he decided to tell Victoria that he loved her, and ask her to forgive him. This thought cheered him up. He turned off Jacci's rollers and fumbled with his shirt studs. His fingers were very thick and clumsy. Jacci wanted him to wear a pink and blue bow tie – 'It's more jollier than black' – but he decided to stick with the thin black tie and the wing collar. The Emanuel dress lay on the bed, a wonderful creation of pink satin and white silk and even seed pearls, with a dramatic hike up the side. It lay on the bed inanimate, its stiffened bodice pointing upwards waiting to welcome and guide her fair bosom. Miles finished the champagne. It was touching, the way she kept appearing for his approval:

'Me hair over to one side or hanging down even? Wotcher fink? Is this too high? Wotcher say, shall I wear both earrings or just the one? 'Ow do I look?'

'You look brilliant.'

She looked like an exquisitely wrapped gift. He tried to kiss her but she skipped away. She had tiny specks of glitter under her eyes.

'The Asian tigers won't have seen anything like us,' he said, trying to be cheery.

'It's lions.'

'Asian lions? They don't have lions in Asia. Tigers.'

'No it's lions, honest. Look at the invite.'

Sure enough the Marchioness of Hereford requested the pleasure of their company at a ball at the Hippodrome to raise money for the Asian lion sanctuary in Gir.

It was a great ball. A giant screen showed videos of the Asian lion and rock stars, who were passionate about conservation, came on stage to sing or to make pleas for generosity. The Hippodrome was decorated with jungle foliage and silk parrots.

'Looks like they cut down the whole rain forest to decorate the place,' said Sting in that nicely ironic way of his. 'But never mind, all in a good cause. Put your hands together, now.'

Luckily the music was so loud and the whole place was so crowded and Miles was so drunk that he was unable to have a proper conversation with anybody, not even with Jeremy and Emma and Mark and Susanna at their table.

At four-thirty in the morning, Miles entered Trafalgar Square too fast, ran Jacci's Renault up a traffic island with a loud metallic noise as the underside was ripped open and spun twice before coming to rest at the base of one of Landseer's lions.

Miles was arrested. 'Solidarity,' he shouted loudly as they forced him into the back of a Vauxhall Cavalier. At the station they took away his shoelaces and his wallet and pushed him firmly into a cell, which was soused with male smells.

The desk sergeant, who was making a list of the contents of his pockets, examined the ticket stubs for the ball.

'Look at this,' he said to the arresting officer. 'You don't earn that much in a week. Fucking Asian lion. What a load of crap.'

'Solidarity,' cried Miles, muffled by the thickness of the steel door and the four courses of Victorian brick which separated him from the world, and – symbolically – his old pal Chua, both of them victims of grave injustice.

The police had not even offered Jacci a lift home as she stood, slightly bruised, her Emanuel dress slashed up one leg and her little Renault sending distress signals from the contorted hood.

CHAPTER EIGHT

Bernie called to say he had a job. I don't know how these actors survive. The most careless among us change jobs only five or six times in a lifetime, but actors look for work with the intensity of a dachshund on the trail of a rat, from morning to night, for years on end. It must be a fix of some sort, with roots in what Jung called the disunity of the personality. It is sacramental. Just as the eagle plunged into the sea from the fiery regions and emerged born again, so the actor submits himself to this ordeal from time to time. Some African kings are reborn every year in a ceremony fraught with danger. Rebirth and renewal are constant human themes, and actors, particularly Bernie, live out the human condition on our behalf.

Bernie is reborn this week in *Cinderella* at the Empire Theatre, Hackney, where he is playing one of the Ugly Sisters. The previous occupant of the part, booked for the whole season, died over a fish supper near the theatre.

I promised Bernie that I would see the show and write it up for *Manhattan*.

'You can explain all about its traditions and so on.'

'Thanks for the tip, Bernie.'

'It goes right back to the commedia dell'arte (commedya dellarty).'

'Almost everything in your business goes back to the commedia dell'arte, Bernie. The rest goes back to the opéra bouffe.'

'That's the one. You've got my drift. I'll leave tickets for you at the box office any night.'

'Thanks a lot. Can I bring my daughter? She's coming from New York.'

'Good idea. Great idea. It's a bit different, innit?'

We fixed on a time a week or two later. Little Gemma would certainly never have seen anything like Bernie in drag, that was for sure.

'Any news on the commercial game?' he asked.

'Nothing yet, Bernie. They're still pissing about.'

I did not dare tell him that he had made a favourable impression on the selected members of the US public who had seen the first commercial. There was no saying what that would have done to his disunited personality, judging by the euphoria the Ugly Sister role had afforded him. He would probably get on the phone to Lennie Weinreb, persuading him out of long overdue retirement and then begin to pester the agency and American Eagle with script suggestions. There is nothing like being proved right in life, particularly in his intuition that i was too stiff and reserved a presenter for the dynamic world of consumer credit. *Nothing personal, Tim. It's just that there's professionals and amateurs in this game. Know what I mean?*

'Do you want any more fish? Jimmy liked you. Any time, 'e said.'

'No thanks, Bernie, not for the moment. Living on my own and so on.'

I had only just got rid of the smell which had offended Victoria. She had rung a couple of times. She was in the throes of a domestic crisis. It sounded like a domestic apocalypse in fact. A ceiling had fallen down flooding the house under a tidal wave of water, caused by a 'cowboy' decorator; her ex-boyfriend had been fired and was demanding that she sell their house at a loss. He was in some sort of financial difficulty. So Victoria had had no time to think about American Eagle. She was living with her sister in Fulham for the time being, while the flood subsided, and she was working evenings at the Tate on her course. She sounded like trouble herself. There are people – I've met plenty of them – who prefer to live in a state of crisis. They encourage crisis because it is exciting to be in the eye of the storm with the barometer plunging still further.

None the less, I was looking forward to seeing her again with her warm, musky conversation and her bruised-fruit lips; she had, I surmised impertinently, had a little too much handling in the sexual domain. Our private thoughts were not intended for exposure to the light, whatever Jung may have said. What is the priest thinking as he hears confession, or the doctor in the AIDS clinic, or the judge in the incest case? For God's sake don't tell us. Keep it to yourself, pal. You keep your Christmas, and I'll keep mine.

What I do in my reporting of London is selective. Nobody in New York, or anywhere else for that matter, wants to hear what I really think about this strange city, with its pinched faces and veinous noses and small eyes and runaway arses and tallow breasts; with its nooks and crannies, its shabby whores, its lamenting brickwork, its vomit-strewn streets, its dribbling skies, and its inexplicable smugness. Everyone is always congratulating themselves on their good fortune in living here, in the great wen: *It's wicked, it's brilliant, it's the business, it's well good*. The families around me with their Labradors and Volvos and green boots, who shoot off to the country every weekend, do not see themselves as Londoners. They may pass the week in town, but they keep London at arm's length, like damp laundry or a baby with a wet nappy. They have circuits of pals, restaurants, dinner parties and places of work, where London is a faint rumour, the scraping of the camels' hooves outside, accompanied by a little desultory barking. To these people, Londoners are rather amusing chaps – little men or little women who fix things – Fred and Doreen, Terry and Doris. They tell tales about the natives in Cockney accents, defunct music-hall Cockney. They learned these accents not from their proprietors but from their chums, who tell similar stories. They probably think, like Bernie, that Cockneys are a good-hearted, jokey race living in colourful slums down the East End. They get a nasty shock when these people turn up in their leisure wear on the first tee in Barbados with their new sets of clubs and slice wildly into the tropical undergrowth. This shower from Essex probably sell stolen lead. Look at these oiks in their sports shirts and gold identity bracelets and Rolexes. Even the piccanins who are forced to carry their immense golf bags are laughing at them.

'Fuck me. Caught it right off the heel of me Ping.'

Something's going wrong. What's happened to the decent sort of Cockney who braved the Blitz? There were real butchers down in Chelsea once. Striped aprons, straw boaters, lovely pink meat, glossy pheasants, hairy venison, still-life mallards, upside-down hares, speckled quail's eggs, old-fashioned service, the whole shooting match. That's the way it used to be.

From where I live it is difficult to have a complete picture of London. You don't see the barristers with their anally retentive tailoring and Lionel Barrymore haircuts; the vicious little bastards in white vans with ladders on the roof; the crazed minicabbers; the child molesters who drive double-decker buses in their sandals; the dipsy old ladies who feed pigeons on sliced white bread; the boys with faces of unbaked dough who beg at the train stations; the policemen with their dead eyes; the febrile gay boys filing into the public conveniences in Clerkenwell; the leather boys on their flying Kawasakis; the wild girls in their torn jeans and nose studs; the black boys with their scalded feet; the black girls with their expressive saunters; the imperfectly blonde old women sitting wheezing in the snug bar. These people don't even come from the same planet as the moonfaced girls with long, straight hair who carry cellos, the cub mistresses eating fairy cakes in church halls, the social workers in Marks and Spencer jumpers, the teachers in John Lennon glasses, the elderly men in tweeds exiting from the British Museum Library; the gypsies selling candy floss beside the dodgems on Hampstead Heath, the schoolgirls in their little green uniforms and white socks.

Where do you stop? You can't even begin. Like the notion of infinite space, London is not susceptible to human reason. Consequently I pass it through the filter every fortnight. Bernie is like a gnat that has been caught in the mesh. He refuses to go through. I am beginning to admire his irreducible quality, but I try to not to give him too much encouragement. I saw a television documentary about camels. They can go nine days without water. Bernie can go months without a refreshing draught of success. Six weeks as an Ugly Sister, second choice, may seem like thin gruel, but it is a huge portion of nourishing elixir which will sustain him through months of drought. The big break is an oasis in the desert where he will lie down under the shade of a thousand palm trees, in camel parlance.

I never cease to wonder at the illusions which sustain

the world. In the death camps when all illusion had been removed in the most unspeakable manner, still the survivors stayed alive by the force of illusion. Sometimes I think this city is closer to holy cities like Kandy or Kathmandu than anyone cares to recognise. Some days the streets seem to me to be full of people as deluded as the lamas of Tibet or the Copts of Alexandria. A large portion of the country's youth lives in dreams of becoming rock stars (perhaps saving the rain forest and some endangered species as a sideline) with the mantic powers which rock and roll bestows on its wise men. Recently a prostitute with a lumpy scarred face, short rat's-tail blonde hair and a square build like a lighter or a tugboat, a cigarette glued to her fingers, approached me at the side entrance to King's Cross at four o'clock in the afternoon. It is inconceivable to me that she can make a living there. And why, I thought as I hurried away, had she picked on me?

Bernie dreams of topping the bill, name above the title. His elderly body is packing its bags untidily but his spirit is unquenchably thirsty. The city is throbbing and humming not – as you would imagine – with the traffic and electrical surges and underground sewers, but with the mysterious anthem of the beehive, a humming which signifies complicity in a great illusion. The illusion is that, like the bees, the citizens live without the knowledge of mortality. A great city is a tissue of immortality; it is the discarded skin of generations, it is countless strata of deception; for it is only in the illusion that it can exist. The bees hum the tunes of immortality while they pursue the paths of mortality. They are immortal – another one will be along in a moment to replace the worn-out body of its predecessor. If you look at it this way, strictly in terms of cells and DNA, we are all immortal. We are only cells which shrivel and die but pop up again in new casings. In the documentary about camels, it did not mention an Arab proverb: *Death is the black camel that kneels at every doorway.* But you got to look on the bright side, ain'tcher? Bernie's credo could be translated very simply: to be human is to live by illusion.

Strangely enough, these were not morbid thoughts. There is something comforting and uplifting about cosmic thoughts, or what passes for them in the state of illusion in which we live. Nor am I plagued and oppressed by thoughts of mortality myself, although I sometimes worry in the night about Gemma's safety. Her hold on life seemed so precarious in the first few years of her childhood. I have watched her small face in the night for signs of irregular breathing and pulled back the bedclothes for fear of overheating, and suffered palpitations beside hotel swimming pools when she has disappeared from sight even for a moment, yet she has blithely survived to be five years old. Five years of appalling risks, many of which I have lived in dramatic detail at a distance, separated by the uncaring Atlantic. This is love of the purest sort: Gemma is the distilled essence of me. I am the discard in the vats – the sediments, stalks and skins – and she is the pure spirit, the few precious drops at the end of the process.

This week I have strayed off my manor, as Cockneys allegedly say, to the fringes of London, to see Darwin's house and look at his letters, instruments and beetle collection. Here the great man worked every day for thirty years. Here he placed his worm stone. Here he refined his glorious theories and grew famous. The voyage of the *Beagle* provided him with so much food for thought that, like his beloved earthworms, he was able to digest it and produce intellectual leaf mould for the rest of his life. Two things struck me about Darwin's house; the letter he wrote to his son Horace's prospective and reluctant father-in-law, in which he said that despite Horace's poor health, poor appearance and lack of prospects, he had the most precious of all attributes, kindness. It is a letter of grace and gentleness. It is not marriage, but parenthood to which he was directing the insensitive burgher's attention.

The other thing which drew my attention, was a picture above the fire by George Stubbs of a lion stalking a horse. What's the connection? This is one of Stubbs' earliest paintings of the theme; at the time he was making an enamel of the same subject with the help of Josiah Wedgwood. Josiah Wedgwood was Charles Darwin's grandfather; he was also his wife's grandfather. On closer inspection it appears that this is a copy of the painting which hangs in the Tate Gallery. 'By Geo. Stubbs' has been overpainted to 'after George Stubbs'. None the less the lion is lurking in the shadows with convincing menace while the horse is rooted to the spot; the electric currents of mortal fear have scrambled the horse's brain – I am no zoologist – as the scent of lion reaches it. The horse is a palomino; it looks like Trigger's elegant European cousin, and the knowledge that this exotic creature is soon to be eaten (*Horse Devoured by Lion* – Tate Gallery) makes the fear more palpable. In Simba Cochrane's case the horse (and Cochrane) escaped by a miracle, confirming that life does not often imitate art.

My appointment with Cochrane at the zoo was postponed again, the reason given was Chaka's ill health. This was a pre-glasnost Soviet-style excuse. Later the keeper called to say that the real reason for the delay was that Chaka was restless. He had tried to swim the moat, which was unusual because lions avoid water as far as possible. The moat is six feet deep and the wall about six feet high, so the lions have no chance whatever of jumping out.

My piece in *Manhattan* about Cochrane prompted a letter from Africa via East 37th Street. It was sent by Chief Phineas Chilingwe, who wished to make my acquaintance. His father, Chief Solomon Chilingwe, knew Mr William Cochrane of the Public Works Department in 1932 in the short reign of George Five. The Chief had some other important and confidential news which he would like to impart to me, if I would write to him. Naturally I wrote to him immediately with some doubts as to whether my letter would ever arrive at Private Bag 7, Uzumbu, Rumunruti District, Kenya. The Chief's letter was cunningly phrased, because, after arousing my curiosity, it ended with a request for money.

'A postal order will help me. Times are hard here because of the rains. The rains have been lacking.'

CHAPTER NINE

Victoria had to leave instructions with the switchboard not to take any more calls from Miles. Because he had been fired for a breach in the bank's rules, he had received no bonus. The bonus had more than monetary value. It was the confirmation of success in the City. It had religious significance. People discussed THE BONUS with hushed reverence. Being deprived of your bonus was deeply humiliating. Miles could not afford to pay. Victoria had had to plead with her bank manager in her most artificial voice for a loan for the flood damage because Miles had let the insurance lapse. She had paid the total cost, £18,000. The carpets had been removed, the walls directly beneath the deluge had had to be stripped and replastered, the wood-block floor had to be taken up, the limed-oak kitchen units had warped and their 'hand-rubbed' stain had oozed out. Nature's way of ageing wood was not as orderly as the kitchen designers', that was certain.

Victoria thought that the soul of the house had been exposed, and found lacking. She resented her involvement in the whole business deeply. She had been against it from the start and now she had been co-opted into the over-exposed young executives' club, a club whose only qualification for membership is foolishness, foolishness of the sort displayed by the grasshopper in the fable.

Miles's new girlfriend had left him. Her insurance did not cover him to drive her little tart's Renault, drunk or sober, and she had sent him a lawyer's letter with three estimates for the repairs. Three thousand, two hundred was the cheapest. Her brother said she might sue him for whiplash as well. Miles was staying with a friend and was naturally desperate to sell

Heron's Beat. He called Victoria six or seven times a day. Her art director, Mike, had told him in plain English to stop ringing, but still he kept on. He wrote her a note suggesting they get back together again. He had only gone out with Jacci because he wanted to prove something to Victoria. Victoria wondered what that could possibly be. She felt sorry for him, however; in the course of two weeks he had lost so much. His vowels had even returned, released from their confinement when the carapace of his self-esteem cracked.

It gave her no pleasure to see that the workings of the City were predictably crude. Nobody – Miles confessed – would talk to him. When he called, his former colleagues were either in meetings or out of the office for the moment. Prospective employers did not return his calls. His letters were answered with such formality that he began to suspect that Arnie had – to use his word – 'circularised' everyone in the City. This tactic of throwing a *cordon sanitaire* around the bank before it could be infected with contagion, would account for his complete isolation. Even a brasserie where he had spent thousands buying champagne had been reluctant to serve him. Victoria suspected creeping delusions.

It was not strictly true that he had not been offered any jobs. He had. The first was a partnership in a bar in Lamu. 'Aren't they Muslims in Lamu, Miles?' The second was as an independent financial adviser. 'Does that mean insurance salesman, Miles?' 'Jesus you know how to twist the knife, Victoria.' 'If you don't want the facts, stop calling me.'

But she had accepted his invitation for a drink one evening. His suit hung on him limply, as though it had been caught in the rain, and his expensive shoes were scuffed; they were missing the attentions of the man who – would you believe it? – used to scuttle around under the young masters' feet with his shoebrushes. Miles's own badger-bristled shaving brush and ivory-handled razor had missed a little thicket of hair under his fine, straight nose; these relatively minor imperfections in his appearance cast doubts, like a fly in a bowl of soup, on the whole. After a bottle of white wine, which he had insisted on paying for with a dog-eared fifty-pound note, he had suggested sexual intimacy.

'No thanks, Miles. Where's Jacci when you need her?'

'Jacci. Jacci. She was just a piece of fluff. Honestly, Vic, there's no comparison. I know it's hard for you to understand, but it's true.'

'Now it's back to solid old Victoria is it? Now that the bimbo has gone. How's her car by the way? A total write-off, I hear?'

'Don't laugh. It wasn't funny.'

'You've got to laugh.'

'What are you doing?'

'I'm very busy with the Tate and with American Eagle. It's my new account. With Tim Curtiz.'

The Admiral Codrington was busy. To Victoria it always had the atmosphere of a private party that was expecting the remaining guests at any moment. Every time the door opened, heads turned hopefully. The new arrival would be greeted by loud shouts of welcome or hoots of derision.

Miles was very subdued. His good looks were working against him now; his strong features, his dark hair and his grey eyes, had all lost their lustre. He appeared to have been dusted all over. He had been shocked by his night in the cells. The desk sergeant had nearly broken his arm when he had asked for a lawyer. They had not let him out until eleven, after a second blood test showed he was sober enough to hail a taxi without danger to the public. When he arrived, Jacci's brother had opened the door, handed him a suitcase and told him to fuck off. Jacci would not speak to him, he said. She had gone home to her mum's in Whitechapel. His trial was in two weeks' time. The fine was going to be at least a thousand pounds and the lawyers' fees about the same.

'When we sell the house, if we sell the house, you will owe me ten or twelve thousand out of your share. And the back payments on the mortgage,' said Victoria.

'Unless I get a job.'

Even as he said it, his red-rimmed eyes shifted uneasily from her face. Victoria was silent.

'I still love you, Vic,' he said, as if talking to the glass in his hand.

'No you don't.'

But she felt a surge of compassion.

'You'll be all right soon, Miles. This will seem like a bad

dream. Now, don't ring me any more and I won't see you again. Not for a time anyway. I've got my own life to lead. We all have, Miles. That's the way things are. I've got to go to my classes now. Thanks for the drink.'

It was impossible to say anything original or even truthful under the circumstances. She left him in the cheerful atmosphere of the Admiral Codrington, more solitary because of the hoots of laughter, clinking of glasses and the shouted greetings around him than if he had been standing alone in a field.

Her classes at the Tate were serious. She was expected to know something about every painter hanging there and a great deal about Stubbs. Art history was an industry. These people knew things about Stubbs he probably didn't know himself. They knew the influences and origins of the horse and lion pictures. They knew which classical sculptures had influenced English painters and which painters had influenced Stubbs. They knew when the first horse and lion sculpture had been done in Rome and they knew its Hellenistic influences. Lions, it seemed, had always exercised the artistic imagination. 'Androcles and the Lion' itself was not an original story, but a common folk legend.

Down in the storerooms of the gallery she was able to breathe her mortal breath on numinous works of art. There were paintings and busts, small bronzes, huge canvases and strange collages, all unseen by the public. There were racks which rolled out so that you could summon up a Turner or a Constable; you could brush past a Degas or Epstein bust; you could stumble over Roy Liechtenstein. There were more paintings in the storerooms than in the gallery itself because of re-hanging. Down there Victoria found girls dressed in painters' smocks with woolly stockings, long straight hair and mulberry-coloured nails and eyes, strange creatures with prematurely grave features who spoke with ecclesiastical affectedness. They were personally familiar with dead artists in the way that nuns are devoted to the body of Christ. They were vestals, feeding the sacred flames of art, and all clad appropriately. The men, like her tutor Tresillian Lascelles, had something approaching a lisp. Proximity to art, Victoria decided, warped the speech patterns, just the way water affected fitted kitchens. Perhaps she would begin to deliver her words in this new way, articulated with mincing fastidiousness. Virginia Woolf probably spoke like this.

She enjoyed it. There was a lot to be said for studying the history of painting and the lives of painters for no obvious gain. Trips were planned to Paris and Madrid. Tresillian was about forty-five with a bald fringe which he wore long. Victoria had never met a real life Tresillian before. He had a mustard waistcoat, with food stains on it. She wanted to tell him that for a messy eater, yellow was a poor choice of colour. He spoke with intensity about Stubbs and his understanding of the anatomy of the horse. He began to pay Victoria little courtesies, which others in the group tried not to notice. He had a flat in Pimlico where, to judge from the state of his clothes, he lived alone. Once he wore a new floppy bow tie. Victoria suspected that he had bought it to appear debonair for her sake. As well as lecturing on art history, he took guided trips to galleries and museums around Europe.

Life had not dealt too kindly with him, Victoria thought. He was jumpy and defensive. In fact most of these art people had a defensive quality which was completely different from the bright, adamantine cheerfulness of the agency. Tresillian had once, he told Victoria, tried to dissect a Shetland pony with a bread knife, such was his admiration for Stubbs. He had ended up with what looked like a rural road accident. That had convinced him at the age of fourteen that he did not have what it takes to be a great animal painter. He asked Victoria if she would like to go to the zoo one to day to look at the lions, applying what she now knew of Stubbs to the real article. They could sketch lions in the postures which fascinated eighteenth-century painters of menageries. Victoria agreed. It all seemed wonderfully unreal to her.

She was working on a paper about Stubbs. Other students in the strangely assorted group were writing papers on Blake and Constable. The American Eagle campaign had bogged down. New York had decided that the campaign was too up-market for the ordinary credit card. The commercial would be run and be researched, but Tim Curtiz was to be saved for the launch of the new Golden Eagle Club, a card limited to people with enormous salaries and senior positions in big companies. This card would prove that these people had arrived. Sometimes Victoria had a vision of advertising as being directed entirely to people who were arriving; those who were departing were as good as dead. Advertising hated bad news. Bad news was for chumps. Over at the agency they believed in the commercial application of the image. Here at the Tate they had removed art from the real world entirely. In her present state, one of transition, Victoria decided she was somewhere near the middle on this issue. Perhaps in sympathy with the Tate she modified her wardrobe and her hair, to produce a more fashionable version of the arts-and-crafts look favoured by the vestals. It resolved her fashion problems and conformed with her serious, reflective mood.

The day after their drink, Miles had sent her a registered letter to the agency. She delayed opening it all day. He appeared to think that she was going out with Tim Curtiz because of something she had said. He wrote, 'You haven't wasted much time, Victoria. I'm desperate to get back together with you, with debts mounting and my life in tatters and you're out every night with some minor celebrity. I've shared your life but now you can only spare me fifteen minutes in a pub.'

She called Miles at the number he had given her to put him straight once and for all. He was drunk.

'Hi, baby doll,' he said. 'Come over, we're having a party here. I knew you couldn't keep away. Come over now.'

There was a loud crash in the background and someone shouted, 'Shit, I've really hurt myself.' Miles laughed.

'Piggy's fallen over his mother's cat. When are you coming?'

'Miles, will you stop writing me ridiculous letters. I do not want to see you and I do not want to hear from you.'

In the background a girl could be heard calling Miles's name. *Miles. Milo. Who are you talking to? Milo.*

'Shh,' she heard Miles say with his hand over the mouthpiece, 'I'm on the phone.'

The whole mawkish scene was clear to Victoria. Miles and his friend Piggy, an unemployed stockbroker, were made for each other.

'Miles, if you want to communicate with me again about the house, get your solicitor to write.'

'He won't. I can't pay him.'

'You seem to have enough to get pissed.'

'Victoria, I'm drowning my sorrows.'

'Don't stop at your sorrows. If I get one more of your calls you'll hear from my solicitor.'

It was an empty threat, and she felt lonely. She called Tim Curtiz.

'Hello, has your daughter arrived yet? OK, when she's gone. No, no. No news yet I'm afraid. You'll be the first to know.'

She slipped out of the staff entrance at the side. The doorkeeper looked up briefly from his pie and chips. 'Night, night, darlin',' he said, his mouth full.

The world had retreated a pace from her. The cold, damp, monumental city outside was in retreat from Victoria. She wrapped herself in the cloak of loneliness and walked up the river. Her sister would be out – she was always out – and she could work on her essay. Harshness had entered her life. Perhaps in a city you could not avoid it. The traffic streamed by, slicing through the wetness with a noise like Elastoplast ripped off. There was a Henry Moore on the river's edge, a giant bronze which evoked the elemental nature of life. Like Picasso, Moore had developed his own, distinctive symbolism which was now part of the language of art. This language of art was a mysterious thing. It seemed to be audible only to the initiated, like Esperanto or Swahili. It could be understood by people like Tresillian who understood so little about anything else, yet the people going by in their BMWs and Volvos were unaware of its vital importance. There was old Henry Moore winking to them, semaphoring important messages from the cosmos, addressing them in the elemental language of the universe, and the bastards were listening for the racing results or the financial news on their radios. She stopped briefly at the Henry Moore, in her new role, and paid her respects in the few halting words of the lingo she had picked up.

The air was loaded with rain. One squeeze and the sky would begin to drip. The river, the self same river which she could glimpse from Heron's Beat, was high and malevolent, its surface like dark slate. It was difficult to imagine where all this water came from. Sure it rained all the time, but this was a huge mass of water, which had lost its rustic innocence on the way to town. In Stubbs's day, London was changing from sprawling villages to the greatest city of commerce and industry in the world. This river had brought the world to London. The lions for menageries had arrived in makeshift cages, donated by dusky princes and bejewelled maharajahs, or despatched by gentlemen explorers and doughty missionaries. Londoners responded to each exotic new arrival enthusiastically. Noblemen claimed some symbolic kinship with these beasts. Her Majesty's consul in Florence, Sir George Davis, formed a lifelong attachment to a lion which was overjoyed to see him when he visited it in the Duke of Tuscany's menagerie years later, where it had been feared as a killer. It was a paradigm of the story of Saints Gerasimus and Jerome, but it also demonstrated the shared nobility of man and beast.

A car slowed beside Victoria.

'You wanna lift?'

Gold teeth, brown suits and King Hussein moustaches were directed towards her.

'No thanks. I like walking.'

'It's cold. We give you ride. How much?'

Behind them other traffic was becoming impatient. Victoria stopped walking so that they were forced on by the inertia. She hailed a taxi. The driver shook his head and muttered when she said Fulham, but she got in quickly anyway.

Her sister had been and gone in a whirlwind. Her underwear lay in the main room, which was dining room, kitchen and living room and now Victoria's bedroom too. Victoria studied it. The bra was black silk, with fancy underwiring and the pants were no more than a small patch front and back. She wondered what this said about little Cressida's private life. Cressida was going out at the same time with an architectural student from home and her boss. This was Cressida's fifth job since leaving school two years before. Her boss ran a shop selling antique watches, which were in demand among financial brokers and bond traders.

There was a note from her sister: 'Gone out, nothing in

the fridge, Love Cress. P.S. Miles rang. Twice. Told him you were in Nepal until Tuesday. Ring Mum.'

She settled down to her books with a cup of coffee. Before she could read a word, the phone rang. Thinking it would be Miles, she answered, 'Cressida, hello.'

'Don't be silly, Victoria. It's me.'

'Hello, Mum, how are you?'

'I'm fine, dear. How are you, that's the important thing?'

'Fine. Working hard at the Tate. I was just about to start my homework.'

'Homework? Isn't it a bit strange after all these years?'

'I don't know. I was just about to begin.'

'Don't be sharp, dear. What news on your lovely house?'

'It's not lovely any more. The plumber flooded it. For twelve hours the mains gushed through it. The damage is nearly twenty thousand.'

'Twenty thousand? Daddy and I bought this house for seven thousand.'

'That was in the Palaeolithic era. Things have got a bit more expensive.'

'Miles said someone was starting work on it.'

'Miles said. Why have you been speaking to him?'

'We had a heart-to-heart. He's very upset. He wants to get back together with you.'

'I suppose he asked you to ring me?'

'Not exactly.'

'What a creep. Do you realise that in the past three weeks he has left me, been fired, been arrested and taken to drink. What possible reason could there be for getting together with him again?'

'Victoria, he loves you. He told me.'

'I don't love him. In fact he's becoming a nuisance. I think he's unbalanced.'

'Who wouldn't be? He's got no job, no home, no money and no girlfriend.'

'Careless, isn't he? Why are you siding with Miles anyway? He behaved like a louse and now he's got his. He was lucky not to be arrested for fraud as well. When he tried to get his bonus, they told him they were considering sending for the

Fraud Squad. His Chinese accomplice is inside. They are beating the soles of his feet with rattan canes every night to get more information out of him. If Miles ever goes to Hong Kong he'll be arrested.'

'Singapore, dear. Miles told me how it happened. Apparently they're all doing it. Miles was just unlucky. He was the scapegoat.'

'God, Miles has been having you on. He was caught in some nasty little fiddle and fired. He then crashed his bimbo's car right into one of the lions in Trafalgar Square and broke all records for the amount of alcohol in the bloodstream. In fact they had trouble finding any blood. Does this sound like ideal son-in-law material to you?'

'Really, where do you get your powers of exaggeration? I suppose they've been useful in advertising. You were always making up stories, even when you were very little. You told Miss Hughes that your father and I were getting divorced so that you could miss gym.'

'Well, I was only about seven years early.'

'Don't be cruel. Have you heard from Daddy?'

'I haven't heard from him for six months.'

Her mother said 'Daddy' in a way which was both contemptible and pitiful, as though she left a lighted candle in the bedroom window every night to guide him home from his wanderings. Her father Lionel was a person who preferred to move on like a nomad, not out of principle, but because he could not bear to be held to account by anyone. It was simpler to up sticks and leave at the first sign of trouble. He had been at different times film producer, hotel owner, arms dealer, and vendor of property in Tuscany. At the moment he was managing a vineyard on the shores of Lake Naivasha in Kenya. Strangely this implausible con man was always supplied with women, who offered to be drawn along by the turbulence he created. The world's backwaters hold numbers of optimistic, unrealistic people looking for an opening.

Her mother was a believer in the individual's true self. This true self was often invisible to the untrained observer, but it was one of her sustaining myths that Lionel's true self had been hijacked by unfortunate circumstances. She blamed herself to some extent: 'I shouldn't have tried to make him settle down so soon, I can see that now. It wasn't really his fault. I pushed him too hard after he lost his job. I wanted him to do well, that's really all.'

Lionel now had a challenger for the job of misunderstood saint.

Still, Victoria had a sneaking regard for her father. At the time of the divorce she had loathed him, but she now saw that, whatever his motives, he had succeeded in unshackling himself from the earth's attachments. He was ahead of his time, instinctively suspicious of the demands which family life was making on him.

'Victoria. Are you still there? I thought we had been cut off. Victoria, what I wanted to say was, Miles is coming to stay with me for a few weeks. He's really desperate. Just until he finds his feet.'

What a lot of people were losing their footing.

CHAPTER TEN

Gemma arrived from New York at seven in the morning, London time, one in the morning New York time. She was wearing a little Laura Ashley dress with a dark blue nanny coat. Mothers – even mothers who dress like Magda – always dress their daughters in the prettiest and most classic clothes. My own mother had me baptised on the principle that you need to know what you are rebelling against. There is a more persistent regard for the folk wisdom than cosmopolitans care to recognise.

I woke early. The alarm was out of a job; I had lain awake for at least an hour in the tempestuous early morning. 'Morning' suggests light expected. None was expected for many hours; London gets a very meagre ration. I was awake all the same in solidarity with little Gemma, unaccompanied minor, zipping over the oily Atlantic towards me, her small face excited but composed. Suppose Magda had changed her mind at the last minute? Or forgotten? Or lost her passport? Or any damn thing. She had not called for a week and her phone seemed to be out of service.

The laurels in the park were taking a beating from the wind. The laurel is a funereal plant, along with the rosemary and the oak. (At four in the morning symbolism looms very large.) It seemed cruel to despatch a little girl into the night, launch her over the ocean into the void. Yet she loved planes. Her duty was clear: to fly like an arrow between her barely trucial parents, a little messenger of bonhomie and love, a belomancer. She accepted these arrangements without question. In fact she rarely asked any questions about anything much. Children's inquisitiveness is simply a need for reassurance, I reassure myself when I hear other children asking questions. Perhaps intuitively she realised that we had no answers. Magda had consumed life so avidly and with so little return that she had probably exhausted her ability to produce fresh answers. Magda bore the same relationship to life as the people who were chopping down the rain forest have to ecology. I worried about the men in Magda's life and their effect upon my Gemma, yet she came to me every few months with her serenity undisturbed.

'Fish,' she said as I kissed her outside the customs hall.

'Yes, darling, as soon as you've had a sleep.'

She was carrying the teddy bear I had given her and a little red rucksack packed with her treasured possessions which included a scrap of blanket so chewed and ragged that I feared it constituted a health hazard.

The stewardess was a big, bony girl with good teeth. She retrieved the minor's tag and handed me some papers to sign.

'She's been a very good girl, haven't you, honey? You take care of your daddy now, you hear.'

She gave me a frank look. She had seen me before.

'You are really great in that commercial,' she said, 'I just saw it the other night. That's weird.'

'Thank you. It's not my real job you know.'

'Sure, sure. You made London (Lundin) look real interesting. I liked the old guy with the fish fry too. You just wait here one second while I get the bag.'

Gemma held my hand with a small and insistent grip, her face as fresh as if she had just been for a short walk. She would soon be seeing the guy with the fish fry in a ball-gown and wig. I picked her up to hold her little body to mine.

'I got a fish now,' she said.

I had never seen her bedroom, but I liked the idea of a fish swimming peacefully in a bowl. It suggested a certain unexpected but welcome domestic order.

'What sort of fish?'

'A red fish.'

'A goldfish?'

'Yes, but it's red really.'

The stewardess returned with the case and gave Gemma a kiss.

'Bye now, honey. You all take care.'

'Goodbye. Say thank you, Gemma.'

We were off in my car, out onto the busy motorway, heading for London. Still the sky was sullen, though lightly brushed with silver from under the clouds. Gemma sat unmoved in the back, strapped in.

'Do you like Daddy's new car?' I asked.

'No,' she said.

She slept serenely. I had bought a little bed from Heal's with a carved bedhead and a patchwork quilt. There she lay, a character from a fairy tale, clutching her teddy and the scrap of blanket. Her lips moved and she smiled and said something I could not catch: I sat near her bed reading so that when she woke she would not be confused. I felt happy, blessed to have this little creature under my roof, breathing the same air, eating the same food, using my plates, spoons and cups and sharing my body-heat. All my anxieties about her were dissipated by her presence. As soon as she woke she would want to be off to the zoo to check out the fish. I was happy to oblige.

I was reading about lions. Lions are much misunderstood. All creatures are misunderstood; this is a truism which doctors of zoology and producers of wildlife films delight in reporting to us. Male lions, Schaller writes, are not lazy. They spend most of the night fighting, marking and patrolling their territory. Indeed, far from being lazy, they are the prototype of the male adventurer – territorially ambitious, aggressive to outsiders, obsessively jealous of their possessions and fierce killers when called upon. As a result they have little time for hunting which is left to the females. This is where the misunderstanding arises. Their brief span as a pride male is an example of sexual selection at its rawest. The pride male has, by virtue of his strength and determination, won the right to pass on his DNA. Others are waiting if he fails. In a few years at most he must take over a pride, kill the cubs, mate with the lionesses and defend his territory to the death. This cast a whole new light on Chaka, London Zoo's dissident.

Of course, the behaviour of lions may be the least interesting thing about them. In the way of symbols, lions are pretty near the top of the tree. But would anyone have followed Richard the Lionheart if they had known how similar lions' behaviour is to that of tomcats? And would anyone have paid to see Simba Cochrane enter Sig. Corleone's ring?

A city is the sum of its history and its symbolism, just as much as its fabric and its industry. I cannot write to my editor to tell him how much significance is contained in the insignificant jockey-bodied, breadmould-headed person of Simba Cochrane. Or even in the boletus-like figure of Bernie Koppel, master of the fish fry: *This your real life, Tim, not your arsey-farty stuff. That's what people want, no offence, not yer hoity-toity highfalutin guff.* I am lumped in Bernie's estimation with all the stiffs who have conspired to keep the real story out of the news, all the pretentious graduates, writers and so-called experts who wouldn't know real life if it stepped up and bit them in the backside: *Life on the streets, Tim, know what I mean.* The only problem, Bernie me old son, is the streets you are talking about don't exist no more, if you get my meaning. The singing porters have been replaced by mute Bangladeshis. The jellied eel has given way to the chapati. The ship's chandlers have been invaded by computer salesmen. My dentist once told me that a British Prime Minister, Edward Heath I think, had lost a general election because of faulty root canal work. You see what you want to see, Bernie, that's the way it is. In your case it's the bright side, which is about as big a myth as any going.

Jesus Christ, lions mate every ten minutes for twenty-four hours when the females are in season, or oestrus, as Schaller calls it. No wonder they have no energy for hunting.

Gemma stirs. I am hoping she will wake. She moves again and turns over with a sigh.

Victoria called me last night. Her tone was rather deliberately businesslike. She and her boyfriend have been separated for a few weeks now. Perhaps she is in a refined form of oestrus. On the lion analogy, I am not sure I am ready. I have taken on the maternal role here. Female lions, says Schaller, are the core of the pride. The males are transient and expendable. They arrive one day out of the savannah, go about their business as ordained and succumb in battle. Chaka's time is up. He is looking towards the goat mountain because he senses the inevitable threat. Little does he know, of course, that they are trying to round up a suitable replacement for him on the Indian subcontinent, not too far away from the emigrating Bangladeshis, as a matter of fact.

She breathes evenly. Every five minutes or so she shifts her position, gulping once for air, her finger instinctively clutching her teddy and her blanket. It is early afternoon. Unseen by me until now, the sun has come out on the park and the mothers and nannies are there trying to look cheerful in that dreadfully strained fashion of the English upper strata. The retired hayloft is flooded with unexpected sunshine. The kilims pick up the light in the way their makers in dusty Tabriz anticipated. The granite tiles glow. My espresso machine, all artful pipes and dials signifying nothing, catches a shaft of light. The stone fireplace, salvaged from a town hall in Cumbria, looks stately. The room is ready for the little princess to wake, but she sleeps on. I fix myself a sandwich. Ready on the work-surface are her bowl and mug, charmingly decorated with bunnies and other little herbivores. As I take my first bite, she appears in the doorway of her bedroom, not at all fuddled by sleep, wearing her white nightdress and carrying her bear.

'Hello, Daddy,' she says. 'Fish.'

'Are you hungry, sweetie? We'll go as soon as you've eaten something.'

I have taken advice on what five-year-olds eat. Junior canneloni is a success. I have also got in a supply of fruits and vegetables, to be administered with tact and in small doses, lest vegetable phobia set in.

We went straight to the fish. Old people in London often sit trancelike in front of television screens watching snooker and cricket, interminable games almost as ritualistic as fish swimming. In the same way, Gemma stood motionless before the tank of mirror carp, entranced as they wheeled and circled, as perfectly regimented as geese in flight or snowflakes on a still night. Then we went on to the coral-reef tank to see the brightly coloured and more individualistic tropical fish. Gemma took communion here silently; I held her hand. A notice warned against pickpockets, but child snatchers were on my mind. Her hand undulated gently as though in time with the fish and their subaqua whims. On closer inspection, fish do not operate on whim at all. They live by rote. Rote is only an old word for route, I imagine. Fish are rotarians. Perhaps we are all rotarians, except that it is easier to discern in fish. Gemma probably sees patterns the way scientists see beauty in atoms, molecules and quarks.

Eventually I coaxed her out into the open air, eager to show her my new pals, the lions. A small crowd had gathered to watch the lions feeding. A keeper had a small bucket of meat and a megaphone. He was standing above the moat inside the restraining fence.

'Good afternoon. These are our three lions at present, Chaka, Ndukwe – we call her Doris – and Leonie. Leonie is an Asian lion. Chaka and Doris are African lions. She is second generation zoo bred, but Chaka, who is fourteen years old, was found orphaned as a cub in Kenya. I am going to feed them in a moment, but only a very small amount so that they will still be hungry when we want to get them to go inside. Lions are very lazy creatures. They spend eighteen to twenty hours a day asleep. The females do the hunting and the males do very little. The ladies present will know what I mean. I am now going to throw them a piece of meat each. Doris and Leonie are eating well, but poor ole Chaka is off his greens at the moment. Still, let's see what happens.'

Chaka was lying just above the moat on a rocky promontory, watching the keeper in that peculiar way of lions with his eyes fixed apparently on something more distant.

'Before I feed them, you are probably wondering why we don't have cubs. The reason is simple. Lions breed very easily in zoos, Chaka has had a vasectomy. Why are your eyes watering, sir? Now, here we go.'

He hurled a piece of meat in the direction of one of the lionesses, which was padding about in a genial fashion. She seized it and trotted off towards the back of the terraces. The keeper then bowled a piece of meat towards Chaka. It landed near him, but he acknowledged it only by turning his head away.

'He's not hungry, but I'll try him once more.'

A piece of meat the size of a soup plate flew through the air towards Chaka. The little crowd, zipped up against the cold, was expectant. The meat struck the lion on the head.

'Oh dear, sorry old boy.'

Chaka stood up. Suddenly he leapt with surprising agility down the promontory to the water's edge and roared at the keeper. The huge front paws were actually in the icy moat. We watchers tittered nervously. The roar, the noise of a truck passing in a tunnel, still rolled in our ears.

'Poor old boy. Who's in a bad mood then?'

How would you like to be smacked in the gob by a flying T-bone, you wanker? (I was thinking in the idiom.) The thin crowd edged closer again as he fed the other lioness.

'Well, that's it, ladies and gents and kiddies,' said the keeper. 'The zoo closes in half an hour. Thank you for coming. Lion feeding is every afternoon at four, except Tuesdays which is the day we starve the lions in order to replicate the conditions prevailing in the wild. Thank you. Come again and tell your friends.'

'The lion is mad,' said Gemma. 'Mad' in the American sense.

'Very cross. Did you get a fright when he roared?'

'No.'

A fat Arab child in a shiny tracksuit was crying because he had dropped his ice-cream in the excitement. Over at the mosque, the muezzin was calling, discreetly amplified, perhaps even recorded. There had been a certain amount of debate at the time of the mosque's building about the mullah's cry, '*Allah akbar*', ringing out over Regent's Park and floating on the prevailing wind towards north London. A compromise was reached.

Gemma and I had an ice-cream which she said was nearly as good as Haägen Dazs. I was over the little awkwardness of the morning. We were just a father and daughter like any other.

'Are you tired?'

'No.'

'You want to see the small mammals before they close?' I asked.

'Sure,' she said happily.

As we left the zoo, Chaka was roaring. Schaller says that lions roar to announce themselves to other lions, to proclaim their territory and to intimidate intruders. They roar most often in the early morning and early evening. They can roar lying down or standing.

'Is the lion still mad?' asked Gemma.

'I don't think so, darling. Lions roar for fun.'

'I think he wants to go home.'

'Where to?'

'To the jungle.'

'I think you are right.'

After a carefully balanced supper, Gemma went to bed without complaining. I read her a story about a farm from a book she had brought with her, but before I was finished she was asleep.

My house was pumped as full as a balloon with the remembered smells of childhood: of milk and cereals, of big printed books, of chewed blanket, of vitamin tablets and moist wool. It seemed so to me, anyway. In her bedroom she was breathing evenly, lying on her back, emitting occasionally the puppy whimpers and whispered confidences of a child asleep. I was happy. The house seemed perfect for the two of us, an ark afloat on the greasy floodwater, uprooted trees, drowned animals and the putrid history of London. I started to write:

My ancestors have wandered the dusty game paths of Africa since life began in the Rift Valley a million and more years ago. My eyes are growing dimmer and my world is growing smaller. Somewhere out there beyond the monkeys on two legs who watch me, lies the great savannah where I was born. I want to go home now. The hyenas will be gathering for me soon. Young lions – I can sometimes see them dimly – are waiting for me beyond the mountains. They can see my weakness. They know that I am old. I roar loudly. My roars which tell of battles won and cubs fathered, keep them at bay, but they are coming closer every night. They become more daring. Sometimes one of the big monkeys comes too close. I can stand their smell no longer. I'm going to eat one soon. That one, with the voice like a baboon who throws meat at me.

Wait a minute. Hold on. She's only five.

Once there was a very old lion called Chaka. His eyes were not very good and he walked very slowly. He lived in a zoo with two mummy lions.

One day he decided he would go home to the jungle to see his friends before he died. Although he roared politely, no one would let him out. He tried to tell them that he was very old and that he would not live much longer and could they please let him out, but the keepers did not understand.

One day a little girl, just five years old, came to the zoo with her daddy. The big old lion was roaring.

'Daddy,' she said, 'he wants to go home to the jungle.'

'How do you know?' asked her daddy, who was rather old and dim himself.

'I can hear what he is saying. He wants to go home and see his brothers and sisters in the jungle.'

Suddenly, before her father could stop her, the little girl jumped over the fence and walked up to the lion.

The keeper came running out with his gun. He was afraid that the lion would eat the little girl. But then a strange thing happened. The little girl whispered in the big lion's ear and the lion lay down. The keeper lowered the gun. The little girl jumped on the lion's back and the lion began to run.

With one huge leap he jumped right out of the lion cage and flew up over the goat mountain. The lion was going home to the jungle at last. The little girl's daddy was very sad, but what he didn't know was that the little girl was really a princess (there had been a mix up in the hospital) who could speak to animals and make them fly.

A few days later she returned from the jungle, after she had delivered the lion safely to his family, guiding by the stars at night and the sun by day. She was a little hungry when she came back and her daddy was overjoyed to see her. He made her some Coco Pops.

I went to bed. Some time later Gemma appeared in my bedroom. I had lost the habit of waking instantly to a child's seismic signals, and was slightly confused.

'What's the matter, darling?'

'I don't want to die,' she said, her eyes as wet as pebbles on a beach when the tide has gone.

'Let me read you a story I wrote for you.'

I wished I could have told her about the angels and so on, but I didn't have the conviction. She settled gravely into the bed beside me and fell asleep before I had finished, her serenity quickly restored.

CHAPTER ELEVEN

Miles was waiting for James Trentham. Nothing new in that. Anyway, Miles was the one with time on his hands. Time to spend, minute by sluggish minute. Time to exhale, breath by laborious breath.

Miles felt like someone who had been evicted into the street, like a refugee carrying all his possessions with him. He sat there in the Kean Club with his whole world in his person. He felt as though he had shrunk. He was an embalmed medical specimen or a pickled walnut in a jar. He was separated from the world by a clear liquid with mysterious chemical properties.

The Kean was James's club. He was already twenty minutes late for lunch. Waiting for people in restaurants is always very unsettling, but worse when you were so clearly unemployed. He was here because James had said he had a plan to help Miles in his predicament. The club was full of loud men in somewhat old-fashioned, loud clothes. They were not dressed like zingari or Bohemians or rock stars, nothing obvious like that, but the stripe on their suits was pretty big and the pinkness of their shirts was pretty noticeable. A lot of silk handkerchiefs fluttered in their top pockets, mute signals from a more turbulent world: *I may be a barrister*, these flags said, *but I've read a few books, once played the piano rather well, done extraordinary things with girls in olive groves on balmy nights, seriously considered applying for RADA, and still go to the National at least once a month. It's too late now of course; once you get on the old treadmill . . .*

Miles had had a devastating insight, which he realised he could never have had if he was still employed: Money has an independent life of its own. It exists in its own right. Sure it coagulated around individuals the way white corpuscles flow towards wounds, but it was – unlike its owners – independent and immortal. Captains of industry and banking – Arnold for example – were allowed to expound their world view because of the amount of money lodging with them. But – this was the ironic part – people were listening to hear the secret harmonies of the money. Major chumps in all sorts of fields of endeavour could command an audience because they had money. Witness Boesky, Trump, Goldsmith, Iaccocca, McCormack; in all honesty none of them had a world view which could be included in the most basic introduction to philosophy, yet millions hung on their words in the belief that they might pick up a few tips on how to look attractive to money. The fortunate few would be dunked in money – like the paint in those Volkswagen adverts – and emerge gold-plated, Buddhas of finance. The joke was, of course, that money was undiscriminating in its affections.

Miles had been the recipient of a lot of affection. His mother had loved him, caressing his limbs and his straight back as he grew up; she had even fondled his little scrotum affectionately. Miles sometimes thought she had sculpted him with her attentive fingers. He had once seen a story in a magazine about Indian mothers massaging their babies with scented oils. They had nothing on his mother. By the time she sent him off to boarding school at thirteen, he was a beautiful child. Inexplicably she had left home and gone to live in America with a man she had met on holiday, as though all those years of personal attention to him had meant nothing to her.

Their housemaster, Mr Le Fanu, had loved Miles in an idealised way. He paid Miles special attention, noticed by the other boys, but there had never been any physical advance. After they had been at school together for two years, James Trentham and Piggy Berens conceived a strategy to make their final years more pleasant. James took the leading part. He and Piggy visited a gay sex shop in Soho and bought a pile of magazines which pictured rent boys and Mediterranean youths with extraordinarily large penises – as though there had been a mismatch in the accessory department – in strange poses.

They began to leave these magazines in Mr Le Fanu's study and on his desk. The combination of circumstantial evidence and sly insinuation by the three friends led quickly to a policy of appeasement, so that the three were allowed to spend nights away from school, smoke dope and have girls from the village in their rooms. After two terms the strain of the whole affair was too much for Mr Le Fanu. He applied to take a sabbatical running the Donkey Haven in Cairo, founded by his mother, Emily Le Fanu, MBE, who presided over a chain of donkey sanctuaries world wide. He never returned to teaching. Miles had often felt guilty about the way they had treated Mr Le Fanu, but he did not tell James this. James's opinion was that the world is a rotten place, dog eat dog, a jungle, no place for the weak, etcetera, etcetera. James was a barrister with a small criminal practice. Miles wondered if this line of work had not confirmed his view of the world, in the way that obstetricians are said to take a narrow view of women.

Miles was the last person left in the bar now as the others, in nervous shoals, scudded into lunch in that awkward but self-satisfied way the English have on such occasions. Miles was ordering his third gin and tonic from the barman, an Irishman with a face which looked as though it had been dusted with talcum powder, like a footman's, when James arrived with some predictably feeble excuse. James's face had grown fatter in the last few years, and his blond hair with its lumpy arrangement like the icing on the top of a Danish pastry, was beginning to look as though it did not quite belong. In this way, middle-aged Midwestern businessmen sometimes have inappropriate, blow-waved haircuts which only emphasise the straining waistbands and turkey necks.

Miles said, 'Jesus you look terrible.'

'Thanks.'

James's slightly battered eyes were undimmed.

'So how's life at the bottom? Do you want another drink before we go in for some swill?'

'No, I'm OK. This is my third.'

'I'll have a kir, Frank,' he said to the barman. 'I suppose you want to know what this is all about?'

'Not much.'

Through his acquaintance with the criminal world, James

had come across a new sport in the East End, Thai boxing. One of his clients had, until his arrest, been a security officer with a fish-trading firm in Billingsgate Market. He was now on remand on a charge of armed robbery at his employer's premises. He had introduced James to the sport. James took a large gulp of his kir and looked at Miles; he seemed to be inviting Miles to congratulate him on his knowledge of London's lowlife.

'So?' said Miles.

This man – James referred to him as 'my client' – had a daughter, Tracy Bilger who was the European champion and a son, Steve, who was the best kick boxer outside Thailand. In Joe Bilger's honest opinion, no bullshit, Steve was the best kick boxer pound for pound in the world, and that included Thailand. Bilger had supplied James with irrefutable evidence that on the night of the crime he was in the corner watching his daughter Tracy knock hell out of the challenger, Cheryl Lombardi. Cheryl, as a matter of fact, had to have a minor operation to relieve the fluid on the brain. Her dad, who was a plumber, had volunteered to put in a tap – *lovely geezer, luvverly sense a 'umour*. He laughed when he told James this story, and James reproduced the laugh now for Miles, a noise like water splashing into a tin bath. *Luvverly sense a 'umour, heh, heh, heh, heh, mmhhm*. His client even had a video of himself in the corner, filmed by Blood Sports Inc. (*Great name, innit?*) He was waiting to see the judge's face when his brief, James, produced the video in court. The police, James explained, knew that Bilger could not be convicted, but they were fitting him up as a warning.

'The thing is Miles – let's go in and eat – the thing is, the son Steve is dynamite. He is going the whole way. My client was just about to go to Bangkok to sign him to fight at Rungkit. There's money in this. It just needs someone with some financial savvy to put it together. You're just the man.'

A Spanish waitress was standing beside them, the way the vultures watch at a Parsee funeral.

'Jew like horder now?' she said morosely.

'Why not,' said James. 'Steak and kidney or fillet of plaice, Miles? Sure? That's what we'll have. What's the matter with you,' he said to the waitress, 'female troubles?'

The waitress left them at a fast shuffle, her short legs very veined at the back. The dining room was stifled by the odour of warmed-up food and furniture polish. Miles wondered what it was that attracted these people here. The obvious answer was that it reminded them of school, but Miles suspected that it was also because they could forget about the Third World outside, lapping at the windows.

'James, why doesn't Bilger do it himself, when you get him off? Or am I being too obvious?'

'Don't be daft, Miles. The police have got his passport. Bilger's an armed robber with a record as long as your dick. The Thais won't deal with some villain. They like a nice English gent. This is where your five years at Uphurst finally pay a dividend.'

'Look,' said Miles impatiently, 'I need money urgently. The house is costing me two grand a month. Victoria flooded the fucking place and she had forgotten to pay the insurance, of course. That's eighteen grand. Jacci's car is three and a half. Even American Eagle are after me to pay last month's bill since the bank took my credit cards. My drunk-driving fine is going to be minimum a grand, my solicitor's bills the same. That's twenty-five thousand I owe right now. So believe me, James, I am not enthralled at the job offer. I don't want to have anything to do with Thai boxing. I do not want to promote a fight for a man who kicks people's heads in. OK, so he may be world champion. How long is that going to take? I've never heard anything so stupid in my life. In fact I can hardly believe you dragged me here to listen to this crap.'

'Hold on. Calm down. Here's the nosh.'

Substantial plates of food arrived and were placed in front of them brusquely. No concessions were made here to the fast-moving world of food presentation. The plates were large and thick, and decorated with the head of the great actor, playing a bearded Macbeth. They were soiled by years of hard use, so that the white glaze had almost been lost. The plates looked to Miles as if they had been recovered from a very deep shipwreck.

'Yam roly poly or treaky tart to follow?' asked the waitress. She was now standing next to Miles, holding a small, grubby pad.

'Yes please,' said James.

'Wish one you like?'

'Both,' said James, 'with lashings of custard.'

James enjoyed sharpening his wits on waiters, barmen and taxi drivers.

'Don't mind her,' he said, 'she's from Barcelona. Look, Milo old son, I don't think I've explained myself properly. We've got the money. The money's no problem. What we haven't got is someone with a little financial savvy to pass the money to the right people. In order to get this deserving young man a crack at the title. The holder of a world title has hangers-on, whole families of them, and they have to be squared before a fight can take place. That's how it works.'

'You've got the money?'

'Yes. We have the money.'

'How much?'

'Three hundred and seventy-five grand.'

'Jesus. Where did you get it?'

'I believe it once belonged to Tibbs and Spockett, white fish wholesalers at Billingsgate. In fact it was a fortnight's takings. This is just a rumour, of course.'

'Your client, as you like to call him, stole it, obviously.'

'Miles, Miles. We never use words like that in the law. My client, as will be proved conclusively at the Bailey in a few weeks' time, is innocent. *Ergo*, he can't have taken the money. Your share will be seven and a half per cent for disbursing the money as it is required until young Steve gets his fight in Bangkok.'

'I'll be the mug.'

'You'll be the banker.'

'It's stolen money.'

'Miles, you have no knowledge whatever of where the money came from. You were asked through a solicitor to consult on this little venture because you were out of a job but had considerable financial expertise. It's only for a few weeks. As far as you know the principals are Swiss business-men. There's free capital movement in this country. It's just a question of moving money about and so on, something which is a mystery to a poor lad from the East End.'

'Tell me straight, can I be done for laundering stolen money?'

111

'Not unless you could reasonably have supposed it was stolen.'

'But I know it was stolen. You told me.'

James looked pained.

'Miles, there's telling and telling. I haven't told you anything officially. I'm not involved. This conversation never took place. We're old school chums having lunch.'

'Grow up, James, for Chrissakes. How long do I have to courier money about the place? Two weeks?'

'A month max.'

'You said two weeks a moment ago. When do I get my cut?'

'Right away. I will arrange for you to get in touch with a solicitor who will give you instructions on how to get hold of the money.'

'I'll think about it.'

'Good. That's the spirit.'

James was in a very good humour. He ordered a large vintage port for each of them. Port was a killer, but Miles did not care. He had nothing to do anyway, but for the sake of his tattered dignity, he insisted he was going to leave at four.

It was almost dark outside in Covent Garden, with couples clinging together in the gloom, their intimacy a reproach to Miles as they hurried past, their heads bent against the weather, holding on to each other as if a gust of wind might blow them apart for ever. Not one of them even glanced up at the high, handsome windows of the Kean, where he and James sat with their Taylor's 1966.

Miles listened to James's tales. James was bursting with confidences about judges, the police and cases which, of course, were never brought to court. But in the back of Miles's mind there was a doubt. James had an underdeveloped ethical sense, that was proven, but did he really have the street smarts he claimed for himself? Somehow the decadence – the good-natured malice was straining his plump facial skin from within – had a juvenile aspect to it, just as when they had stitched up Mr Le Fanu, donkey curator, years ago. It had still never sunk in, as far as Miles could see, what havoc might have been wreaked in the poor man's life.

'How's Victoria? Do you ever see that stuck-up tart?' asked James.

'No. She's gone all arty.'

'Typical. She always looked as though there was a bad smell under her nose when I was around.'

'There was.'

'Ha, bloody ha. Not such a bad smell that she wasn't up for a quick bonk.'

'You didn't screw her did you?'

''Fraid so. When you were at Glyndebourne, with Jacci, ho, ho, one evening. We got pissed,' he added, in explanation.

'Jesus.'

Miles gazed out of the window. In the gloom Christmas shoppers were seething in and out of shops laden with parcels. The paper and card shop across the road attracted girls in their scores, going on their errands like busy shoals of fish.

'Jesus, you are the pits,' said Miles.

On the question of morals, Miles knew that he did not really have a case, but he felt hurt and demeaned all the same. He looked out at the hurrying, heedless shoppers, and wondered exactly what sexual activities Victoria and James had practised. He did not ask, guessing anyway that James would have forgotten the details. James treated women with what he took to be amusing scepticism. Women, as far as he was concerned, had to prove themselves human. They could be divided into three categories, old bats, bluestockings and tarts. He had some sub-categories, such as would-be intellectual, scrubber, and fluff. Victoria had always made it clear to Miles that she regarded James as a fat boor. That's women for you, he thought. They're always making a fuss about faithfulness and love, but give them half a chance and they behave like stoats. Like the men they profess to despise, in fact.

The volume of people passing underneath the window had become a torrent. It was rush hour. He glanced at his Rolex. He imagined Victoria applying her lips, which had always reminded him of those crushed-ice Italian sorbets, to James's cock. He had been a witness to James's nakedness for years, in the showers and masturbating in the craft room at school, on holiday, in swimming pools, in the bath and even in bed with two or three Australian girls in Verbier. He had seen his cock in almost all the relaxed and anguished postures of the

113

male organ. He felt sad. The port seemed to have entered his bloodstream clumsily. It was barging its way around, bumping into his vital organs.

'You don't mind, do you?' said James. 'Just picking up the crumbs from the master's table.'

'Course not. Silly tart. I'll do your business as long as I can get half my money next week.'

'Good man. No prob. Another port, Milos?'

'Sure.'

'You'll get a call from a chap from a firm of solicitors acting for my client. Check with me first thing tomorrow morning. They will ask you to sign some documents setting up a trust in the Isle of Man or the Caymans or somewhere. I don't know the details. This trust will receive some funds. Again I don't know where from and nor do you. All you have to do is make sure it gets to the right people and go to Singapore or Hong Kong to make sure it's handed over in stages. That's the way they do business. Someone must be there in person with the cash.'

'Not Singapore, I'm afraid.'

'Well, wherever. That's not the point. It's the personal touch they appreciate.'

'I'm the bagman.'

'The executor of the trust set up by interested, but anonymous parties, Miles.'

'Where is the money at the moment?'

'I don't know. I don't even want to know, but my guess is it's probably in a lock-up in Walthamstow.'

'James, just theoretically, what's to prevent me running off with the lot?'

'You wouldn't want to do that, Miles. Believe me. You have to understand that these guys have lots of friends where you would least expect to find them.'

'Like Gray's Inn.'

'Maybe. And also people to whom violence is a way of life. Merrie old England doesn't mean a fuck to them.'

Miles thought, It doesn't mean much to you either. James was predisposed to a dramatic view of life.

'Of course, James, of course. I was just asking. You promise me I can have my money next week?'

'I promise. Now where's the old Spanish boiler with our port?'

The waitress had gone home. They had to move back to the bar, which was filling up again with many of the people who had been there at lunchtime.

When Miles woke the next morning he was lying on the sofa in James's flat without a clue as to what had gone before. James's bed was unmade and a pile of crumpled clothes lay on the floor. James had made some small attempts to make his flat look like the home of a serious lawyer. There was green Regency wallpaper around a marble fireplace and half-completed bookshelves on which stood a few leather-bound books about torts and wills.

It was nearly midday. Miles bathed and looked out of the window at the mean streets. West Hampstead was deserted except for a man changing the wheel on a Cavalier. He had no money in his wallet so he rang for a taxi using the bank's account number and Arnie's name. Serve the bastard right. He was still trying to get his bonus, which would have been forty thousand at least. Bastard.

As the taxi sliced its way through the wet towards Piggy's place, where his things were, Miles remembered his conversation with James. It might have taken place a month ago, under water. His head was throbbing. His eyes were filled with grains of sand. His skin was dry and itchy and he felt nauseous. James had been bullshitting of course, about his contacts with the underworld. James had said that the Bilgers were one of the hardest firms in London. Done more jobs than you've had hot dinners, etc. etc. James wanted to believe things like that. Yesterday Miles had believed James that he could make thirty thousand.

'Cheers, guv,' said the taxi driver. 'You Mr Zwitters? You don't look like him. I've driven him before.'

'I've had a head transplant.'

'You look pretty rough. Mind how you go.'

Miles was spending the weekend with Victoria's mother. The perfidious Victoria. He felt a stabbing pain in his heart. He was supposed to get down to Farnham for dinner. Plenty of time. He would pack later. He turned on the television to watch the racing and soon fell asleep.

It was already dark outside when the phone rang. Miles was confused. There was a children's programme on the television. The presenters were painting pictures with toothbrushes.

'Miles. Miles, is that you?'

'Yhh.'

'God you're a wanker. Where have you been?'

'Here I think. I was at your place until lunchtime.'

'I rang you there fifteen times at least before I had to go to court.'

'Didn't hear a thing. What's up?'

'What's up? Four hundred grand, that's all. You were supposed to ring me at ten this morning.'

'I didn't think you were serious. I just thought you were pissed.'

'You really are a prize plonker. Look, get some clothes on, get over to this address. Yes, get a pen. It's forty-eight Doughty Street, WC1. Granville and Brostoff. See a Mr Jonas. He's expecting you. Now. Yes, now. It's almost too late. We're not playing games, you know.'

'Did Victoria give you a blow-job?'

'I should think so. Don't they all? Get moving and call me later at the flat. I'll be home by eight. I've had a hangover all day. I've got to get to bed.'

Mr Jonas looked depressed. He had stooped shoulders as though he had spent a lifetime poring over legal documents, yet he was probably only about thirty-three. His dark suit rode up at the back of his neck, and his white collar was keeping its distance from his Adam's apple. He looked at Miles, whose own suit was somewhat crumpled, without curiosity. He had a very small office at the top of the first flight of stairs. The ceiling of this office had been lowered with pressed tiles from which fluorescent lights hung. It had a small window which looked out on to a jumbled and darkened landscape of backyards and clumsy extensions.

'You must be Mr Goodall,' he said eventually in a tired, light tenor.

'Yes.'

'I've got some deeds of trust for you to sign, sir. I'll witness. Just sign here where you see the pencil marks. That's it. And here. Now I sign and seal it. Good. Do you want a copy?'

'No.'

He handed Miles an envelope.

'What's this?'

'I've no idea, I'm afraid. It's sealed.'

Mr Jonas stood up slowly, like a man who has just finished some violent exercise. His face was prematurely wrinkled, not with age but with fatigue. He shook Miles's hand drily.

'That's it then. Good evening.'

He was already packing his briefcase and reaching for his raincoat as Miles turned to go.

'Irene will let you out,' he said.

'Thank you,' said Miles. Miles wondered what he had signed. He could not ask Mr Jonas. It was obviously some legal paper to remove the Bilger firm a few steps from the money.

Miles walked down Doughty Street until he found a pub. He ordered a beer and sat down at a small table. A few people were playing darts. He opened the envelope. It had been sealed with red wax, which was quaint. Inside was a ticket for the left-luggage department at Euston Station. He tried to find a taxi but failed, so he walked up to the station and handed in his ticket to a fat black man who was bulging out of his British Rail uniform.

After a brief search the attendant handed him a small suitcase. When he opened it later in the back of a taxi he discovered the money which was still in little canvas bank bags, neatly sorted. He shut the suitcase fast.

The money had found Miles. It had swarmed to him for its own, unfathomable reasons. A faint fishy smell had escaped from the case.

Miles laughed so violently, so painfully, that the taxi driver looked around concerned.

'You all right, guv?'

CHAPTER TWELVE

Pantomime may be the only uniquely British theatrical form. It is played around the Christmas season and grew to its greatest popularity in Victorian times, when its peculiar mixture of nursery tales, jokes from current events, music from popular songs and sentiments from the patriotic rag bag, really developed. The principal boys are girls and the 'dames' are old comics in drag. Got the idea? No? Don't worry; my encyclopedia of the theatre tells me that pantomime is greatly enjoyed by the British but completely incomprehensible to the foreigner.

The better to understand it, I turned to Bruno Bettelheim. Bettelheim believes that Cinderella is a sexual tale: Cinderella's penile foot slipping into the Prince's vaginal slipper. (This may go some way to explaining why the Prince is played by a girl.) Bettelheim also warns parents against trying to explain fairy tales to children; in his opinion Disney committed a crime by naming the dwarves in Snow White. All such tales send important messages to the conscious and unconscious minds of children about growing up. The dwarves represent stages in this process, instantly recognized by children. 'Each fairy tale is a magic mirror which reflects some aspect of the inner world and the steps required by our evolution from immaturity to maturity.' You could probably see the hand of Jung in this high-octane intellectualizing. Anyway, in the interests of better informing my readers, I went equipped with Bettelheim's insights to the Hackney Empire.

Hackney is not a part of London the average tourist sees. In fact quite a few Londoners of my acquaintance have only the vaguest notion of where it is located . . .

* * *

My readers, I believe, like a small dose of European intellectuals once in a while. Bettelheim is the sort of name you can take seriously.

As guests of one of the Ugly Sisters, we were shown to the front row of the stalls, plumb in the middle. I hoped Bernie had not arranged any special attention for us from the stage, like those plays where the actors used to run naked through the audience inviting you to take part and throw off your inhibitions. You do your job, pal, and I'll do mine.

Gemma was excited. Her hand pulsed in mine just as it did at the fish tanks under the goat mountain. She was dividing her affections now between the fish and the lions since my fairy tale. (What would Bettelheim make of this?) The orchestra struck up. Music in a theatre has an electrifying effect. it is like the opening of a tomb. The audience stiffened and quietened. The Empire smelled of its history. The thick and richly decorated velveteen curtains, the skewed seats, the brass railings, the elaborate oriental plaster decoration and the worn carpeting were infused with the body odour, tobacco smoke and warm breath of hundreds of thousands – perhaps millions – of our predecessors in this shabby palace. On this stage Marie Lloyd, Little Tich, Tom Thumb, Isadora Duncan, Charles Bertram and the vanishing lady, the Two-headed Nightingale (singing Siamese twins), and Léotard himself, the daring young man who gave his name to the work-out costume, had all performed.

Gemma was entranced as the curtains opened to reveal Cinderella hard at work. I decided to follow Bettelheim's advice and explain nothing. He obviously had something, for Gemma seemed to follow it all except for the jokes about the Prime Minister. She hissed at the Ugly Sisters. She turned to me, her face convulsed with the merriment of it all; I was hissing and booing up a storm. Bernie was instantly recognisable, although his face was plastered with white make-up and his head was covered in an elaborate wig, so big that it housed ribbons and balloons and small, stuffed birds. Bernie would have been recognisable in a deep-sea diver's suit. His chest was contracted by a corset to produce a cleavage and his bustle was hugely exaggerated so that the other Ugly Sister was constantly becoming entangled in it. Poor little Cinders scrubbed the floor, but the look on her face was knowing. Buttons clowned camply. Gemma was captivated when the first transformation scene came. Transformations are an essential part of pantomime: the pumpkin became a golden coach, Cinderella's rags became a ball-gown by the Emanuels, and – most magical of all – the rats became real Shetland ponies covered in lights and feathers. Away they went to the ball; the coach swayed alarmingly and Cinderella clutched the woodwork.

The prince was a Euro-playboy intent on debauching our Cinders, but she seemed pretty eager. Gemma will be a teenager in only eight years, I thought. Here time was compressed and speeded up the way it is in a child's world. The more the Ugly Sisters appealed to the audience for sympathy, the more we rejected their overtures. We were definitely not on the side of these crones. This is another old theme: an evil parent or guardian must be foiled so that true love can find a way.

We were invited backstage: 'Of course, wotcher expect, you're my personal guests.' Bernie was loosening his stays. Two very elderly actors were removing their make-up and wigs. They looked tired and unhappy. Close up the props and costumes were unbearably cheap and soiled and the dressing rooms were crowded. The dancers had large thighs, like German *bierwurst*, and big mouths, heavily painted. The air backstage was hard to breathe, full of smoke and fuller's earth and particles of a theatrical sort. Bernie pulled on a dressing-gown and took Gemma's hand.

'Come on, my darling, let's go and see the ponies before they go to bed. You'd like that, wouldn'tcher?'

The ponies were nipping irritably at the stagehands who were removing their lights and feathers, and the air was strangely rural with their vegetable gases. A woman still in costume but without her wig passed by. Bernie greeted her.

'Lovely job, Cynth. Real professional,' he said to us. 'She was the fairy godmother. Lovely lady. Do you like the ponies, Gemma? Better not stroke them, they bite, the little buggers.'

Bernie said he was still coming down after performing. Still happened, every time, after all these years.

'Right, Gemma, you can see the coach now.'

The ponies were being led away, their dwarf heads tossing.

My little princess sat in the coach. Not much had been spent on the interior. The plywood was exposed and Cinders obviously had to sit on a large box. Someone had written 'Millwall' and 'You shall go to the ball, Cinders' on the bare interior. Gemma didn't seem to notice the austerity measures.

'This is Gemma. She's from New York. And this is 'er dad.'

Bernie led us off on a tour. He introduced us to everybody. 'Personal friends of mine. Tim Curtiz, the writer. *Manhattan* magazine. The tops. Now let me introduce you to Cinderella. Trudi Bastin, this is Tim Curtiz and his daughter Gemma. He's a writer. Very big on the other side of the pond.'

Trudi was removing her make-up. She was wearing a towelling robe which had *Hotel Ritz* on the back. She offered Gemma her hand. Gemma shook it gravely.

'Did you enjoy it, sweetie?'

'Yes.'

'We did. Very much, thank you,' I said.

'You were really fantastic tonight,' said Bernie. 'Fa-an-tastic.'

'You are a love,' said Trudi. She was probably twenty-eight but her hair was arranged like a little girl's, tied with a ribbon and two slides. Her face was as pert as a squirrel's, like Natasha's in *War and Peace*, but there was an abstracted look about her. She was the wistful sort.

'Are you going to write about this?' she asked me.

'Probably. Something to explain pantomime to my readers in Manhattan.'

'Did you see my Beatrice at the Barbican? With McKellen?'

'Missed it unfortunately. My, you are versatile.'

'Well, just in case you thought I only played panto.'

The worm is eating their souls. It's not enough for her to be entertaining eager children and undiscerning adults. She has, like all actors, a Platonic form in mind, which floats above the reality. (Actually, I think we all have, but not as obviously as actors.)

'Bernie, you were terrific too.' I said. 'Wasn't he, Gemma?'

'Yes,' said Gemma.

'Ta. I've enjoyed it. I always used to do panto every season. It's great fun, innit, Trudi?'

'Yes,' she said languidly, 'great fun.'

She made it sound like five-finger exercises for Alfred

Brendel. She rubbed her cheeks lightly with cotton wool and then looked searchingly at her rodent face in the mirror. She was looking to see if she had removed the traces of Cinderella which had lodged with her receptive features for the evening. She was merely a receptacle, as little able to explain her gifts as a medium. Sometimes she found it quite spooky, the way a part took her over. Bernie listened to her in real admiration.

'Lovely performance, Trudi. Luvverly. Every one different. What a range.'

Actors have a sentimental streak.

'Where do the ponies live?' asked Gemma.

'Where do the ponies live, Bernie? I should know. I'm afraid I have no idea,' said Trudi. We saw the caring squirrel now. 'How silly of me.'

'They live in a trailer at the back. Every morning they get a run on 'Ackney Marshes,' said Bernie. 'That's a story in itself, innit, eh?'

Trudi stood up.

'I'm afraid I must go now. My car will be waiting. I'm so glad you enjoyed it.'

A voice came over the tannoy: 'Minicab for Miss Bastin. Blue C-reg. Cavalier outside, cab for Miss Bastin.'

Trudi slipped off the robe and left bravely for the journey down to her mother's house in Sydenham.

'What a trouper. Two shows on Wednesdays and Saturdays. Four songs. Five dance routines and she does Shakespeare. Fantastic.'

The nasal tympany: 'fa-anne-tastic.'

'Bernie, it's been a great evening. You're a pal. Wasn't it marvellous, Gemma?'

'Do you give the ponies their food?' she asked.

'Not me personally, darling. No. But they get plenty. That I do know. Did you see how fat they are?'

'We had better go. It's way past her bedtime.'

Bernie plucked at my arm.

'Before you go, can I have a word in your ear?'

'Can it wait? She's nearly out on her feet.'

'It can wait,' he said, 'course it can wait. I'll give you a ring tomorrow.'

As we left the theatre by the stage door, a group of black boys, tall and athletic in huge new track shoes, called to us.

'Wassyername? You in the panto whatsit? Got any free tickets?'

Their voices were Cockney, but with a Caribbean additive. They walked on, laughing. Their feet were reluctant to linger on the broken pavement; they were moonwalking through tumbledown Hackney. I installed Gemma in her seat belt and we glided away. She was tired but concerned about the dinner arrangements for the bad-tempered Shetland ponies.

We drove through a succession of run-down streets, bombed by plastic rubbish bags, past tracts of land overlooked by East European concrete apartment blocks. The concrete tells the inhabitants something about their relationship to the gentler world which the disordered old streets still manage to conjure up. It's a straightforward message, which they acknowledge with their garbage and graffiti.

From Hackney we suddenly found ourselves in the still streets of the City of London, where even the most ardent brokers and dealers had gone home. A pub coughed smoke and beer breath on to the road and two drunken girls stumbled out to catch the last bus, but the mausoleum stillness, the polished granite, the marble doric columns, the window boxes of early narcissus, the clean streets, the bronze statues and monuments could have been a million miles from Hackney, rather than a few hundred yards. In Hackney they were sauntering off to the kebab houses and fried chicken huts; they were stealing cars and kicking empty beer cans along the streets; they were throwing up in pub toilets and rapping in church halls; they were waiting for minicabs, eating chilli tacos; they were gunning the motors of their little Ford XR3is, pretending they were in *Miami Vice*; they were filing out of the urine-stained cinemas for a curry. Here in the City – St Petersburg – the money had gone calmly to bed. It was resting until morning in its marble and granite palaces. These buildings were solid, constructed of materials which were resistant to doubt. Why don't they all rush in from Hackney and smash the place up? Posters in Hackney urged the workers to do just that. The Tory industrial military complex was keeping the workers down; multinational corporations must be confronted, and so on.

Unfortunately nobody was listening. The workers had drowned in garbage and Australian lager. The money was anyway immortal, a substance as mothproof as titanium. The brokers and bankers, who would appear respectfully to attend to the money's levée, were not immortal, but somehow they had got their relationship to the money round the wrong way; long after they were pushing up the daisies these palaces, these acropolises of money, would be here, joined by a lot of new ones. The City was growing daily. The lanes and alleyways led to Banks of Baroda and Brunei and Bangalore. Every nation in all the world was represented here.

We were approaching Trafalgar Square now, with its watchful lions. Gemma was asleep. Columbine and Harlequin were on their way home. The Ugly Sisters were in transit too. I realised that I had no idea where Bernie lived in this huge city. Perhaps he lived above a jellied-eel shop in Bermondsey. How was it I had never enquired?

Bernie's performance had been robust. He tried a little too hard for laughs, probably inhibiting the other sister, but he was irrepressible. To have survived, spirit more or less intact, he must have had to keep his eye on the ball. Only the leisured classes – now proliferating around the globe – can afford to look about them. We sped through the quiet streets, the dashboard controls glowing like the Lloyd's building, and then through Hyde Park, cold and frosty.

What a pleasure to carry a sleeping child to bed. I undressed her, slid her fragile limbs into a nightdress and bedded her down with her teddy. In her sleep she mumbled 'goodnight'. My heart was full. It was stretching at the seams.

I read some more about lions. Lions are the only co-operative hunters in the cat world. Lions have extremely acute hearing. Lions breed when game is plentiful and practise abstinence when game is scarce.

Simba Cochrane knew none of this when he despatched the lion to the other world. Nobody studied the behaviour of lions in those days. Nobody studied the behaviour of anything much. But it is not true that the scientific chaps with their behaviourism and DNA don't see the big picture. Schaller writes: 'Male no 134 is to me not merely a nomadic lion who gained or lost a territory, but a living entity, a part of the vastness of the plains; he represents memories of the immense silence at night, of the heat waves at noon transforming distant granite boulders into visions of castles, and zebra into lean Giacometti sculptures.' Nothing could be less scientific than the grandeur of nature. For Cochrane the lion was just a great big, dangerous brute. So much had changed in his lifetime. Who knows if he, or anyone else, could keep up with the gyrations in the popular perception?

There was a message from Victoria on my machine, asking me to call her at the agency. Her musky voice, with its crumbling edges, summoned a picture of her soft-fruit lips. (Is it permissible to think of women in these crude terms?) I wanted to see her, but it would have to wait until Gemma had gone back home. The fastidiousness was because I detected a need for intimacy. Sex to her would be, I guessed, a necessary preliminary to intimacy. Nothing wrong with that, but the only intimacy I wanted at the moment was with Gemma, breathing very evenly in the next room, when I last visited her. A friend once told me that he had given up his mistress because he had been in bed with her the very moment his wife had taken their child to hospital with convulsions. He had climaxed in her mouth as the child's life was saved by an injection of pentathol.

There they lie, trusting and defenceless. A newly born wildebeest can get up and run three minutes after birth. The human baby can barely walk after a year. Gemma needed my full attention at five. No question, there was a lot of self-esteem in these thoughts. I lay in bed to listen to the resonances of our hayloft. I knew I was kidding myself, but I could hear them, and they were of a different timbre entirely. Perhaps we were echo-locating like bats and porpoises, bouncing sonar signals off one another. Of course, my side of the deal was the more intense. My signals were more frequent, more like radar than a porpoise. If anything happened to Gemma in my house, my life would be over. I scanned the horizon for trouble, but instead found only serenity. I tried to read Schaller but became bored by the details of lion movements and predation in Serengeti. The big picture is my preference too.

Chaka escaped that night. There were two theories about how he got out. A newspaper suggested that an animal rights movement might have done it with some long scaffolding planks. Another theory was that the moat had frozen solid in the night and he had leapt out. The zoo admitted that he had been left outside because the weather forecast had not predicted intense cold. I had seen Chaka's leap after the horsemeat incident. It was surprisingly athletic, but I could not imagine him leaping ten feet off ice. I had another theory. Schaller observed lions climbing trees, upwards with no difficulty, but downwards in disarray. There was a large tree in the lion terraces. Perhaps he had climbed that and dropped on to the roof of the enclosure behind. No sign of the escape had been found and Regent's Park was sealed off until the lion had been darted and captured. I felt sorry for the lion. He may have imagined Serengeti lying beyond the goat mountain, but he would be disappointed. That way lay the mosque, Lord's Cricket Ground and the business school.

Bernie called me.

'Did you enjoy it?'

'We loved it.'

Gemma was watching television, a manically cheerful show which interspersed puppets and games with rock videos and conservation stories. Madonna was lying at that moment in the surf of Malibu, her ample Italianate body dressed in a waitress uniform, her breasts becoming wetter and plumper before my very eyes. What sort of children are we bringing up?

'Gemma loved it. You were particularly good.'

'Listen, can I come round and see you this morning?'

'Is it urgent? I haven't had a chance to think about the script for *Bombed*, I'm afraid.'

'*Bombed*? What's that? It's called *Buzz Bomb*. *Bombed* makes it sound like we was pissed during the war. Mind you, many a true word spoken in jest, as the bard says. As a matter of fact it's a business matter. It's about American Eagle.'

'No news, Bernie. Not yet I'm afraid.'

'You don't get my meaning. They've offered me me own commercial. Apparently it's going to be the authentic – no offence – guide to lots of countries. I'm London. The inside story. Lennie hasn't got a clue about the dosh on this one. How much did you get?'

'You'd better come round.'

CHAPTER THIRTEEN

Miles paid in cash. He paid the builders (they had become distinctly plural); he paid Victoria; he paid the arrears on the mortgage and he paid for Jacci's car. Twelve thousand pounds, in cash.

Everyone knows what cash means: something a bit clever, the little columns in the ledger ignored, the tax man given the two fingers. Cash has mystical appeal in London; the boys with the wads don't want anybody else telling them what to do with their money. No chance. You must be joking. They make big money where the punters fear to venture. The wad is the proof. The wad looks big, in today's money. So, some of it isn't strictly legal, but what do you think those big companies get up to every day? What do you think happens in banks and stockbrokers? How do you think property developers get their permissions? Wake up. The only difference is they don't think of it as crime. There's the hypocrisy.

Everyone in London is acquainted with this line of thought. It is the price exacted for living in the city. There is even a little self-congratulation involved: the bumpkins have no idea of the street smarts you need to operate successfully in London.

'Where did you get it, Miles?' asked Victoria.

'Fnnh. What are you suggesting, mmnh?'

At the sight of his newly acquired wealth, Miles's vowels had apparently taken fright again.

'I'm not suggesting anything. I just wondered if an elderly relative had died or something.'

'Hhmmnh, very funny. Vics, now that I've got things straightened out a bit, will you have dinner with me soon, mmnh?'

128

'I've got to go, Miles. Miles, I'm very glad you've come into money, but I don't want to see you. And if I'm honest, I don't like the fact that you're staying with my mother.'

'She's been very kind to me. Don't worry, it's only for a few days more. I'm off to the Far East.'

'To Singapore?'

'Mnnh. Very funny. What are you working on?'

'American Eagle.'

'With that writer chap?'

'No, as it happens; he's been dropped. I've got to go. Bye.'

'Victoria, what did you and Trentham do in bed? He can't remember.'

'Goodbye.'

Miles rang back immediately. For the second time she had to give the switchboard instructions not to take his calls. So typical of Miles. So typical of men. He's off screwing his bimbo at every opportunity and then when he finds out she had been doing something similar, admittedly a big mistake in this instance, his pride is hurt. In truth, Victoria did not believe that male pride was such a big deal. Some of her friends in the agency talked about it as if it were a visible defect, like spots or sagging bottoms. Male pride seemed to them antediluvian, as redundant as adenoids. But male pride was only self-esteem in one of its many guises. Paradoxically, self-esteem could only be achieved through the esteem of others. In the agency – proving the theory conclusively – a brightly attractive and extrovert attitude prevailed. Ugly people did not do well, because ugly people reflected poorly on the self-esteem of the less ugly. Introverted people cast gloomy shadows. And old people carried a contagion, absolutely fatal to the self-esteem of those around them. The agency was famous for its gloss. The prospect of working in a glamorous agency was a more powerful incentive than money in attracting creative people.

Female anxiety was just as open to crude misrepresentation. Miles's real problem was not male pride, but gross insensitivity. Not the usual things like farting in bed or leaving dirty clothes on the floor or turning up late for dinner or forgetting birthdays, but insensitivity on a more cosmic scale. He was never able to take Victoria's preoccupations seriously.

'Honestly, Victoria, who cares what Stubbs thought about

horses' anatomy? Why can't you just accept that he was just a bloody good painter? End of story.'

Victoria had tried to explain to him that painters sometimes suppressed what they knew of the world to concentrate on what they saw.

'Twaddle, Vics. Over-analytical rubbish. Anybody could do a Picasso. So-called art experts are afraid to admit what every normal person can see with their own eyes.'

Miles failed to understand – refused to understand. ('Don't get heavy, mmhhnhh, Vic.') Whenever she brought up the question of art, in any of its manifestations, Miles said: 'You're in advertising. You're selling things, but you think you're in ART. Whatever that is.'

Another mistake. Victoria did not think she was in art. True, quite a lot of people in the agency, like Mike, believed they were plumbed directly into a higher consciousness, but Victoria had come to see that most people in their own profession suffered from this delusion. Even Miles and his chums thought they were making the wheels of capitalism go round. That belief was probably shattered, now that Miles was reduced to doing shady deals with his wads of funny money.

Miles had once told her how he and James had blackmailed a schoolmaster. Big joke. The poor man had to resign to run a donkey sanctuary in Cairo. She should never have slept with James. (Why do we say 'slept' when we mean something very different?) Not because of any moral qualms, but because James was even less aware (and much less attractive), than Miles. What Miles had said was probably true too: James wouldn't remember the details at all. She could, all too clearly; James had tried to sodomise her. According to James, aggrieved at her refusal, everyone did it. What a thought. *All those girls in the King's Road with their pearls and dark blue jumpers over floral green skirts, James?* Men of James's type seemed to think sex was a supermarket where they could pick anything off the shelf.

She would have to talk to Tim about American Eagle today. New York had decided that Tim should do tasteful press ads for the new up-market card; the main television campaign was to go middle-market for the States. It needed to have 'characters' in London, Paris and Rome. The fish-fryer in the first ad, who had overacted in an exaggerated music-hall fashion, was the one they wanted for London. Victoria had looked at the rushes. He was an elderly extra type, full of dreadful suggestions and desperate good humour. No doubt in Paris they would be looking for a Maurice Chevalier lookalike and in Rome for a singing ice-cream vendor. That was the way Europe – *Yurp* – looked to the people from the sixty-fifth floor of the De Soto Tower. They were the sort of people who thought Frank Sinatra was a major figure in world culture.

The phone on her desk rang.

'Mike, answer will you, it may be Miles again.'

'Yeah. Yeah. Just a moment. I'll just see if she's here.'

He put his hand over the phone: 'It's Tim Curtiz for you. Do you want to speak? He says you called him?'

'Yes please. Hello, Tim.'

'Hello. You called?'

'Yuh. We've had some news from our lords and masters in New York. They want you to do the gold-card launch, the Golden Eagle Club card. Five press ads with expensive locations and some high-class copy.'

'No TV?'

'No. Sorry. The ordinary card is going to be given away to anybody who can spell dog.'

'And the money? I hate to be mercenary.'

'Don't worry about that. It's not my department, but believe me, their pockets are deep. You're a celebrity, you've got class, etcetera etcetera. You're perfect for the gold card. How are you by the way?'

'I'm fine. My little girl is still here so I'm a bit tied up.'

'Can we meet to discuss the copy and so on? I'm working on drafts but they've got to be in your inimitable style. Do you remember the loudest noise is the ticking of the clock ads for Rolls Royce?'

'Not personally, but I've read about them.'

'Well, we think, that is my brilliant art director Mike and me, we think that a sort of walnut-and-leather, gentleman's club look at London is what's needed. London your average Joe Soap doesn't see kind of thing. He's doing layouts even now.'

Mike was in fact reading a magazine called *Focus*, which purported to be the work of serious photographers. As far as Victoria could see, these photographers were serious about bondage and rubber. Mike's large ox-blood shoes, which Victoria knew came from Comme Des Garçons, lay on the desk, their tractor soles raised defensively towards Victoria, the better to conceal an erection stirring in the baggy Jean-Paul Goude (or was it Galtier?) trousers.

'OK,' said Tim. 'Whenever you're ready.'

Tim was subdued, she thought. Perhaps he had been seduced by the siren song of film, the excitingly expensive celluloid ripping through the camera.

'Next week?' she asked tentatively.

'OK. We'll meet next week. Mail me what you've done so far.'

'Right, I'll get the boy genius here to photocopy – do you say Xerox? – his layouts and I'll bike the lot over to you. Is that all right, Tim?'

'Sure. Whenever you like.'

'Are you busy?'

'Busy looking after Gemma.'

'I would like to meet her.'

'That's nice. I'll call you back about that. We've got a pretty crowded schedule.'

Mike looked up over his magazine. He pursed his lips, and cocked his head, in what he took to be a genteel fashion.

' "Do you say Xerox?" Bosh, bosh. "I'd like to meet Gemma." Jesus, Victoria, you want to play house or something? I've never 'eard you squeaking like that.'

'Fuck off. Get those layouts done and copied. We've got to get them over to him.'

'OK. After lunch. I'm going to the Brasserie.'

'Try and get back by nightfall.'

'Mr Curtiz mustn't be kept waiting. May I kiss your arse Mr Curtiz. And the lovely little Gemma, 'ow's she faring today?

'One day they're going to rumble you, you lazy wanker. If they don't, I'm going to grass on you.'

'No you're not. I've got too much on you.'

It was true. They had worked together for four years and

132

had no secrets. In the beginning they had had a brief fling, but without any conviction and no residue of rancour. It sometimes troubled Victoria, perhaps for reasons of self-esteem, that it could have fizzled out so completely.

Mike was a dedicated follower of fashion. He knew every famous photographer in London, Milan, Paris and New York. He was a barometer of up-to-dateness. Nothing escaped him. If he declared a designer or photographer dead, the account people never mentioned his name again in public. In these matters he was as restless as a snake, whose tongue is its main sensory organ, testing and sniffing the air for the new and important. And yet he was almost totally uneducated in the conventional sense. In the beginning Victoria had been amazed at the depths of his ignorance: history, literature and science were to him simply sources for visual ideas. They had no standing of their own. He had once asked Victoria who Einstein was 'in real life'. He had seen images of him with his electric shock hair, but had no idea what his day job had been. There was a whole subculture based entirely on the image. It had its own magazines, shops and clubs. Victoria was uneasy about this aspect of advertising. Sometimes she saw the work she and Mike produced as advertisements for Mike's taste. He didn't give a fuck about grammar or punctuation. The words were really just to set off the visuals, like the *salade de mâche* or arugula in the restaurants he frequented.

George Stubbs, slightingly known as 'the horse painter' for many years, had resolutely refused to change his style to suit changing fashion. He had pursued his own notion of truth in art, based on his anatomical studies, with fantastic dedication. His landscapes and portraits were masterly too. The trouble was, Victoria was not sure what useful moral to draw from this.

Miles had been dismissive of any dilemma Victoria felt. The real world – where he was located of course – created the wealth to allow people like her to speculate about art and have a guilty conscience about advertising. She did not have a guilty conscience about advertising. Far from it. She was simply trying to see her way through the welter – the storm, the tempest – of style, fashion and image which lashed her every day in the agency. Literature and art were supposed to be signposts in the murky cosmos. She was wondering if the signposts were pointing in the right direction: were the destinations still there? Would Shakespeare have written for television? Would anybody have spent five minutes in the Globe if they could have gone to the movies? Would Holbein have used a Leica or a Hasselblad? Not such idiotic questions really. And, most important of all, was her ambivalence healthy?

Mike sauntered off to lunch. How he loved this world. Here he was, boy from Deptford (a part of London so dismal it was only known, if at all, as the birthplace of some of the Stones a long time ago), strolling out to lunch through the fabulously expensive lobby (the marble alone had cost one and a half million and the bamboos had been bred in Florida), out into Berkeley Square and round to a restaurant so famous that it had become one of the sights of London. It rivalled the Tour d'Argent or Maxim's as a must for the well-heeled traveller.

There he would be ushered to his favourite table under a Hockney picture of the late proprietor peering drunkenly at Hockney. There he would have a *vin blanc cassis – not too much of the Ribena, Jean-Paul –* which he called a 'cur', and then he would lunch off quail's eggs *followed by the liver and bacon.* This betrayed his origins, in Deptford. A head waiter had once told Victoria that all the yobs liked something with bacon in it; this was well known to restaurateurs in London. They could see them coming, with their aggressive, ill-at-ease walks, their shoulders rolling a little, like a boxer going into the ring; the quick crack, the ready wit half formed on the face, the legs perhaps a little short, the hair looking a touch suburban. They knew in their hearts they weren't supposed to be in these palaces guzzling quail's eggs and drinking Californian Chardonnay. *Very tasty. Not bad. Don't ponce about wif the bottle, Jean-Paul, splash the 'ole lot in. That's the game. That's it, mate. Not a bad geezer for a frog, Jean-Paul. I'll have me usual. Try and make the bacon crispier than what it was last week, orright?*

Mike was thirty. He had, Victoria thought, peaked too early. There was nothing in his locker now except his refined, pop-porno taste. The account people, who were frightened of him, also hated him. They were waiting for the first signs of weakness, the first misjudgement, the first lost account, the first major fuck-up in fact, to get him, because he was really just a pretentious little oik from south of the river where his mum was a telephonist and his dad worked as a hospital porter. 'Worked' was a joke too. He had a desk job organising the rotas of porters, a task which could have been done by a baboon – said Mike – only his dad was in the union. Not that that was the scam it used to be, neither. The Prime Minister's cold breath had blown down there too. In the good old days the hospital supplies used to go missing, the drivers ran cab services, the porters worked about twenty-five hours overtime a day – 'Amazin' scams, you wouldn't believe what was going down.'

Victoria guessed it had always gone down. The purse-snatchers and pickpockets, the footpads and sneakthieves, had not just vanished. The archetypes were still around, even if their appearance and habitat had changed. A real Londoner was a crook. *That's the game, innit?* A real Londoner took great pride in his game.

Victoria wrote some nonsense about the quiet clunk of car doors, the warmth of rosewood veneer, the discreet coughing of the butler, the crystal port decanters, the scent of aged leather, the aroma of new-mown grass, the cricket ball which had inadvertently killed a sparrow in flight, the venerable shoe lasts at Lobb's, the claret bins at Berry Bros, the single malts from a private peat bog, the four-year waiting list at Purdey's, the royal enclosure at Ascot. Jesus, she could go on for ever. The Golden Eagle Club card would get you in, with a discount. This world she could conjure up so easily, probably existed, but it was an illusion none the less. She had never independently verified any of it. It was to her as much a mystery as Einstein's professional life to Mike. It was anyway increasingly difficult to distinguish between the image and the reality. And London (formerly known for mulled wine and chestnuts roasting by the fire), was the world capital of fakery. There were things which were so real you could not be sure if you had experienced them yourself or not, like seeing a minor celebrity in the street and saying hello. Her mother said goodnight to the weathermen. Perhaps Miles joined her in chorus on the chintz sofa.

What would Tim Curtiz make of this twaddle about rosewood and twelve-bores? She wanted to see him. He was sheltering behind his precious daughter, the ineffable Gemma. Divorced men were always the same about their children. The egotism of it. Without their undivided attention for a couple of days a week or a couple of weeks a year, the little angels would be deprived of a vital element, an element more important than calcium or iron or fibre to the development of complete human beings – paternal love. They doled it out like the Salvation Army with soup on a winter's night, and with the same questionable motives.

Men were no more peculiar than women, but they were peculiar in a different way. Men had wanted to come on her face, and beat her, and cry between her legs, and tie her up. Men had made love to her and vanished semi-clothed. Men had claimed to love her too much to have an erection. There was no end to it. Any girl who had lived in London a few years knew the score. Men dreamed through sex. Their dream life was no less vivid than an aborigine's. In their own estimation they were practical, no-nonsense, unsentimental chaps, but the erraticism of their sexual selves proved that they had dark dreams. Sex was the window to their souls. Artists tried to capture these elusive shadows in paint, but most men could only lunge after them in sex. Victoria had done her bit to help them dream, it was true. Perhaps she had done too much, and been too understanding of their longings for them to want to marry her. Because they were ashamed of them. In their non-sexual lives they opted for order and restraint. It was the madonna and whore business. Tim was probably not too different.

There were three floors of creatives, 230 of them paired like Lorenz's geese. She and Mike were separated from the others on their floor by a system of movable dividers of matt grey. The rest of the floor was now completely deserted. She and Mike, in recognition of their importance, had a larger space, with a sofa and a view on to the square. In bigger offices, with only one desk and solid walls, lived the creative directors. The term had lost some of its original lustre, because there were now ten of them. Above them were group creative directors and finally the executive creative director. It was Ruritania, really.

Mike collected Lalique car mascots. He had fourteen, some of them worth a grand or two. He also collected arty porn magazines like *Focus*, and cars which had special qualities, religious significance, like Austin Healeys and Jaguar Mark IIs. Around his drawing board, which hogged the north light of Berkeley Square, stood ranks of coloured pens, exquisite pencils from foreign countries, Royal-Sovereigns, Magic Markers, jumbo Pentels and his small but growing collection of antique Mont Blancs. They had totemistic value mostly, because Mike did not draw well. But he could make a few bold, sweeping lines on his pad; he also fiddled with his pens during meetings, a brooding impatience emanating from him as the poor stiffs talked about segmentation and market-slot. They knew that at the end of the day they would have to rely on Mike and Victoria to produce something which they could then adapt to their purposes. Some of the account people used language the way Pol Pot used human rights.

She wrote:

Combine your stay in London with a great British invention, the country weekend. You can now be the guest of Lord and Lady Gravetye at Elmscott, their historic fifteenth-century manor on the banks of the River Kennet, Britain's finest chalk trout stream, only an hour from London.

Lord and Lady Gravetye had been persuaded by the prospect of huge piles of dollars and yen to allow the barbarians in. Lord Gravetye had lost a bundle when the family stockbroking business collapsed after Big Bang and, in a way that naturally engaged Victoria's sympathy, was worried about estimates for replacing the roof of the stately pile. Its hammer beams had been fatally weakened by a flood and six centuries of beetles of Plantagenet descent. It sounded to Victoria more like the script for an Ealing comedy than a country weekend.

The 'Country Weekend' entitled you to stay in a wing of

137

the house and fish with the help of a gillie. Mike said a picture of Tim Curtiz and the gillie landing a brown trout on a misty morning was just the sort of image to get their motors racing. (A 'guest' of Lord and Lady Gravetye should be interpreted loosely. They were only contracted to make a brief appearance at dinner.) The newly affluent did not appear to be slighted by having to pay to be someone's guest and having to pay to belong to the corporate section of once aristocratic institutions, any more than they felt cheated by mechanical hippos and plastic castles at Disneyland. Membership of a golf course where the Duke of Windsor himself had been a member was now being sold to Japanese. Come to that, Mrs Calvin Klein was wearing the Duchess's jewellery.

The account people loathed Mike because he was so fucking up to date. Yet what were the components of his vision of the world? There were none. Unlike Stubbs, he had no enduring values. His only value was up-to-dateness. He could tell within days of its launch if a watch or a car or a magazine was properly attuned to the contemporary world. This hit parade, this *FT* Index of style was an obsession. He had once commissioned his own typeface for the launch of a tampon. He said that none of the six thousand typefaces already invented was suitable for this new product. The copy, written by Victoria, was (like the tampon) short and to the point: *For Today's Woman, Today's Confidence. Today*. It cost nearly fifteen thousand just to set that one line. Victoria had suggested he register it under the name of *Sanitary Italic*. Mike's religious faith in design had no theoretical basis. He could not explain why he preferred Mont Blanc pens to Parkers, and Austin Healeys to MGs, and yet he had a wall of plaques testifying to his taste. Victoria could see, even if Mike couldn't, that he was conforming to some unconscious ideal, what de Chirico had called the 'ghostly and metaphysical aspect' of objects. He was a shaman in relation to the spiritual properties of these things, while the benighted account people could see only the surface aspect of them.

Horse Attacked by Lion (to be followed closely by *Horse Devoured by Lion*) was not a new theme in art. It was Greek in origin. Lions had roamed the remoter part of Greece until comparatively recently. But *Horse Attacked by Lion* represented far more to the Hellenic mind than a danger to livestock. It was symbolic of the struggle which is life itself. Lions represented courage, nobility and danger. Later they came to be seen as the embodiment of evil: *Your adversary the devil, as a roaring lion, walketh about seeking whom he may devour*. Tresillian pointed out the sexual aspect of the lion and horse pictures: the quiveringly beautiful horse and the violently masculine lion. In early Christian times the lion had come to represent Christ himself. Later, lion statues guarded churches, because lions were believed never to sleep. The lion as a symbol was very adaptable, no question about it.

The phone rang.

'Yuh?' she said warily.

'Victoria, there's a huge bunch of flowers for you at reception. You are a lucky bunny.'

'Thanks. Send them up.'

CHAPTER FOURTEEN

I looked through the index of Schaller, from *Anal Sniffing* to *Zebras, predation of* without seeing any mention of captive lions.

Chaka had been gone for two days. He had fled the coop. An unidentified truck had been seen in Regent's Park, which led to a theory that animal rights fanatics had removed him. His replacement by a pure-bred Indian lion from Gir was simply a matter of time. A suitable lion had been found, but the paperwork in New Delhi would be some while. There were no tracks. A retired game warden from Tanzania had been called to check the zoo grounds for what he called 'spoor', but the paths were concrete and tar. He had sniffed the ground, gateposts and trees for signs, but had found none. This was probably a good line of enquiry; in Schaller there are many references to marking, scraping, spraying and even dung-rolling. I wondered what dung-rolling could be. Perhaps some form of recreation. In fact it is an attempt to disguise scent by rolling in the vegetable dung of ruminants.

'He's gone to the jungle to see his friends,' said Gemma.

We had only a few more days together and I felt I must give her a large ration of my affection, to last until we met again. The zoo, our favourite outing, was closed until the lion had been found. Residents of the elegant terraces near by had been advised to keep their dogs at home. People were advised not to walk along the canal or anywhere in the park. Primrose Hill was closed too, but there were no tracks to prove that a lion had been there. The frosty ground made tracking difficult, said the game warden, whose name was Mordaunt Spear. He had not had so much fun since Tanganyika became independent thirty years before. The press had taken up position with long lenses all around Regent's Park. They were hoping that the lion would kill a duchess; failing that they were hoping that it would kill a duchess's poodle. At the very least they were hoping to see it shot. Ironically, the last thing that could be done to it now was to kill it.

A letter arrived for me, postmarked Uzumbu, North East District, Kenya. I looked at it carefully before opening it. The envelope was of rough blue paper. The paper looked as if it had been made in Eastern Europe; something in the milling process was not quite right. It was slightly shiny, like institutional toilet paper, so that the address had spread over the surrounding paper like an African watercourse. The stamp, by happy coincidence, bore a picture of a male lion, gazing over the vast savannah towards President Moi, who occupied a corner of the design grumpily. I was reluctant to open the letter too quickly. I sniffed it. I could smell woodsmoke and old-fashioned ink of the sort you used to buy in sturdy, sensible jars. The postmark was faint, but the letter from the middle of nowhere had taken only eight days to reach me.

The Chief wrote:

Dear Sir

I would like to commence by thanking you for the speedy reply to my previous correspondence. The weather here has been unseasonable. It rained in the dry season and it has been dry in the wet season. The rotation of crops has suffered a cruel blow. We are not dispirited although it is very difficult to get diesel at this time. We also cannot get rice, soap and cattle dip. I am frequently in correspondence with Nairobi, but to no avail. They are not like you, because they do not answer promptly. I am the chief of this district, Uzumbu. The people are mostly Samburu (Maasai) and Somali. The chief before me was a Luo man from Naivasha, but I was born here. I am the son of Solomon Chilingwe, who was the chief at the time of which you have written. Mr William Cochrane was working for the Public Works Department. He and his colleagues were in charge of the drainage and water

141

system of Uzumbu, which unfortunately does not operate any more. At that time Uzumbu was a very small place, only six manyattas (villages). The government wished it to become the administrative centre of North East district. That plan was not carried out. We had a census recently which I organised, and we have found four thousand people in this area. This was a big surprise to everyone. I am pleased to see that you live in London, Sir. My father attended a meeting with the King Edward in Nairobi in 1935. He came from London for hunting. There is no hunting permitted now. My father died in nineteen sixty-seven from buffalo wounds. I would like very much to visit London. I am writing this letter to ask if you can assist me with some money for the fare. I have applied to the British Council in Nairobi, but unfortunately the funds are dry, like our wells. I have many matters to discuss with you if you wish to know about Mr Cochrane. Mr Cochrane has a daughter living here in Uzumbu. She is my first wife. Her name is Daisy. She has never seen her daddy unfortunately, because he was transferred after the lion problem. She is blind now from the cataracts, but she is a good wife. She is very pleased to know that her father is still living and she would be pleased to receive some money to help with the school for his grandchildrens, which are my children also. I am expecting your reply. Please do not cock a snoot at my request.

Yours faithfully,

Chief Phineas Chilingwe.

Private Bag 10, Uzumbu.

'Gemma, let's go. We're going out.'
She was watching a rock video.
'OK. This is stupid (stoopid).'
She turned off the television with disdain and jumped down from the sofa. Her dress hiked up over her legs to show her pants, which were blue and embroidered with roses, like my mother's tablecloths. Helping her dress each day – finding the shoes and the armholes and operating the slides for her hair –

142

was as intimate as moving in with a lover. She was a delicate, yet complete being. I had tried to ring her mother to beg for an extension, but she was not at home. A man answered. He was just staying for a while. He had no idea when she would be back or where she had gone.

Victoria called to tell me about Bernie's promotion, just as we were going out, but I already had all the details from Bernie himself. He had had a discussion with the agency about his new role. He was concerned about the money. Lennie had handled it in the past, starting with three pounds ten shillings at Collins Music Hall way back when, and once getting to a hundred and fifty quid a week for a stint on the Black and White Minstrel Show.

'What the hell was that?' I asked.

'That was a good show, but the racial equality people didn't like it. Done me career no blooming good neither, I was dressed up in a black stocking for a month, like a golliwog. I coulda been the Elephant Man in there, nobody would of been the wiser.'

They had offered Bernie £8,000 for the American Eagle job. The immensity of the money made him suspect there was a lot more where that came from. Of course Lennie was in a pension in Nerja waiting for his villa to be completed, concrete shortage in Spain, as much use as a bacon rasher at a barmitzvah.

'To tell the truth, Tim, he's not used to playing in this league. With the multinational boys. Unfortunately – let's be candid – 'is best days as an agent are behind him. Do you mind me asking how much you got?'

How could I tell him the truth without wounding him? He was a jokey character actor; I was a personality, as the agency called it. Personalities got more money, more dosh, more spondulicks. Fame is a marketable commodity in our age; even modest quantities are commercially viable. Bernie's view of the matter was somewhat different: he thought that the agency had finally seen sense and brought in a professional. And professional equals lots of money, know what I mean.

I lied: 'I got ten grand Bernie. You could get twelve if you play your cards right.'

'Twelve? Straight up? You don't think that's pushing me luck a little?'

'No, I think it's right. It is the mass-market card after all. There are three hundred million people in America. Anyway, all they can say is no. No harm in trying.'

There are plenty of occasions when I find myself talking in alien tongues.

'Faint heart ne'er won fair maid, as the bard said,' said Bernie.

'Absolutely.'

'He's got hair in his ears,' said Gemma, but Bernie wasn't listening fortunately. The hair in his ears had maybe filtered out what he didn't want to hear in his long life. He smiled at her charmingly, the way busy, active people do to show that they have not lost touch.

'I've done a bit of a script for them. Will you look at it for me? Me spelling's going off, although I won the spelling cup at yeshiva.'

'I don't think that's the way it works, Bernie. They like to write the script themselves.'

But I wasn't so sure any more.

Gemma and I sped across the Saturday streets which were as deserted as Serengeti, although colder and lacking the Modigliani shapes described by Schaller. Everything here was squat, with a lot more mass, growing out of the streets slowly and painfully. But the second-hand bookseller was already setting out his wagon of books and the traffic was becoming thicker as we approached Simba Cochrane's tenement.

'Where are we going?' asked Gemma.

'We're going to see a man who once fought with a lion.'

'It smells,' said Gemma as we climbed up the brick and concrete steps to Six D. I wanted to tell Cochrane about his daughter. *Daughters aren't too bad, Simba, look at mine*. But there was no answer. We retraced our steps, Gemma counting each one, to the caretaker's flat. She took a long time coming to the door. There was activity behind the spyhole, coughing and the clunking of chains. It might have been the London Dungeon in there. She had been cleaning the budgie's cage and was lightly speckled with excrement. I withheld from her the latest news on psittacosis, namely that it wasn't just carried by parrots.

'Yes?'

Her face had a raw look as though she had just come in from a gale and her eyes were smarting from the same cause. She inclined her face downwards to take in Gemma for a moment and, reassured that she was too small and the wrong colour to be a mugger, opened the last chain and coughed loudly. I feinted to avoid the flying microbes of parrot virus which had obviously caused her bronchial troubles. She placed her cigarette back on her lower lip where it clung like a marsupial to its parent. The cigarette end was wet through and the wisp of smoke coming from it was scented like damp lawn clippings on a bonfire.

'I've come to see Mr Cochrane, Six D, but he's not in. Do you know where he's gone?'

'That little bastard. Excuse my French, darling. 'E's gone off to tell his lies to somebody else, I should think (fink).'

'When did he go?'

'When did 'e go? Two days ago. 'E didn't tell me nothing (nuffink) of course. His meals on wheels come round, very nice piece of fish and 'e wasn't here. So guess who gets called out? You've got it. Muggins 'ere. Mrs bloody Muggins. The meals on wheels was ever so pissed off, I can tell you.'

She had a voice which thumped down on alternate syllables, like a fishmonger gutting fish.

'I think he's gone to the jungle too,' said Gemma.

In fairy tales as in dreams, connections are made which do not exist in real life. And yet they have their own logic. Jung suggested that dreams had prophetic powers which you ignored at your peril, an idea so absurd that it contributed to his decline in the scientific world and his rise in the mystical.

'Gone to the jungle, and good riddance. I hope the bleeding lion finishes the job this time,' said the caretaker.

'If he comes back will you ask him to call me?'

'Does he know your number?'

'Yes, but I'll write it down for you. It's important.'

'Important?'

She couldn't believe it.

'I need to speak to him urgently,' I said as she slipped my note negligently into her pocket, a quark into a black hole.

'Would you ring me when he gets back?'

I gave her £10.

'That's very kind of you, sir. Thank you. This isn't much of a job you know. The Trust never do nothing (nuffink) to help me. Thank you.'

'Have you had this job a long time?'

'I used to work at Billingsgate. In the old days. I won't say the good old days, but compared with this, it was.'

'Is it true what they say about Billingsgate, about swearing?'

'Is the Pope a Catholic? Enough effing and blinding there to turn the air blue. You had to really, else the porters would treat yer wrong. But you're talking about a hundred years ago and more when the fishwives was a law (law-er) to theirselves. When I started in nineteen twenty-three we 'ad a few of the old timers left. One of them sold an 'addock to Charles Dickens. So she said. But she was as big a liar as him in Six D. I used to open oysters, Colchesters. Look at me hands.'

Her hands were calloused, lumpy and damaged by life. They reminded me of dried apricots.

'Do you want to come in?' Her voice had crumbled.

'No thanks. My daughter's got a dancing class.'

My daughter doesn't want psittacosis either.

'Goodbye, darling,' she said, groping in her way for human warmth. It was in short supply in this poisoned building. Selfishly, I took Gemma's hand, my own portion of that priceless commodity.

Old people were living in these buildings alone and exposed, like gulls' eggs on a cliff face, to the cold winds of loneliness which presaged death. Simba had not gone to the jungle but perhaps Gemma's intuition was correct; he probably wanted to get away to a warmer, more magical place before the wind blew to hurricane force. Simba might be out roaming the savannah, searching for his son on the very day I wanted to tell him he had lost a son, but found a daughter, Daisy. Or he might have heard about the lion's escape and gone to lend his particular expertise to the search party. Why not? My own grandfather packed his suitcase with one book and an apple and set off to enlist in the Moonies at the age of seventy-six. (I have often wondered what the book was.) I should have asked the caretaker to let me into Simba's flat to see if there were any clues to his destination. This woman knew a woman who sold Charles Dickens a haddock. And Charles Dickens was a friend of Edwin Landseer, whose mighty lions were now coming into view. There was no end to the connections you could make if you knew how. None of them in truth was less tenuous than those of a fairy tale or a dream. Simba had gone off to the dreamscape, yet in my pocket was the letter from his son-in-law the Chief.

'Do you want to see the big lions, Gemma?'

We played for a few minutes on the lions. Generations of children have played on the lions so that their bony backs are burnished by countless small buttocks. Gemma did her bit. I thought of the recumbent figure of François Villon at Père Lachaise, whose penis – so prurient Parisians say – had to be protected from the attentions of amorous girls. *And perhaps not only girls, hein?* It had embarrassed the authorities that his privates were being worn away in this fashion, and they are now protected by a small cage. The lions, close up, have that overbearing quality of Victorian art, yet Landseer has captured their faraway look, the inattention to the foreground, very well. The ears are not so good. All around the lions the pigeons were fossicking or working the tourists. At all hours and in all weathers there are hundreds of people at Trafalgar Square, but none of them except the man who sells the pigeon feed and the policemen's helmets, is a Londoner.

Behind Nelson's Column, the final decorations were being placed on the Norwegian Christmas tree with the help of scaffolding. Out-of-town religious people, with pinched religious faces, were building a crib of hay bales and wicker. The city was humming like a top. The great city had its rituals and its nasty habits, which produced sounds like lovers in a distant room or turbines inside a Swiss mountain. In all big cities you can hear this throbbing and pulsing if you withdraw to a park; city people find sleep difficult without this great generator going in the background.

We went to look at the Christmas tree rising in front of the National Portrait Gallery.

'It's from Norway. Where Santa lives.'

'Santa doesn't live in Norway.'

'Well, up there where it's snowing.'

'Santa lives in Alaska.'

'Same difference.'

I felt such a welter of love for her as we stood there in the cold, damp morning beneath this huge tree that tears almost started – the ducts began to prickle – in my eyes. Her small neat figure, framed in the dark blue nanny coat with her hair falling corn coloured, popcorn coloured, from beneath a knitted red cap, was so tiny in front of this huge tree that I thought of the pictures of the giant sequoias of California which rose a thousand feet into the air and showed man his proper place in the natural world, as it had said in *National Geographic*.

By the crib some carol singers broke into song. Something has gone wrong with religious people. They all look as if they haven't been given a full rucksack of life's essential supplies. Far from being the most serene and the most spiritual of our kind, they appear to be crackpots. The strain of religiosity shows clearly on their faces, like the unconvincing smiles of circus acrobats; or the lunatics in an asylum who sit replaying their tormented lives on their faces. Religion in our time has acquired a cut-price, perverted aspect. We, the heathens, feel they owe us an explanation for their behaviour, and they know it. We've got all the answers now, from the DNA, molecular biology, quantum theory, astrophysics and natural selection. And they are left with the argument that faith cannot be explained in these terms. Nor can dreams, not yet anyway.

Gemma took my hand. It slid into mine with the greatest confidence, a perfect fit. We went to see the changing of the guard, not much of a substitute for the fish, but the best I could manage. I parked the car near the Foreign Secretary's neglected house and we walked down the huge granite stairs beneath a statue of George VI towards the palace. There is a country feel here – overhanging chestnut trees with a few wet leaves, squirrels racing about and horsemen trotting grandly to their military duties. The Scots Guards came down from their barracks in full flower; we followed their wild noise and their mascot, a goat, to their appointment. The bagpipes played a lament, with only the kettle-drums accompanying them quietly; it was very moving. Gemma tried to keep abreast of the goat. It was the leader of this strange band of men in skirts and bearskins, she could see that. We marched down the Mall, level with the caprine commander, our ears filled with the plangent cries of the Highlands – deforested, depopulated, despoiled by the Hanoverians – towards whose pile the Guards were marching, not to exact revenge for these outrages, but to amuse the tourists gathered by the railings and around the monument which dominated the view with that same Victorian overkill.

I have been inside Buckingham Palace myself, for the reception for George Bush. The vast stairway was peopled by Life Guards with breastplates and drawn swords, and the long reception rooms were decorated with glorious paintings by Rubens, Van Dyck, Constable and Rembrandt. (I don't remember seeing any Landseers.) The palace was draughty. I would have liked to see where they watched television and played whist. The Queen spoke to me. She was very small and quite plump and her face had a lot of powder on it close to, like my mother's. I also chatted to a major general in the British Army who was fascinated by the old-fashioned wiring.

'Look. She's in. The Queen's at home. See that flag there, that's the royal standard. That means she's at home,' I said.

'I like goats. Can we have a goat? What does he get for his dinner?'

The goat wore a small regimental overcoat. With its long white beard and pale eyes it looked like Trotsky. It tried to eat the orderly's kilt as the soldiers went through their rituals, and the bagpipes cheered up.

Having Gemma to stay led me to think about marriage. Men always think that they can get married when they want to, while women fear that they may not succeed, their intensity repelling the object of their attentions. It seemed to me, as we stood together, that nothing could be more natural or desirable than to join the ranks, the regiments, of normal parents with children. But is there such a thing in reality, or is this as much a fiction as the other myths which sustain us?

As we drove home, I saw a billboard: *Lion sighted*. I bought a paper. Chaka had been seen by a Miss Janice Showering

149

who walked her dog Donut on the towpath every morning at six. The dog's back hair had stood up and the lion had slunk away into some trees. Rain had obscured any tracks there might have been but experts with dart guns were making a close search of the area. The dart was loaded with a dose of succinylchlorine chloride which had been calculated by the zoo's scientists to tranquillise the lion in four minutes. Just in case, dying for an excuse, police marksmen carried live ammunition.

Landseer painted for Queen Victoria a vast canvas of the performance by a Dutch American lion tamer, Isaac Van Amburgh. This gentleman would enter a cage dressed as a Roman gladiator and lie down with the lions, tigers, leopards and a lamb. He was all the rage in London for months and Victoria visited his show four times, staying to see the animals fed after each performance. It probably would have been smarter to feed them before each performance, but that was the way Van Amburgh did business.

The lion's escape has had a disastrous effect on traffic in the area, not seen since President Bush stayed at Winfield House. North–south road communications have been cut by the police cars, wildlife experts, marksmen, photographers, and TV crews pressing around the zoo. Hampstead can only be reached by a back route involving the *terra incognita* of Kentish Town. Even Hampstead is suspect. People point out that Hampstead Heath is well within a lion's range. Schaller says that lion walk at least ten kilometres most nights. I will do a piece on the precautions the US Ambassador is taking in his twelve acres of lion country. My editor will like that.

I wondered if Simba was somewhere in the scrum, a mouldy old man who looked as if he had nothing better to do:

'Come on, pop, get off home now, there's nothing to see.'

'But I was nearly eaten by a lion meself. I'm Simba Cochrane. Look, I'll show you me scars.'

'Of course you are, grandad. And I'm Buffalo Bill. Nice to meet yer. Let's get going now before you catch a chill.'

'I can help you, honest.'

150

"Ow? Would you like to be the bait?'

The lion hunter slips off unnoticed through the crowd, through the barriers, into the now deserted hinterland of the park. The vast football savannah stretches before him and he believes he is in Samburu country again. He is going to find the lion. Or maybe he is going to find his son/daughter.

I started on the piece about the Ambassador's residence. I wrote a few lines. Then I went to Gemma's room. She was not there. She had joined the general exodus to the jungle. I checked my bed but she was not there either. Anyway she could not have emerged into the nave of the hayloft without my noticing. I checked the window in her room. It was closed. I felt like a man drowning in a closed compartment of a capsized ship. The walls of the hayloft were coming closer. It was early Polanski. My eyeballs seemed to be full of a heavy liquid; a cold sweat stood on my brow. I felt, like the dog Donut, physical reactions which were quite out of my control. And it was my idle fairy story that had set her off.

Suddenly I saw a piece of her blanket poking out from under her bed. She was sleeping soundly holding her teddy and the morsel of chewed blanket. Any experienced parent could have told me that night migration was not unusual. I carried her to my own bed. My knees were weak. I endured her movements and noises and insistent feet with all the gratitude of a flagellant at the time of the Black Death, which incidentally killed off one eighth of the population of London.

Lion sightings were frequent in the next few days. It was sighted in Fortis Green, Highbury Fields, Hackney Marshes and Hampstead Heath and even south of the river at Richmond Park, Blackheath and Ham Common. Dogs' hackles were working overtime all around town.

The babble of conservationists, the appeals for the endangered habitats, for ecology studies, for preservation of species; the magazine articles and television films; the lectures and scientific papers – none of these could dispel the primitive thrill aroused by the likelihood that sooner or later the lion would kill someone. Sure, lions are part of the delicate balance of nature; but there is no mistaking the fact that they are great big fuckers with teeth unambiguously designed to eat meat and tear hide. I had also seen the ammoniac eyes; I would not like to meet Chaka on a dark night in old London Town.

This unworthy sensationalism was not much different from the thrill experienced by Queen Victoria when she saw Isaac Van Amburgh lie down with his wild beasts. Landseer's picture may suggest something biblical, but the public knew full well that instead of lying down with Mr Van Amburgh in his toga, flanked by a woolly lamb, the lion would have preferred to eat them both. The reasons for this frisson are as old as the folk memory of small knots of nomads crouching by their fires, or closing the mouths of caves with branches of thorn trees.

And another reason is that only human beings know they are mortal. Lions, in common with all animals, have no inkling of their own mortality.

CHAPTER FIFTEEN

The fighters kicked bags of sand for two hours a day to toughen their legs. Steve often kicked the bags for longer. Why this punishment did not weaken the legs, was a mystery to Miles. These Cockney boys – roofers, plumbers' mates and delivery drivers – also studied Buddhism. At least they studied enough to help them kick someone's head in. This was the Ram Muag. The fighter knelt to beg help from above or walked around the corners of the ring to ward off evil spirits. The gym was scented with joss sticks. From the outside this temple of orientalism looked like any other condemned building in Bethnal Green. But inside, Thai boxing was flourishing. The Rungit Gymnasium was an old music hall, more recently a cinema called the Roxy. The stage was used to store equipment, including the bags of sand which weighed so much that two men were needed to carry them. The place smelled of sweat and blood and embrocation, overlaid with joss. Its former incarnation as a place of entertainment had, in the Buddhist tradition, been respected. The velveteen curtains which framed the stage were tied back with hemp ropes, and a row of the old seats lined one wall.

There was a group of black boys who favoured long flashy trousers with stars down the side, as worn by Benny the Jet Urquidez. Benny the Jet retired undefeated despite the fact that the Thais never allowed a foreigner to win if they could avoid it. If a Thai was still standing, he was invariably the winner.

'Luckily none of 'is opponents has ever been standing at the end of a fight. Most of 'em have 'ad to be carried out. A couple of them never made it back from the 'ospital as a matter of fact. Mind you, if you've seen the inside of an 'ospital in Thailand, you would know the reason,' said Joe Bilger.

Joe, Steve's dad, had got off at the Bailey, no problem. His only regret was that the prosecution had withdrawn their case before James could produce the video of him in the corner of the ring on the night of the crime. He wasn't bitter after his few weeks on remand in custody; not at all. It was a victory on points, but there would be a return match with the Bill sooner or later, no question. Miles stood beside him while Joe watched Steve train. Steve had muscles which seemed to have attached themselves to his frame like a cluster of oysters to a jetty. He was basically a thin boy, but his muscles crouched uneasily, like living animals, inside a delicate membrane of pale skin. His skin was so fair it looked as if it could split or tear. His face was knocked about a bit, with scar tissue over the eyes and his nose was not correctly positioned in the available space, like a car parked at an angle to the kerb. His eyes were cold – cold in the sense that a trail has gone cold or a story has gone cold.

Joe had been a pretty fair boxer himself, winning the British middleweight title and defending it once successfully. He was still involved with boys' clubs and boxing, but kick boxing was the future. There were nine hundred million kick-boxing fans in the East. It was a way of life. And Steve, along with Dutchman Ari van Oosten, was the only boxer in Europe to be in with a chance of a world title. Steve was employed part-time as a bodyguard for the royal family of a Gulf state. Whenever the Sheikh arrived to watch his horses race, Steve was at his side. No weapons, just his hands and his legs, hardened by kicking bags of sand. In Thailand they had played a joke on him when he had first arrived to train at Lumpini. Would you believe it, they put rocks in the bag? He had kicked it for half an hour, much to the amusement of the Thais, until the pain was unbearable. ''Airline fracture of the tibia. Little fuckers. But you get used to their sense a 'umour after a bit.'

While Steve flailed and kicked the air, Joe drew Miles aside to the edge of the stage to discuss the timetable for the payments to the boys in Bangkok. Rain dripped from the roof into a bucket, in which Miles could see pale pink water;

154

between rounds a small stocky man, built like a coal miner, spat into the bucket and the blood suffused the water with red for a moment, just like the cassis going into a kir.

'It's full contact. That's where the money is. But to get into the ball game you got to put up a stake. You got to see a few people right. No visa, no work permit, no hall, that sort of game. Once you're in it's a different matter. You can name your price.'

'What's full contact?' asked Miles.

'Give the opposition the full treatment. You can 'it where you like with your feet or 'ands. You can use your elbows or knees to the 'ead.'

'Don't people get killed?'

'Sure, a few. One fight not so long ago both the fighters handed in their dinner pails. One in the ring and the other the next morning.'

'And Steve. Can he take it?'

'He's a quiet boy, but he's got the instinct. Do you know what he does for his free time? He goes round releasing animals from laboratories. Anti vivi whatsit. Crazy innit?'

Miles enjoyed the conversation. He had stumbled into a world of hard men, a world nobody at the bank knew existed. Death was not something you pretended didn't exist. Death – Miles felt a manly intuition swelling – was part of life.

Joe was not very concerned about the details of the money transfers. He had self-assurance. As James had said, you wouldn't want to try anything funny with these people.

''Ow you do it is your business. Why 'ave a dog and bark yerself? Just get the hundred and fifty grand to this geezer by Wednesday. Where's it stashed?'

'It's not stashed, it's in seven Swiss accounts.'

'James said you was the man. That's what I like to hear. You've 'ad yours already I 'ope?'

'I have had some. And the plane ticket. Is that all right?'

'That's my boy. Enjoy.'

Miles had arranged to go to Hong Kong with the money. He had to hand over one hundred and fifty thousand in cash and the rest when the contract was confirmed. Somebody would call him to tell him that it had been faxed through. He would have no paper. He was just the bagman; he was under no illusions. The money had to leave the country by untraceable routes at one remove. He was the remove.

What Bilger did not realise was that it was not complicated at all. A few calls, a few deposits and it was done. Anyone could have done it, but of course Bilger couldn't walk into a bank in Bethnal Green with a pile of notes, smelling of fish, and ask for them to be sent to Bangkok. Miles had tumbled the money in the dryer at Heron's Beat with a wet towel for a few minutes. He went there on the pretext of viewing the builders' progress. Property prices had taken a terrible dive in Docklands and Victoria anyway showed less than no interest in selling. She was probably putting buyers off deliberately. Her mother was being very kind, but sometimes she spoke in a small, flirtatious voice, which set his teeth on edge. She was not bad looking for fifty-two or three and she enjoyed, as she put it, having a man about the house. This involved him sitting watching television while she brought him toast and home-made cake.

One night he had taken her to an Italian restaurant near Farnham and they had got very drunk on Pinot Grigio. He had kissed her a little too warmly and then got into bed with her. He had gone through the motions; it had been quite cosy. But it had changed their relationship for the worse, which he could have predicted. She was tremulously expecting him to come wandering down the corridor every night. He would have to leave, but at least he had some money. If the builders would get a spurt on, he could go back to Heron's Beat. Victoria did not answer his calls. It wasn't difficult to guess what she was up to. He was surprised that he cared. Since James told him he had shagged Victoria, it had begun to prey on his mind.

Steve finished his training. His lethal body was covered with a film of moisture. His shins were red and his chest was completely hairless. He looked otherworldly: pre-natal, something from a science fiction movie.

'Gooboy,' said his dad. 'You look sharp.'

'I felt good.'

Bilger introduced them. Steve gave Miles a cold smile.

'That's the merchandise,' said Bilger affectionately as Steve went off to dress. 'He's a gooboy. OK, you're the banker. You're the front. They won't ask you nothing about Steve.

That's not your job. It's all in the bag except for the money. All right?'

'I've got it.'

'You look the part, I must say. Public school and all that. Smartest thing your mate James ever done, if you ask me. Maybe the only one.'

Joe laughed, a noise like water poured into a tin bucket.

He gathered up the training equipment. His features were not perfectly arranged either, but there was a shrewdness about the knotty, boxer's face, and a calm, unhurried manner. Perhaps his serenity was a result of inhaling joss smoke. The smell was still on Miles's suit as he got into a taxi. You couldn't piss about with these guys, James was right. They had a simple code.

Miles had to go to court that afternoon. He was fined £1,000 and lost his licence for one year. James made a pompous statement in mitigation about the fact that his client's promising career in the City had ended unexpectedly that day, an innocent victim of foreign adventurism in the venerable City of London. The judge was not impressed. If James hadn't finished when he did, Miles might have lost his licence for two years. Bilger was right: James was not much of a brief. He radiated misplaced confidence without either the vocabulary or the incisiveness to back it up. Still, James wasn't charging him for donning his robes and wig. Miles refused a consolation drink at a lawyers' pub. He had had enough of James.

He took a taxi to Berkeley Square and waited outside the agency for Victoria. He wanted to apologise and make some promises. She finally came out alone at about six-thirty. She jumped into a waiting cab before he could speak to her, but she looked right at him as the cab pulled away. Her face was caught for a moment in the interior light before she turned to the driver. It looked, in that cold light, frozen and panicky, as though a paparazzo had photographed her. The taxi disappeared and he was left with the after-image of her startled face. It entered his head and developed there like a print in a photographer's tray. He thought he would never forget it. He was standing alone in Berkeley Square, his career finished. Bilger had told him that Steve's Thai name was Singnum, the Young Lion. He rang Jacci's number, but a man answered smugly, the way men do when they are caught fucking:

'No, she's a little busy at the moment. Who shall I say rang?'

'The young hyena, you dipstick.'

As he put the phone down he could hear giggles.

The phone box was decorated with little cards: *Busty Lynn. Caribbean Massage. Detention for naughty boys. Big and bouncy. Schoolgirl needs extra lessons.* Jesus, what a city. It made you puke. He went down to the Admiral Codrington and found Piggy. They got completely pissed and Miles forgot that Victoria's mother – her name was Joyce, but he had never used it – was making something special for dinner. He ended up at Piggy's place with a girl who kept pushing his head down between her legs, which was some fucking nerve from a nineteen-year-old. In the end he managed to get her to blow him, but it was a struggle. When he woke up she had gone. These girls from the Cod always seemed to get nervous before first light. This one had tried to make him wear a condom, which she had produced from her bag. It was a first for him.

He thought of Victoria's face, her lips as black as ripe mulberries in the taxi's light, and his chest felt swollen as though something in there was fermenting.

'Piggy, let's go down to the brasserie for some breakfast. Piggy, wake up, you wanker.'

Piggy was lying sideways across his bed, completely naked.

'God you're revolting, Piggy. You look like a bag of manure.'

'I feel like one,' said Piggy without moving.

The cleft of his buttocks was trimmed with fur. Looking down on him, Miles could see that his hair was thinning at the crown, but he said nothing about that. His misfortune had given him a greater sensitivity to other people's problems.

The brasserie had those old-world green cups with gold rims and real French waiters. The whole town was full of pretend brasseries, tapas bars, Tex Mex restaurants, diners, delis and places where you could eat chicken or swordfish blackened on genuine mesquite wood. The old-fashioned kind of food, with root vegetables and double cream had gone on the defensive. But the brasserie was as close to the real thing as you could get in London, Miles thought. It was old for a start; it had been going ten years, which was an ancient pedigree in the restaurant trade. The waiters were eccentric; they had no idea at all of effacing themselves in the interests of service. They were characters and you were expected to acknowledge that. If they were in a good mood they might talk; if not, well, that was their business. As they entered, an elderly waiter was snipping hairs from his ears with some Gallic clippers, looking carefully at the results in the mirror above the table that held the newspapers with their wooden spines.

'Let's have the whole works,' said Piggy.

He was not as fat with his clothes on. The blazer and the red checked shirt concealed his small paunch effectively.

'How come a fry-up is what the system craves most when you've got a hangover, Miles?'

'It's the grease. It mops up the alcohol. Like an oil slick in the North Sea. Did you score last night? I can't remember?'

'Nor can I. No I didn't as a matter of fact. Her boyfriend came back just as I was trying to get her into a taxi. How was yours?'

'Presumptuous.'

There were other men in the brasserie who had also had hard nights. The skin on their faces was tender, the blood vessels straining. There were young wives with lustrous hair having coffee together after visiting Conran and Joseph, and there were property developers or estate agents with portable phones on the table, apparently unaware that portable phones were as unfashionable as over-cooked vegetables.

Miles watched Piggy eat his eggs. His feelings about Piggy were mixed. Piggy had lost his job with a stockbroker about eleven months before. It was an aristocratic family firm, Gravetye and Co., run by partners who did nothing but hunt, shoot and fish. They had made a deal with a Japanese bank, but had completely lost their way after Big Bang. Piggy had been one of the first to go. He had hardly tried to find another job and was living in expectation of milking a few hundred thousand from the family trust. What Piggy did not realise was that a few hundred would hardly buy you a one-bedroom flat in

Chelsea. It would certainly not keep anyone afloat for more than three years. This town was like a black hole into which money vanished. In Singapore the Buddhists put paper money into ovens at their temples, so Chua had told him. Not so different here, my old china, he had thought, except that we put real money in. Piggy was falling apart. He was drunk most days by lunchtime. Some of their more successful friends had given up alcohol and made a dreadful show of drinking Perrier and knowing the names of a dozen different mineral waters.

Piggy had been a very amusing companion when Miles was working but now that he had seen the down side, he thought he should distance himself a little from the Pig; his condition might be catching. Miles was going to use the rest of his windfall sensibly. Property prices would recover. He could sell up and live modestly. He felt cheered by his own good intentions. Egg ran down Piggy's face and dripped on to his blazer. He wiped it with a paper napkin, which certainly helped. Piggy ordered a strong Carlsberg. Miles just had a small bloody Mary.

By the time they left the brasserie, the day had turned from flannel grey – low light levels, excess damp in the air – to rainy and blustery. People were coming in to lunch as they exited.

'What you doing now, Pigs?' asked Miles.

'I've got a few things to do. And you?'

'I've got to go down to Victoria's mum's and get my clean clothes. Then I'm going to look at a flat in Fulham.'

'OK. Call me this evening.'

'Excuse me, sir,' said a man in a blue raincoat.

'Yes?' said Piggy irritably.

'Not you, the other gentleman.'

'Yes?' said Miles. The rain was stinging his tender face, but the rawness of his face was as nothing compared to the pain which had invaded his heart.

'Are you Mr Miles Goodall?'

'Yes.'

'I would like you to come down to the station, sir.'

'What do they want?' asked Piggy.

'I'm being arrested, Pigs. He's a policeman,' said Miles. 'Call James quickly.'

160

'You're not being arrested, sir,' said the policeman. 'Not yet anyway. We just want to talk to you.'

Arnie had done this to him, because he had tried to press for his bonus. The vindictive shit. The policeman walked with him to a blue Sierra, where another man was sitting at the wheel. He held Miles's arm lightly as he opened the back door. Miles wished he would forgo this little intimacy. It suggested all too vividly their true relationship. Piggy stood by the car, dazed.

'Get on to James. Where are we going, officer?'

The policeman shut the car door and his friend drove off fast.

'Don't worry. I'll tell you all you want to know about commodities. Don't worry about that. They've got nothing on me.'

'You what?' said the policeman.

Miles stopped.

'Are you from the City Squad?'

'No. Drugs,' said the policeman.

Drugs. For a moment he had thought it was something to do with Bilger. Drugs. Typical fuck-up. He would sit this one out quietly and see what they were on about. He looked back. Piggy was circling on the pavement trying to get his bearings as they turned the corner. There was still coffee and fried eggs lingering in James's mouth and his clothes were dirty. They had him at a disadvantage. This sort of thing was happening every day. A friend of his had been thrown to the ground and had a gun pointed at his head by the diplomatic squad a few months ago for no reason at all. *Sorry sir, mistaken identity, hope you appreciate, just doing our job, you would be the first to complain if we didn't.* Merrie England.

'Where are we going?' asked Miles.

'Just to the station.'

'Yes. I know that. Which one? I would like my lawyer with me.'

'You won't need a lawyer. You're not being charged.'

'I would still like a lawyer.'

'Would you want James Trentham?'

'Yes. Well he's a barrister, but he would find someone for me.'

161

The driver was quite young. He had short hair. Miles noticed that he had just the suggestion of gel on the front bits as he half turned to smile at his colleague. They were enjoying this; this was probably the high point of their day, when they bundled someone into a car and took him to the station, before the tedious process of form-filling began.

The car made its way out of Belgrave Square and into Piccadilly. They slowed at the Naval and Military Club, known to taxi drivers as the 'In and Out' because of the legend on its gates. The police car was unmarked, but with its aerial and the arrangement of its passengers, no one was fooled. People stared in. There was no doubting which of the three was the criminal: the one in the crumpled suit who hadn't shaved. The two officers, one in a blue raincoat with a large blue tie, the other, the driver, in a double-breasted light grey suit, both had neat, dependable hair. Miles's hair needed a wash and his eyes were hurting.

The car pulled into a yard at the back of Savile Row.

'This way, Mr Goodall.'

He was flanked by the two policemen as they walked down the corridors. A policewoman glanced at him; otherwise he was ignored by the traffic. There was a functional feeling about the place. It was like the service area of a large hotel.

'Would you mind waiting in here for a few moments.'

He was shown into a small room with a table, four chairs and a huge cast-iron radiator (the sort of thing decorators were rediscovering), beneath a barred window. The radiator gave off a fierce heat, which made the tender skin of his face glow, as if he had just come in for a glühwein after skiing the deep powder.

'Can I make a call?'

'Mr Trentham will be along soon. He's on his way.'

After a few minutes, the door was opened and there was James, as promised.

'Thank fuck. What's going on? I haven't done any drugs.'

'It's serious, Miles. Sit down.'

'What's this about? It's Bilger, isn't it?'

'They say you have sent money abroad for a drug purchase.'

'Drugs. For kick boxing, for Chrissakes, James. You know that.'

'Miles, we're both in trouble. We've got to do a deal with them.'

'You knew it was drugs, you cunt.'

'Ssh, for God's sake. Don't say anything.'

'Are you under arrest too?'

'Look, neither of us is under arrest. Just let me do the talking.'

An older policeman came into the room. He was wearing a dark, pin-striped suit and carrying a brown, manila file.

'Right. Sit down. I'm Detective Inspector Munday. Drug Squad. You probably both know why we've asked you to come in.'

'Nobody asked me,' said Miles.

'We would like to hear,' said James, still standing.

The policeman looked at James and Miles. His face was weary.

'You have been handling the proceeds of a robbery.'

'My client was found not guilty,' said James.

'Don't piss about, Mr Trentham. This isn't the Bailey. This is the real world. Let's get on with it.'

The Inspector's hair was thin. His face was large and covered with tiny pockmarks, probably the legacy of bad acne years ago. He spoke with the contorted vowels of an earlier generation of policemen and public officials. With his pin-striped suit and cheap shirt he wore a dark red tie with a small badge a few inches under the knot.

'Let's get straight to the point. Your involvement in this is minor as far as the Drug Squad is concerned. It would be the finish of your not very promising career, Mr Trentham, to go down for a few months. And I don't suppose it would make much difference to your prospects, Mr Goodall. But there's a lot of money gone missing. Not only could we get it back, but we could crack a major drug ring and put a few people away for a long time. So I am offering you the chance to help us in these worthy aims. What do you say?'

'Let's hear the whole deal,' said James, smiling at Miles.

Miles felt tears welling up inside him. He could not control them.

'Don't blub,' said James. 'The Inspector needs us. We'll get a medal.'

'You're a bastard,' said Miles. A completely aberrant thought came up on him unbidden. He thought about Mr Le Fanu. He felt terrible remorse, but the remorse was probably prompted by self-pity; he could not be sure. James was chatting to the Inspector. James seemed to imagine he was making a good impression. He had entered into the 'we're all realists' spirit with gusto.

'*Ergo*, Inspector, it couldn't be stolen money. Of course if the verdict had gone against my client I wouldn't have touched it. You know that. I was just helping Miles here, who has considerable financial expertise, make a few quid. Nothing in it for me. The solicitors brought the subject up. I'm not saying I thought the money came from the Sieff Foundation or anything like that. I'm not a complete pratt. But Miles was a bit down on his luck. Thai boxing promotion was what we were told. Nothing whatever about drugs. If Miles helps you out, it would be as good as admitting he knew (a) that the money was stolen and (b) that it was for a drugs deal. He didn't and I didn't. As a barrister you may have suspicions but that's not enough.'

'You're a better brief than I had been led to believe,' said the Inspector.

'You could try and charge Mr Goodall, but it would be a long time coming to trial and the money would have vanished,' said James, pushing his luck.

Jesus, James actually had him on the defensive. He went on:

'I can't grass up a client, Inspector. But Mr Goodall here might be able to help you. He might if you made it clear what you're offering in return. In writing.'

'You put Mr Goodall in touch with your client. You are in trouble.'

'I am not. I simply recommended Mr Goodall to my client's solicitors for his financial expertise.'

'What for, his fucking insurance policies? Don't piss about. The Prime Minister herself has declared war on crack. Not that she has the faintest idea what crack is. Let's get on with it, or you both get nicked.'

'Come on, James,' said Miles.

'That's a gooboy,' said the Inspector.

'It's not as simple as that,' said James. 'What's going to happen when they find out Miles grassed?'

'They aren't going to find out. When are you supposed to be going to Bangkok, son?'

'Next week. I'm going to Hong Kong, not Bangkok.'

'Miles.'

'Fuck off, James, you wanker. Next week, on Wednesday. British Airways.'

Miles wanted to tell the Inspector everything to relieve the ache in his chest, which was close to bursting. The Inspector was tired too; he looked chronically, pathologically tired. His skin, his hair, his eyes were all completely exhausted.

He and Miles ignored James. The Inspector explained that he had power to exempt people from prosecution. He believed Miles when he said he hadn't the faintest idea drugs were involved. That was the way they worked. He wasn't so sure about the stolen money, but he would let that pass. These things could drag on for months, years.

'You don't want that any more than I do, do you?'

'No,' said Miles, 'I don't.'

'Wait a minute,' said James.

'Fuck off, James. You got me into this.'

'They tape-record these conversations,' said James.

'Only if you've been charged, Mr Trentham. You should know that. This is off the record. This is information from a concerned citizen.'

'Wonderful,' said James. 'Let's not drag the Director of Public Prosecutions into this. Let's just make off-the-record promises. Until the Bilger firm hears about it.'

'You've got the idea now. Just remember, if I get the DPP involved, you're both going to have to make affidavits and then we're going to have to wait for immunity, by which time the deal will be off. Then all we'll be left with is you two, and the money, to show we got something out of this.'

Miles felt as if he had wandered by chance into a police series; the words they were speaking were all too familiar, yet now they seemed less real than on television.

James was standing in that way he had adopted, with his calves pushed backwards. It looked fine in court when he was wearing a gown, but here it seemed to Miles offensive. He and the Inspector were getting on well, and James was standing there, rocking slightly, trying to look aloof from all this.

'This is completely confidential, isn't it?' asked Miles.

'Of course. I'm not even taking a sworn statement from you.'

James snorted. It was the sort of noise plumbers and builders make when they examine other plumbers' and builders' work. The sort of noise the workmen made at Heron's Beat when Miles enquired about the flood damage.

'And nobody here is going to mention the fact that Miles grassed up Bilger? Are you serious?' James said, pushing his thick thighs forwards.

Miles saw that there were endless complications. He thought of the squat man spitting into the bucket and Steve kicking a bag of sand.

'Perhaps we should just get the arrangement a bit straighter first,' he suggested lamely.

The Inspector's features were already in motion; inside the skin his tired facial muscles agitated.

'Look,' he said. 'We can do this by the book, or we can do it in a grown-up way. Which do you prefer?'

The Inspector had fallen back on the script. Perhaps Miles was right. Once he had given the Inspector the information, he might be very amused to let the Bilger family know who had grassed them up.

'Do you know what they call Steve Bilger in Thailand?' Miles asked.

The Inspector gazed at him sadly. His expression said, Now I've heard fucking everything.

'No, please tell.'

'They call him the Young Lion. He kicks bags of sand for two hours a day.'

'The Young Lion. Bloody marvellous, innit? Now that's really something. Don't worry about him. I'll put him back in the zoo. Can we get on now, please.'

In the next room they could hear the sound of a scuffle, subdued by the thick walls, and ending with a door banging sharply. The Inspector lifted his eyes irritably from his notes for a moment, as if he was listening to the neighbours having another domestic row.

CHAPTER SIXTEEN

Schaller says that lions can go five days after a large feed. He has observed lions eating as much as seventy-three pounds of meat at one sitting. Seventy-three pounds is the size of one nine-year-old child or one large dog. Gemma weighs thirty-four pounds. A snack. *Vorspeise*.

It was therefore no surprise that the reports of sightings increased in number after four days. But nothing had been proved. The lady who owned Donut admitted that she had not actually seen the lion. An anonymous caller reported that a vicious Rhodesian ridgeback, the property of an expelled South African diplomat, was living rough on the towpath. There was a theory that the lion had followed the towpath until it came to the tunnel, where it was now holed up, venturing out only at night. A Highland terrier and two rabbits were missing from houses in Camden Town. A Chinese waiter who worked on a floating restaurant claimed to have seen the lion trying to get into the aviary one night. Nobody believed him because the Cantonese term for lion has a number of meanings. Strange, incandescent eyes were seen on several nights by patrols in Regent's Park and some tracks were found. The police proposed leaving a goat tethered on the towpath, because its piteous bleating was sure to attract a hungry lion, but the method of capture after it had killed the goat was not fully explained. Later the police public relations spokesman announced hastily that the use of live bait was not a viable option. Instead, experienced conservationists baited traps and loaded dart guns every night. Nights went by and nothing happened.

However, Simba Cochrane came back from the savannah

where he had wandered. He was picked up, half frozen, two nights after setting off on his mission, near St Paul's, a walk of less than a mile from Jubilee Buildings. In the hospital he had asked the way to Thompson's Falls. They placed him on a drip and fed him; after a few days when his memory returned, the hospital staff were very anxious to get rid of him because he told anyone who would listen (a rapidly diminishing group) his tall stories. The ambulancemen delivered him back to the tenement in a wheelchair with a rough grey blanket wrapped around his knees.

'And guess who's (ooze) lookin' after 'im? That's right, you guessed it, Mrs bloody Muggins. 'Is sworn enemy. I told 'im you come round to see 'im the other day. Chuffed to buggery 'e was. You comin' again soon? 'E said you was going to make him famous in America. Can't imagine why you would do a t 'ng like that, I'm sure, but the world's a funny place, innit? I never seen 'is scars before. Did a lion really do that to 'im?'

I promised to send the caretaker some money to help her over her inconvenience and asked her to tell Cochrane that I would visit him as soon as I could. Gemma was going back to the jungle too, in a manner of speaking. From this vantage point, New York seemed like no place to bring up a child. I probed gently to discover the nature of their domestic life, but Gemma gave nothing away. Magda's sex life was probably as lively as ever, yet it had not impinged on Gemma's consciousness as far as I could see.

The domestic arrangements were shrouded in mist and I could glimpse them only partially through Gemma's account. They sometimes went out in very big cars driven by Larry, a chauffeur. Sometimes they went for ice-cream in the Park. She was starting school soon at Brierley. This was interesting, because I had been paying huge sums for school fees for more than a year now. Anyway Gemma was swaddled so tightly in serenity that even the wayward Magda had been unable to unsettle her. Was I disappointed? I abandoned the enquiries guiltily in the face of her innocence.

During his absence on the savannah, Cochrane had acquired a fifty-year-old blind daughter, not the sturdy son he imagined. Nothing had turned out the way Cochrane planned it. Still, nothing much ever does for anybody. If you want to make

God laugh, tell him your plans. I had become moderately rich by doing very little, a minor celebrity. In reality, a very minor celebrity, about to be eclipsed in that firmament by Bernard Koppel. They were shooting his plain man's guide to London two weeks before Christmas. Bernie was going to appear as Father Christmas, Mr Pickwick and a Yeoman of the Guard, just for starters. But of course underneath he was still going to be lovable old Bernie with the hairy ears. His greatest pleasure had been telling them that he would have to have a car to get him back to the theatre by six-thirty each evening.

'Have you told them you're appearing as a transvestite? American Eagle don't go for that kind of thing.'

'For Gawd's sake don't say a word. I said I was in *A Christmas Carol*.'

'You're very ecumenical, Bernie.'

He ignored my little jest. He was a man with a mission too. His faith had paid off. They had given him fifteen thousand, a 'buyout', he said. He liked the word. It sounded opulent: 'world buyout'.

He now told me that he had lived in a hostel in Whitechapel run by a Jewish charity for the last eight years, rent and cooked breakfast £14 a week. Sudden fortune had given him the confidence to tell me this secret. He had brought a present for Gemma, a Dent edition of *Richard III* signed by Laurence Olivier, Ralph Richardson and John Gielgud.

'Bernie, you can't give this to Gemma. Really. I appreciate it, but I can't accept,' I said.

'I got the signatures in 1950 at the Old Vic. No use to me. Let Gemma have it, Tim. You'll have to explain to 'er who these poor old geezers was. And Bernie of course.'

'I'll keep it safe for her, don't worry. You're a pal, Bernie.'

Bernie, in his sly way, thought that maybe he was edging into the Laurence Olivier bracket. There was a vacancy. To me the three knights were as unreal in their lives as they had been in their acting. Brilliant actors, all three, but left over from another London, a world so remote now it could only be guessed at by those living in the last decade of the century. Their London is as remote as the Abyssinia of Emperor Haile Selassie, the Lion of Judah, seen in old newsreels.

'Where are you going to live now, Bernie? Moving out?'

'Not yet. It's a dump but I've grown to like it. I share an electric ring with a boxer who's lost most of his marbles. Ever 'eard of Kid Blumenberg? No. Not surprised. Well 'e's my neighbour. 'E can't remember nothing much since 'is fight with Maxie Schmelling in 1938. Nowadays not too many Jewish boys get in the ring with gloves on. The Kid is in *Buzz Bomb*. I call him Kid Rosen. He dies in the war before he can challenge for the world title.'

'Great scene when he's going off to fight. *Don't ring the bell.* Lovely scene.'

'You like it?'

'I do. I'm not sure I can help you with the script, but . . .'

'Don't worry I can give you the lingo. You just run your eye over the spelling and so on. A fresh eye. Any suggestions you want to make, I'd be honoured.'

My main suggestion would have been to forget the whole project. I also noted that my role had changed. Where I had been the great hope of bringing the project to international notice, I was now the rewrite man. But just as Bernie had grown to like his lodgings, I had grown to like Bernie. He sometimes reminded me of a fish which had just been landed, gasping in the alien atmosphere. Into the old familiar ether of London new gases had escaped which he could not breathe. Yet he refused to accept these chemical facts. He had wanted to be my guide to the real London, but now I saw him as the pointer to something more valuable: Bernie demonstrated very clearly the power of myth. It is this inclination to live according to a series of illusions which distinguishes us from the animal world.

Of course we don't necessarily see our own illusions too clearly; it takes a Bernie to come along and throw the whole business into relief. This can be a cheering insight or depressing, according to your mood. My mood was sombre because Gemma was leaving in a few days. Anxious calls to New York to confirm the arrangements had so far produced no results. I would keep her until Magda got back. I wasn't going to despatch her into the void without knowing that the reception committee was waiting. In my mind, Larry the Chauffeur conjured up a Yoko Ono or Bianca Jagger demi-monde to which my little angel was to be returned.

'This lady from the agency, Victoria, she asked me quite a lot of questions about you. You're on to a winner there, me old son. I took her to a proper fish restaurant (restrong). She was impressed. I don't think she had eaten middle cut of plaice before. Sort of restaurant she goes they serve the fish raw. So she says. Can you believe it? Japanese. Anyway, I've got to go to Berman's for a wardrobe call. All the costume is being specially made. Gawd knows what it's setting them back.'

'Thanks for the Shakespeare. She'll appreciate it when she's a bit older.'

'That's nothing, Tim. It's been lucky for me knowing you. I won't forget.'

Did he mean he wouldn't forget me after he was famous, or did he mean he wouldn't forget my help? It did not matter.

His face was more expertly shaven than I had seen it. The tufts of hair on the upper slopes of his cheeks were still there, but thinned out, and beneath his strong nose, on one side at least, the razor had passed close. When he told me about Victoria, his lumpy features, each one under independent motor control, jostled one another with cheery innuendo. If his face ever cooled down, it might fall like a soufflé. It was warmed from within by his animation. At the moment the elderly and very visible blood vessels were coursing with vivacity and his eyebrows were trembling with kinetic energy. After the wardrobe call he was taking the Kid on a shopping trip in a taxi. The Kid had not left Whitechapel knowingly for sixteen years. Not that today would be any different; he was slightly meshugga. What would Oxford Street make of these two neanderthals shambling into John Lewis's to spend American Eagle's dosh on a nice new jumper for the Kid? I wondered if it had occurred to Bernie how close in consonance 'Kid' was to 'saucepan lid', and 'yid'.

The wealthy Bernie, with enough money before tax to buy a middle-priced family car outright, was going to buy his old pal a sweater. Bernie was born to be a prince. There had been a mix-up in the bulrushes and he had been delivered to the East End of London instead of Luxor. Also, there's something in the refugee memory that needs this kind of gesture: *middle cut of plaice, nice new jumper, eat as much as you want, Kid, don't worry about the cost of the cab.*

171

I had become richer too, and from the same source. The capitalist *milchkuh* had suddenly spurted into our mouths. No complaints, but the arbitrariness of it was unsettling. Bernie expressed his good fortune in generous gestures; I bought an S-type Mercedes. I would sell it soon; I knew enough about cars to have discovered that the resale value was likely to be good. (If the boys who kicked empty Coke cans along the sullen streets didn't do it over first.)

There have been periods in my life when I have been short of money. The tyranny of the attendant worries has oppressed me. It is a waste of time, an appalling imposition: the sleepless nights, the letters to the bank, the reassessment of dwindling assets and, in my dealings with Magda, the lawyers' bills. In the last ten years wealth has exploded like an accident in a kitchen, spattering the bystanders unevenly. A university professor friend of mine, studying the secrets of the cerebral cortex, is earning £26,000 a year. This man may have the clues to the location of our notion of beauty; he may uncover the liaison between art and illusion; he may establish a connection between the chemical structure of the brain and the higher emotions. Yet I earned more money for saying 'London, my kind of town', etcetera than he will earn in years. But I can't worry about it too much. I can't subject myself to another tyranny of our times, the tyranny of guilt.

Perhaps he will discover the relationship between the higher emotions and money. That will be something.

Gemma was going to dancing class at Knightsbridge twice a week. Magda had enrolled her from New York. She herself had been there as a little girl, when Madame was in her middle sixties. Now she was in her eighties. She descended a staircase in a ball-gown with a stiffened skirt and the little girls curtseyed. The little boys, who were fewer in number, bowed. Some of them wore sailor suits. As she descended, an elderly party, evidently a great admirer of Madame, played the piano with fierce attack. Her bony fingers touched the ivory keys of the Bechstein as if they were scalding hot, so that the metacarpals bounced off them and regrouped in the air for a fraction of a second, like a high diver going into a tuck, before plunging down again. The children hopped about and mimed to nursery rhymes and rounds. The parents were encouraged to watch the self-expression.

'Five currant buns in a baker's shop.' 'Puff the magic dragon' and 'London Bridge is falling down'. The children sang, as we sat on hard chairs around the perimeter of the room. The room had something of the feeling of Madame's youth in Budapest, a world of extravagant balls and hand-kissing and piano music and dashing hussars, the memories of which could be seen on Madame's face, not so much etched as modelled, in the clay of her stringy but refined features.

I was the only father present. A young wife talked to me in that slightly suspicious way of the English, listening for the sonar signals that would reassure her. Evidently I did not give them off. She turned away. But a young American woman wanted Gemma to come to her child's fifth birthday party. Her husband was a banker and she found the English 'kinda tricky and wimpy at the same time'. The children curtseyed and bowed and Madame progressed up the staircase with the hauteur of a Habsburg princess, which she was rumoured to be. She paused half-way up while we wrote cheques and handed them to the accompanist who placed them in a tin box on the piano. The accompanist's face was furrowed by the years, but she did a good job on the make-up; not quite as dramatic as her employer's, who had strikingly arched eyebrows, but the colour and powder were applied imaginatively.

As she thumped the ivories, her face had a convincing serenity, like a ballerina's, but close up it was clear there were strains in living in Madame's shadow. Madame was an institution. There were middle-aged men and women in governments, in merchant banks, in embassies and palaces who had bunny-hopped around this draughty room. Some of the young mothers, I realised a little late, were in fact young nannies. This became obvious when they reclaimed their charges and the alien vowels of Glasgow, Durham and York were aired.

Gemma enjoyed it all. It did not seem strange to her that she was wearing a party dress from the White House in Bond Street, curtseying to a staircase. Still, after the life she had been living, this probably seemed like fairyland. I buckled her into the leather seats at the back which now seemed to me

173

unnecessarily plush. Four or five cows with perfect hides had been sacrificed for these seats. The song of the engine, which had seemed so harmonious, now sounded over-orchestrated, appealing to the vanity of nouveaux riches. Bernie had done this to me. Some of the mothers at dancing class had silver mascots on the hoods of their cars, race horses and gun dogs. These heraldic beasts told the world that they were only passing through London; their true homes were out in the shires. If my car had carried a mascot, it would have been a laughing cow, as on that French cheese, *La Vache qui rit*.

There was no message from New York. I tried to call Magda, but her answering machine was on. I left my sixth or seventh message, barely suppressing my impatience: 'I cannot send Gemma until you confirm that she will be met,' I said primly. I left the flight details again. This uncertainty was paralysing. I needed to work and Victoria was pressing for meetings, but somehow everything had come to a halt (just like the traffic around the American Ambassador's residence), while I waited to hear from Magda. I decided to take the flight with Gemma. Then I decided to keep her until Magda showed some interest. Then I decided to postpone a decision. Parenthood, which I had experienced only in bursts, was a serious, worrying business. I had become used to thinking for one.

I called Victoria and asked her to come over for dinner, seeing she was in a hurry to settle the copy for the Golden Eagle Club. She offered to pick up something tasty from a little place in Notting Hill on the way, but I volunteered to make my *spaghetti puttanesca* instead.

'No symbolism intended, I hope,' she said.

'No. Good God no.'

She laughed. Her laugh was quick and explosive, uncorked by the pressure within.

'OK. What time do you want me?'

'Say about eight-thirty, after I've got Gemma to bed.'

My motives for asking Victoria were mixed. I wanted to get the American Eagle stuff settled before she vanished to film Bernie. I didn't get any money until the copy was agreed by New York. Also I looked forward to spending an evening with her with the excuse of discussing the words I was supposed to have written. I could advance along the path of intimacy safely with Gemma asleep in the next room. Let's face it, I could hedge my bets.

Gemma's dancing had tired her. She asked plaintively if we could go to the zoo in the morning. She was missing the fish and her lion friends.

'The big lion hasn't come back yet. He's still in the jungle.'

'Do you think he's going to come back soon?'

'I don't know darling.'

'I'll go and get him.'

'Don't do that. No, I think he may be happier in the jungle.'

'I guess he is. Will you tell me another story?'

Once you have acquainted yourself with Bettelheim's advanced thinking on the subject, it becomes very hard to make up fairy stories at all. You can't get away from the fear that you may be casting a long shadow where you least wish to tread, in the unconscious.

My story was as conventional and lacking in undertones as I could manage. She resisted the mysterious process of sleep like a patient going under an anaesthetic, her heavy eyelids opening once or twice in a doomed rearranged action. Madame's *ancien régime* eurythmics and my tedious story about a rabbit and its burrow – no foxes, no bloodthirsty farmers – took care of that.

With Gemma asleep I chopped tomatoes and pitted olives happily. Italian food has been rehabilitated in the last decade. Olive oil is practically an elixir. The ingredients for *salsa puttanesca* are the sort of thing small farmers in the Mediterranean have been growing for hundreds of years, which have suddenly become so right on every count. I had some bottles of olive oil which cost more than vintage Burgundy. They had been cold pressed by elderly women in black, aided only by a faithful mule, in a remote corner of the Mediterranean where German tourists had inexplicably failed, as yet, to upset the local economy.

One of these oils tasted of lawn clippings. The olives were so young and so virginal that only a thousand bottles a year found their way on to the market. It was an acquired taste, but apparently closer to what the Romans had enjoyed than anything available in supermarkets. I added a tablespoon to

175

the bubbling tomatoes and removed more stones from large Greek olives with a little implement designed for that purpose. It could do cherries equally well. A bottle of Barolo was breathing deeply on the granite work-surface. Large, flat-leaved parsley was roughly chopped ready, and I lit a fire; the whole lot flooded and eddied in the air of my hayloft, integrating happily with the childish smells which I prized so highly.

I opened Schaller and read some more about lion predation. Each lion, Schaller estimates, eats about seventy antelope a year. At the time of his study there were probably six hundred lions in Serengeti: plus or minus fifty thousand ungulants a year eaten. Yet, as Schaller points out, thousands upon thousands of wildebeest drown in the annual migrations without any help from lions. The lion is an agent of natural selection. Actually, almost everything is an agent of natural selection, in some humble capacity. The process of natural selection has no aim in mind; it is entirely random, but within the randomness, order – of the sort we crave – can be detected. A lion loose in this great city was an event so random that it had blown life on to the embers of the city's dreamlife, which Carl Jung said we ignore at our peril. (Jung's theory is tantamount to blackmail: you dream, therefore your dreams have significance, therefore you must study them. If you don't, don't say you weren't warned.) London had an intimate relationship with lions in its dreamlife. Only the other day this special relationship with lions was demonstrated: at St Katharine Cree Church in Leadenhall a sermon was preached as it has been every year since 1646 to commemorate the miraculous escape of a Lord Mayor of London from a lion in the Turkish dominions. All over town, lions guard bridges and churches, because lions never sleep. There was no end to this symbolism once you started looking. The lion's friend is the jackal. I was becoming the lion's friend, in Bernie's estimation.

Victoria arrived on time, but with a flurry of apologies. She hadn't had time to change. She had had a terrible day. The flowers she brought were all she could get in a hurry, and so on. She was aware of her attraction; she made herself approachable by the deprecation. Her hair was arranged more severely than I remembered, and her lips were bursting with autumn

176

fruit. Seeing her come through my doorway, I knew that this would not be the last time. She had come for intimacy. She needed it. Her body was a receptacle for it. The crossing of the threshold was a turning point. She sized up my hayloft. Women always do this in a single man's house. They test the air and make a quick reconnaissance. Single men are practitioners in a woman's world, with their own cooking equipment, their own recipes, their own bedding and their own towels and soap. Women perhaps prefer a man whose domestic taste is unshaped, like a potter's clay which they can turn on the wheel and then fire. They also suspect men who have made their own domestic arrangements of being fussy and precise. 'Set in his ways' is an English term which carries a heavy load of unpleasant implication.

'What do you think?' I asked.

'I love it. It's wonderful. Where does Gemma sleep?'

'In there.'

'Can I see her?'

'Of course.'

We inspected her in the crepuscular light which entered the room with the opening door.

'She's beautiful. At least I think she is, I can't really see.'

Gemma was clutching her blanket and her teddy, curled like a cochlea. Victoria stood close to me as we peered down at the Conran bed with the colourful duvet. We stood for a moment longer, just touching.

'Do you want a drink?' I whispered.

'Love one. What goes with a *putta*?'

'Barolo.'

'I'll have some.'

We discussed the copy, all about places I had never stayed and sights I had hardly seen, as we ate. Victoria's lips, hard at work on the spaghetti, were wonderfully erotic to me. Little Gemma lay asleep, but we advanced towards a day when our bodies would meet and we would share the other's fluids and the dampness produced by skin pressed on skin. To me this had a serious aspect to it, although I was not sure that Victoria saw it that way. It is probably a sign that your youth has slipped away when you begin to think there is something sacramental about sex. However you look at it, the exchange

177

of cells and epigenesis are intensely sacramental. In these ways the non-religious are able to see what the religious are going on about.

Gemma woke me in the morning. Her body slid in beside mine. She had my morning newspapers. They were disintegrating fast in her chubby hands. The Animal Liberation Front had sent a note to the newspapers. It was made of individual words cut from magazines and circulars, pasted on to typing paper, like a ransom note. The words were in a variety of typestyles, which made the note more sinister. The government's fascistic inhumanity to animals was being exposed. The lion had been tranquillised and removed in a crate (like a former Nigerian finance minister) to be liberated in Africa. It was already at sea.

The constraints of the ransom-note format were all that saved the whole industrial-military complex from more severe censure. The *Independent* printed the curator of mammals' view that it was an inside job. A temporary assistant keeper had failed to show up for work. The zoo deplored this dangerous action which would certainly be fatal to the lion's declining health. The lion had been on a controlled and monitored diet which involved scientifically prepared supplements. (And the flying T-bones for variety.) The zoo's statement was carefully worded, marshalling the accumulated prestige of science to the cause, but it contained the unmistakable assumption that euthanasia, correctly administered, was preferable to a sea voyage in a Panamanian freighter.

There were no sightings of the lion in the next few days. Nobody was eaten. The plaster casts of the tracks turned out to be those of a large Doberman with canine pedalbone dysplasia, disease of the pads and claws. The newspapers were trying to trace all likely movements of shipping on the Lloyds Register in order to photograph the release of the monarch of the jungle. What a scoop that would be.

Londoners were on the side of the liberated lion. I wrote a piece called 'Cockney lion's knees-up'.

CHAPTER SEVENTEEN

Victoria loved Heal's. It was all ready for Christmas. The shelves were groaning with tastefully chosen gifts. There were wooden boxes of French and English soaps, chocolates from Belgium, gleaming espresso machines, no-nonsense cooking equipment, woven baskets, exquisite recipe books, colourful jams, confectionery fish, gift hampers and greetings cards made from recycled paper. And yet, despite the profusion, there was an economy. There were not fifteen varieties of coffee maker, but three or four, all chosen by a higher sensibility.

From the lush and scented flower shop right through to the tribal rugs, there was almost nothing Victoria would not have liked to possess. The shop had an aura. Conran's down in South Kensington was, if anything, even more pleasurable. She had seen an old olive tree there in an antique Chinese pot, for £900. Sometimes Victoria just wandered around these stores for the soothing effect they had on her. It was pretty pathetic, she knew. She suspected it might be because she was twenty-nine. These places cooed uxoriousness quietly but insistently, like turtledoves in a tree. They were a eulogy to tasteful, prosperous domesticity. You didn't find any lavatory cleaner or nappy steriliser here, but you found vinegar with tarragon, Provençal herbs, red peppers or raspberries.

Her mother liked to visit National Trust properties and gaze at the framed photographs on the piano and the heavy silverware on the dining table with the same sort of personal interest.

Victoria was looking for a gift for Tim Curtiz. She chose a pasta pot, deep and capacious, in polished aluminium. She enclosed a card saying, 'Spaghetti puttanesca seems to suit me. Can't think why. Lovely evening.'

It was wrapped by an Asian boy with glistening curls. His neck was like a tree trunk, like the trunk of an old olive tree, and his white shirt was bursting with laterals and pectorals. Suddenly the whole town was full of body-builders.

When she got back to the agency she had the despatch department send the pot over to Holland Park. He would ask her again when the sleeping beauty had gone back to her loopy mother in Manhattan. He had told her a little about his ex-wife. She was English and only thirty-one or two. She seemed to have left a few nasty scars.

Mike, for once, was in before her. She had hardly settled back at her desk when the phone rang. It was her mother.

'Have you seen Miles?'

'No, why?'

'He was supposed to come by for his things, but he hasn't appeared. I'm worried.'

'That sounds like Miles. Don't worry about him. He's not worth it, really.'

'This is more serious than you think, Victoria. He hasn't rung or anything. He was coming for dinner.'

'Oh dear, that is serious.'

'Don't be sarcastic, Victoria. Miles may have behaved stupidly but I don't think he's all bad. I'm sure he's in trouble.'

'Trouble is his middle name. I don't want to upset you as you've obviously taken a shine to him, but he probably met some eighteen-year-old bimbo in a wine bar and forgot all about your chicken Kiev with rosti in the excitement. However, if he rings, I'll tell him you're anxious.'

'Victoria, I have a feeling for these things. Will you ring his friends and find out if he's all right?'

'No I won't. But you can call his disgusting chum James Trentham if you like. Here, I'll find his number for you.'

Victoria felt as though she were watching a ship leave for a distant shore. James, Piggy and Miles were standing there waving, and their image was fading fast. From Heron's

Beat, before the intrusive building works, she had watched the rubbish barges nosing downriver to the dumping grounds. What cargoes of discarded intimacy they carried, mountains of forensic evidence of a city's follies. In the old days, in Stubbs's day, there had been an under class who removed the nightsoil across the river to the south bank where it was used to fertilise the vegetable fields. Mountains of excrement, both human and animal, were picked up on the river banks to be recycled by these unfortunate people. There were other strange trades too, like the purefinders, women who collected dog turds for use in tanneries. Miles no longer had a trade, but his former employment was the modern equivalent. Miles and his friends were moving off downriver, out of sight and out of mind.

Miles as a lover had already faded from the memory. It was extraordinary how all that intimacy could evaporate, like water in the desert, leaving barely a trace of a mineral deposit. Miles had joined the seventy-five in anonymity. They were the threads in the needlework her mother admired in stately homes, merely the elements in an illusion, which is really just self-esteem. Art was illusion. Stubbs could produce a scene of the greatest tension and beauty, lion devouring horse, simply with paint on a flat surface. This was the oldest puzzle in art, the puzzle of illusion.

'Victoria,' said Mike.

'Mmh?'

'Is your mother screwing Miles?'

'Mike, I know you read, well look at anyway, porn mags all day, but I don't want you to start speculating about my mother's sex life, OK?'

'You can never think of your parents doing it can you?'

'Is that it for the day?'

'Yuh. That's me uplifting thought for today.'

Mike was cutting out shots from what he called 'source material', but most people called magazines.

'Mike do you ever think about what you're doing? I mean not like is Bailey better than Avedon or is a Lagonda more sexy than a Hispano whatsit, but about the nature of illusion?'

'Victoria. Victoria. You've got to give up this Tate Gallery crap. Honest, it's bullshit. People painted for money, for prestige, for style, for fashion, I don't know, all the same things we are in this biz for. Then along comes some ponce in a striped shirt and suede shoes and rationalises it all. It's crap.'

'And advertising? What's that?'

'It's straight. It's using whatever you can to sell something. You don't piss about. You try to make it as attractive as you can and, wallop, the punters buy it. Sure you use art and so on and styles and fashion, but you are not saying this is for the greater glory of the human race or nothing like that. You are really just in window dressing. I don't buy the big manipulator story. We don't manipulate fuck all. We just tart it up.'

'But why do you take it so seriously?'

'Because it's me job. I enjoy it. I love it as a matter of fact. Most of me mates from school work as roofers or plumbers or decorators. I can do about two hours' work a day and the rest of the time I'm feeding references into my computer.'

He tapped his head.

'Two hours a day. Don't flatter yourself.'

'You're becoming really ratty. You should hear yourself on the phone. If you're not getting enough, I can maybe make a little space for you in my diary.'

'What do you want me to wear? A rubber raincoat and six-inch heels?'

'That's good. Jesus, I'm getting a hard on.'

Mike stood at his layout pad, in the best light. He was wearing a suit which looked as though it had been made by someone who had failed tailoring school in Bucharest. The crutch hung down about a yard; the shoulder pads fell off the end of his shoulders and the body of the suit was equally generous. In the Third World they could have made three suits out of the material. As Mike knew well, someone dressed like this had to be taken seriously in advertising. His hair, which was fair and long, was today tied back in a ponytail. The skin of his face was very white, almost papery, with a disturbed surface as though the flesh beneath was simmering. His eyes were smoky. They reminded Victoria of the surface of a mirror on which you have just breathed. It was surprising that he could see out of them.

Her mother called back.

'James Trentham says he's gone to Hong Kong on business. I must say, I think he could at least have rung.'

'I told you. Parents are all the same. You'll never take advice; you have to find out the hard way.'

'You really are being very unpleasant today. Why has Miles gone to Hong Kong?'

'I don't know. He came into some money suddenly and he had to go to the East.'

'He made some money. When?'

Her voice had been constricted to a thin squeak. Miles had borrowed a thousand pounds from her more than a week before. She was deeply hurt that he could treat her so lightly. He had promised to pay it back when he came down for his clothes. Victoria was angry too.

'Victoria, I know this isn't the moment, but I'm very lonely down here sometimes. This is definitely not a country for single women. I've probably been silly lending Miles money, but I enjoyed having him to stay. That's all.'

This confidence made Victoria feel older. She could see the wheel turning. Mothers became their daughter's daughter in time. It was the remorselessness of age; her mother had passed on to her the childbearing genes and instincts. It was a natural process, but knowledge of it was hurtful. For 'single' woman, you could read 'middle-aged'. Middle age was lying in wait for her too, like one of Stubbs's lions. (The lion was full of symbolism, as Tresillian said.) Still, Victoria felt that her mother's emotions were undignified. A person of her age should have acquired a little serenity. At the very least she should have shuffled her emotions to the back; they were not going to get her anywhere. But at twenty-nine, Victoria also knew that self-esteem was not just the property of the young.

'What's the problem?' asked Mike.

'Miles conned my mother out of money.'

'How much?'

'A grand.'

'That's not too bad.'

'For my mother it's quite a lot.'

'Why don't you give it to her?'

'I can't. Until I've paid the bank off.'

183

'I'll give you some.'

'That's OK, Mike. It's not necessary. I'll get Miles to pay her back.'

'OK. Whatever you say.'

Victoria was touched. Mike was looking at some slides of models on his light box. He believed it was important to know every model in Europe and quite a few from beyond. Victoria kissed him, just forward of his ponytail.

'You're a pal, Mike.'

Outside in Berkeley Square the light was going fast, rolling away, drawing in the gloom behind it. It seemed to get dark just after lunch at this time of year. The square was tricked out in small lights, hanging in ropes from the giant plane trees, frogspawn in neon.

Victoria tried to finish the copy for Lord and Lady Gravetye's exclusive Country Weekend. Victoria had suggested that Tim go down there for a weekend to authenticate the copy: *Have kedgeree for breakfast, served by Fred Noakes the butler. Catch a brown trout before tea with the help of Alf Windlass the head gillie. Between them they have been with the family, man and boy, for one hundred and nineteen years.*

Mike had already discussed the trout picture with a photographer: *All the gear, the green waders, the business. Bosh. Clean out Hardy's. The best cane rods, a lovely box of flies. One of them silly hats, a wicker fishing box. Bosh. And a shooting stick. And a few thoroughbreds wandering about on the other bank, like a Stubbs, for Victoria. Yeah, she's an art expert. Yeah, yeah, make up. Get that Marlene, she's good for a laugh. OK, stay lucky.*

Just as she was going, the switchboard called. They had Miles Goodall from Hong Kong for her.

'I don't want to speak to him.'

'Victoria, he says it's life or death.'

'OK. But if it isn't it will be.'

'You what?'

'Put him on.'

'Vic. Is that you?'

'It depends.'

'Don't muck about. I'm in big trouble. This is serious.'

'Go on then.'

Miles's voice was strangled. He was drugged or drunk or jet-lagged, or perhaps all three. He sounded like someone speaking in a face-mask, like Jacques Cousteau or Lotte Haas, reporting from under the Red Sea. He started to sob, then he began to laugh bitterly. What he said made very little sense.

'Miles, what are you talking about?' Victoria asked in the middle of this farrago.

'I'm talking about life. They are going to kill me. I'm not going to come back alive.'

'Who's going to kill you?'

'The Bilgers. Steve can break a pile of bricks with his bare hands. I just wanted to speak to you once more.' He began to sob again. 'One last time. He kicks bags of sand for three hours a day.'

'Who kicks bags of sand?'

'Steve. He does it to toughen his legs. Tell your mother I've left her money in the top drawer in the bedroom. I forgot to mention it.'

'Which bedroom?'

'The one at the back with the bunnies on the curtains.'

It was Victoria's bedroom. He had been sleeping in her bed! It was the story of the three bears, transposed to Surrey.

'Miles,' she said, but Miles could not stop. He rushed on, out of control.

'I've grassed up the Bilgers. They are going to kill me when they find out. I'm waiting here for Mr Battong, who is the big fish. He's coming to see me this evening. What day is it in London, Wednesday or Friday? He's coming on Friday. Then the Hong Kong police are going to arrest him. And then Steve's going to kick my head in. It's all James's fault. He's a sod. And you slept with him.'

'I've got to go Miles. Get to bed, it's just jet lag.'

'Jet lag. You must be fucking joking. I'm going to be fucking killed. I just wanted to call you to tell you that I love you.'

'Miles, for Chrissakes. There are Christmas lights outside.'

This information made him choke: Jacques Cousteau's oxygen supply had been cut off at fifteen fathoms by a barracuda.

'Get some sleep, you'll be all right.'

As she said this, Miles was gurgling. The phone went dead.

For a moment she heard him say 'I can't sleep at all . . . Donkey sanctuary . . . Bastard.'

Victoria felt tired. She could have slept with no trouble. Her mother was asking her – sending her messages on her own frequency – to acknowledge that they were no longer mother and daughter in the old way. The new arrangement was not yet clear, but it involved admissions which Victoria did not want to make. And Miles was calling, stoned and mawkish. What had she done to attract this unwelcome attention? Miles had slept in her bed, the little bed that had seemed to her so vast when she first spent a night in it; that was before her father Lionel had started on the long winding road which led to viticulture in Kenya. He had brought the bed down from Tottenham Court Road on the top of his Triumph Dolomite, a company car which had soon after been reclaimed. Her bedroom and her sister's had stayed inviolate until now. It was pathetic, but the idea of Miles snuggled up in her bed, with her mother bringing him tea in the morning, upset her.

Outside it was now completely dark. That is to say, the sun had long gone down out of sight. In fact you seldom saw the sun set in London. Long before dark it had been smothered, a pillow of cloud pushed over its face. Sometimes you saw bands of colour in the sky, like the flashes on a duck's wing, marking the spot of the interment. Usually the sun just slipped quietly away unnoticed. Spotlights lit the mottled plane trees from below. From the creative floor you could see the glow, the halation, that still hovered over the city. Victoria had never worked this high up before. London was not concerned with vistas.

When Lionel went she had sobbed in that bed (which had mysteriously shrunk over the years). She had masturbated in that bed and once had sex in it with a boy from up the road who was now a manager at the new Sainsbury's. He was married with two children, who had red hair like his wife's. Whenever he saw her he waved cheerily. Once he had asked her how 'that funny little bed in that funny little room' was while she was buying ugli fruit. Victoria had escaped into university and advertising and life had been wonderful. Ten wonderful years, and now, suddenly, unbidden, shadows were falling across her youth.

She looked at her face in a small mirror to see if she could see the effects. She swung Mike's battered aluminium light towards her. She couldn't see anything new, but that was because the mildew was on the inside. He had salvaged that lamp in Albuquerque, when they were pulling down the Cattleman's Hotel, so he said. Albuquerque and Taos and Phoenix were towns that art directors liked. They like to shoot there and buy Zippo lighters and Justin cowboy boots and Navajo jewellery.

Her lips, she saw, were dark brown, the colour of coffee grounds.

The Dolomite would break down on the way to the office and her father would be back, or he would say he was working at home today, or he would be avoiding the marketing manager, an unimaginative person. One way and another, Lionel was often at home when she came back from school and it was always a pleasure to see him. He was so interested in every detail of her day, perhaps because of the poverty of his own day. And then nothing. Lionel left. Sixteen years later, her mother was renegotiating the terms of their contract, and Lionel was growing Californian Chardonnay in Kenya. A lion had visited his vineyard one night from a nearby reserve. There were tracks between the rows of vines. Heaven knows what it was looking for in a vineyard, said Lionel on his postcard. Actually, it was a miracle the postcard had arrived at all, because he had the address badly wrong.

Just as she was going out of the door a fax was delivered from New York:

Lord and Lady Gravetye will welcome you into their gracious parlor for English muffins and preserves. Before traditional British tea, you may ride an English thoroughbred, led from the stables by His Lordship's head groom, or stroll down to the River Kennet to cast a fly upon the waters. May I commend my own particular favorite, Gravetye Green Goddess, a hand-tied fly with a pedigree almost as long as your hosts'.

'Read this crap,' said Victoria. 'Tim wouldn't say stuff like this.'

Mike read slowly.

'Surprising what people will do for money,' he said.

That reminded her to call her mother about the money in the bedside drawer.

CHAPTER EIGHTEEN

Cochrane did not fully understand what I was telling him.

'You have a daughter in Africa.'

'No, I never 'ad no daughter.'

'Yes you have. You remember you said you might have a son?'

'Yes,' he said, doubtful.

'Well in fact you have a daughter. She is married to the Chief at Uzumbu. He wrote to me.'

My own daughter was dancing with Madame at this moment, before going to a birthday party at Mrs Lehman's, the banker's wife. I was happy to spare Gemma the noxious air in Jubilee Buildings.

'No. I never 'ad no daughter.'

He was weakened by his spell in hospital. Hospital frequently has this effect. I tried to give him the news of the lion which was now on its way to Africa in a container ship, but he had no interest in lions today. The hospital had indicated that his time was up. It is not the fault of people who work in hospitals; they know when the game is up, and their demeanour cannot hide it. When an old boy like Cochrane comes in, what choice do they have? These hospitals are not too personal at the best of times. An old chap walked into a London hospital not so long ago for an X-ray and died in the lavatory while he was waiting for the pictures to be processed. He was not discovered for six days. His last photograph alive was of his bladder, pictured *in situ*.

Only the wealthy can afford consultants and surgeons and private nurses to tell them, despite the evidence – the accumulated evidence of medical history mind you – that they are good for a while yet. Cochrane was not good for much longer. It made me reflective. I had seen Cochrane the lion killer as a way of getting closer to the real story. But there seemed to be so many real stories. Chekhov said that philosophy, history and religion were subjects too big to have a view on; he would content himself with describing how people love, marry, give birth, die and speak. How Cochrane spoke was to me as revealing as archive film. I love archive film. I look at the buildings, the streets, the clothes, the incidental animals. I listen to the words. Politicians were so much more articulate in the recent past. Now politicians talk without precision. President Bush, when I was invited to Buckingham Palace, was one of the worst. Mrs Thatcher is banal, as if she has just culled the *Reader's Digest* of snippets. Cochrane spoke the authentic language of pre-war London. It was a language developed without the help of the church or the government or education. It contained a wheedling note, a descant, running through it, a plea in mitigation against any charges the big city could bring.

He lay in his bed waiting for his meals-on-wheels, watching a small black and white television whose picture was composed of shadows in a snowstorm. It looked like avant-garde ballet from Czechoslovakia, but was, I could tell from the soundtrack, an Australian soap.

Cochrane had come back chastened from the endless savannah. In another sense he appeared not to have returned fully from the endless savannah. They had tidied him up in hospital. The fuzzy growth on his head had been trimmed, and his face looked well scrubbed. The net result was not good; they had wiped away some of the life. He had a nasty cut above one eye which was blue and yellow. The yellow was the colour of Dijon mustard. He was wearing pyjamas which had ST BARTHOLOMEW'S HOSPITAL embroidered on the pocket. What are pockets in pyjamas for anyway? St Bartholomew's Hospital is sited in the middle of Smithfield Market, where my other old pal from pre-history, Bernie, wanted to take me for some cut-price ribs of beef. What am I doing with these old chaps? Simba Cochrane is dying, Bernie Koppel is trying to take the bread out of my mouth, yet somehow I feel I must cherish them. Perhaps 'nurture' is a better word. I am like a farmer, hoping to get a pay-off from my nurturing, just like the farmers who send their cattle to Smithfield.

The tenement swirled with its greasy, pea-soup odours. The caretaker had told me that the building was going to be pulled down. All the old folks would be moved to comfortable, centrally heated accommodation on the outskirts of London, so she had been informed. It had dawned on somebody that this site, within a few minutes of the City, was worth a bundle.

I showed Cochrane the Chief's letter. He held it listlessly.

'Do you remember his father?' I asked.

''Is father. Can't say as I do.'

'Yuh. The Chief's father was Chief when you were out there. He is married to your daughter. As a matter of fact she is his first wife, his most important wife.'

Cochrane was reading the letter, his lips moving like a monk's at matins. He gave up after a few moments, despite the neatness of the Chief's ballpoint handwriting. The effort of reading made his face look pained. Londoners often look like this when they are eating too; they cock their heads and open their mouths laboriously, as though they had been ordered to open wide by the doctor, as if they had never previously eaten anything so demanding.

'No, I don't remember 'im,' he said reproachfully as though the letter had failed some test. 'I've got a letter an' all.'

He reached into the drawer beside his bed. In there were pill bottles and rubber bands and tubes of cream. He handed me a large envelope, it contained a letter from the Circus Hall of Fame in Orlando, Florida:

Dear Mr Cochrane

In recognition of your achievements in circus and your contribution to circus history, the Circus Hall of Fame has elected you to Associate Life Membership of the Academy.

On receipt of a once-and-for-all payment of $100 we will be sending you an illuminated scroll, individually inscribed with your name and signed by the President of the Academy, a statuette in one hundred per cent gold-plated cupro-nickel, a short illustrated history of the Circus Hall of Fame, founded in 1971, and a program of exciting attractions and events at our showpiece headquarters here in Orlando, Fla.

You have truly been a part of circus history. We honor your achievements and look forward to welcoming you to the Academy.

Yours faithfully

Louis F. Corleone Jnr.
(Life President)

'What an honour,' I said without irony.

'Is it better than *The Guinness Book of Records*?'

'Much better. I'll pay it for you, so you get your membership.'

'I would be much obliged. Thank you.'

'The Circus Hall of Fame. Fantastic.'

'To be honest,' (he aspirated the aitch) 'I was only in the ring for a few minutes.'

'That's not the point. What you did was unique. Anyway, you are being honoured for much more than five minutes in the circus ring.'

'That's true.'

'It certainly is.'

The meals-on-wheels arrived. A plate of haddock with boiled potatoes and peas was delivered by a cheery black boy wearing brand-new Converse basketball boots with his jeans. By a coincidence he was wearing a Florida State sweatshirt. These Converse boots cost £60 or more a pair.

''Ere you go, grandad. Wotcher fancy for sweet?'

'Wotcher got?'

'It's steamed pudding or fruit salad.'

'Steamed pudding.'

He nipped out of the room and after a brief tympany of the aluminium lids, reappeared with the steamed pudding.

'Is 'e your dad? You 'ave been a naughty one going walkabout, ain'tcher?'

'No. I'm just a friend,' I said.

'Nobody never takes the fruit salad,' said the boy. 'Don't know why they put it on. Back in a few minutes for the plates, grandad. Eat up.'

The fish smell was circulating around the building as I left. The caretaker waylaid me. I gave her some money for Cochrane's laundry. She and Cochrane had come adrift and were floating directionless in the soup, I thought, as I climbed into the Mercedes.

I imagined the Chief, Cochrane's relative by marriage, minding his wives and children back in Uzumbu, each phase of their lives marked by a little ceremony, a natural progression. Like Bettelheim's fairy tales. But here in Jubilee Buildings the rituals had long ago been ditched. The next one in the cycle was the unmarked van with the unadorned coffin. Family, I mused as I piloted my bachelor's £48,000 Mercedes, was very important.

I sped to my rendezvous with Gemma as fast as the traffic and the rain allowed. Since the very hot dry summer it had rained non-stop. The new decade has been libated, the old stones drenched, the crumbling sewers inundated. When Mercedes put in those dinky wipers, they could not have known what a workout they were going to get. Still, I was right on time for the party's appointed end. Small children in fancy clothes were coming out of the gleaming front door. Balloons fluttered on the massive brass door knocker. I could see more balloons downstairs in the basement kitchen, and a half-eaten tray of cookies with unnaturally bright green and pink icing. Mrs Lehman, who found the English so tricky, came to the door wearing a plaid skirt and a cashmere sweater.

'Oh,' she said.

'Hello. Good party? I hope I'm not late.'

She looked flushed.

'Gemma behave all right?' I asked.

'Gemma's not here.'

'What do you mean?'

'She's gone.'

'Gone. Where's she gone?'

I felt a beating of wings in my chest, a bird trapped in a confined space.

'A chauffeur came for her. I thought you had sent him.'

'I don't have a chauffeur.'

'He said he was supposed to pick up Gemma.'

'How long ago was this?'

'About ten, fifteen minutes. Maybe twenty. He waited a moment while I got her leaving present. They all get leaving presents at these parties.'

She was shaking.

'Did she know this chauffeur?'

'She seemed to. She went along happily. She held his hand.'

My heart broke. It exploded in fragments.

'I must get to a phone.'

'Oh my God. She hasn't been kidnapped? Oh my God. I didn't think of asking.'

'It's not your fault.'

Larry. Larry the chauffeur, sent by crazy Magda, my nemesis. Why do they do these things to you? How can they keep such appalling tricks up their sleeves? It's because they want to hit you where it hurts. It's because they know that nothing is so painful. I must call the police. I must make sure it's not some nutcase who has objected to something I wrote. I once wrote that a Palestinian leader looked like Eleanor Roosevelt in a tea-towel.

The police were ponderous and methodical.

'What sort of car was it sir?'

'I wasn't here or I would have stopped it.'

'Yes, sir, but did anyone witness the incident?'

A call was put out to all airports.

'New York flights will be checked for a man and a small girl. A car is on its way to take a full statement. It sounds like a custody dispute, sir. Matrimonial.'

'There's no dispute. She's been staying with me. As a matter of fact I've been trying to speak to her mother to arrange the details of her return.'

'Can you contact her mother now?'

'I've been trying for two weeks.'

'Sounds a bit casual, sir.'

'It's not fucking casual; the woman's crazy.'

'Don't get over-excited, sir, that's not going to help. Give a full statement to the officer when he arrives. Is that your

194

permanent address? Where exactly do you live, sir? Now let's check on the description again.'

What a moment to be dealing with Sergeant Buzzfuzz.

Gemma Curtiz. Five years old. Fair hair. Last seen wearing a party dress, pink and green panels. Green shoes. No distinguishing marks. May be with a man called Larry, US citizen.

That's what it comes down to.

I called Magda's apartment, but the machine was on. I was still talking when the tape came round again. It was not so much talking as ranting. Deep-seated resentments rose to the surface. It was lucky the tape lasted only a few minutes. If it had been longer I might have issued threats, which I could never carry out. I wanted to drive to the airport and watch every flight. But which airport? Larry the chauffeur had my little girl. They were walking through immigration even now, her small hand clamped in his large, insistent hand.

When I had finished with Magda's answerphone, there were still stragglers being picked up from the party. Mrs Lehman ushered them to the door, handed them a present and spoke a few words with the parent or nanny. She could have been giving children away to anybody. The Filipino maids were clearing the remains of the party, and her own child was wrecking her presents. Gemma and I had bought her a small hamper lined with silk, which contained a miniature tea set. It was a copy of the one Queen Victoria's children played with in the Swiss chalet at Osborne. When all the children had gone, Mrs Lehman came into the drawing room.

'I am sorry. My God, where are we? Is this Beirut? I was expecting something different in London. I don't know. I am so sorry.'

I comforted her by holding her hand, but my soul had dispersed.

'Don't worry. It's my ex-wife, I'm sure.'

In some respects a kidnap by an anonymous lunatic would have been preferable.

A small police car arrived. When he removed his hat, the policeman's fair hair stood almost straight up, as if leaving his thin and stretched features; the bone in his nose dressed urgently against his skin. He took out his notebook and we went over the same information as I had given on the telephone. Mrs Lehman had seen the car: it was nothing special, a light blue kinda little economy.

It took a long time. While the policeman was writing laboriously, barely concealing the difficulty, I could picture Larry the chauffeur and Gemma boarding a plane, taking their seats, fastening their seatbelts, the plane's engine roaring and the plane moving slowly down the taxiway. The policeman was finished.

'That's it, sir. Thank you very much.'

'What's happening?' asked Mrs Lehman, obviously expecting to see something more dramatic.

'I've just filled in the report. I've got to get the information over to them right away.'

I could see him sitting in his little car reading his report over the air. There was nothing reassuring about the sight at all. I could only blame myself however: I had gone to tell Simba Cochrane about his daughter and had lost my own in the process.

'I'll go home now and wait for news. Have you got my number?'

'Yes,' she said. 'This is the worst thing that's ever happened to me.'

Americans feel the need to place themselves right in the centre of the emotional action.

'It's not your fault. You can't ask for identification from everyone who comes. Don't worry.'

She hugged me. There were tears in her eyes. Her anxiety had released wafts of Tiffany's perfume.

'You loved that little girl, I know.'

'Don't worry now. I'll call you as soon as I have some news.'

As soon as I got home I called my brother in New York to tell him what had happened.

'Try and find out where Magda is. I've been calling her for more than a week. Have you seen her?'

'Not for months. There's just one thing I must remind you of.'

'Don't. Please just find out where Gemma is. OK?'

'Sure. Leave it to me. If she's coming to New York, I'll find her.'

'I want custody now. She's gone too far. You can't believe what this is doing to me.'

'One thing at a time. I'll get somebody on to this.'

I sat in my hayloft waiting for the phone to ring. My phone rings two or three times every hour on a normal day. Now it was silent. I picked it up to make sure it was working. Outside in the park all I could see was grey wetness, trees dripping, pathways greasy, squirrels in retreat. I tidied Gemma's things. They were pitifully skimpy. Her nightdress, embroidered with owls, lay on the pillow. Tears came to my eyes. Only humans cry, because only humans have a true awareness of their predicament.

The hayloft had lost its resonances. Perhaps I had only imagined the infantile fragrances. But when I picked up her nightdress and held it to my face, they flooded straight in to occupy the space vacated by my spirit. I felt as desolate as the last person on earth. And I felt guilty. I felt the guilt of holocaust survivors reported by Primo Levi: the awfulness of these events must have sprung in some way from my own failings. The tears now rose; there was nothing pleasurable about it. Women have directed tears towards me. I can't say categorically that they have drawn pleasure from the experience, but they have willed it, that's for sure. But these tears of mine came from a deep pit where they had been accumulating, incognito. They were a different class of tear.

Of course I know that vanity and self-regard are present in the love of one's children. Sometimes in the streets of London I see mothers hitting their children on the side of the head. ('If yer do that again I'll really belt yer.') In Spain I once saw an aristocratic man hit his young daughter (of little more than Gemma's age) hard on the face many times in the course of a Sunday lunch in Escorial. These parents do this in public because they regard the child as part of their own self; they have an instinctive understanding of DNA. It is the obverse of the self-regard with which parents invest their children. For weeks I woke in the night ashamed that I had not attacked the hidalgo with the remains of my Sunday lunch, an immense scapula of roast mutton. I would have done it, but I feared it would frighten the child far more than being struck by her handsome papa (while the women in the family looked silently and tensely on).

A torrent of the most basic emotions flooded the empty space I had once inhabited. Losing Gemma in this cheap, made-for-television fashion, snatched by someone called Larry the Chauffeur, plunged me into guilt. By my self-regard, I had set this in motion. I had wanted the love (what a clapped-out word) of a child when I had done nothing to deserve it. Larry the chauffeur had come over from the real world to teach me a thing or two about life. Magda's ambivalence towards my modest renown had definitely come down on the side of malevolence. I could hear her reasoning – her logic has always been wonderfully self-sustaining: if I wanted Gemma to visit me, it must be because I had some unpleasant motive connected with my insatiable desire for public recognition. This was proved by the fact that I had now appeared in a commercial on network television. It would be no good reminding Magda that I had achieved this small fame accidentally after steady application to my fortnightly columns.

Magda had herself contracted one of the epidemic ailments of our times, the desire to mix with the famous. She had dragged me to meet all sorts of up-and-coming people in the world of popular culture, none of whom has, as far as I know, survived in the public consciousness. It followed from this – my feigned reluctance to fraternise with the future big hitters – that I was capable of any deception. Larry the chauffeur was therefore despatched to retrieve Gemma from my clutches, and no doubt all the bills would make the return journey, just as soon as the lawyers and travel agents could get them out. These bills would be in proportion to the huge amounts I was making by recycling old London Town.

All this and more passed through my thoughts as I sat waiting for the telephone to ring. My brother had a reassuring familiarity with the ways of the world. He would speak to Magda and find out what had brought this on. When he spoke to people, he actually said very little, but they felt obliged to explain themselves to him. This is an asset in business.

Nobody called. The phone began to loom large, the way it does in cheap television dramas, with the anxious actors sitting out of focus in the background. I looked at my watch. Only ten minutes had gone by, not enough time for the workings of the Metropolitan Police or my brother's people. I wanted to call

Victoria, but I had to restrain myself in case of incoming calls. When this was over, I would not hang back prudishly. I would gorge myself on her autumn-fruit lips. What a fool I had been, with my Mercedes and my expensive suits, and my daughter, the ultimate accessory. I had been an accessory to her kidnap by my foolishness. I hoped she was not bewildered or confused. I tried to take comfort from the fact that children can be tough, as earthquakes and civil wars have shown, protected from the world around them by a clingfilm of mysterious properties.

The phone rang. It was my brother.

'I have spoken to Magda. She's in California, studying aromatherapy. She sent some guy to get Gemma because you have not been in touch. She was worried about how you were treating Gemma. You're too busy with being a celebrity, she says.'

'She's crazy. I've been trying to call her every day for the last ten days. I was going to send Gemma back to New York two days ago, but I couldn't find her.'

'You know Magda.'

'Did you tell her I want custody?'

'No. I spoke to a lawyer. You can apply to the courts for custody or more access, but you don't have much hope. Do you want me to see if she's interested in some sort of financial settlement?'

'No. Just try and make sure Gemma gets safely home, wherever that is. Probably a fucking trailer at Venice Beach.'

'She's not a bad mother. You know that. She may be a little weird, but she's kind to Gemma. This lawyer says if you can snatch Gemma at your end you can probably keep her as long as you like, because the courts always favour the home country.'

'I'm waiting for the police to call. They're watching all flights.'

'She's going to LA via Dallas. Tell them that. Magda had no idea when she was supposed to arrive.'

'Typical.'

I called the police. I gave them the flight details. While they relayed them to Gatwick, I held on.

'Good news, sir. We've arrested a man. The police at Gatwick had already spotted him. You had better get down there as soon as you can.'

By the time I got to Gatwick, they had released Larry the chauffeur. He and Gemma were in the air for Dallas. A senior policeman took me to a small, bare room.

'He had committed no crime, sir. He had a sworn statement, properly notarised, from the child's mother asking him to pick up the little girl. And copies of the court orders. You were late returning her to the United States, sir. We checked the airline reservations. Her mother was beside herself with worry, apparently.'

'And Gemma. What did she say?'

'She looked happy enough, sir. The girls brought her a little present while we were questioning Mr Larry Agnello. She said she wanted to go home to her mother.'

'You don't know what you've done.'

'Sir, it is always difficult in these disputes about custody. But my advice is, next time you accuse people of kidnap, be more careful.'

'What do you call it? This Larry took her away without a word. I call that kidnap. I had been trying for ten days to find her mother.'

'I'm really sorry, sir. It went to the highest level. It was thought best to let her go back.'

'Couldn't you have waited until I spoke to her?'

'She's very small, sir. She seemed quite happy to be going home. The plane was held up nearly twenty minutes as it was. I've got small children myself.'

He was telling me that we were both part of the human herd, and that as far as he was concerned, that was that.

I stumbled back to the Mercedes. Some small boys were looking at it, peering into the exotic interior. On the back seat was Gemma's pink and green rucksack which I had packed with her teddy and blanket. What would Bettelheim make of these discarded things?

I drove home again. In the course of the journey the stubborn fish smells emerged from the heating system. And through the rain on the windscreen I saw shoals of mirror carp, swimming in unison.

CHAPTER NINETEEN

Her tutor, Tresillian, had a theory. It was that Stubbs was influenced by the notion of the sublime, advanced by Edmund Burke. Victoria had difficulty distinguishing between Burke, Locke, Berkeley, Hume and others of the same time. Tresillian said that Burke had challenged the idea that beauty could only be pursued through classical forms. Burke believed that the sublime and the beautiful were different. Tresillian was very familiar with these abstract concepts; he moved more easily in this atmosphere than in the terrestrial realm, where he encountered difficulties. He could place every picture in the Tate neatly in the history of ideas.

Tresillian had more difficulty directing the Tate's wholesome fare into his mouth. A lot of his egg and cress sandwich came out again at the corners of his mouth. His attempts to recycle his lunch were disastrous. Victoria wondered how someone who spoke like this – a seedy Plato in a paisley bow tie – could eat like a child in a high chair. Then she wondered if there was perhaps some connection. Still, when you looked at Stubbs, armed with this new information, you could see that the lion and horse pictures were meant to stir up all sorts of pleasurable emotions, including terror, as an introduction to the sublime.

This notion also accounted for some of the backgrounds in Stubbs's paintings, said Tresillian, in one of those leaps with which he bounded from crag to lofty crag, and to his decline in popularity. Victoria could not follow the connection.

Tresillian kept asking her to dinner at his flat. She had used up her excuses. She had to tell him that because of her boyfriend, she could not go to his flat alone.

'Well, bring your boyfriend, that would be delightful,' he said. 'I'll ask some chums. Come tomorrow.'

The next morning Victoria approached Mike.

'Mike, will you come with me to dinner with my tutor?'

'Whatsis name? Peregrine Fauntleroy Massingberd?'

'Something like that.'

'No.'

'For God's sake, Mike, I helped you out with that girl from the TV department. He's only my tutor for another six weeks.'

'All you did was tell her we were getting married.'

'Exactly. All you have to do is come to dinner with Tresillian and pretend to be my boyfriend.'

'Tresillian. Fuck me. OK. It sounds good for a laugh.'

'I doubt it.'

Mike was leafing restlessly through his pile of magazines.

'Bernie the American Eagle actor called. 'E's a fruitcake. 'Ow did we get lumbered with 'im?'

'Our masters ordained it. He's a typical Londoner, according to them.'

'Typical old fart vintage 1947 if you ask me. Anyway he wants to come in and discuss the script. He wants a script conference. Those were his very words.'

'A script conference? What does he think this is, the Royal Shakespeare?'

'I told him you were in charge of the script. He's coming by later. He is in a play this afternoon. *Matinée*, don'tcher know. Unfortunately I'm going out to lunch. I wish I could put it off. What a shame.'

'You are such a little shit. I suppose for the next six months I'm going to hear nothing but how you went to dinner with Tresillian as a huge favour whenever you want something. Who is doing the stills at the Gravetyes'?'

'I've got a new guy called Lysenko. He's Russian. Black and white only, but he's great.'

'Good choice. Helping glasnost too. I wonder if a black and white trout is as evocative as a brown trout? Still, that's just my personal opinion. As you say, I'm only a humble wordsmith.'

'And art lover. Cheers. See you about three-thirty, four o'clockish.'

Victoria looked at her watch. It was ten-thirty.

'Where are you going to lunch? New York?'

'No. I'm going out to the Riverbank. It's a champagne launch of fifty pictures by famous photographers to save endangered species. Something like that.'

Victoria sat down at her table. She tried to write the copy for the next ad, about Lock's the hatter in St James's, where Tim was supposed to have his headgear made. She thought, instead, of her mother. When Victoria told her the news that Miles had left her money in a drawer, she burst into tears. Her good opinion of Miles had been vindicated.

'You are far too quick to find fault,' said her mother. 'I just could not believe he would deliberately not pay. Everybody goes through a rough patch from time to time.'

'He says he's going to be murdered soon.'

'Have you spoken to him?'

'Of course. That's how I knew he had left your money.'

'Where is he?'

'In an opium den in Hong Kong by the sound of him.'

'Oh, Victoria. Why did he say that?'

'I don't know. He sounded drunk.'

'Jet lag can have some strange effects. I was reading about businessmen who cross too many time zones. It affects their judgement.'

'That's what I told him. But I didn't mean it. I think he's flipped his lid.'

'What do you mean?'

'I think he's having paranoid delusions.'

'I knew he was in trouble.'

It was snowing outside in the square. It was falling heavily, so that her view seemed to be through a lace curtain, but it was not sticking. The moment it hit the ground it vanished. There were Christmas trees in windows, on the outside of buildings and in the Rolls Royce showrooms. In the falling snow the lights twinkled. The snow lent a deceptive perspective. The lights might have been from a distant village.

She wrote: '*Since 1676 Lock and Co. have been making hats for some of the most notable heads in Britain. Crowned heads . . .'* Her mother was in love with Miles. *'Notable heads'* was not quite right. How about *'distinguished heads'*? Reception called before she could grapple successfully with the problem.

'There's a gentleman here for you, Victoria, a Mr Koppel.'

'Gentleman' was a clear warning from reception.

'Yes, I know him. Ask him to come up. I'll meet him at the lift.'

Bernie emerged beaming from the lift into the marble lobby. He was wearing a bright red sweater over mustard yellow checked trousers. He was carrying his short brown coat, but his rakish hat sat on his head, suppressing, with only partial success, the volcano beneath.

'Morning. Very nice of you to see me at such short notice,' he said.

'That's OK,' said Victoria. 'I just have to tell you that the script has had the blessing of the people in New York.'

'No problem,' said Bernie. 'Don't worry.'

She led him out of the lobby. He smiled at everybody and wished them a good morning. Some of the elegant young people passing by were taken aback for a moment. Bernie was large and awkwardly packaged. He trod the marble like someone new to ice-skating. Victoria led him to her little nook. She was glad Mike had gone out; Bernie seemed to absorb most of the available space.

'Matinée today,' he said with a shrug of his shoulders, which suggested the burdens of the actor's calling.

'What is it?' asked Victoria.

'It's a Christmas show. Traditional. Trudi Bastin is in it. Lovely show.'

'Right, what's the problem with the script?'

'Problem? Who said anything about a problem? Don't get me wrong, there's no problem with the words, none at all.'

Bernie produced one slim page from somewhere in his overcoat. It was tattered and covered with notes, in red and blue. Then he fished about for a pen in his pockets. Victoria handed him two of Mike's Ultrafine Pentels.

'Here. Keep them.'

'Right,' said Bernie. 'Thanks very much. Hot in here isn't it, considering it's snowing outside?'

Bernie did not appear to have any sort of familiarity with central heating. He held up the script.

'I was just thinking, you know about the character.'

Outside, the snow was now beginning to gather in drifts at the base of the plane trees. Bernie removed his hat carefully and placed it on the floor next to the low chair in which he was sitting. The chair was not designed for Bernie, any more than a bidet would have been. It gave him a hunched, uncomfortable appearance, but this did not deter him.

'The thing is. I was thinking that the character could be made a lot more jollier.'

'I'm all for that. What do you suggest?'

'I think we should do it all to music. A musical. So instead of just saying 'at the Tower of London' and so on, the character – that's me – would sing it. I've written some music for it already. All we need to do is make it rhyme. You won't have no problem with that, a gorgeous intelligent gel like you, willyer? Have you got a piano here?' ('Pee-enner 'ere?')

'No we haven't. Why don't you hum it or something?'

'Right.'

Bernie moved. It took him a while to get his centre of gravity up and forward enough to stand up. He sang in a style that had probably been popular before the war, with plenty of handwringing and features which spoke (or sang) volumes.

'Wotcher fink?'

Bernie was sweating after his sixty-second performance. People were looking in at them from the neighbouring spaces.

'Lovely tune. Did you write it?'

'Matter of fact, it's not an original composition. It's a song I used to hear in me childhood. I've adapted it for the theme in my musical.'

'You've written a musical?'

'Yah. It's called *Buzz Bomb*. It's about the East End of London and the war. What people are looking for is not all the problems and politics, but the good things. Know what I mean? That's what the war was. Funny that, innit? Our finest hour.'

Oh fuck, thought Victoria. Tim had warned her about Bernie.

'The thing is, Vicky – you don't mind me calling you that? – the thing is Americans, begging their pardon, need to see London a little differently than what it is normally.'

Bernie was into his stride now.

'They want to see the real London. I'm not saying London hasn't changed. Of course it has. But people don't change. The basics is still the same. The way I see my character, he will convey that over. The real London.'

Bernie plunged onwards. Victoria was aware of a faintly briny whiff coming from him as he spoke. It was not unpleasant. He was like some sea creature, a manatee or a dugong, which had clambered up a muddy bank to communicate with her. He sang his song again, and she found herself putting the words into rhyme, under his direction, while he beat time with a large freckled hand. His hand reminded her of a flipper. The melanin spots had congregated on his brow and hairy ear lobes as well. They were the first rainspots of mortality. Victoria was always on the alert for signs of deterioration in her own physical aspect, but Bernie was in another league in this regard.

'You're wasted in this game,' said Bernie, gesturing around the lavish offices. Victoria followed his gesture. It did all look a little self-congratulatory when compared with the heroic struggles Bernie was outlining. The struggles were no less than the triumph of the human spirit over adversity.

'You've got a talent for lyrics. Rodgers and Hammerstein. What a team.'

It only took about half an hour. Bernie sang the completed work. Victoria felt as if she was auditioning for something. His idea was that he would sing the song right through, but appear in different places – 'locations as we call them' – in different costume. 'Nothing wrong with the costume. Musta cost a bomb.' He had one further request.

'Can we get my old mate Kid Blumenberg into the film? 'E would love that. He fought Maxie Schmelling you know. Any chance?'

The way Bernie put it, all the other stuff was settled and this would just be the icing on the cake.

''E doesn't get out much. Matter of fact I took 'im up

Oxford Street and bought 'im a new jumper. Bought meself one too, wotcher fink?'

'It's nice and bright,' said Victoria.

The red sweater was already showing signs of wool fatigue at the neck and the elbows, but no ordinary raiment could contain Bernie Koppel.

'Bernie, I'm prepared to fax your suggestions to New York, but don't hold your breath.'

Victoria wondered what they would think in New York. They might go for it, particularly if she told them the music rights were free. She would have to fix some kind of test recording for Bernie. It was true Bernie had not changed the script that much. There were still five scenes: the Tower of London, Billingsgate Market, the Prospect of Whitby pub, Horse Guards and the Royal Hospital, Chelsea. But Bernie had hijacked every scene. This was Bernie's story, writ small. Sixty seconds was scarcely adequate for the significance and the symbolism with which he was endowing it. The audience were to understand that Bernie had lived the triumphs and disasters of London. This might be the weak point, thought Victoria; they might not care. Jacques Brel, Charles Aznavour, Bud Flanagan, Eddie Cantor, Sinatra and so on had represented a whole city, but they had arrived gradually at their place in the public's esteem. Bernie's greatest success to date had been the Black and White Minstrel Show in 1965, which he had played entirely incognito inside a bank robber's face mask. Victoria did not know how to go about making clear the distinction between a music-hall leftover and a public icon.

Victoria looked at Bernie sitting hunched in his sway-backed chair. He had come to a halt. There was a hush for a moment. The barnacled old sea creature had had an idea. It was so good it had stopped him short.

'That's it,' he said. 'I've got it.'

'What?'

'A transformation scene. Just like in the pantomime – which comes from the commedia dell'arte originally – the transformation 'appens as I sing in each scene.'

Victoria had come to a stop herself on the words 'commedia dell'arte'. The way Bernie pronounced them she thought he was talking about another old friend, perhaps a retired boxer or fishmonger. When Bernie rose excitedly from the chair for the second time, his seaweedy, herring vapour seemed to have grown stronger. He explained to Victoria, with kindness, the nature of the transformation scene. As Bernie sings, London is transformed from Dickensian to modern day, from midsummer to midwinter, from day to night.

'They can do anything with special effects. I'll be in each scene with the backings and the lighting and the costume changing. Magic. It'll be magic.'

Oh shit, thought Victoria, they might just go for this.

'It'll be a case of the more it's changed the more it stays the same,' said Bernie. 'As the froggies say.'

By the time Mike came back from his lunch and the first showing of the conservation pictures (all done on an expenses only basis), Victoria had spoken to New York and arranged a music recording.

'How did you get on with the old codger?'

'We made a few changes.'

'Oh yes? Do tell.'

'How was the conservation binge?'

'It was good. Great pictures. Fuck me I had no idea so many things was on the way out. Ring-tailed lemurs, the Mauritian pink pigeon, the pygmy hippo, the Asian lion. You name it, it's on its bike. So what are the changes?'

'Well, just a minor one to start with. It's a musical now.'

'Oh, that's nice.'

Mike's breath was heavily laden with expensive drink.

'Yuh. And it's all transformations. The commedia dell'arte and so on.'

'You're having me on.'

'No. Serious. While you were saving the pink pigeon I sent it off to New York.'

'We're going to get fired.'

'You're clean. You weren't even on the premises at the time of the offence. In fact you're not on the premises very much, ever.'

'Don't get heavy.'

'All you do is go to lunch and talk crap to fucking

photographers. You don't do a damn thing yourself except act as some sort of self-appointed arbiter of taste in your silly arse, yobbo clothes. You're pissed as a newt most of the time and you're a pain in the bum and I can't stand another five minutes sharing an office with you.'

'I suppose this means we won't be going to Tresillian's little wine and cheese do this evening? What a pity.'

'God, you're a little wanker. Now get a load of this script. I want some pictures fast. We need an animatic by tomorrow for New York.'

Mike was fiddling with his Magic Markers and Pentels, perhaps counting them.

'Jesus,' he said, 'this office smells of herring. What did you have for lunch?'

Tresillian's flat was on the top floor of a huge house in Pimlico. The hallway was damp. On a shelf below a tarnished mirror lay some junk mail and demands from Telecom and British Gas to departed tenants. A plastic over-carpet had been laid to protect the decaying carpet underneath. A racing bike rested against a radiator. The hallway was a dead zone, a DMZ, where the communal odours, the misdirected mail and the unwanted telephone directories congregated. The tenants never congregated. These huge houses were as hermetic as Japanese capsule hotels; the hallways were a limbo where the tenants flitted past each other uneasily. Victoria had lived in houses like this. She was living in one now with her sister as a matter of fact. The hallways filled her with gloom. In one house where she had lived, the tenants below – he was a news photographer and she was a demonstrator – had violent fights almost every night, yet in the hallway they always passed by shyly. Even when she came by one day with a puffy eye and a cut nose, the girl smiled demurely at Victoria. The hallway was neutral territory; what you did in your own flat was not acknowledged there.

'It's only five floors up,' said Victoria. Mike always claimed to be a fitness fanatic, yet Victoria had never seen any evidence for this claim.

'Shit. OK, let's go. I'll do the first abseil,' he said.

He was wearing one of his capacious suits, in gin-bottle

green. As they mounted the first flight of stairs, the front door sprang open. They looked back. These were Tresillian's friends. The man was wearing a cloak and bicycle clips over a velvet suit of dark burgundy and the woman was wearing a blanket.

'Quick, get moving,' said Victoria, hoping she was mistaken, but knowing she was not.

By the time they reached Tresillian's front door, they were both panting. Tresillian was flustered too. He was cooking and it was not going well. He kissed Victoria inexpertly, so that his purplish lips landed just below her cheekbone. He shook Mike's hand vigorously.

'Ah, the lucky man,' he said.

Behind Mike the other guests had now arrived. There was a small scrum on the landing. As Tresillian leant forward to kiss the woman in what now appeared to Victoria to be a hairy curtain, the door of his flat clicked shut. There were five of them standing cramped together on the landing while inside the cracked wheat was boiling over.

The man in the cape began to laugh. His teeth were not good. (The men in the art world had very poor skins too. Victoria wondered if there was something turbulent and restive in the blood which erupted from time to time, the way eczema affected certain people under stress.) Tresillian laughed too, but his laugh lacked conviction. He was wearing a butcher's apron over his generous new corduroys. Corduroys were not a good choice because they emphasised his old-fashioned body: narrow shoulders and heavy thighs and bottom. The cords had already lost their spruceness; they looked like a field flattened by a storm.

The lights suddenly went out.

'Just a minute,' said Tresillian, 'the switch doesn't work on this floor.'

He set off down the stairs to find the press switch, but tripped and fell heavily in the gloom far below. The half-introduced stood awkwardly in the dark, terrified of touching in the confined space. The light came on again. From some floors below, Tresillian shouted:

'I'll hold it; can you get the door open?'

'How do you suggest we do that? asked Victoria.

'Hold on. I'll come up.'

Before he had reached them, the light went out again. There was nervous laughter.

'The television chaps use a credit card,' said the man in the cape. 'They sort of slip it into the lock. Unfortunately I don't have any.'

Mike was not going to produce his new Golden Eagle card for this purpose, Victoria felt sure.

'Fuck me. Stand back,' said Mike. In the dark they shuffled obediently. There was a thump and the door flew open.

'You're a genius. Quick let me get to the kitchen. Something's burning.'

'This can't be for real. They're all fucking loopy,' said Mike. 'I'm going 'ome.'

'No please, Mike, stay until we've had dinner.'

'Dinner. You must be joking. It's like a baboon's armpit in 'ere. You could get salmonella.'

There were tribal rugs and swags of dry flowers and dry leaves which looked like the remains of a *fête champêtre*. Pictures were stacked around the walls or lying unframed in heaps on the floor. The man in the cape, Haldane, had been here before. He found some wine and handed it round. The woman in the curtaining was also an art lecturer. Her name was Ferelyth Ffrancon-Headley.

'That's a tongue twister,' said Mike. 'Fucking hell, I bet you get called all sorts.'

'Everybody had a drink?' asked Tresillian emerging from the kitchen. 'I'm doing something Hungarian this evening. It was going to be Serbian chicken with cracked wheat, but I'm afraid the cracked wheat caught fire.'

'Never mind,' said Victoria. 'I love your flat.'

'It's a bit of a mess,' said Tresillian. 'I'm very behind.'

'It's been a mess since nineteen sixty-three,' said Ferelyth. Her voice was surprisingly light considering her ravaged face. No question of it, a love of art worked its way out to the features. Haldane looked like a gypsy guitarist who had overdone the absinthe for many years, with long, wiry grey hair and rather crowded features, competing for space as in an Ibo carving. He spoke with that slight lisp that Victoria had come to know.

'Lovely suit,' said Ferelyth to Mike. 'Interesting colour.'

211

'And your, what you call it, looks nice and warm,' said Mike.

'It's a traditional Moroccan wrap which I adapted as a dress. Very practical. Angora.'

Tresillian was standing some way back behind what Victoria thought must be a camel saddle, swaying slightly, a bottle of red wine in his hand. He appeared to have no idea what to do next.

'Nuts anybody? There are some delicious nuts,' he suddenly shouted.

'Don't say it,' said Victoria to Mike.

Ferelyth was holding a small canvas to the light. She put it down abruptly.

'Tresillian, the Johns must go back to the gallery. When are you writing your report?'

'Tomorrow. Next week, at the latest.'

Mike stood up.

'Won't be a moment,' he whispered loudly to Victoria. 'The only way I'm going to get through this is to shove something up me nose. Hold the fort, old girl. Super party what?' He nudged Ferelyth playfully as he went by.

The dinner was eventually spread over the table in haphazard fashion. The food was probably Hungarian, but vital ingredients appeared to have been omitted. Victoria wondered if this was not the motif of the evening.

'How long have you two been together?' asked Tresillian.

Mike put his arm round Victoria. His mood had changed.

'Nearly four years. I dunno. It's passed in a blur,' he said.

'Are you in the fast-moving world of advertising too?'

'Yeah.'

'What do you do?'

'I'm an art director.'

'Art director.'

Tresillian sampled the words like an Arab taking snuff. Haldane actually did take snuff, from a small ornate box. Mike looked at it hopefully.

'Art director,' said Tresillian again. 'What does an art director do?'

He practically sang a little chorale with the words 'art director'.

'Art director is an American term originally. It means the person responsible for the visual side of an advertisement,' said Victoria quickly.

'Is it well paid?' asked Tresillian.

'Not too bad,' said Mike. 'Can't complain. What about your game?'

'Not very good, I'm afraid. *Ars artia artis.*'

'You what?' asked Mike.

'Snuff?' asked Haldane.

Mike looked startled for a moment.

'Oh yeah. Love some. That Serbian chicken was magic. Pity the cracked wheat went up in smoke, but that's it with cooking, innit? It's a lottery. Shit this is powerful. What's it supposed to do?'

Mike's eyes were streaming.

'Are you an art director too?' Ferelyth asked Victoria.

'No, I'm a copywriter.'

'Another world. We're so terribly insular, I'm afraid. We know very little about what's really going on.'

'I suppose everybody just sees part of the picture,' said Victoria. She felt a little let down. These people had not risen above the mundane anxieties she had been trying to escape.

'I suppose so,' said Ferelyth gloomily.

Later, in the hallway as they were preparing to leave, Haldane tried to direct Victoria's hand on to his cock somewhere under the Carpathian cloak. It seemed harmless enough to her.

'Now, now, Haldane,' she said, 'You've had too much snuff.'

Mike insisted on holding her hand as they walked towards the river to find a taxi.

'Four years. It's been marvellous darling. Absolutely top-hole. Lovely dinner. Super chicken. Fabulous snuff. Lovely chums.'

'Put a sock in it for Chrissakes.'

'Art director. What's that? American term. Serbian chicky wicky, Victoria? You look lovely, like a Titian, tonight.'

'Very funny.'

'I enjoyed it, honest. It's not every day you get invited to meet the inmates. But I think the camel blankets had fleas.'

The river was low. In the beaded lights off Albert Bridge they could see the mud of the riverbank. A supermarket trolley was lying there. She wished she were walking here with Tim.

'Do you want to come back to my place, Victoria? asked Mike.

'No thanks. It wouldn't be a good idea.'

'No problem. Just thought it would be matey.'

'You're a sweetie.'

When Victoria got back to Fulham and was fumbling for the keys, Miles stepped from behind the hedge which separated the small paved front garden from the street. In the half-light coming through the coloured glass panels of the door, Victoria could see that something was amiss. He had a look her mother had worn for months after Lionel left. It was a look of vegetable blankness.

'Miles. What's the matter?'

'The young lion. He's going to kill me.'

CHAPTER TWENTY

My place had the melancholy of a swimming pool which has been drained, or a seaside resort in winter, or a cinema left derelict. And outside, London was crouched, a primitive and toxic growth, clinging to the earth's surface like a melanoma. Some cities have been flung down on the bare plains like grains of wheat; some have vaulted skywards off the backs of naked capitalism; some have been planned on aesthetic principles; some have been drawn up by bureaucrats. London had grown organically and stealthily. Like an agaric or a boletus. Like Simba Cochrane's hair. The damp, the mouldering brickwork, the greasy roads and the dripping trees; the very quality of the pavements, seemed to me perfect for the evolution of fungate life. The civic symbol should be a newt. (The newt – aka salamander – has quite a respectable symbolic pedigree.)

The city oppressed me. Its sprawl was menacing. In the face of it I felt alien. I had spent almost ten years here and I had made a little corner for myself, but now I looked at Londoners as I did when I first arrived. I felt again my incredulity that Londoners could speak the way they do. They must have a motive for garrotting their vowels. Nobody could speak like this by accident. *No chance. You must be fucking joking mate.*

I had landed up in here by chance. Now it seemed as whimsical as settling in Minsk or Reykjavik. What had I seen here to hold me? As the trees in the park jostled each other in a genteel but determined manner – like travellers on the Underground – I felt London stirring menacingly. This was how science fiction gets a start, I thought. This is how Jung got interested in dreams. It was clear to me that you could adopt these modes of thought all too easily when you were emotionally disturbed. The big picture, the big metaphor, became very attractive. By popping in from the real world for a quick practical on how-it-is, Larry the chauffeur had made me see my life in London more clearly: I *was* the silly arse in the American Eagle ads. What an illusion!

And another thing: who are Londoners anyway? If you looked at it in a certain light, there weren't any. Nobody I know is actually from London. Only Bernie and Cochrane, and they belonged not to London as it existed now, but to a London so remote it might never have existed. Who really believes now that bombs fell and sirens sounded and St Paul's was in flames? Only old people with unreliable memories.

With Gemma asleep in the next room, or listening to my stories attentively, ready to catch the significance (I had been morbidly taken by Bettelheim) London had seemed to me a place where I was taking root. With Gemma gone, snatched by Larry the chauffeur, London had become completely foreign. Sometimes you see an expatriate speaking of lost Bosnia or Latvia or some other half-remembered state and you think, no matter how well he speaks English: what a quaint, unrealistic old fellow. He is inhaling our air yet exhaling the air of a foreign country. Everything he eats and breathes and touches is metamorphosed into something foreign. Look at the way he breaks bits of bread and drowns them in his pea soup; he holds his cup like a bowl of goulash; he reads *The Times* with close attention for the occasional references to his lost homeland; he recasts every political event into its significance for the restoration of King Casimir or Prince Albin. He looks at the Thames and sees the Vistula or the Lodl. But we don't give a monkey's fuck (as we say in London). Now I felt as if I had joined the company of chess-playing, bowel-troubled, furrow-browed outsiders. London had given me a poke in the eye. London was completely indifferent to me.

I finally heard from my brother a few days later. Gemma had arrived safely and was living with Magda in a friend's house in San Diego. 'She likes the zoo there apparently.'

I could imagine her making visits to the zoo to pass the time while her mother investigated the intricate relationship between aromas and spirituality, a connection that had been wilfully overlooked for far too long. As I was thinking these thoughts, my phone rang and it was Gemma; she said they had lions in the zoo and fish. This was her big news. My voice would not come out at once. Finally it lurched:

'I hear it's a nice zoo, darling?'

'Where's the daddy lion? Is he in the jungle?'

'No news yet,' I croaked.

An unfamiliar voice came on the phone.

'Hi, this is Lawrence Agnello. I just want to assure you that Gemma is just fine and I empathise with you if you were upset or disturbed by the action we were obliged to take.'

'Mr Agnello, I don't know your precise relationship to my ex-wife and I don't care,' (which of course was a lie) 'but just let me assure you that I care very deeply about Gemma and what happens to her.'

'Sure, sure. I can relate to that, no problem. Message received. You want to speak to her tomorrow? Sure, we'll call you tomorrow, won't we honey? We're just kinda getting settled in again. Getting our feet on the ground. You can say goodbye now, Gemma.'

I called my brother and asked him to check out this Larry Agnello. In my imagination I was becoming dangerously assertive, but in reality I would have to rely on my brother's good sense and know-how to achieve anything. I did not even know how he had found out where Gemma was living.

The hayloft was drained; it was like the dry pans of the Kalahari I had seen, hard to believe there had ever been life here. My essence had certainly dribbled away. I had forwarded Gemma's things to LA by Federal Express. They barely made one large parcel, but there was a lot packed in there none the less.

I wanted Agnello sewn up in a bag and thrown into the moat of the lion enclosure at San Diego Zoo. When he marshalled my daughter to say her goodbyes, my blood began to slow ominously and I was shaking as the phone went dead. He and Magda were in cahoots to torture me. Agnello was now rationing my conversations with Gemma. Clearly he had not been apprised of all the facts in the case. He had been recruited from the decent, manly world of chauffeuring to bring some order in to the *Sturm und Drang* of Magda's world, and no doubt he was getting a leg over as a reward for his troubles.

Of course his view of the facts is somewhat different to mine. What he sees is some pretentious jerk who has got lucky writing arty-farty pieces for *Manhattan*, who wants his daughter when it suits him in his adopted home of London. Just what Gemma doesn't need right now. I'm not one of your writer types, but I believe I know what kids need – their feet on the ground. He and Magda are concerned that my lifestyle, as Agnello calls it, is not providing the stable environment a small child should be exposed to. Magda is trying to put together the pieces of her life right now, and the last thing she needs at this time is hassle, this disruptive influence. I have probably begun to enjoy life in the public eye. Who wouldn't? But look, he's just a guy who has tried to make a living in limousine service, you can ignore everything he's saying, but he prides himself that he's got his feet on the ground. Magda thinks maybe they should cut down on the visits, you know, until she's more settled.

I haven't had this conversation with Larry Agnello yet, but I know it's coming. The puzzling aspect is why Magda would nominate Agnello as her spokesperson. She has never shown any reticence about speaking her mind before. In fact, in all our dealings, Gemma has been her trump card, usually played early in any negotiation. Agnello's voice worries me too. He may be thinking vile, aggressive thoughts about me, but they are not in his voice. Admittedly I have heard only a few sentences, but they are enough. It is one of those carefully modulated, very reasonable voices which chorus all around the offices and banks and marketing enterprises of America. These are the voices of the brain dead. They are the voices of people who believe that language should be deployed like muzak, and for the same purposes. Agnello is not a chauffeur at all, but a caring individual. God knows, this kind of crap has been parodied often enough, but I feel the tide of empty verbiage rising to ceiling height every time I visit my old home. Soon there will only be a few old fools sitting on the roof with their furniture, marooned by the floodwaters of inanity. And this reasonable monster has his hooks into my daughter. He wants to keep her feet on the ground: i.e. he wants to lobotomise her.

I enquired at Moorfields Hospital about cataract operations for the Chief's wife. The British High Commission in Nairobi was trying to find her and arrange a flight. Simba Cochrane's caretaker called to say that he was going back into hospital for tests.

'I don't like the sound of tests. I've never 'ad no bleedin' tests in me life,' she said. Her voice was as harsh as a parrot's. 'Mr Cochrane says you told 'im 'e 'as a daughter in Africa.'

'Yes, he has.'

So it had registered with Cochrane after all.

'What colour would she be, black or 'alf-an'-'alf?'

'I don't know.'

'Probably an 'alf-an'-'alf. I done 'is laundry again.'

'Right, I'll send you some money.'

'That's very kind, thank you.'

I would have liked to see Victoria but she was busy with Bernie: She said it was some sort of musical now and they were auditioning the chorus of washerwomen and beefeaters. My ads, the up-market ones, have been postponed. I will, however, be photographed catching a trout, eating kedgeree at the Connaught and trying on a fishing hat at Lock's. Fish have moved up-market, the way they used to move up-stream.

My thoughts were disordered. Outside, the park was drying off. The timid natives were emerging diffidently to air their children. A man from the Foreign Office rang to say that the High Commission in Nairobi had located the wife of the Chief. They were applying for a passport for her. This might take some time.

'Bit of a shambles out there at the moment apparently,' he said. 'We'll be writing, but I just thought you would like to know.'

'How long does a passport take in Kenya?'

'How long's a piece of string?'

Past experience told me that the Foreign Office specialised in this type of smart alec, *broad of mind, broad of behind*.

* * *

I also sent money to Orlando, Fla. to the Circus Hall of Fame. I paid the full whack so that Simba Cochrane could be a life member and honorary vice-president, with all amenities. In a shop in Islington I purchased a lion skin, laid on green baize. The head lay flat, with crude glass eyes. It was a young male. The price of lion skins has dropped dramatically, as you might guess. I felt as shifty as a man who has just bought his mistress a snow-leopard coat. Paralleling the proliferation of lions in zoos, there is a surplus of lion mementoes. The trophies have accumulated over the years. In one memorable season an American sportsman shot seventy lions in Kenya. Karen Blixen killed a lion with Denis Finch-Hatton's gun as a 'declaration of love'. I, however, stuffed the lion skin, pale with age, hastily into the trunk of the Mercedes, thinking one of my favourite thoughts: how quickly things change. History has gone into high speed. Only a few years ago you could have shot a lion and hung its head on the wall and shown it to your friends. Better still if you could make an attractive arrangement with a couple of rhino heads and a zebra skin. Now the government of Europe can turn on the sale of deodorants. A man with a lion skin is about as welcome in polite society as a child molester.

I left the scene of the crime and made for Jubilee Buildings. The streets were, like my thoughts, in uproar. It looked as though someone was strip-mining the pavements. No street in London is free of building and excavation works. Under the old streets miles of plastic tubing and orange cabling are being stuffed. God knows what goes on down there. I must write about subterranean London. I must write something soon, but I cannot. I am paralysed by my loss. I can only think about how events are spiralling out of control and London's innards are being stuffed with brightly coloured pasta, and how Cochrane's caretaker knew a woman who had sold a haddock ('an 'addock') to Charles Dickens, and what a pleasant surprise it will be for Cochrane to come out of hospital and find his lion skin, a Circus Hall of Fame statuette and certificate in place. I hope I haven't been too impulsive. Quite a lot of people don't come back from a visit to a London hospital. - -

The ground floor of Jubilee Buildings, except for one

window at the front belonging to the caretaker, was boarded up. Nothing could have been more expressly designed to tell the world that the knackered soul of Jubilee Buildings had flown the coop. The caretaker was perversely delighted by this proof that the pace of change had speeded up.

'Bleedin' dump. They start movin' us out after New Year. Not a moment too soon if you ask me.'

'What about the people on the ground floor?'

I imagined them boarded up like mushrooms in the dark until the festive season was over.

'Nobody, only me on the ground floor (flaw-er). Only me. Mrs Muggins. Too dangerous. People was throwing (frowing) lighted matches in the winders and pouring beer in and that. Someone even peed in one winder. I don't never go in the front room at night no more. Wotcher got there then?'

'It's a Christmas present for Mr Cochrane.'

'I don't fink e'll see Christmas, if you ask my opinion. What is it?'

'It's a rug. Can you let me into his flat?'

'Come on then, I'll give yer an 'and.'

'That's all right. I can manage.'

I didn't want her with her budgie-scombered housecoat and her thinning, world-weary hair, watching me unroll the lion skin. She would think I was crazy and with some justification. But she insisted.

The flat, Six D, released a powerful gust of mildew as she opened the door. Never mind Cochrane, the lion skin might not see Christmas.

'Thanks for letting me in,' I said, looking around as if I might take some time weighing up the various options of perspective before laying down the rug.

'Come on then. Let's 'ave a look at it.'

I untied the string and unrolled the lion skin in the available space.

'Fuck my old boots,' she said. 'Excuse my French. Is that 'im?'

'That's the one,' I said.

'It's 'uge.'

'The male can weigh nearly five hundred pounds,' I said, quoting Schaller.

I shifted it around.

'If the 'ospital don't kill him, this'll do it,' she said cackling. 'Wait till 'e sees that.'

The lion lay in the small, condemned flat. It looked best with its head and the sightless eyes, like scuffed marbles, turned towards the door.

'Do you want to come in for a cup of tea?' asked the caretaker.

'Not today, thank you. I've got to get back to do some work, Mrs . . . What is your name? I'm so sorry I never asked?'

'Doris. Doris Pollymoss.'

'Pollymoss' was a name right out of Dickens. Londoners even have their own names, which never penetrate into the community at large.

'Next time,' she said. 'It makes no difference to me.'

As I drove home I wondered why I had bought the lion skin. Who cares? You could make too much of this business of operating strictly on the rational level. I might try aromatherapy myself.

There was a message on my machine from the American Ambassador's social secretary. I had forgotten to reply to a dinner invitation to meet the Vice-President who was on a private visit to Europe. I accepted for myself and my 'partner'. I called the hospital; Cochrane was not in any danger, they said. They seemed to be surprised that anyone should be interested.

I wrote a piece about Christmas in London. I started with the cheeses in Paxton and Whitfield and moved on via the boy sopranos of the Chapel Royal to Bernie's pantomime, but my heart was not in it.

My room could not support life. The air was thin and grated in the lungs. Anyway, the festive season was as attractive to me as another dinner (I guessed) to Vice-President Quayle. The annual dusting-off of Dickensian sentiment was a sham in a city inhabited by Bangladeshis and Pakistanis and tourists. Aliens, like me. Actually it was done for us. Fortnum and Mason tricked out like a scene from Disneyland; Harrods owned by an Arab; Selfridges by Sears. We were all hopelessly caught up in an illusion straight from a Victorian Christmas card, a skating party; a transformation scene, as favoured by Bernie. If the snow fell it turned to slush; nobody has skated on the Thames in a thousand years; anyone who could afford it was either in the country or skiing; yet London, like an old whore, donned the clapped out threads, applied the garish make-up and puckered the tripe skin around her mouth hopefully. Like Scrooge, I thought: Keep Christmas your way, and let me keep it mine.

Over at the zoo they were sprucing the place up too. Crowds were thin at this time of year. They were using the lull to build more modish attractions. Chaka's former companions would be outside; lions thrive in the cold. I saw Chaka sniffing the dry air of Africa and stepping out into the savannah. I saw him ambling off towards the distant hills, his huge paws for the first time feeling the dry and individual grains of sand and the cropped stubble of Africa, his nose filling with the intoxicating scent of a million wildebeest, and his mane ruffled by a dry wind which had combed a thousand miles of thorn trees to reach him. But wait a minute. What's this clip-clopping, this familiar musty smell, coming towards him? It's Simba Cochrane mounted on his sturdy horse. Chaka stiffens and flattens himself in the grass, which is just the right colour to camouflage him perfectly.

Unless the Animal Liberation Front has put him on the wrong ship, for Gujarat, and he finishes up with his Asian cousins, of which only one hundred and seventy-six still exist in the wild. With his great mane and huge head he would scare them to death. Asian lions have rather small manes, like the one on Cochrane's floor waiting to greet him. My thoughts would not settle down. I was like Jung, like Gemma, like Bettelheim, trawling for significance in all the inconsequence and menace which assailed me, but having no luck at all.

That evening, Victoria and Bernie came by directly from the studio where they had been rehearsing fish porters. In the liquid world he inhabited, like a friendly whale or a benign porpoise, Bernie had heard my sonar signals and come straight over. He had come in the role of Pandarus.

'Vicky didn't want to come. No offence. She thought it would be bad manners. Bad manners. So you can't blame 'er. Isn't she a picture (pitcher)?'

'I'm really sorry,' said Victoria, standing awkwardly, perhaps unbalanced a little by the turbulence Bernie created, like a beached cetacean with the tide departing.

'I've got the night off,' he said. 'Me understudy is doing my part.'

'Understudy' is a word actors can savour. I wasn't going to spoil the fun by enquiring why the third Ugly Sister should rate an understudy these days. He was wearing a red sweater under his short brown coat. When he had taken the coat off and placed it carefully on the back of a chair, he invited me to admire the sweater. The sweater was large but it had not been made to accommodate the undisciplined frame that gave lodging to the unquenchable spirit of Bernie Koppel.

'It's new,' he said. 'I got one for the Kid in yeller.'

'It's very seasonal,' I said.

Victoria started to laugh.

'Ain't she a picture?' he asked, drawing Victoria closer with a large freckled flipper.

She was. She was wearing jeans and a smock of jungle foliage, like a small section of a Rousseau or a Gauguin.

'How is it going?' I asked.

'It's great. Bernie's music is being arranged and choreographed and the sets are being built.'

'Gawd alone knows how much it's all costing,' said Bernie cheerfully. 'Right. As soon as you've made some coffee, not too strong, I'm off. Before you can say Jack Robinson. I'm taking the Kid to a charity night.'

Little Gemma had lain here next to me with her flannel and cereal smells, her exquisite smooth skin, the warm scent of her hair, the curve of her fragile back, the long lashes of her eyes, the sweetness of her breath, the little night sighs, the alarms and whispers, and the preoccupied expressions of sleep. Next to me now lay Victoria. Her skin smelled of life itself. I wondered how long it would be – I could scarcely imagine it – before Gemma would one day be lying beside a man, her skin exhaling the vapours of life in this way, like the mist rising off a pond in winter.

Victoria's scents and aromas were now adhering to my body, so that in this regard we had become one. On my hands were the richer, more female tinctures, yet all over our bodies we had been glazed by lovemaking.

I was thinking of the quick transformation from little girl to musky woman, when Victoria woke and held my hand.

'Are you all right?' she asked.

There is a camaraderie in fucking, shared by people who have been in a car crash or through a bush war together.

'I'm fine. And you?'

CHAPTER TWENTY-ONE

Miles had visited the police station three times now. He recognised the Desk Sergeant. When he gave his name, he was waved negligently to a bench to wait; just another piece of garbage in the steady stream that flowed through here every day. The Inspector kept him waiting deliberately. When Miles was working in the City he had felt as if he were in charge of events. Now he was completely at their mercy. It was difficult to understand how this could have happened so quickly. The Sergeant had barely looked at him. He was accustomed to dealing with people who had lost control over their own destinies. A Swedish tourist came in to report a bag snatch. The Sergeant wrote down the details without enthusiasm. Over in Gothenburg they obviously did not understand how the real world worked.

Miles felt an obligation to speak to the Sergeant, to demonstrate that he was jumping to conclusions by treating him so lightly.

'Could you tell Inspector Munday that I'm a bit pushed for time?'

Miles glanced significantly at his watch as he said this. The Sergeant looked up at him wearily.

'He knows you're here. As soon as he wants you he'll let me know.'

'I can only wait a few minutes longer.'

'That's up to you.'

He did not even look at Miles as he said this. Miles had been subpoenaed to appear in court at Bilger's trial. The Inspector had expressly promised him that he would not have to appear. His statement would be enough. Miles had asked for a meeting. He waited twenty minutes before he was summoned to an interview room.

The Inspector's face was chalky. He was probably unwell in that chronic way of middle-aged Londoners. Years of poor diet and smoking and gaseous air did it to them. This condition could not be banished by a good holiday; it was pathological.

'I know what you're going to say. Don't bother. It was orders from higher up. Nobody wants Bilger to get off this one. CID is still smarting about the fish job. Really pissed off. Juries won't accept uncorroborated police evidence these days. Even unemployed Greek minicab drivers who've got nothing better to do think they're on some sort of fucking clean-up-London crusade the moment they get on a jury. It's a matter of principle. Wonderful, isn't it? And of course they never stop whingeing about the crime rate.'

'You said my statement would be enough. You said you were only going to use it to make the arrest.'

'Things have changed. I'm afraid. By the way, we need your passport.'

'What the fuck for? You can't have my passport.'

'It's for your own safety. To protect you from threats.'

'What do you mean?'

'You're a grass, son. We've got to look after you. You would be amazed how many witnesses are approached and handed plane tickets. That's no life. By midday tomorrow, latest. If anyone tries to talk to you, let me know right away.'

As Miles walked down towards Piccadilly, uncontrollable fears entered his bowels and writhed there painfully. His body had become a playground for uninvited electrical currents and chemical reactions.

Steve Bilger had asked to meet him at a club at the Angel. Now he knew why. Communications between the police and the Bilgers were very prompt. Miles went over to Gray's Inn to find James, but James had taken an unscheduled holiday in Marbella. His room at chambers was locked and the clerk spoke about him with a flat, grudging intonation. James had let him down too.

The club had the sort of glamour Miles associated with the suburbs. The girls serving the drinks were a little overweight. The extra flesh – just an extra five or ten per cent – could not quite be contained by the little ra-ra skirts and pants they wore. They were not Californian girls, that was for sure. They were Cockneys. Their legs were nourished on crisps and McDonald's and exercised only by short walks to the number 19 bus.

Steve had a very poor dress sense. He was wearing a maroon woollen jacket with thin lapels. Underneath the jacket he wore a blue nylon shirt. He looked as though his face had been worn away by the training, like a rock in a stream. His eyebrows had thickened with scar tissue and his nose was not quite aligned to the rest of his pale features.

He was affable.

'Look, mate,' he said. 'It's business. You grassed up my dad, now you owe us one.'

'You don't seem to understand. The police knew all about it long before I told them anything. I didn't even know it was drugs. I really thought it was for Thai boxing. What could I do? They had me over a barrel,' said Miles.

'You grassed, mate. You shouldner done it. Wotcher going to drink?'

The waitresses' hair was fantastic. It had vitality all of its own, independent of their heads. It was hard to believe it actually grew from their scalps. The girl who took their order – Steve had a Perrier – had hair teased upwards to give her more height.

' 'Ello, Steve, 'ow yer doing?'

'Can't complain. Nice gel, Sharon,' said Steve. 'She's got a little gel indoors. Nice little gel. Only three (free).'

The waitress looked about sixteen to Miles, as she wobbled off to get the drinks.

'The fing is, like, Miles, you're the only one can give evidence against me dad, right?'

'I told you, they knew all about it. They had been watching the bag at Euston. The British Rail guy was a policeman.'

'You're the only one who can link it to me dad.'

Miles was not sure about that.

'Miles is a very posh name, innit?' said Steve. (Real people were called Steve and Wayne and Terry.) 'No one in London is going to give evidence against me dad. No one. All they have is the stuff and you. My dad was in Birmingham at a boxing promotion the night they seized the gear. None of those guys has grassed. It's business, Miles. That's how it works, mate.'

'If I don't give evidence, I'm going to be charged.'

Steve blew air through his closed lips, which produced a rubbery, derisive sound.

'What with?' (Wot wif?)

'With handling stolen money.'

'You didn't know it was stolen. You was just doing someone a favour.'

'Yes, but your dad was the one who set it up.'

'Hold on, hold on (Hoe-don, hoe-don). You got your instructions from your mate James. James was asked by a solicitor to find someone to administer money from a trust. A trust in the Isle of Man. The executors was accountants. You might get a rap over the knuckles for somefink, but not much. You just deny you ever seen me dad. It was silly of 'im to talk to you. 'Is fault. But it never 'appened, right?'

'The police know it happened.'

'The police have to give evidence in court too. Everyone knows they're trying to fit up me dad because of the fish job. You keep very quiet until you get in court, then you say the police forced you to say you had seen me dad. They put a lot of pressure on you. They threatened to bring other charges, all that stuff. They said it was the only way they could get me dad, because 'e done the fish job. Our brief will ask you all the right questions, don't worry.'

'I thought James was your brief?'

'You must be joking! We got a QC an' all for this one.'

'I've got to stand up in court and say the money in the left luggage was from a trust? Do you think they're going to believe that?'

'You just done what you was asked. You may've 'ad your suspicions, but you was asked by a friend and you got your instructions from some solicitors. The jury will understand. The police are going to try and get you in and out of there quick, to say that you got your instructions from me dad.

229

They aren't going to want to talk about the fish job and the money in the bag. Our brief will say that you made the deposits and so on, and then the police tried to involve me dad. You 'ad no idea where the money come from. You 'ad to make a false statement because they threatened you. Don't worry, our brief will be in there like a rat up a drain. By the time 'e's finished the jury will fink the police set this 'ole fing up. You're all they've got, Miles. You been dragged into this. You been badly used.'

'That's right.'

'That makes it more easier, don't it?'

Nothing was easy. Steve might see it this way, but Miles could envisage an altogether different outcome.

'What if I don't do it?'

'That's not a good idea, Miles. Did you read about that boxing promoter who was killed the other day?'

'Yes.'

'Well he was killed because 'e didn't do what 'e was supposed to. 'E thought 'e was too important. The man who killed 'im is sitting right in this club. You can't believe it can yer? Must be some kind of joke. That's what you're finking. This isn't Chicago, this is supposed to be Merrie England.'

Miles knew it was not a joke. In Hong Kong he had met two men who had made his blood run cold. When he picked up the phone from London and heard there was a delay – someone was late at their end because of traffic – these two talked among themselves and Miles had felt the sweat burst spontaneously from under his hair. He had sat in a hotel room with them for an hour before the call came through, and in that time they did not speak a single word to him. Miles had gazed transfixed out on the busy harbour below; cargo boats, junks and tugboats stitched lights onto the black warp of the water. What if the police moved in before the deal was done and he was out? These two would kill him, he had absolutely no doubt. Their eyes were like dead dogs or stagnant water. Nothing in his life had prepared him for this. Nothing in anybody's life could prepare them for this amount of fear.

When he finally handed over the money and took a taxi for

the airport – almost missing the plane – he was shaking and his shirt was drenched. The Hong Kong police were supposed to be waiting at the airport for the two men, who were leaving later that night for Bangkok. As he slid into his seat on British Airways, he shook with the shock and relief which engulfed him. The stench from his own body was revolting. He had to go to the lavatory and sponge himself all over with the paper handtowels. They left knots of paper under his arms.

'Steve,' he said, 'I believe you. But you've got to see it from my side too.'

'Sorry, Miles, but me dad can't go down. He'll get fifteen years minimum. And look at it this way; if the jury acquit my dad, the police are not going to do you for a much smaller job. They're just trying to frighten you. Listen, the police don't even investigate crimes under a hundred grand no more. That's the truth. Sure they take a few statements and run around a bit, but they stick the file away somewhere and forget it. You helped them to get the money back; they ain't going to go after you.'

The way Steve explained it, honour was about even. The police only had Miles and that was because he was an amateur. They could get nothing out of anybody else, much as they would like to fit Bilger up with this one. The way Steve explained it, the individual jobs meant little to the police. They would try to get Bilger for something or other, even if they had to invent it. They had once got his brother-in-law, who was a jewel expert, for a bank job.

'I mean, can you believe it? 'E don't run around with shooters doing banks. 'E's an expert with jewels and alarms and things. And they fitted 'im up with a bank. He's in Maidstone now doing twelve. They told the witnesses to the bank job it was 'im at the identity parade. Simple as that.'

Steve shook his head sadly at the injustice. *That's the way they do it.*

Sharon with her spun hair came over. She leant forward towards Steve. Her breasts were very soft, without any supporting tissue in them.

'Any more drinks, Steve?'

'Same again, Sharon, thanks.'

'Didyer know we was being redeveloped? The 'ole block's going. Big noo offices,' she said.

'I 'eard,' said Steve. ''Ow's yer little gel then, Shar?'

'Right little monkey.'

'Ere, give 'er this. Buy 'er somefink nice for Christmas.'

'Thanks, Steve. Ooze yer friend?'

'This is Miles. I think she fancies yer, Miles.'

'Shut yer mouf. I was only being friendly.'

She teetered off, her ra-ra skirt thrashing about above her milk-stout legs.

'Nice gel, very nice gel,' said Steve, ever on the lookout for the elusive spoor of human goodness.

Victoria had dismissed all this when he tried to explain it. He could see how it looked to her. Sometimes – in very brief spells and in daylight – he wondered if it was all as improbable as it sounded to Victoria; a London of bent policemen, Thai boxers, bank robbers, jewel thieves and girls like Sharon. Steve talked about 'shooters' and 'fitting up' and 'tooled up'. Steve had told him about a very senior policeman – *Freemason and all that game* – now suspended but very unlikely to be charged, who helped himself to six bars of silver from a bullion job. He, like James, was on holiday in Marbella. You only had to say 'Marbella' and eyebrows began to hop about significantly. Victoria had advised him to go to the police or get a lawyer.

Miles woke. He was cold. His neck ached from sitting here in Victoria's mother's Honda and his back ached from not being able to sleep. Since he had returned from Hong Kong, he had not slept more than two hours consecutively. He had tried homoeopathic sleeping pills, but these had made his heart flutter and his urine yellow and pungent. It smelled strongly of seaweed which was one of the principal ingredients in the pills. He had found some other sleeping pills and tranquillisers in Victoria's mother's bathroom and he was now eating a small handful of these every night. He felt unbearably tired during the day and unbearably alert at night.

It was three-thirty. Victoria was still in there with the minor celebrity whom she had denied going out with. 'Going out'

232

was a ridiculous phrase. Miles decided to go and bang on the door. First he turned on the engine to warm himself. Victoria was in there fucking and he was out here freezing to death. He could not go back to Victoria's mother's. For two nights he had lain there in agony, apparently hearing her anxious breathing through the wall. He had even thought about getting into bed with her again, but he knew that with his pill-fouled breath, his nervous sweats and his rampant insomnia, he would frighten her terribly. He needed somewhere to leave his things and have his washing done. She was all he had left.

He became bitter. This should never have happened to him. Despite the cold he felt the sweat start under his hairline. Something had gone wrong with his sebaceous glands; they were connected directly to his fears. These sudden starts took place ten or fifteen times a day.

He had to speak to Victoria. It was understandable that she had been upset about Jacci. She had to know the facts. She had been crazy about him once. He would admit that he had made mistakes and tell her that he still loved her. He had to convince her that his life was in danger. The pills concentrated his thoughts on the big things.

A light came on in the house briefly and then went off again; the little domestic by-products of intimacy. He wanted to go in and tell her the real facts of life. He picked up the tyre wrench which he had ready in order to break in if necessary.

'This your car, sir?'

'What?'

A policeman was shining a flashlight on to his face.

'No. I borrowed it.'

'Just step out of the car, sir.'

Miles released the wrench. He opened the door of the Honda and stood up unsteadily. There was another policeman standing beside a police car. He hadn't even seen the car pull in behind him. He stumbled.

'You all right, sir?' said the policeman. It was not really a friendly enquiry. The second policeman was speaking on his radio. After a few moments he came over.

'This isn't your car, sir.'

'I know that.'

233

'What are you doing with it?'

'I borrowed it from the owner.'

'And who is that?'

'It's Mrs . . .'

He couldn't remember. He couldn't even remember her fucking name!

'It's Victoria's mother's. Sorry if I sound a little confused officer. I was having a little nap.'

'Have you been drinking, sir?'

'No. No.'

'What's your name.'

Miles for a moment thought of giving Arnie's name, but he imagined suddenly where that could lead.

'You can call the owner of the car. She's my girlfriend's mother. My ex-girlfriend. Ring her. She'll tell you that she gave me the car. She lives in Farnham.'

'Can we see your driving licence, sir?'

'I haven't got it on me.'

'I think you had better come down to the station with us.'

'For God's sake. No, no, for Chrissakes. I'm a police witness in a big case soon. Don't arrest me. Ring Detective Inspector Munday. He'll tell you.'

They made him lock the Honda and then one policeman guided him firmly to the back of the blue Sierra. He had his arm in what had become for Miles a familiar grip, light but insistent.

'Do Ford supply all your cars?' asked Miles, his mind snatching clumsily for normality. Actually he was happy in a fashion because they had not found the gun he had put under the seat. The tyre wrench had diverted them.

234

CHAPTER TWENTY-TWO

The horse's mane streams out like a tattered ensign on a stricken man of war. The two creatures, the lion and the horse, are joined planimetrically. The landscape and the horse's relationship to it are invocations of the sublime.

Victoria's notes invoked only the poorly sculpted figure of Tresillian Lascelles. Since the evening at his flat, and the fleabites which she and Mike had compared next morning, and the disasters with the cracked wheat, she had taken his pronouncements on the big questions of art less seriously.

She was working on her paper, 'The Notion of the Sublime in the Horse and Lion Paintings of George Stubbs'. Mike was reading a new issue of *Focus*. It had pictures of bar girls in Bangkok, some of them as young as twelve, photographed with great integrity by a French photographer. Mike wanted to commission him for something: 'Look at these faces. Look at the way he uses the light.'

'Look at the way he uses underage girls, Mike.' Mike was wearing a Comme des Garçons suit in apple green. Victoria found the suit offensively unseasonal.

'Did you hear what happened to Andy?' asked Mike.

'No.'

'Well you know that new secretary of his? The one who spoke with an amazing horsey accent from the country somewhere?'

'Not really.'

'Well anyway, she's straight from Cheltenham or some-where, right, about eighteen years old, and she goes into 'is office, this is day three, and he says to 'er, "If I put my dick in your mouth, what flavour would you like me to come in?"'

'Sounds like Andy.'

Andy was the Creative Director.

'Yeah, but unfortunately she goes off 'ome deeply shocked and tells 'er dad, who is a Colonel in the 'Orse Guards, and he gets on the blower to the Chairman demanding that Andy should be fired.'

'He sounds like a man of sense.'

'Andy's only had to write a grovelling letter saying 'e didn't mean it, 'e was insensitive, just the silly way people talk in advertising, bosh, bosh, bosh. 'E's shitting himself because the Colonel told the Chairman 'e's going to the police.'

'I can tell you, "Disgusted of Cheltenham" has my support.'

They were waiting to hear from New York. The board of American Eagle was seeing the commercials today. About now probably. If the white smoke was sent up the chimney, they would get a call within the hour.

The sets had cost a fortune. They were way over budget. God knows what would happen if the board rejected the ads. Anything could happen with these people. It depended on which board member made the first comment. After that the others would all line up according to their estimation of the best side to be on.

The transformation scenes had had a certain magic. The snow fell out of a clear sky, day turned into night, and the chorus line's costume changed magically. Through it all Bernie sang and danced, as eager to please as a performing seal, and similar in his movements.

'That's the real London, Victoria.'

'I can see that, Bernie.'

'Wotcher think?'

'I love it.'

She did. The London that Bernie was tying to conjure up had probably never existed, but if anyone had the credentials for the part, it was Bernie. Tim had told her in confidence that he lived in a rooming house, a Jewish charity, with other survivors of this vanished age. Some, like the Kid, had not survived as well as Bernie. The Kid had sleepwalked around the set, dressed as a fish porter.

* * *

When they had first made love, Tim had wept salt tears which had fallen on her face and breasts. She knew enough about men – too much really – to know that this outpouring should not necessarily be taken seriously. Men could produce tears and semen and flush themselves out with great effectiveness. It was not the same thing as love. And yet she was sure they were in love. It was a physical, sensual feeling. One day, like the notion of beauty, they would be able to pinpoint its exact physiological causes. The feeling of being in love, at twenty-nine and a half, was overwhelming. She understood the notion of the sublime which Tresillian had tried to explain. The sublime was first experienced though the senses, just like love. Perhaps they were the same thing.

Her mother had found a gun in the drawer beside her little bed.

'Victoria, he was also arrested in my car the other night.'

'Oh my God. Why did you let him take it?'

'I didn't know he had taken it. I didn't know he had lost his licence.'

'You usually do nowadays if you drive round Trafalgar Square completely drunk and bash into the lions.'

'You're always so quick to criticise.'

'Oh sorry. Yes, I am being unreasonable, I can see that.'

'He really believes his life is in danger.'

'It is. Mostly from himself. He's always drunk, he's stealing cars, he's harassing me, he's . . .'

'He's not trying to harass you, dear. He just wants to talk to you. You won't talk to him.'

'Of course I won't talk to him. He thinks I've done him some grave injustice. I mean, Jesus Christ, can you believe it?'

'Victoria, your language, really.'

Their conversations always followed the same pattern. They were allotted characters from which they could never escape. There are actors who are remembered for a part they have played twenty years before. Nothing will shake off the memory. She and her mother were still reading from the same dog-eared script, except that her mother was now trying to change the relationship of the two principal characters. She was now trying to load Victoria up with the responsibilities which had formerly belonged to her character.

'Victoria, I am not sure what to do about him,' she said in her small voice.

'I think you should kick him out.'

'I can't. I feel sorry for him. I can hear him moving about at night. He never sleeps. He looks like death. He says that he has to give evidence at some trial and if he does he'll be killed and if he doesn't he'll go to jail.'

'He's got ideas above his station. Why would anybody bother to kill Miles?'

'He also says that you are going out with that journalist. Is this true?'

'It is, but I can't see what business it is of his. Or yours.'

'Well, he was waiting outside this person's house for you when he was arrested in my car at four in the morning.'

Victoria felt a heavy lump like pig iron in her stomach.

'You're not serious are you?'

'That's what he said.'

'What for? What does he want?'

'He wants to talk to you.'

'What about? There's nothing to talk about. The house is fixed, more or less and it's for sale. I am going out with someone else. What can I say to him? Have you got any ideas?'

Victoria was worried now. She didn't want Tim to think she was some kind of flake whose ex-boyfriends followed her around with guns. It was awful. It was far too soon to explain to Tim what came with the package: a deranged and unemployed City dealer, who was keeping a gun where she had kept her Peter and Jane books and her diary with a lock. Her mother, of course, was wallowing in the drama. Mind you, Tim's daughter was snatched by someone called Larry the chauffeur. Tim would understand that there are turbulent undercurrents in any big city. Nobody who lived in London a few years could avoid the chemically scented torrent of sexuality of the city. There were noxious elements floating in it. And Victoria had sometimes ventured out beyond her depth in these polluted waters. She had woken up in beds daubed with shame; she had taken the Underground in her guilty party clothes amongst early-morning commuters; she had visited clinics harshly lit with neon and loud with significant silence.

She had been a city girl for ten years. She had skirmished with the city. She had discovered its indifference, but she had been unable to detect its soul. All cities were supposed to have a soul, but London's had taken a walk. The real London, whatever that was, lived on only in the imaginations of people like Bernie and in the minds of advertising agencies, who specialised in this kind of illusion.

New York called. It was the Account Director, Henry Sprockett.

'Victoria, they love it. They are mad for it. The President thinks it's the greatest commercial ever made. They love the snow and all that stuff. Great idea. Congratulations, darling. They want to fly Bernie over here to appear on television. They think he's better than Gielgud.'

And the same age. Victoria told Mike the news. He laughed.

'What a load of cobblers. Holy fuck. You've put back advertising about thirty years with this one.'

'What you mean is, it's too corny for you. People in Podunk, Ohio, might actually like it.'

'You've made London look like *Mary Poppins*. The only thing missing is Dick van Dyke.'

'The only thing missing is piles of plastic bags and yobbos puking on street corners and mountains of dog shit. Do you really think the world you are trying to portray, of smirking male models in silly clothes with silly haircuts, is real? The whole world is made up. It's all a fake, Mike. It's an illusion.'

'You're becoming very philosophical. Is it because you're in love?'

'Could be. Let's go and celebrate. Look at it this way, Mike, we've probably saved our jobs for a few months.'

Mike had never considered the possibility that he could be fired. He regarded himself as immortal, but he would find out the truth soon enough. As they strode together along Berkeley Square, the snow was falling. The square, too, was magically transformed. Victoria was transformed.

Miles was waiting outside after a long session with Detective Inspector Munday at West End Central, and they did not see him. In a sense he was transformed too: his head was encrusted with snow; his hair had congealed into a sort of helmet, which was melting underneath, even as it accumulated more substance on top. Victoria and Mike passed by him so close that he could smell her warm perfume. He tried to speak, but they hurried past. They were laughing. He heard Mike say something but he did not catch its significance: 'Mary fucking Poppins.' He tried to hurry after them, but he could not move. He tried to shout, but his tongue had swollen in his mouth. It filled his whole mouth. Instead he stood on the pavement, his shoes, the ones with the multiple holes, letting in the melting snow in multiple places. He felt like a man in a dream who was invisible to passers-by and unable to communicate with them.

Nobody made you sign nothing. No pressure was applied. Bilger personally told you what to do with the money. That's it. Dead simple. Gottit?

The Inspector treated him with contempt now. He had gone slowly over the statement, warning him what the opposition brief would say. Above all he must not make anything up or deviate from what they had agreed under cross-examination. 'And get your suit cleaned up before Monday, son. You look a right mess.'

Miles had nowhere to go. Literally nowhere. He had imagined that if he waited for Victoria and talked to her the whole thing could be revealed for what it was, a terrible mistake. He could not go back to Victoria's mother's because Steve had called him there this morning for a friendly chat. He had signalled frantically that he was out. Victoria's mother had said that he might be back later, but it wasn't very convincing. He could not go to the City for fear of running into his former colleagues, and he couldn't go and hide at Piggy's because Piggy's mother had turned him out at last. He was anyway avoiding places where he was known.

He moved one foot with great deliberateness, and then began to walk woodenly down towards Green Park. He took a train for Uxbridge. The Underground was half full of shoppers.

The English were once a nation of shopkeepers; now they had become a nation of joyless shoppers. To Miles it seemed as though the straining shopping bags and the holly-wrapped gifts were a reproach to him personally. A woman looked at him, stopped speaking for a few moments, and fussily gathered her three children together just eighteen inches further away from him. The people in the train had the authentic suburban look: crumpled anoraks, down-at-heel shoes or trainers in black and green, short overcoats, plastic sports bags and cheap handbags. Yet they all had friends. And rat-faced children. Only a tramp, asleep in a corner, was alone. The rest were in knots or pairs on the badly scarred seats. There was no menace down here at this time of day; the atmosphere was more of a waiting room at the doctor's in some provincial town: the same uneasy glances, the suppressed impatience, the out-of-date fittings, the transience, the quietened voices, the dead smell. The seats on either side of him were empty; he had slumped right across them. He sat up and smiled, self-deprecatingly, but no one met his gaze.

Hours later he got out at Victoria and wandered around the station. Eventually he bought a Camembert and prosciutto baguette. He was astounded at the activity; these thousands of people were all in a tearing hurry to get home to Surbiton, Sutton, Cheam, Croydon, East Grinstead and so on. But on the fringes of this crowd, working the bins and looking around the benches for leftovers, were bag ladies and tramps, mad people who had none the less a mission to find all the unwanted sandwiches, cigarette ends and small coins in London. When Miles had worked at the bank he had often passed a black tramp with dreadlocks who lived near the exit of the Light Railway in a cardboard box. One night some boys going home to the Isle of Dogs had doused the box in methylated spirits and ignited it. Miles sometimes thought dispassionately of the box and the tramp in flames, like a Christmas pudding, like an illustration on a Christmas card, like the wrapping paper on the presents the hurrying commuters were carrying.

On his way to the police station, terrified by Steve Bilger's proposal for a friendly chat, he had decided to tell the Inspector that he had changed his mind. The Inspector could not charge him with handling stolen money, because he had already accepted a sworn statement saying he had no idea the money was stolen. It was a bluff, as Steve had said. He tried to bring the conversation around to his change of heart.

'I've been thinking, Inspector.'

Inspector Munday, as always, looked tired. His features were tired, absolutely whopped out in fact. His eyes, when they shifted reluctantly towards Miles, which was as seldom as possible, seemed to be bathed in a clear spirit, so that they were like tropical fish, refracted in an aquarium some unreachable distance away, sunk in little pools in his exhausted head.

The Inspector ignored Miles. In front of him he had a brown file.

'We have been in trouble, haven't we? What were we doing driving around in someone's car without permission after losing our licence? We have been a silly boy.'

The Inspector's clumsy irony was even more menacing than he intended.

'Look,' said Miles, 'don't come on all heavy with me. I don't want to give evidence. I've done nothing. The worst that can happen to me is a suspended sentence.'

·'I don't think you understand.'

'For Chrissakes don't say that to me again. You've said it too often. I do understand. I understand perfectly. You're trying to force me to give evidence when I don't want to. If you want to fit Bilger up, do it yourself.'

'Fit up. Fit up. We've got all the lingo, haven't we? You shouldn't talk to that Steve Bilger, you know. Criminals will say anything. Any bloody thing. You would think we were the ones who went round selling drugs and robbing old ladies, not them. I have here' – he had to fumble with some papers for a long time to find it – 'a report to the Director of Public Prosecutions on some fraudulent trading you are alleged to have engaged in. Your record is not getting any brighter, son. I have asked them to hold this back. There may be a request from Singapore for an extradition hearing too. The DPP doesn't think at the moment that he will proceed. But it doesn't look good, does it? Do you see what I mean?'

Miles saw all too clearly. Arnie had made good his threats.

'Right, son, let's get back to business. All right? Nobody made

242

you sign nothing. No pressure was applied. Bilger personally told you what to do with the money. That's it. Dead simple. Gottit?'

As Miles wandered around Victoria Station this conversation replayed itself, unbidden, endlessly. It began to fragment and re-form in the wrong order. The sentences writhed and contorted in his head, with a primal vigour of their own. There was no end to their frenzied activity; long after the sentences had been chopped and rearranged and played backwards, long after they had lost any meaning, they kept up their desperate, protozoan life. Fear had given his thoughts an electric charge of energy. At the same time, fear had drained Miles. For the last two days he had not slept more than half an hour at a time, and when he did fall asleep he woke only minutes later, fully alert, his heart pounding. He could feel his nervous system – incandescent wires in the tired, tired flesh – glowing with fear.

He put his hand into his pocket. He found a few loose coins and bought half a bottle of Bells'. The woman in the wine store wrapped it in a thin sheet of tissue paper. Her hair was basically grey, with a pink, unnatural shine, like a hybrid rose.

'There you are, dearie.'

'Thank you,' said Miles, his treacherous tear ducts tickling his eyes with static. 'Thank you very much indeed.'

He sat on a bench facing the huge noticeboard which told the ordinary people – the people with home and beds and wives – how long they were delayed. He drank deeply without trying to conceal the little bottle. Fuck it. Fuck them. He was going to shoot himself anyway, so what the fuck. *The train on Platform Fourteen is the delayed eighteen forty calling at all stations to Portsmouth. Platform Fourteen. The delayed eighteen forty for Portsmouth.*

The whisky spilled down his mouth and on to his suit. Fuck them. There was a surge of commuters towards Platform Fourteen. Some of them made a detour to avoid him as he slumped sideways on to the bench. Victoria. Victoria Station. Victoria. What a joke. Fuck them. But with all his heart he wished he were going with them.

There was a rule which had never been articulated, let alone written, about when people could charge champagne to the agency. Victoria ordered a bottle of Dom Pérignon. It would have been a mistake to buy a bottle of vintage champagne if the reaction from New York had been unfavourable. Never mind that reactions from the board of American Eagle, and indeed most of their clients, were completely arbitrary. It didn't work like that. The creative people were always nibbling away at the restraints. They only found out what these were when they were fired. This, Victoria knew, would be Mike's undoing.

As Mike drank, Victoria looked at his damp mouth, his thin lips and the large stumps of his whiskers. Mike shaved with a special attachment to his razor which did not cut too close. It left a permanent pointillism of whisker stumps. It was difficult to believe that his mouth had fastened on to hers and on to her breasts. Mouths and tongues were very intimate ways of expressing affection. In this way, she thought, we are not one person all the way through our lives at all. She was certainly not the same person who had fumbled eagerly for his cock one night.

She was in love now; when she looked at Mike (talking about the French photographer and how great he would be for something hard-hitting and punchy, like an AIDS campaign) she was briefly saddened, because she felt nothing at all for him. That made her wonder if being in love might not be an illusion; as much of an illusion as the simple one produced by paint on canvas: the evocative landscapes, the planimetrically linked protagonists, the grapeshot-raked mane and all those things. And, of course, the tons of artificial snow falling on old London Town (as dreamed up by Bernie Koppel) which had so entranced the board of American Eagle. As Tresillian said quite often, we can never separate what we see from what we know.

As they walked back to the agency, real snow was still falling. Conduit Street was thronged with expensive cars and richly dressed shoppers who, as they passed, gave out a warmth from the rich folds of their clothes and the cosseted intimacies of their skins. She caught many languages – Spanish, Italian, German and Arabic – and for the first time in her years at the agency, she saw someone drive away in a Rolls Royce from Jack Barclay on the corner.

'Do you know, there's six miles of copper pipes in a Roller. It's amazing the fucking things can reach sixty at all. Six miles of copper pipes and seventeen perfect Andalusian cow hides. I wouldn't have one if they gave it to me,' said Mike.

There existed a constant state of tension between Mike and the artefacts of this world. It was like the process of cellular division as Victoria dimly remembered it, a never-ending dance of attraction and repulsion. It seemed to Victoria, as the marble sarcophagus of the agency loomed, a pretty silly form of kinesis. But she was tolerant. She was in love. Her own cells were rearranging themselves fecklessly all the time, dancing to a music that had come down the millennia with its harmonies intact. So what if it was just wasps buzzing in a bottle? It was a miracle. A transformation.

Nigel Johnson-Partridge, the Managing Director, had sent some flowers down to her office. They were in a white plastic bowl, lots of small, expensive flowers arranged with the naturalness of a funeral wreath. Victoria usually threw about eight huge flowers into a tall vase, but Nigel Johnson-Partridge was from the stockbroker belt, where wives dressed up for dinner and poured sherry into cut glass.

She sent a motorcycle messenger round to the Hackney Empire with a note for Bernie. She wrote: 'Bernie you are the toast of New York. Congratulations, your biggest fan, Vicky.'

She ordered a taxi. She was emitting powerful waves of affection. She was like a porpoise echo-locating. She rode off into the night on a tide of happiness; she surfed away and crested the breakers. The traffic was moving slowly because of the snow. Lights were leaving slug trails behind them in the air. The taxi driver said: 'Amazin' innit, every fucking year it's the same. Snow? Never 'eard of it. What a surprise. 'Ow yer supposed to make a living? This is me last job of the day, I can tell you.'

Victoria did not care. She thought it was beautiful, perhaps even sublime. When they finally threw off the clasping arms of Mayfair and entered the park, she felt as if they were out on the steppes of Mother Russia. The snow stretched away for ever before them, right to the bridge over the Serpentine. The park was luminous, the snow light and volatile, drifting in the hollows. The lights along the paths appeared to flutter in the falling snow. The cab driver cursed the snow again, but she blessed it.

Tim was waiting. The hayloft breathed a welcome. The fire was burning with huge logs which gave off the scent of a Nordic country. It was the right scent, Victoria thought, for a night like this. Tim kissed her. He had just brushed his teeth.

'Why are you laughing?' he asked.

'Because you have brushed your teeth. I wonder why?'

They didn't bother to go into the bedroom. Their flesh was incandescent; every fibre and muscle (and the nervous system which sparked the whole business) was glowing.

CHAPTER TWENTY-THREE

Now I can see that things were coming to a head. I can impose a crude taxonomy on the events of the period just before Christmas. The impulse to fashion the stuff of existence into a recognisable artefact is almost universal. There are exceptions, however: the Maasai and the Samburu are allegedly exempt from this impulse. They will not speculate beyond the first level, the existential level. As a result they are the happiest people on earth. This may not be true – I personally doubt it – but the notion is appealing. Why knock yourself out looking for significance?

The significance I was looking for in the Cochrane story seemed to have come to nothing in Bart's Hospital. It had petered out the way streams and watercourses in Africa simply spin themselves to nothing. In any event Cochrane had been pushed back in my order of importance by my worries about Gemma and her deluded mother, the student of aromatherapy. (She was not studying aromatherapy, as it turned out, but this must wait a while.) I was also deeply in love with Victoria. Perhaps I had thought I would never be in love again. I certainly did not expect the bruising intensity. Victoria made love as if she were intent on suicide. It was a point of honour with her to rip her heart and soul out and throw them on to the bed.

Each evening I waited for her to return from the agency, musky, champagne scented, lips bruised (lips that the night before had actually had spots of blood on them) her hair smoky and almond scented, her pussy (what else can you call it?) as warm and pungent and delicate (yet surprisingly resilient) as . . . as love itself. (When you talk of love you

247

end up with a tautology, like a Muslim talking about religious belief.) As the time came round for our bodies' secretions to commingle, I began to tremble. My breathing quickened. My temperature dropped.

Where I had lain next to the night-startled Gemma, I now lay next to Victoria. As we recovered some sanity in the armistice, she told me that her ex-boyfriend was carrying a gun and had been following her. I told her that Larry Agnello had a record for minor drug offences. (My brother was on the case.) We shared a pious hope that neither of us had done anything to deserve these dark, primal, threats. (I am sure we both thought privately that we were guilty in some way.) Love anyway conjures up guilt: it is impossible to be so possessed without being presented with the bill. Sometimes I had less elevated thoughts: for example, how sensational that this ecstasy was free and available.

The gathering clouds, the things coming to a head, were presaged by a telephone call from the Foreign Office. The Chief and his wife were on their way to Nairobi. The passport office in Nairobi had had a sudden rush of blood to the head. They would be here in three days' time; space had been found for them by Lufthansa who had deposited a khaki army on the game parks. The mercy flight had been written up in the *Kenya Times*. The chap from the Foreign Office was tickled by the whole thing. The High Commissioner was making capital out of it. I checked with the hospital and they confirmed that they could operate quickly when Cochrane's daughter had been examined.

The Foreign Office official sent the copy of the *Kenya Times* around to me. It read: 'Chief's wife to be flown to London for eye operation by well-known television personality.' Lower down on the page was a picture of two elderly Maasai, primitively bandaged in what looked like torn bedlinen, under a caption which read:

It's survival of the fittest. These two men, Mzee Parimai, 62 and Mzee Malhohlo, 63 were attacked by a lion while inspecting their cattle. The two old warriors speared the lion and drove it off. Although they will bear the scars of this beastly attack and the knowledge that all is not safe in the jungle, they have learnt a lesson. The law of the jungle is survival for the fittest. Only the fittest will survive, man and beast alike.

I studied the pictures of the battle-scarred old men. One had blood on his tattered shirt, but his face, sparsely bearded, was serene. The other had a bandaged head and a wary expression. There were scars on his face from previous problems with wildlife. In his extended ear lobe hung an ornament, a rounded stone on a filigree of wire. The newspaper said that wildlife attacks on humans were on the increase. In fact they were rampant.

I visited Cochrane to tell him the news of his daughter's arrival. He was due to be released from hospital in time for Christmas. Nobody had any objection to his being released earlier. Nobody would have minded if I had taken him away right then. He was sitting in bed looking at a copy of the *Sun*. He was looking at a porky girl with immense breasts who was planning to start her own tapas bar in Ilford. *Caramba. Tastee.*

'Look at the tits on 'er,' said Cochrane by way of a greeting. 'Look at 'er, Doctor.'

I did not need to look at her. I had my own erotic larder, seasonally stocked.

'Good news,' I said. 'You can go home soon and your daughter is coming to London for Christmas.'

'I ain't got no daughter, Doctor.'

Gently, as if he were a traveller lost in the interior, I guided him down the tracks and trails of his personal history. I recounted to him the story of his horse and his victory over the lion. (*Only the fittest shall survive.*) I told him about his unexpected blessing of a daughter (mindful of my own loss in this department) and his son-in-law the Chief. I then told him that the Circus Hall of Fame had honoured him by making him a life member. There was nothing in his eyes at all, except a little tadpole activity when he glanced down at the newspaper. I arranged with the hospital to have him home the next day. I would hire an agency nurse to look after him over Christmas at least.

The light was failing as I left the hospital; the afternoon was dying of boredom. I walked through the meat market to find my car. The great vaulted halls were hung with carcasses. They reminded me of aldermen or Freemasons. There was nothing repulsive about the sight, nothing that would encourage vegetarianism. Instead I saw a hundred stout John Bulls, the old roast beefs of England, hanging in rows. My car, soon to be sold, was just about to be hoisted on to a truck and taken away. A short discussion took place on the jumbled pavement, before it was unhitched. I wondered if money was supposed to change hands. Who knows how to operate in this town now? Cities have always lived on sweeteners, deals, fiddles, games, numbers, fixes, grease jobs, schmeers and straighteners. *That's the way it is, innit? What can yer do?*

The car was mercifully free of the fishiness which had plagued it for weeks. These weeks now seemed to be gathering intensity, like cattle driven down a lane to market, or water approaching a ravine. As I drove home I was troubled by the thought, a rogue thought, that Victoria was perhaps a sack artist. It was a term I had heard many years before, but now it came back to me uninvited. Victoria had plenty of sexual inventiveness, but did this make her a sack artist? It was an absurd, even insulting thought. She had said, 'Oh my God, I needed that,' the first time we had made love (after Bernie's manatee courtesies). At the time I was myself thinking the same thing and the remark seemed natural enough. (After all, I did not know then if there would be another time.) But now I thought that it suggested a somewhat impersonal approach. It troubled me, as I drove through the traffic. Love can demand a searching examination of small details. Stendhal said that love produced 'fresh perfections in its beloved at every turn of events'. In our time it also produces fresh worries. I had a long and gruelling experience of an authentic sack artist to draw on. Perhaps I attracted sack artists. Perhaps they are the women of today.

So far, Victoria and I only had one friend in common, Bernie Koppel. But we were going to the American Ambassador's dinner for Vice-President Quayle. Bernie loved us. Surprisingly, he lacked a family. Someone would still be clinging on, you would have thought, but they had all gone. I think Bernie saw us as his creation. He had certainly been in at the conception, a clumsy Pandarus. He was going to America to appear on various cable television shows, a Cockney character. He was hoping to use the trip to raise money for his musical. He was talking of a one-man show for charity. Soon he would be President of the Koppel Foundation, with branches in New York and Tel Aviv.

The Mercedes was on borrowed time. Normally I drove defensively, even nervously. One small nick meant a very high-minded discussion at the body shop. Now I scanned the faces of girls passing by anxiously, grateful for the traffic. True it was Christmas, but the streets seemed to be swarming with young girls. London was alive with them, the way Hamelin was overrun by rodents. Some of the girls looked like rodents. (Many Londoners do: the pinched features, the ratty hair, the small, close eyes, the noses which, while not necessarily large, none the less push insistently against the skin.) Were all London girls sack artists? Was it a necessary condition of life for a girl today? If they were, their faces gave no clues. Some of them had no coats despite the cold. (Many Londoners have no raincoat or weatherproof shoes.) They wandered, happy geese gaggling down Oxford Street, their bottoms not always in the sort of condition you might wish for girls so young, in short skirts, in black tights and chains; in hundreds of varieties of jeans; in leather jackets, in cycle shorts, in workman's boots, in T-shirts, in baseball outfits. They did not look to me like sack artists. Like the wine drinkers of the Mediterranean with centuries of steady drinking behind them, London girls do not go overboard sexually; sex has always been part of the fabric of London, as quietly persistent as the damp and greyness. Take the girl in Cochrane's newspaper: she sits there innocently, her buttery breasts more evocative of the dairy than the erotic inferno, her mind on snack food. *You gotter laugh, ain'tcher? You can't take it too serious, can yer?*

I saw a boy and girl kissing. He was smaller than she was; their haircuts were similiar, huge exaggerated cows-licks and short, shaven sides. In his hand, behind her back, he was carrying a film can. As she manoeuvred to engage his mouth her skirt revealed a large hole in her black tights, with her

251

white, white flesh showing through. It was so white and soft it looked like ricotta. (In my Mercedes Sports I was at thigh level.)

I drove into Mayfair, towards Victoria's agency, which was busily renegotiating the terms of my contract in line with my demotion. It was another continent. The girls here were quite different. Their hair gleamed. Their boots and shoes were of the shiniest leather and somebody had distributed a truckload of expensive coats to all comers. But these were not real Londoners. They deported themselves differently; they were sack artists every one.

Propelled by the traffic I glided past the pantheon where Victoria worked. Two nights a week she was also grappling with more metaphysical and aesthetic problems. She was studying the horse and lion paintings of Stubbs. I contributed a little of my knowledge of lions from Schaller.

For the first time Victoria was home before me. We stumbled to the bedroom, drunken tangoists. Half dressed she crouched on the bed. I saw a little line of fuzz at the bottom of her backbone.

'Go on,' she said, 'stick it straight in.'

There was for a moment some resistance and then I found myself in her. She was irrigated from within by desire.

'All the time we were talking about Stubbs, I was thinking about this. All day as a matter of fact,' she said. 'What a *putta* I am.'

I wished I could speak, but I could not. '*Putta*' is Italian for 'sack artist', I thought, delirious. I held her hips, my hands full, my heart full, and wondered if there was any end to the topography of lovemaking. Like the notion of outer space, this territory might be boundless. What a thought.

We lay together, survivors of a plane crash, stunned but miraculously alive. When I looked at her from this angle, her face had that sensual, foxy profile. Her lips were bursting, but her eyes were tender as if she had been rubbing them.

She looked so young, although she said that she had lost the bloom of youth. I felt old. I felt I should be out there pumping iron or something to merit this abandon. I also felt a little guilt. We had driven out Gemma's childish aromas with something more adult. Victoria had moved in. There had been no discussion. Over a few days all her surprisingly few things arrived and found places for themselves. Her own house was for sale down in the great dereliction of Docklands. She was here to stay, for a while anyway. I told her about the Chief, his wife, and Cochrane.

'Where's the Chief going to stay?' she asked.

'I've found a place in Regent's Park where foreign students live. The Foreign Office suggested it. The chap with the plump voice.'

'Why have you got them over here?'

'That's a question.'

'I'm interested.'

'I haven't honestly thought why. I just decided to do it.'

I remembered that when you are living with someone you can't just do things for no reason.

'I was looking for significance,' I said, lamely.

'Who isn't?' she asked. 'I'm studying George Stubbs and you're importing African chiefs.'

The world outside was running wild with kidnappers and men with guns but we were in an ark.

'What was your wife like?' she asked.

'She was a sack artist.'

Her face ceased its minor motions; for a moment it was as if the blood and the vital cells had ground to a halt.

'Do you think I'm a sack artist?'

'I was wondering.'

'I do my best.'

'Have you got something to wear for the Veep's party?'

'Are you offering?'

'I am.'

When you buy a woman clothes, you are cementing a relationship, no question of it. Also, I didn't want to get on to the subject of my relationship with Magda. She was now only an unpredictable but inevitable cause of trouble. My brother was preparing a case with his usual thoroughness.

The next day I formed the welcome committee for Cochrane's return from hospital, with a Jamaican nurse at my side. The nurse was dismayed by the surroundings, but I promised to pay her a substantial Christmas bonus. Perhaps to prepare him for his outing, the doctors had plumped him up with drugs. He looked fatter and livelier. He was wheeled into the gloomy hallway and pushed backwards up the stairs by two overweight ambulancemen. They complained, but more to draw attention to their efforts than anything else.

''Ere we go, grandad. Up, up and away.'

I hoped the sight of the lion skin was not going to kill him as the caretaker had predicted. His eyes fell on it as the ambulancemen wheeled the chair around.

'That is beautiful (bew-i-ful),' he said.

'Fuck me, what's that?' asked one of the ambulancemen.

'It's a lion killed by Mr Cochrane out in Africa.'

'You killed that, didyer, grandad?'

'I did. Look at me scars where the bugger bit me.'

He started to fumble with the buttons of his pyjama jacket, but the nurse stopped him. The ambulancemen gave her some papers and left. She took Cochrane's temperature and felt for his pulse, which I imagined was very weak, like the gasping of a stranded fish or the soughing of kelp in an ocean current.

The nurse was not as jolly as you might have expected. She said that Cochrane did not have long to live. I wondered if I could take him out to see his relatives. *Why not. It hain't goin' to make no difference like*. When we had settled him with a cup of sweet tea, the Londoner's elixir, I showed him the certificate from the Hall of Fame and the statuette, a little Oscar depicting a trapeze artist standing as they do on tiptoe to receive the plaudits. Cochrane held it in his hand. His thoughts were shuffling themselves into order, like someone playing patience badly.

'When I went missing, you know, before I got sick, I was looking for that lion what escaped, you know . . .'

'I thought so.'

'But I got lost.'

He looked wistful. He held the statuette now. I told him that he could visit Orlando any time, admission free.

'That's good. I'm a honorary life member now.' (He pronounced the aitch.)

'That's it. And if you're feeling all right I'll take you to meet your daughter when she comes. Day after tomorrow.'

'Is that me daughter?' he asked.

'No, that's the nurse.' The nurse did not look pleased to be caught up in this conversation. 'Your daughter's coming from Africa. She's married to Chief Phineas Chilingwe. His father knew you. His father was the Chief in your day. Chief Solomon Chilingwe.'

'I remember 'im. Yes I do.'

'What was he like?'

'Big bugger. 'Uge. He had a big stone hanging from his ear. 'E was an 'unter.'

The lion skin, as in life, was dominating. It sprawled all over the tiny flat. Cochrane wanted the door of his bedroom, his rathole, left open so that he could look out at its malevolence, partly lost in the cheap taxidermy, but still impressive when the light caught the glass eyes. Taxidermy and taxonomy had the same root, I realised. *Taxis*. Many things seemed to be coming together like amorous protozoa, but this is perhaps the effect of hindsight. The next few days were so full of incident that as I look back I see order where none existed.

Africans often travel with elaborately trussed brown cardboard boxes, which bulge and strain and cause customs men to shuffle warily out of sight, or advance menacingly, depending on their mood. Sometimes Africans check in for planes with huge quantities of kitchen appliances and television sets. These appliances are the new household gods of Africa.

The Chief and his wife Daisy came through the arrivals hall carrying two parcels, long, lumpy shapes, wrapped in brown paper and tied with string. They also had two new suitcases made of blue plastic. The Chief was wearing an army greatcoat and his wife was wearing a print dress in the Kenyan national colours, with a heavy shawl around her shoulders. Underneath the dress her legs were warmed by socks and shod in sandals. She followed just behind the Chief her hand resting lightly on the arm of his greatcoat. A Lufthansa official shepherded them through the traffic towards me. I introduced myself. The Chief's face was weathered, so that it was difficult to guess his age. He was not overawed by the seething congestion of Terminal Three.

In fact he was a master of protocol. He thanked the man from Lufthansa graciously and introduced his wife to me. Her face was lighter in colour than his. Her nearly sightless eyes were tobacco-coloured. They gazed timidly straight ahead. Around her neck were five bands of beads and shells. I scanned her face for signs of her patrimony but I could see none. Her hair was close shaved, so that her face looked very strong. In her right ear was a round piece of ivory, perhaps a wart-hog tusk, and attached to that was a filigree of copper wire holding a triangle of metal. Her ears had been pierced frequently in unlikely places. Her mouth had set over the years in a defensive, downward curve.

The Chief's ears had also once borne ornaments. The ear lobes were stretched, but unadorned, like a sideboard that has been cleared of trophies.

'My wife, she enjoyed the journey very much. She is looking forward to the medical care.'

'I bet she is. Come, let's find my car and I'll take you into town.'

With the help of a porter we made it to the car park. The Mercedes was a little small for the three of us, with luggage.

'What sort of car is this?' asked the Chief.

'It's a Mercedes.'

'Mercedes. Cheap Mercedes. Too small. My father came to London in 1935. He said it was raining.'

'He was right. It is usually.'

We set off.

'What is that, there?'

'That is the Trust House Forte coffee shop.'

'And that place, that side?'

'That is the interdenominational chapel for travellers.'

The Chief was a born sightseer.

'Where is Buckingham Palace? Not so far?'

'I'll drive by it. You'll be just in time to see the Changing of the Guard.'

We mounted the M4.

'Have you got children?'

'I've got one.'

'I've got eleven. Six from this wife.'

So Cochrane had six grandchildren living out there in Samburuland. His family was extending.

I showed the Chief Buckingham Palace, patrolled by men in bearskins – and greatcoats like his – and drove him up the Mall, which was crisp and wintery, into Trafalgar Square. He sometimes spoke to his wife to tell her what she was missing. Landseer's lions did not detain him. He was looking for Nelson on top of his column, a difficult feat from the low front seat. The car had acquired the scents of an African village, as though the departed fish had created a vacancy. I remembered these scents keenly; they reminded me of so much.

The undersized Mercedes would have been a strange sight, had anyone been looking. In the back crouched the sightless Daisy, and in the front still holding his awkward parcels, was the Chief; the trunk was propped open to hold the suitcases. For the Chief, the British Empire was springing to life from linen-covered schoolbooks. He conveyed this transformation to his wife.

'Is she looking forward to seeing Mr Cochrane?'

'Yes. She has brought him some medicines. Family business.'

He laughed. It was a two-way traffic, this health business. We had the laser, but they were equipped for the more human medical emergencies.

I dropped them off at the students' residence in Regent's Park. The Chief was not tired, he said, but I suggested a night's rest and some food before we took Daisy to Moorfields Hospital. And then on to see Cochrane.

Besides, I was keen to get back to the erotic inferno.

CHAPTER TWENTY-FOUR

The free-range chickens lived in two barns in semi-darkness. They were able to have a walk in the surrounding quarter-acre of muddy field. On sunny days a few did. Most days more died in the gloom than went exploring. In one barn all the chickens were now dead, after first going bald as suddenly – and with the same patchy effect – as if they had had chemotherapy. There did not seem to be much hope for the surviving chickens in the second barn either. As a matter of fact the whole landscape had given up hope. It was the sort of area on the fringes of London where smallholdings coexisted with DIY warehouses, garden centres selling koi carp and retirement bungalows with colourful flowers in white-painted wheelbarrows. It was clapped-out country, waiting for the property developers. But the property developers had their hands full for the moment.

In the first barn, secured by a small cage of heifer gates, lay Chaka the lion. The straw around the lion was mouldy, fouled not only by the deceased poultry, but by the lion itself. Its turds were huge, with white granules like aspirin in them. Nobody dared enter the makeshift pen to clear them, even if they were inclined to do so. Its urine, which was sprayed backwards in jets, was pungent. All these stenches together were unbearable. The lion's fur was beginning to fall out in patches. The mane around its neck was thinning, so that it looked like the beard a mullah or an orthodox Jew might wear. Its head, at the same time, had emerged from its cover and looked far smaller, like the inmate of a gulag's, than it had done previously.

In one respect, however, the lion's upkeep was not a

problem: dead or moribund chickens were plentiful. These could simply be pushed through the barriers. More often than not the lion did not eat the chickens. One chicken had escaped from under his paw and survived for a few days on top of some bales of hay, where it succumbed either to its wounds or to the malaise which had overtaken the rest of the chicken farm.

The lion rarely moved. That is to say, it seldom walked about its limited quarters, but it blinked and twitched and suffered minor convulsions like a dog asleep in front of a fire, all the time. Occasionally, for no obvious reason, it stood up unsteadily and stared in the direction of the M25 orbital motorway, whose digestive rumble could be heard clearly even by human ears. If you were to guess the lion's state of mind, you would probably conclude that it was depressed, or perhaps fatalistic. But how could you really know? Despite the condition of its coat and mane, its eyes had become more intense, the yellow deeper and the irises darker. When it was fed or watered it would sometimes rise to its feet to snarl; at other times it would snarl from a prone position. The noise was like a jet of water and steam released from a pipe under high pressure. Between the enormous pads of its feet there was a fungal infection, probably from the chicken shit which covered the floor of the barn to an unknown depth. As a result its paws had become yellow, the colour of expensive mustard.

The lion stood up painfully on the infected pads as the large doors of the barn were opened. The uncertain light flooded in. A small, closed truck, was backed in. It stopped. A man in an army-surplus jacket, with a little *Wehrmacht* flag on the shoulder, got out of the truck, closed the doors of the barn and directed the driver, who manoeuvred the truck right up to the makeshift cage. The driver then got out of the truck and the two men had a short discussion before opening the back of the truck and lowering a ramp to the edge of the lion's pen. Then, with baling wire and more calving barriers, they constructed another crude cage around the back of the truck and the ramp, and secured that to the existing barriers.

The lion had moved away while all this was going on, and now sat beneath the hay bales where the escaped chicken's carcas lay decomposing slowly. The chicken's head, which retained a thin ruff of feathers, actually hung down over the edge of the top bale like some cruel surrealist composition designed *pour épater les bourgeois*. Down below the lion was sitting with its back legs splayed out to one side as if it no longer had complete control of them. Anything less like a heroic painting of a lion would be hard to imagine: *Lion and dead chicken*. The mouldering hay, the mouldering guano, the mouldering chicken and the mouldering lion, were far from sublime. There was no planimetric association between lion and chicken whatever. If anything, this was a study in the relentless microscopic activity of spores and bacteria. If you could have speeded the whole process up – condensed a week into five minutes the way they do in nature films – it would have been an object lesson in decay.

When the tunnel was finished, one of the barriers was freed with pliers and lifted out of the way, so that in theory the lion could now enter the back of the truck. All that was lacking was a lion tamer with a whip and a chair. The two men stood as close to the lion as they could without entering the rickety cage and prodded the lion with broomsticks. The lion snarled and lowered its head, but eventually, with some difficulty, it mounted the ramp and entered the darkness of the truck. Now the men had a tricky thirty seconds or so as one raised the tailgate of the truck while the other freed the barriers they had constructed, leaving a large hole until the back of the truck could be closed. But the lion did not seize its opportunity. The men then padlocked the truck and drove it out of the barn.

Outside it was already becoming dark. The sky was fat, like a fish about to spawn, the colour of a carp, or an eel. On the side of the truck the words *Farm Fresh Free Range Chickens and Eggs* were stencilled in blue letters beside a picture of a chicken, fully feathered.

Miles Goodall had spent the last four nights at different addresses. He had taken a lot of pills to try to sleep, but he had not had much luck. The best night was the one he spent in the cubicles of the Turkish bath at the RAC Club. (It reminded him of his school dormitory.) He pretended to be James, who was a member. He was able to sleep for a few hours with the comfort of the night noises and escaping gases of sleeping businessmen all around him. The cubicles were only £15 for members. He had spent one night at Victoria's mother's house, not sleeping at all, and two over the weekend at Heron's Beat on his old bed which was damp and covered with plaster and the builders' moist copies of the *Sun*. London workmen left a mouse-trail behind them of cigarette ends, heavily greased wrappers, chirpy newspapers, woodshavings and polystyrene coffee cups. They marked a place with their beer-bellied masculinity; they sprayed it liberally with their discount musk.

Private dinner for the Vice-President. Private visit. Victoria and Tim had been invited to a private dinner at Winfield House. Miles had spent the afternoon at Victoria Station. Nothing private about that. Victoria's mother had told him about the dinner. She had also told him that Victoria and Tim were living together. He already knew that from his own observations. Their toothbrushes were living together. Their stray pubic hairs were living together. Their saliva was living together. He wanted to see this; he wanted to see them going into their private dinner at Winfield House. He would be there, with a message from the public world he now inhabited. He could be summoned at any time to the police station. He could be traded between the City Squad, Drugs and CID at will. He had become a commodity, just like soya bean futures. He could be required to turn up in court. He could have his pockets searched and his shoelaces removed whenever they liked. He could be sent for trial or not as they wished. He could be told to sit down, stand up, get into the car, get out, wait here, sign there. He was public property.

From among the swaying, narcoleptic shrubs in the park, Miles had caught glimpses of them, half-dressed. He had once seen Victoria's head rising and falling just above the frame of the bedroom window which opened on to the park. His blood had drained into a sump. He had worked out the geography of the building from their happy movements past this window and the others which opened on to the street. They flitted past like bats with – he could imagine but not hear in the wet, swishing plants – the same shrieks of happiness and absorption which bats utter. No doubt Victoria was treating him to her full vocal range of ecstatic woofs and tweets, which in his foolishness he had once imagined could only be produced for him.

Victoria's mother also told him that Tim had paid for an Emanuel dress for Victoria. He wanted to tell a young, bearded tramp who was working the bins near the croissant shop this exciting fashion news. Miles no longer had the disdain for tramps he used to feel in his previous existence: *Jesus, why doesn't somebody do something? This is supposed to be a great capital city. They're bloody everywhere. Came down for an England/Scotland match and lost the return ticket.* It was true, they were everywhere. They begged at stations, outside supermarkets and in the streets. There were tens of thousands of them loose on the streets. Most of them were mental or alcoholic. A few seemed simply to be suffering from a complete loss of self-esteem. Some muttered and swore, some gathered in convivial groups drinking. Some busied themselves obsessively collecting scraps. Miles had read that we are all mad; it was only a question of degree. He now knew that we are all outcasts: it is only a question of degree. He was mortally tired all day long and violently awake all night. When he lay down, his statement, rehearsed so many times, spun round and round in his head like a prayer wheel, like verses from the Koran, like train wheels, and it was impossible to stop them.

The Inspector was worried about him. He didn't give a fuck about Miles, but he was worried that he might mess things up. ('You look awful, son. Get a haircut. Get some sleep.') Piggy said he had had a visit from someone looking for him. And his conversation with Steve kept coming back. He could never end these conversations. They were part of the ceaseless motion, the atomic world, the biological world. Nothing except death could end them.

When he said he was going, finally, Victoria's mother's face split apart, like a pomegranate falling to the ground to reveal its hidden contents.

'I know you're in trouble, I can help you.'

He was in trouble. But 'trouble' was not an adequate description. Nor was trouble liberating or stimulating or romantic as she imagined.

'Joyce,' he said. (It was the first time he had used her name.) 'I appreciate everything you've done. You've been wonderful. But I can't stay here. It's not safe. When I go to court on Tuesday I'm finished. Believe me.'

'Won't you come back for Christmas?'

Evidently she did not understand what he meant by 'finished'.

Her face was wrecked, empty wrapping. She had made him brown toast with grapefruit marmalade. He could not eat. She was screaming 'I love you' silently and he could do nothing to help her. Her mouth, where his tongue had so stupidly ventured, was puckered; her head was straining slightly at the tendons which moored it to her shoulders. After nights of sleeplessness, her eyes were slightly tipsy. Her lips, probably once as plump as Victoria's, were thin and supersensitive to emotion so that they moved before she spoke and sometimes when she was restraining herself from speaking.

The tramp passed him muttering loudly: 'Focking conts. Focking conts.' All over London there were people convulsed with the inability to speak their true feelings. He could feel London seething. He could hear London groaning. He would speak his true feelings. He took a shower in the washroom. He combed his hair carefully and sponged his suit with the corner of the roller towel. The rest of his stuff was in a left-luggage locker. He set off for Regent's Park, an envoy from the under class with an urgent message.

The chicken-farm truck was parked near some tennis courts not far from the Ambassador's residence. Next to the tennis courts Telecom had been digging holes for their plastic pipes, which were stacked in pyramids beside a couple of yellow vans. The man in the *Wehrmacht* jacket locked the gates to the site with a large padlock and chain. There were more police cars than usual because of the Vice-President's dinner party – the diplomatic protection squad, speeding by in their maroon Sierras. The two men sat in the cab of the truck, waiting for the traffic on the Outer Circle to ease. From time to time they could feel the heavy, uneasy movements of the lion rocking the whole truck. The truck was backed right up against a temporary fence on to the park itself. After perhaps an hour, the driver climbed out of the cab with a pair of bolt cutters and cut through the fence immediately behind the truck. The other man lowered the ramp into the gap, but they had no means of getting the lion out of the truck. They climbed back into the cab and waited.

The familiar scents which, we can assume, had already reached the sensitive nose of the lion, now flooded in. It could smell the goats and the Ambassador's Shetland ponies strongly, but also the myriad smells – seals, owls, hyraxes, penguins, gibbons, tapirs, etcetera – which it had inhaled for years from the lion terraces. Directly out of the back of the truck it now had a view, partially obscured by tennis courts, over the football fields towards the boating lake and the hostel where the Samburu Chief and his blind wife were quartered. The night was damp, but the moon was present behind the clouds. Every so often as the clouds tumbled by, the moon flashed like a fish glimpsed in deep, murky water; like carp or bream which turn suddenly so that you see their underbellies catching the refracted light. The park was a wetland.

The lion did not leave the truck. It lay gazing carelessly out on to the plain, apparently hardly engaged by the empty vista. The lion closed its eyes and opened them reluctantly, but its ears were working hard. Sometimes they were back in the position favoured by Landseer, turned away from the open door; immediately afterwards they would flick forwards, sifting the sounds of the zoo's nocturnal life, ignoring the thrum of the city (which sounded like a ship's turbines), listening for male lions, perhaps the Asian usurper.

The air around Winfield House crackled. The marines were in their finest. Secret servicemen with microphones in the sleeves of their raincoats conferred with each other gravely. The diplomatic protection service had positioned two of their cars near the gates. Seven photographers had gathered because Michael Caine was expected. From the road Miles could not see the house. He had imagined that he would be able to walk up to the front door, but he was not allowed within twenty-five yards of the gates. These private people at their private dinner party needed plenty of distance from the public people.

Miles edged closer until a photographer spoke to him: 'Wassyour game then? I'm doing this for a fucking living you know.' A Jaguar arrived, paused briefly at the gates and was saluted by the guard. The photographers looked at each other and shrugged. 'Fucking nobody.' They got word on a walkie-talkie that Michael Caine was coming. A Bentley appeared and they rushed forwards to the gate. Miles got a view of Michael Caine, his face bleached by the photographers' flashes, waving cheerily. He looked like a deep-sea fish in an aquarium peering out. As a matter of fact, the whole world, of which he was no longer a part, seemed to Miles to have retreated behind the thick glass wall of an aquarium, from where it carried on with only the occasional uncomprehending glance out at the terrestrial world. His view had been restricted to a porthole.

The photographers were leaving. 'Useless fucking assignment.' 'I told the prick they don't let you nowhere at a private do.' 'Wotcher got?' 'Fuck all. Back end of a fucking Bentley. And you?' 'I got his missus, I think.' 'Fancy a quick one?' 'Why not, where's the nearest boozer?' The photographers barely glanced at the Mercedes, low and dark blue, as it turned towards the sentry box. Only Miles rushed forwards. A marine was checking the invitation. He straightened up and saluted. Miles bent down to look in the window. Before him was Victoria's cleavage. He looked right down into its soft, remembered warmth as the car slid away up the gravelled driveway. Victoria's face turned towards him at the last moment. She was gone before he could see her reaction. He stepped towards the house.

'I'm sorry, sir,' said a marine. 'You can't go any closer.'

'Private dinner is it?' said Miles. His voice snagged somewhere in his throat.

'Yes, sir. Step back please.'

A policeman was coming towards him.

'OK, OK, I'm going.'

Miles walked along the Outer Circle away from the residence. Winfield House had been given to the American people by Barbara Hutton. It had twelve acres of gardens. Twelve fucking acres in the middle of London. Miles followed the railings towards the zoo. He passed a temporary car park near some tennis courts before he came to an open section of railings. Nobody was watching; he climbed over as quickly as he could. In his haste he tore a long garfish-shaped hole in his trousers and gashed his calf. He ran through the wet grass until he was out of sight of the road. His heart was pounding. Until recently he had not realised that your heart could pound. It hammered against his rib cage, begging for release. He doubled back towards Winfield House past the tennis courts.

The lion stood up. It stumbled down the ramp and into the park, where it paused for a moment, the corners of its mouth curling upwards. Stiff-legged, its ragged mane like a pennant shot to ribbons, it was a tentative figure. Its weeks in the chicken farm had reduced its physical presence greatly, the way some men come out of hospital after a serious operation looking like their own fathers. It scented the air. The zoo was to its left. It moved off cautiously, fearing who knows what? It walked with difficulty keeping to the trees. It paused opposite the goat mountain and the seal lake. It moaned quietly, but there was no response. It was far too unsure to roar. None the less it sniffed a tree for signs of interlopers from some distant savannah, but all it picked up was signs of Jack Russells, Labradors, dachshunds, old English sheepdogs and so on. When it reached the children's zoo – where the goats and rabbits lived and a cow was milked to keep London children in touch with real life – it stopped again. Now it was directly opposite the lion terraces. In the intricate skein of scents it could pick out the particular aroma of the surviving lioness, Dukwe. The lion moaned again, louder, but there was no response. It followed the line of the fence past the wolf run and the rare pheasants and then doubled back, looking for a way in.

Its skin was too big for its frame; the skin caught on the high points of its shoulders and pelvis. The unaccustomed walking and the play of scents (after the ammoniac gases of the chicken farm), roused its hunger. It was probably Pavlovian. When it reached the end of the zoo, nearest the residence, it again caught the scent of the Ambassador's fat little Shetland ponies. (All Shetland ponies, like zebras, are fat.) But then it saw some movement ahead and flattened itself close to the damp grass to watch.

Miles was aware of the unnatural stillness of the park. From the zoo came noises he could not identify. (It would have needed a Fellow of the Royal Geographical Society to identify some of them.) Around the park, but not quite entering into it, he could hear the bee-music, the giant hydro-electric motors of London. His heart had settled down. He was still conscious of it, but it had stopped beating against his ribs.

(Suicide is a form of release for bottled up despair. But the notion of suicide rather than the act itself, is usually enough. Let me admit it, I don't know how serious Miles was about killing himself.)

Miles felt calmer. The park was a landscape from a dream; it lay in the middle of town, housing all sorts of exotic beasts. There were animals here that belonged in icy crevices in the Hindu Kush and turbid creeks on the Orinoco. He walked through damp grass. His shoes were soaking up the moisture. Even his trouser legs were drawing the moisture upwards.

Winfield House was surrounded by a double fence and thick planting. Inside there – he could picture it – they were gathering for a drink around a huge fireplace. Cocktails. Huge Christmas tree by the stairs. The Vice-President, Michael Caine and Mrs Caine, Victoria and Tim, Ambassador Woodrow E. Fos and Mrs Fos, a few friends from the racing world, a Duke and so on, all privately invited. Victoria with her Emanuel uplift, her breasts voguishly visible in a nest of lace and silk, is chatting to the Vice-President who is determined to relax after some tough official business in Eastern Europe.

Miles tried to climb the railings. There was nothing to hold on to. He thought that if he could climb a tree and drop down in to the space between the two fences, he would have a better chance with the second fence which was of mesh. He found a tree which overhung the fence. Its bark was wet and slippery. He jumped up and grabbed a branch. He tried to heave his legs up.

'Miles.'

He turned around. There was no mistaking the London

features, sandpapered and very white, even in this half-light. Miles let go of the branch.

'Steve.'

'You shouldner done it, mate. You shouldner, 'onest.'

Miles tried to explain, but there was no time.

The rest you know.

CHAPTER TWENTY-FIVE

It is a Sunday night. Bernie has taken the Empire Theatre, Hackney for his one-man charity show. It's not strictly one-man, but there's only one who counts and that's Mr Entertainment, Bernard Koppel. He has paid £2,000 of his own money to hire the theatre.

They have all come. The place is jammed to the roof with the non-people. They are wearing party hats and waving Union Jacks. These are the people who sheltered down the Underground during the war. Very little has been seen of them in the intervening fifty years. I recognise their faces, however; they are straight out of the catalogue. The men are mostly small, weasel-faced; their hair (in whatever quantities), is plastered close to their heads. They hold cigarettes between their discoloured thumbs and second fingers. They are quieter than their women, who are both more numerous and more animated. The women are larger, too; their hair is almost universally grey and permed into thinning curls. A lot of them cough. A hypochondriac would feel very ill at ease, because the bronchi all around are in poor condition. They rasp and grate.

Almost the only black faces, apart from the theatre's staff, are in my group. The Chief and his wife (her eyesight with her new plastic eyes is about sixty-five per cent) are also wearing party hats. He is wearing a fez in red tissue paper. So am I. The air is thick with humour. It crackles and zings as the old folks rib each other. An elderly woman with a face so jumbled it rivals the pavements outside, taps Victoria on the shoulder: 'You get tired of 'im, darlin, pass 'im over 'ere. I'll know what to do with 'im, I can tell yer.' Her three companions, all with the tortured, thinning hair of discount hairdressing, laugh until tears come into their eyes. It sounds like gravel hitting the bottom of a bucket. It's quite a production. God knows what it takes out of old people to laugh like this. 'I'm only jokin', darlin',' says this old card, dabbing her eyes and coughing. 'Oh dear. I'm jus' jokin'. You're a lovely gel an' all.'

Victoria is wearing a short black dress. She *is* lovely. She reaches back over the battered seats and places a friendly hand on a bandaged knee. 'I love him,' she says seriously. 'But we can share him.' This sets them off again. It is surprising in all the years they have been hiding we haven't heard more from them.

The Chief is, I think, having a good time. He is waving his flag and has removed his greatcoat. His wife is gazing out of her new eyes, happy but bemused. Her reaction after years of blindness may be like that of the Japanese Sergeant Yokoi discovered hiding in the Philippines, believing himself still at war.

Bernie has had a pretty lavish programme printed. There are pages of ads wishing him luck. His local corner shop wishes him luck on his big night; Ali and Benazir are thinking of him. The launderette, Dallas Coin Op, is rooting for him; Express Car Service suggests he breaks a leg. American Eagle, courtesy of Victoria, wish their new star all the best on this wonderful night in such a good cause. A golden eagle adorns the page, the only full colour ad in the programme. All proceeds are to be shared equally between the King David Homes and the Princess Alice Mission. The show is called *My Kind of Town, by Bernard Koppel. A talent to amuse.* Not content with taking my job, he's stolen my lines. The show contains, it says, some of the best-loved songs of the East End and some original material. It has Titch Rabinowitz on the Steinway, the fastest left hand in the east (end); the Cedric Mason tap team; the Harry Green Quartet; and a number of surprise guests.

Only Simba Cochrane is missing from the story. He has made his last journey to the hospital, the courtesy stop, never longer than a few days. They need the beds. He's not going to make it to the suburbs. It may appear to be callousness, but

I am pleased. His life would have lost the little distinction it possessed if he had ended his days in a home.

We did get one outing together. I drove Cochrane to Regent's Park for a family visit to the zoo. The Chief insisted on pushing the wheelchair all the way from the hostel to the lion terraces. He was wearing his greatcoat. We crossed over the bridge where lonely people were gourmandising the ducks with sliced white bread, apparently gratified by their power to attract a milling, paddling, honking, squawking flock of ill-assorted birds in the *Erbsensuppe* water. Then we set off across the football fields towards the goat mountain. Both the Chief and Cochrane wanted to see the lion, which was under lock and key, not allowed out on the terraces for public viewing. I wondered if the keeper of mammals had a sneaking desire to cash in. The lion was under sentence of death, but there had been such a blizzard of protest that the zoo had stayed execution. The lion, I was told, had only a few weeks to live in any event. In India man-eaters are big attractions at zoos. Track record counts for a lot with the public there. In negotiating a private view of Chaka, I had not explained my relationship to the dead man, which anyway was tenuous. My story was called 'Cockney Lion on Death Row'.

We were shown into the lion quarters by the back route. Chaka lay listlessly on the scrupulously clean concrete floor. He had been medicated and injected and his more obvious medical problems were apparently in check. We looked on from the safety line painted on the floor. His eyes were fixed, without much interest, on a spot some miles past Cochrane's head. The Chief clicked his tongue: this lion was not really much of a specimen. In the bush it would long ago have been eaten by hyenas.

Cochrane gazed at the lion from his wheelchair.

''Ow much did 'e eat?'

'He's not eating well,' said the keeper.

'No. I mean 'ow much of the geezer what 'e killed?'

The keeper was uneasy in the strange company I kept.

I wish I could say that Cochrane's meeting with his daughter had been a success. She spoke to him respectfully in Swahili, her new eyes cast down. The Chief translated. She said that she was very happy to meet her father after such a long time. It all came to nothing. The occasion passed Cochrane by completely. In the flickering cavern of his condemned flat, the lion skin already showing patches of damp, there was an unbridgeable gap between father and daughter. The clumsy parcels which the Chief had brought with him contained two Samburu spears, gifts for Cochrane. He unwrapped them on the lion skin, rolling the string carefully and slipping it into the pocket of his coat. His fingers were strong and sure. They were accustomed to taking their time. The spears were about eight feet long when assembled. The head was shaped like a small sole or flounder, with a spine in the middle. It was attached to a tapered piece of wood from a very hard tree, which grew along the course of the Ewaso Ngiro River. At the other end was another piece of iron, long and thin and spiked. This was customarily stuck in the ground when the spear was at ease. He himself had killed lions with these spears, before hunting was banned. Cochrane was not interested.

I was saddened by the gulf between Cochrane and his family. They were on the other side of the river waving to him, but he could not pick them out. What had happened out there so long ago had passed from the realm of reality. The death of the lion, the heroic walk with the confused and winded horse, even the conception of this woman (who was now waving the Union Jack as a stagehand came and set a microphone in front of the curtain) – all these things had undoubtedly happened, yet they were irretrievably in the past. I had tried to retrieve them, imagining I would better understand the sprawled city outside in this way. Even as I write these words, I ask myself if that was my true motive. As with so many good intentions, the result has not been as planned. Before we die, I wondered, is it necessary to chuck a lot of baggage overboard? Do we want to go off encumbered, or do we perhaps just keep a few essentials for the journey?'

Of course, Cochrane was leaving that baggage behind for us, who are still here. Along with his trinkets – the lion skin, the statuette and the kindling furniture – he would leave behind his whole life intact. He was like the flying ants of Africa which shed their wings, leaving little piles of what look like shavings of mother-of-pearl behind on the ground where they have embarked on their new lives. London would receive Cochrane's life, stack it unseen into its catacombs, somewhere beneath the deformed, vomit-stained, disordered streets; a mausoleum of bricks. Sometimes I wonder how many bricks exactly. It is hard to imagine, as difficult as the notion of endless space, that every one of these seeping bricks was placed there by hand. Whole buildings are prefabricated now, panels swung into place on cranes, but still London is largely a city of bricks. And every one of them is suffering.

My brother has made headway. Aromatherapy proved to be in a sense a metonymy. The aromas Magda had been inhaling (and shooting up) were altogether more lethal. She is in the Betty Ford Clinic. Larry the chauffeur is contesting our custody claim. He has requested blood tests to prove that he is Gemma's father, but his claims have not been admitted in evidence, because, even in Palm Springs, *pater est quem nuptiae demonstrant*. The court will finally award me custody in a few weeks and Gemma will be in the air again. Of course, any talk of marriage – there has been plenty – has been postponed until this is settled. Victoria, if she fears it, gives no sign of resenting Gemma's return.

As for the death of Miles, I could refer you to Schaller on the purely physical level:

> Large animals are usually held by the throat, the most effective killing site. Small animals with weak bones, tend to be bitten through the nape, which during a pounce from above, is easier for a lion to grab than the throat. After having killed, a lion either begins to eat immediately, or else moves the carcass to another location. The viscera are often eaten first.

The coroner at St Pancras was not aware of any significance in the fact that Miles's body had no marks at all on the nape or the throat, although he had been eviscerated. A Chinese intern was called. He listed the injuries in that peculiar can-opener English. I could have stood up and read some Schaller. (I could have read some Sherlock Holmes.) In fact this little court, packed with reporters, was as much a leftover from the old days as Cochrane himself. The coroner was heavily browed, stooped, and very courteous to the witnesses. An attendant whispered to me that he had two university degrees.

I call Mr Timothy Curtiz. Call Mr Timothy Curtiz. The gas lamps are flickering. Call Mr Timothy Curtiz. Nobody called me and I was not going to volunteer unwanted forensic evidence. This court specialised in the deaths of tramps and prostitutes from the surrounding mean streets, streets which themselves were about to be the subject of the biggest redevelopment since Docklands.

The coroner returned a verdict of death by misadventure. The hearing had taken twenty minutes. As he was speaking, I noticed two lions and a unicorn on the crest above his desk.

The next case was of a woman who had jumped under an underground train. By a terrible coincidence the policeman who found the body reported that he recognised the woman as someone he had retrieved alive a few months before from under another train at another station. Her legs were severed.

I left the court. The reporters were long gone. In the garden outside, yellow crocuses were pushing up through the heavy black soil, soil which you would have thought would have had difficulty providing succour to even the most primitive forms of plant life, like fungi and algae.

Victoria and I seldom talk about Miles. I have not told her what I know about the killing sites of lions. So already we have secrets. I don't fret about this. I know that it is part of the human condition, the hoarding and secreting in the gloomy corners of the heart. Victoria has secrets, and she has asked me, without so much as saying so, to accept her as she is. I am happy to do so. After all, although neither of us willed it, we were certainly complicit in Miles's death. Also we are both bound by the absurdity – to a disinterested spectator – of the whole business. Neither of us wants this sort of publicity.

Behind the curtain the Harry Green Quartet strikes up. It sounds smaller than a quartet. The audience stiffens and quietens. Bernie appears, but he chooses a novel route. He catches us all by surprise by entering from the back of the stalls, singing in his corncrake voice into a microphone, as he progresses down towards the stage. He is wearing a yellow tuxedo (the colour of a crocus), and singing the theme tune, the show-stopper, from *Buzz Bomb* the musical, with additional lyrics by T. Curtiz.

Julian Barnes
Staring at the Sun £4.99

A fighter pilot, high above the English Channel in 1941, watches the sun rise; he descends 10,000 feet and then, to his amazement, finds the sun beginning to rise again. With this haunting image Julian Barnes's latest novel begins. It charts the life of Jean Serjeant, from her beginnings as a naive, carefree country girl before the war through to her wry and trenchant old age in the year 2020. We follow her bruising experience in marriage, her questioning of male truths, her adventures in motherhood and in China; we learn the questions she asks of life and the often unsatisfactory answers it provides.

'This small, packed book is impossible . . . to "summarize"; markers, merely, can be placed, to suggest its teasing fullness, its wit, incisiveness, gentleness and generosity. Julian Barnes is forty now; a cheering aspect of the twenty-first century'
TIMES LITERARY SUPPLEMENT

Russell Hoban
The Medusa Frequency £3.95

'Russell Hoban's *The Medusa Frequency* is the sort of hyper-kinetic feat of the imagination that runs on high octane fuel and thunders across its surreal landscape at a dangerously high speed . . . In the course of this tour through the imaginative outback of Mr. Hoban's mind, we are treated to brilliant flashes of mordant humour, not to mention splendidly baroque evocations of present day London' THE LISTENER

An inexplicable message flashed onto the screen of his Apple II computer at 3 a.m. heralds the beginning of a startling quest for frustrated author Herman Orff. Taking up the offer of a cure for writer's block leads him 'to those places in your head that you can't get to on your own' – and plunges him into a semi-dreamland inhabited by a bizarre combination of characters from myth and reality: the talking head of Orpheus; a lost lover . . the young girl of Vermeer's famous portrait – and a frequency of Medusas.

'*The Medusa Frequency* sparkles with classical allusions and a wisecracking American humour at times suggesting the Marx Brothers' THE DAILY TELEGRAPH

'Short, smart and fizzy, the novel seeks out the roots of creativity with none of the solemnity that phrase implies' NEW STATESMAN

'Russell Hoban is the most original novelist that we have' THE TIMES

'The rollicking rhetoric . . . is entirely captivating' TIME OUT

All Pan books are available at your local bookshop or newsagent, or can be ordered direct from the publisher. Indicate the number of copies required and fill in the form below.

Send to: **CS Department, Pan Books Ltd., P.O. Box 40, Basingstoke, Hants. RG21 2YT.**

or phone: 0256 469551 (Ansaphone), quoting title, author and Credit Card number.

Please enclose a remittance* to the value of the cover price plus: 60p for the first book plus 30p per copy for each additional book ordered to a maximum charge of £2.40 to cover postage and packing.

*Payment may be made in sterling by UK personal cheque, postal order, sterling draft or international money order, made payable to Pan Books Ltd.

Alternatively by Barclaycard/Access:

Card No.

Signature:

Applicable only in the UK and Republic of Ireland.

While every effort is made to keep prices low, it is sometimes necessary to increase prices at short notice. Pan Books reserve the right to show on covers and charge new retail prices which may differ from those advertised in the text or elsewhere.

NAME AND ADDRESS IN BLOCK LETTERS PLEASE:

....

Name————————————————————————

Address————————————————————————

————————————————————————————

————————————————————————————

————————————————————————————

3/87